Burned

Thomas Enger lives in Oslo and previously worked as a journalist. *Burned* is his first novel. As well as writing, he composes music. *Pierced*, the second novel in the Henning Juul series, will be published in summer 2012.

Praise for *Burned*:

'This debut from Norwegian journalist and composer Thomas Enger has real strengths: the careful language, preserved in the fine translation; and its haunted journalist hero . . . This could be an intriguing series.' John O'Connell, *Guardian*

'Thomas Enger is an intriguing new voice. *Burned* . . . offers another scary insight into the realities of the Scandinavian experience.' N. J. Cooper

'The story is solid, the characters very well drawn, and I found myself reading this at all hours when I should have been doing other things . . . Enger has reserved a real surprise in *Burned* to the end . . . hooked me to want to read the next book (as if he hadn't already).' *Shots*

'[Henning Juul] is a bewitching lead. Extremely perceptive and with a flair for his work, he has enough moral fortitude to be sympathetic, but not so much that his presence in a newsroom is implausible . . . [*Burned*] easily holds the reader's attention throughout. The real masterstroke is in the plotting . . . The finale is inspired, with Enger teeing himself up nicely for the next in the series. Enger leaves enough unresolved in *Burned* to ensure a smooth transition into the second Juul book, *Pierced* (as yet still a work in progress), and abides by the golden rule of all the best performers, leaving us wanting more. Enger is a fine talent, and *Burned* is a reminder of exactly why we love Scandi crime.' bookdagger.co.uk

THOMAS ENGER

Burned

Translated from the Norwegian
by Charlotte Barslund

faber and faber

First published in 2011
by Faber and Faber Ltd
Bloomsbury House
74–77 Great Russell Street
London WCIB 3DA
This paperback edition published 2011

Originally published in Norway as *Skinndød*
by Gyldendal Norsk Forlag in 2010

Typeset by RefineCatch Limited, Bungay, Suffolk
Printed and bound by CPI Group (UK) Ltd, Croydon, CRO 4YY

A CIP record for this book
is available from the British Library

ISBN 978-0-571-27225-9

⌣

2 4 6 8 10 9 7 5 3 1

To my other hearts –
Benedicte, Theodor & Henny

My life, I promise you with all my heart
to belong to you
until death extinguishes my burning passion
for you and for joy.

Halldis Moren Vesaas, *To Life*, 1930

Prologue

He thinks it's dark all around him, but he can't be sure. He can't seem to open his eyes. Is the ground cold? Or wet?

He thinks it might be raining. Something touches his face. Early snow? The first snow?

Jonas loves the snow.

Jonas.

Shrivelled carrots in snowmen's faces, clumps of grass and earth. No, not now. Frosty the Snowman, it can't be you. Can it?

He tries to lift his right arm, but it won't move. Hands. Does he still have them? His thumb twitches.

Or, at least, he thinks it does.

His skin is crisp and delicate like snowflakes. Flames everywhere. So hot. His face slides down like batter on a sizzling frying pan.

Jonas loves pancakes.

Jonas.

The ground is shaking. Voices. Silence. Wonderful silence. Protect me, please. You, who are watching me.

1

It'll be all right. Don't be scared. I'll take care of you.

The laughter fades. He is out of breath. Hold my hand, hold it tight.

But where are you?

There. There you are. We were here. You and I.

Jonas loves that there is a 'you and I'.

Jonas.

Horizons. Blizzard rain on an infinite blue surface. A plop breaks the surface, line and bait sink.

Cold wood beneath his feet. His eyes are still stuck together.

It'll be all right. Don't be scared. I'll take care of you.

He feels the balcony under his feet. He has a firm foothold.

Or so he thinks.

Empty hands. Where are you? Rewind, please – please rewind.

A wall of darkness. Everything is reduced to darkness. Siren sounds approach.

He manages to open one eye. It's not snow. It's not rain. There is only darkness.

He has never seen darkness before. Never really seen it, never seen what the darkness can conceal.

But he sees it now.

Jonas was scared of the dark.

He loves Jonas.

Jonas.

2

Chapter 1

June 2009

Her blonde curls are soaked in blood.

The ground has opened up and tried to swallow her. Only her head and torso are visible. Her rigid body is propped up by the damp earth; she looks like a single, long-stemmed red rose. Blood has trickled down her back in thin, elongated lines, like tears on a melancholic cheek. Her naked back resembles an abstract painting.

He takes hesitant steps inside the tent, glancing from side to side. Turn around, he tells himself. This has nothing to do with you. Just turn around, go back outside, go home, and forget what you've seen. But he can't. How can he?

'H-hallo?'

Only the swishing branches of the trees reply. He takes a few more steps. The air is suffocating and clammy. The smell reminds him of something. But what?

The tent wasn't there yesterday. To someone like him, who walks his dog every day on Ekeberg Common,

3

the sight of the large white tent was irresistible. The strange location. He just *had* to look inside.

If only he could have stopped himself.

Her hand isn't attached. It's lying, severed, next to her arm as though it has come undone at her wrist. Her head slumps towards one shoulder. He looks at them again, the blonde curls. Random patches of matted red hair make it look like a wig.

He edges up to the young woman, but stops abruptly, hyperventilating to the point where his breathing stops. His stomach muscles knot and prepare to expel the coffee and banana he had for breakfast, but he suppresses the reflex. He backs away, carefully, blinking, before he takes another look at her.

One eye is dangling from its socket. Her nose is squashed flat and seems to have disappeared into her skull. Her jaw is dented and covered with purple bruises and cuts. Thick black blood has gushed from a hole in her forehead, down into her eyes and across the bridge of what remains of her nose. One tooth hangs from a thread of coagulated blood inside her lower lip. Several teeth are scattered in the grass in front of the woman who once had a face.

Not any more.

The last thing Thorbjørn Skagestad remembers, before staggering out of the tent, is the nail varnish on her fingers. Blood red.

Just like the heavy stones lying around her.

Henning Juul doesn't know why he sits here. In this particular spot. The crude seating, let into the hillside, is hard. Rough and raw. Painful. And yet he always sits here. In the exact same spot. Deadly nightshade grows between the seating which slopes up towards Dælenenga Club House. Bumblebees buzz eagerly around the poisonous berries. The planks are damp. He can feel it in his backside. He should probably change his trousers when he gets home, but he knows he won't bother.

Henning used to come here to smoke. He no longer smokes. Nothing to do with good health or common sense. His mother has smoker's lung, but that's not what stops him. He wishes desperately he could smoke. Slim white friends, always happy to see you, though they never stay for long, sadly. But he can't, he just can't.

There are people around, but nobody sits next to him. A soccer mum down by the artificial turf looks up at him. She quickly averts her eyes. He is used to people looking at him while pretending they aren't. He knows they wonder who he is, what has happened to him and why he sits there. But no one ever asks. No one dares.

He doesn't blame them.

*

5

He gets up to leave when the sun starts to go down. He is dragging one leg. The doctors have told him he should try to walk as naturally as possible, but he can't manage it. It hurts too much. Or perhaps it doesn't hurt enough.

He knows what pain is.

He shuffles to Birkelunden Park, past the recently restored pavilion with its new roof. A gull cries out. There are plenty of gulls in Birkelunden Park. He hates gulls. But he likes the park.

Still limping, he passes horizontal lovers, naked midriffs, foaming cans of beer and wafts of smoke from disposable barbecues burning themselves out. An old man frowns in concentration before throwing a metal ball towards a cluster of other metal balls on the gravel where, for once, children have left the bronze statue of a horse alone. The man misses. He only ever misses.

You and I, Henning thinks, we've a lot in common.

The first drop of rain falls as he turns into Seildusgate. A few steps later, he leaves behind the bustle of Grünerløkka. He doesn't like noise. He doesn't like Chelsea Football Club or traffic wardens either, but there is not a lot he can do about it. There are plenty of traffic wardens in Seildusgate. He doesn't know if any of them supports Chelsea. But Seildusgate is his street.

6

He likes Seilduksgate.

With the rain spitting on his head, he walks west towards the setting sun above the Old Sail Loft, from which the street takes its name. He lets the drops fall on him and squints to make out the contours of an object in front. A gigantic yellow crane soars towards the sky. It has been there forever. The clouds behind him are still grey.

Henning approaches the junction where Markvei has priority from the right, and he thinks that everything might be different tomorrow. He doesn't know if it's an original thought or whether someone has planted it inside his head. Possibly nothing will change. Perhaps only voices and sounds will be different. Someone might shout. Someone might whisper.

Perhaps everything will be different. Or nothing. And within that tension is a world turned upside down. Do I still belong in it, he wonders? Is there room for me? Am I strong enough to unlock the words, the memories and the thoughts which I know are buried deep inside me?

He doesn't know.

There is a lot he doesn't know.

He lets himself into the flat after climbing three long flights of stairs where the dust floats above the ingrained dirt in the woodwork. An appropriate transition to his home. He lives in a dump. He prefers it that way. He doesn't think he deserves a large hallway, closets the size of shopping centres, a kitchen whose cupboards and drawers look like a freshly watered ice rink, self-cleaning white goods, delicate floors inviting you to slow dance, walls covered with classics and reference books, nor does he deserve a designer clock, a Lilia block candleholder from Georg Jensen or a bedspread made from the foreskin of humming birds. All he needs is a single mattress, a fridge and somewhere to sit down when the darkness creeps in. Because it inevitably does.

Every time he closes the front door behind him, he gets the feeling that something is amiss. His breathing quickens, he feels hot all over, his palms grow sweaty. There is a stepladder to the right, just inside the hall. He takes the stepladder, climbs it and locates the Clas Ohlson bag on the old green hat rack. He takes out a box of batteries, reaches for the smoke alarm, eases out the battery and replaces it with a fresh one.

He tests it to make sure it works.

When his breathing has returned to normal, he climbs down. He has learned to like smoke alarms. He likes them so much that he has eight.

Chapter 2

He turns over with a disappointed grunt, when his alarm clock goes off. He was halfway through a dream which evaporates as his eyes glide open and the dawn seeps in. There was a woman in the dream. He doesn't remember what she looked like, but he knows she was the Woman of his Dreams.

Henning swears, then he sits up and looks around. His eyes stop at the pill jars and the matchbox which greet him every morning. He sighs, swings his legs out of bed and thinks that today, today is the day he'll do it.

He exhales, rubs his face and starts with the simplest task. The pills are chalky and fiendish. As usual, he swallows them dry because it's harder that way. He forces them down his throat, gulps, and waits for them to disappear down his digestive tract and do the job which Dr Helge enthusiastically claims is for Henning's own good.

He slams the jar unnecessarily hard against the bedside table, as if to wake himself up. He snatches the matchbox. Slowly, he slides it open and looks at its contents. Twenty wooden soldiers from hell. He takes out one, studies the sulphur, a red cap of concentrated evil. *Safety Matches* it says on the front.

A contradiction in terms.

He presses the thin matchstick against the side of the box and is about to strike it when his hands seize up. He concentrates, mobilising all his strength in his hands, in his fingers, but the aggravating splinter of wood simply refuses to shift, it fails to obey and remains unimpressed. He starts to sweat, his chest tightens, he tries to breathe, but it's no good. He makes a second attempt, takes out another tiny sword of evil and attacks the matchbox with it, but soon realises that he doesn't have the same fighting spirit this time, nowhere near the same willpower now, and he gives up trying to turn thought into action. He remembers that he needs to breathe and suppresses the urge to scream.

It's very early in the morning. That explains it. Arne, who lives upstairs, might still be asleep despite his habit of reciting Halldis Moren Vesaas's poetry day and night.

Henning sighs and carefully returns the matchbox to the exact same spot on the bedside table. Gently, he runs his hands over his face. He touches the patches where the skin is different, softer, but not as smooth. The scars on the outside are nothing compared to the ones on the inside, he thinks, and then he gets up.

*

The sleeping city. That's where he wants to be. And he is here now. In the Grünerløkka district of Oslo, early in the morning, before the city explodes into action, before the pavement cafés fill up, before mum and dad have to go to work, the children are off to nursery, and cyclists run as many red lights as they can as they hurtle down Toftesgate. Only a few people are up and about, as are the ever-scavenging pigeons.

He passes the fountain on Olaf Ryes Square and listens to the sound of the water. He is good at listening. And he is good at identifying sounds. He imagines there is no sound but the trickling water and pretends it's the day the world ends. If he concentrates, he can hear cautious strings, then a dark cello slowly inter-mingling before fading away and gradually giving way to kettledrums warning of the misery that is to come.

Today, however, he doesn't have time to let the music of the morning overwhelm him. He is on his way to work. The very thought turns his legs to jelly. He doesn't know if Henning Juul still exists, the Juul who used to get four job offers a year, who made the mute sing, who made the days start earlier – just for him – because he was stalking his prey and needed the light.

He knows who he was.

Does Halldis have a poem for someone like me, he wonders? Probably.

Halldis has a poem for everyone.

He stops when he sees the yellow brick colossus at the top of Urtegata. People think the huge Securitas logo on the wall means the security firm occupies the entire office block, but several private businesses and public bodies are located here. As is www.123nyheter.no where Henning works, an Internet-only newspaper which advertises itself with the slogan '1-2-3 News – as easy as 1-2-3!'

He doesn't think it's a particularly good slogan – not that he cares. They have been good to him, given him time to recover, time to get his head straight.

A three-metre-tall fence with black metal spears surrounds the building. The gate is an integral part of the fence and slowly slides open to let out a Loomis van. He passes a small, deserted guard booth and tries to open the entrance door. It refuses. He peers through the glass door. No one around. He presses a brushed steel button with a plate saying RECEPTION above it. A brusque female voice calls out 'yes'.

'Hello,' he says, clearing his throat. 'Would you let me in, please?'

'Who are you meeting?'

'I work here.'

A period of silence follows.

'Did you forget your swipecard?'

He frowns. What swipecard?

'No, I haven't got one.'

'Everyone has a swipecard.'

'Not me.'

Another silence. He waits for a continuation which never comes.

'Would you let me in, please?'

A shrill buzzing sound makes him jump. The door whirrs. Clumsily, he pulls it open, enters and checks the ceiling. His eyes quickly identify a smoke alarm. He waits until it flashes green.

The grey slate floor is new. Looking around, he realises that many things have changed. There are big plants in even bigger pots on the floor, the walls have been painted white and decorated with artwork he doesn't understand. They have a canteen now, he sees, to the left behind a glass door. The reception is opposite it, also behind a glass door. He opens it and enters. There is a smoke alarm in the ceiling. Good.

Behind the counter, the woman with red hair in a ponytail looks fraught. She is frantically hammering away at the keyboard. The light from the monitor reflects in her grumpy face. Behind her are pigeonholes overflowing with papers, leaflets, parcels and packages. A TV screen, hooked up to a PC, is mounted on the wall. The newspaper's front page clamours for his attention and he reads the headline:

Then he reads the strap-line:

Woman found dead in tent on Ekeberg Common.
Police suspect murder.

He knows the news desk has yet to cover the story,
because the title and the strap-line contain the same
information. No reporters have been at the scene,
either. The story is accompanied by an archive
photo of police tape cordoning off a totally different
location.

Neat.

Henning waits for the receptionist to notice him.
She doesn't. He moves closer and says hello. At last, she
looks up. First, she stares at him as if he had struck her.
Then the inevitable reaction. Her jaw drops, her eyes
takes it in, his face, the burns, the scars. They aren't
large, not embarrassingly large, but large enough for
people to stare just that little bit too long.

'It looks like I need a swipecard,' he says with as
much politeness as he can muster. She is still staring at
him, but forces herself to snap out of the bubble she has
sought refuge inside. She starts rummaging through
some papers.

'Eh, yes. Eh – what's your name?'

'Henning Juul.'

She freezes and then she looks up again, slowly this time. An eternity passes before she says:

'Oh, that's you.'

He nods, embarrassed. She opens a drawer, riffles though more papers until she finds a plastic cover and a swipecard.

'You'll have to have a temporary pass. It takes time to make a new one and it needs to be registered with the booth outside before you can open the gate yourself, and, well, you know. The code is 1221. Should be easy to remember.'

She hands him the swipecard.

'And I'll need to take your picture.'

He looks at her.

'My picture?'

'Yes. For the swipecard. And for your by-line in the paper. Let's kill two birds with one stone, right? Ha-ha.'

She attempts a smile, but her lips tremble slightly.

'I've done a photography course,' she says as if to pre-empt any protest. 'You just stand there and I'll do the rest.'

A camera appears from behind the counter. It is mounted on a tripod. She cranks it up. Henning doesn't know where to look, so he gazes into the distance.

'That's good. Try to smile.'

Smile. He can't remember the last time he did that. She clicks three times in quick succession.

'Great. I'm Sølvi,' she says and offers him her hand over the counter. He takes it. Soft, lovely skin. He can't remember the last time he felt soft, lovely skin against his. She squeezes his hand, exerting just the right amount of pressure. He looks at her and lets go.

As he turns to leave, he wonders if she noticed the smile which almost formed on his lips.

Chapter 3

Henning has to swipe his shiny new card no less than three times, going from the reception area to the second floor. Though the office is where it always was, there is nothing to remind him of the place he had almost settled into, nearly two years ago. Everything is new, even the carpet. There are grey and white surfaces, a kitchenette, and he would bet good money that there are clean glasses and mugs in the cupboards. There are flat screens everywhere, on the desks and on the walls.

He checks out the room. Four smoke alarms. Two foam extinguishers, possibly more. Good. Or good enough.

It is a large, L-shaped room. Work stations by the windows, tables and chairs behind coloured glass partitions. There are tiny individual cubicles for when you want to conduct an interview without an audience or any background noise. There are lavatories, disabled ones as well, even though he can't actually see anyone even mildly infirm. He imagines there are rules about such things. They have always had a coffee maker, but now they have the state-of-the-art version, which takes twenty-nine seconds to make a fancy cup of black coffee. Not four, like the old one.

Henning loves coffee. You're not a proper reporter unless you love coffee.

He recognises the buzz immediately. Foreign TV stations, all reporting the same news over and over. Everything is *breaking news*. Stock exchange figures scroll along the bottom of the screen. A collage of TV screens show what NRK and TV2 are reporting on their strangely antiquated, but still viable text TV pages. The news channel runs its features on a loop. It, too, has a ticker which condenses a story into one sentence. He hears the familiar crackle of a police radio, as if R2D2 from the Star Wars movies intermittently makes contact from a galaxy far, far away. NRK News 24 can just about be heard from a radio somewhere.

Bleary-eyed reporters tap on keyboards, telephones ring, stories are debated, angles suggested. In a corner by the news desk, where every story is weighed, measured, rejected, applauded, polished or heavily edited, lies a mountain of newspapers – new and old – which the newly arrived reporters seize upon while they sip their first coffee of the day.

It is the usual controlled chaos. And yet, everything seems alien. The ease he felt after years of working in the streets, of being *in the field*, of showing up at a crime scene, knowing he was in his element, has completely disappeared. It all belongs to another lifetime, another era.

He feels like a cub reporter again. Or as if he is taking part in a play where he has been cast as The Victim, the poor soul everyone has to take care of, help back on his feet. And even though he hasn't spoken a single word to anyone, except Sølvi, his intuition tells him no one thinks it's going to work. Henning Juul will never be the same again.

He takes a few, hesitant steps and looks around to see if he recognises anyone. It's all faces and fragments from a distant past, like an episode of *This Is Your Life*. Then he spots Kåre.

Kåre Hjeltland is looking over the shoulder of a reporter at the news desk. Kåre is the news editor at *123news*. He is a short, skinny man with messy hair and a passion which exceeds anything Henning has ever known. Kåre is the Duracell bunny on speed with a hundred stories in his head at any given time and an arsenal of possible angles for practically anything.

That's why he is the news editor. If it had been up to Kåre, he would have been in charge of every department and worked as the night duty editor as well. He has Tourette's Syndrome, not the easiest condition to manage when you're trying to run a news desk and have a social life.

However, despite his tics and various other

symptoms, Kåre pulls it off. Henning doesn't know how, but Kåre pulls it off.

Kåre has noticed him, too. He waves and holds up one finger. Henning nods and waits patiently, while Kåre issues instructions to the reporter.

'And stress that in the introduction. That's the hook, no one cares that the tent was white or bought from Maxbo last March. Get it?'

'Maxbo doesn't sell tents.'

'Whatever. You know what I mean. And mention that she was found naked as soon as possible. It's important. It plants a sexy image in people's minds. Gives them something to get off on.'

The reporter nods. Kåre slaps him on the shoulder and bounces towards Henning. He nearly trips over a cable running across the floor, but carries on regardless. Even though he is only a few metres away now, he shouts.

'Henning, good to see you again. Welcome back.'

Kåre extends a hand, but doesn't wait for Henning to offer him his. He simply grabs Henning's hand and shakes it. Henning's forehead feels hot.

'So – how are things? You ready to chase web hits again?'

Henning thinks earmuffs might be a good investment.

'Well, I'm here, that's a start.'

'Super. Fantastic. We need people like you, people

20

who know how to give the public what they want. Great. Sex sells, coffers swell! Tits and ass bring in the cash!'

Kåre laughs out loud. His face starts to twitch, but he carries on all the same. Kåre has coined a lot of rhyming slogans in his time. Kåre loves rhymes.

'Ahem, I thought you could sit over there with the rest of the team.'

Kåre takes Henning by the arm and leads him past a red glass partition. Six computers, three on opposite sides of a square table, are backed up against each other. A mountain of newspapers lies on a round table behind it.

'You may have noticed that things have changed, but I haven't touched your work station. It's exactly the same. After what happened, I thought that you – eh – would want to decide for yourself if there was anything you wanted to throw out.'

'Throw out?'

'Yes. Or reorganise. Or – you know.'

Henning looks around.

'Where are the others?'

'Who?'

'The rest of the team?'

'Buggered if I know, lazy sods. Oh yes, Heidi is here. Heidi Kjus. She's around somewhere. In charge of national news now, she is.'

Henning feels his chest tighten. Heidi Kjus.

Heidi was one of the first temps from the Oslo School of Journalism he hired a million years ago. Newly qualified journalists are usually so bursting with theory that they have forgotten what really makes a good reporter: charming manners and common sense. If you're curious by nature and don't allow yourself to be fobbed off with the first thing people tell you, you'll go far. But if you want to be a star reporter, you also need to be a bit of a bastard, throw caution to the wind and have enough fire in your belly to go the distance, accept adversity, and never give up if you smell a good story.

Heidi Kjus had all of the above. From day one. On top of that, she had a hunger Henning had never seen before. Right from the start, no story was too small or too big, and it wasn't long before she had acquired sources and contacts as well as experience. As she began to realise just how good she was, she added a generous helping of arrogance to the heavy make-up, she plastered on every morning.

Some reporters have an aura about them, an attitude which screams: 'My job is the most important in the whole world and I'm better than the lot of you.' Heidi admired people with sharp elbows and soon developed her own. She took up space, even when she was working as a temp. She made demands.

Henning was working for *Nettavisen* at the time Heidi graduated. He was their crime reporter, but it was also his job to train new reporters and temps, show them the ropes, put them straight and nudge them in the direction of the overall aim: turning them into workhorses who wouldn't need micromanaging in order to deliver top stories that attract web hits 24/7.

He enjoyed this aspect of his job. And *Nettavisen* was a great first job for young journalists, even though most of them had no idea they were driving a Formula 1 car around increasingly congested streets in a media circus that grew bigger every day. Many were unsuited for this life, this way of thinking and working. And the problem was that as soon as he saw the beginnings of a good on-line reporter, they would leave. They would get offers of new jobs, better jobs or full-time employment contracts elsewhere.

Heidi left after only four months. She got an offer from *Dagbladet* she couldn't refuse. He didn't blame her. It was *Dagbladet*, after all. More status. More money. Heidi wanted it all and she wanted it now. And she got it.

And she's my new boss, he thinks. Bloody hell. This is bound to end in tears.

'It'll be good to have you back in the saddle, Henning,' Kåre enthuses.

Henning says 'mm'.

'Morning meeting in ten minutes. You'll be there, won't you?'

Henning says 'mm' again.

'Lovely. Lovely. Got to dash. I've another meeting.'

Kåre smiles, gives him a thumbs-up, and leaves. In passing, he slaps someone on the shoulder, before he disappears around the corner. Henning shakes his head. Then he sits down on a chair that squeaks and rocks like a boat. A new red notebook, still in its wrapper, lies next to the keyboard. Four pens. He guesses that none of them works. A pile of old print-outs. He recognises them as research for stories he was working on. An ancient mobile telephone takes up an unnecessary amount of space and he notices a box of business cards. *His* business cards.

His eyes stop at a framed photograph resting at an angle on the desk. There are two people in it, a woman and a boy.

Nora and Jonas.

He stares at them without seeing them clearly. Don't smile. Please, don't smile at me.

It'll be all right. Don't be scared. I'll take care of you.

He reaches for the frame, picks it up and puts it down again.

Face down.

Chapter 4

Morning meetings. The core of every newspaper, where the day's production plans are defined, tasks distributed, stories up- or down-graded, based on criteria such as topicality, importance and – in the case of *123news* – potential readership.

Each news desk starts by holding its own morning meeting. Sports, business, arts and national and international news. Lists of potential stories are drawn up. At this stage, a morning meeting can be inspirational. A good story often matures through discussion, while others are discarded – by common consent – because they are bad or a rival newspaper ran something similar two weeks ago. Afterwards, the editors meet to update each other and inform the duty editor of the kind of stories that will unfold throughout the day.

The one thing Henning hasn't missed is meetings. He knows before it has even begun that this meeting is a total waste of time. He is supposed to cover crime; murders, filth, evil. So why does he need to know that a sports personality is making another comeback? Or that Bruce Springsteen is getting divorced? He can read about it in the paper – later – if he cares, and if the reporter in question writes something worth reading. The finance editor or the sports editor is often clueless about arts and vice versa, which ruins any chance of a productive meeting. And secondly, each editor is too preoccupied with their own area of interest to offer each other valuable ideas or suggestions. However, the paper's management insists on such meetings, which is why Henning is now entering a meeting room with a table whose surface shines like a newly polished mirror. A stack of plastic cups and a jug of water are placed in the middle. He hazards a guess that the water is stale.

He sits down on a chair that isn't designed for lengthy discussions and avoids making eye contact with the others who are taking their seats around the table. He doesn't do small talk, especially when he believes everyone knows who he is anyway and isn't entirely comfortable with his presence.

Why is he here?

He's not an editor?

I heard he had a breakdown?

Kåre Hjeltland is the last to arrive and he closes the door.

'Okay, let's get started,' he shouts and sits down at the end of the table. He looks around.

'We're not expecting anyone else?'

No one replies.

'Right, let's kick off with foreign news. Knut. What have you got for us today?'

Knut Hammerstad, the foreign news editor, coughs and puts down his coffee cup.

'There's an upcoming election in Sweden. We're putting together profiles of their potential new prime ministers, who they are, what they stand for. A plane crash-landed in Indonesia. Suspected terrorist attack. Crash investigators are looking for the black box. Four terror suspects have been arrested in London. They were planning to blow Parliament sky high, I heard.'

'Great headline,' Kåre roars. 'Sod the Swedish election. Don't waste too much time on the plane crash. No one cares about it, unless any Norwegians were killed.'

'We're checking that, obviously.'

'Good. Push the terror story. Get the details, planning, execution, how many potential deaths and so on and so forth.'

'We're on it.'

'Great. What's next?'

Rikke Ringheim sits next to Knut Hammerstad. Rikke edits the sex and gossip columns. The paper's most important news desk.

Kåre ploughs on.

'Rikke, what have you got for us today?'

'We'll be talking to Carrie Olson.'

Rikke beams with pride and glee. Henning looks at her and wonders if she is aware his face is one big question mark.

'Who the hell is Carrie Olson?' Kåre demands to know.

'The author of *How to Get 10 Orgasms a Day*. A bestseller in the US, top of the sales charts in Germany and France. She's in Norway right now.'

Kåre claps his hands. The room reverberates.

'Bloody brilliant!'

Rikke smiles smugly.

'And she has Norwegian ancestors.'

'Can it get much better? Anything else?'

'We've started a survey. "How often do you have sex?" It's already attracting plenty of hits.'

'Another magnet. Sucks in the reader. He-he. Sucks, get it?'

'And we have another web hit: a sexologist says we need to prioritise sex in relationships. Might run it a little later today.'

Kåre nods.

'Well done, Rikke.'

He carries on, full steam ahead.

'Heidi?'

Henning hadn't noticed Heidi Kjus until then, but he does now. She is still skinny, her cheekbones are gaunt, the make-up around her hollow eyes is far too gaudy and she wears a lip gloss whose colour reminds him of fireworks and cheap champagne on New Year's Eve. She leans forward and coughs.

'Not much doubt about our big story today: the murder at Ekeberg Common. I've been informed that it is murder. Quite a brutal one. Police are holding a press conference later. Iver is going straight there and will be working on the story for the rest of the day. I've already spoken to him.'

'Great. Henning should probably join him at the press conference. Right, Henning?'

Henning jumps at the sound of his name and says 'hm?' The pitch of his voice rises. He sounds like a ninety-year-old in need of a hearing aid.

'The murder at Ekeberg Common. Press conference later today. Would be a good start for you, wouldn't it?'

From ninety to newbie in four seconds. He clears his throat.

'Yes, sure.'

He hears a voice, but fails to recognise it as his own.

'Super. You all know Henning Juul, I presume. He needs no further introduction. You know what he's been through, so please give him a warm welcome. No one deserves it more than him.'

Silence. The inside of his face is burning. The number of people in the room seems to have doubled in the last ten seconds and they are all staring at him. He wants to run. But he can't. So he looks up and concentrates on a point on the wall, above all of them, in the hope they might think he is looking at someone else.

'Time's flying. I've another meeting. Anything else you need to know before you go off chasing clicks?'

Kåre is addressing the duty editor, a man with black glasses, whom Henning has never seen before. The duty editor is about to say something, but Kåre has already leapt from his chair.

'That's it, then.'

He leaves.

'Ole and Anders, would you send me your lists, please?' The duty editor's voice is meek. There is no reply. Henning is thrilled that the meeting is over, until the chairs are pushed back and a bottleneck is created at the door. People breathe down his neck, they bump into him accidentally, his breathing becomes constricted and claustrophobic, but he holds it together, he doesn't push anyone out of the way, he doesn't panic.

He exhales with relief when he gets outside. His forehead feels hot.

A murder so soon. Henning had hoped for a gentler return, time to find his feet, read up on stories, check out what has been happening, get in touch with old sources, re-learn publishing tools, office routines, discover where everything is kept, chat to his new colleagues, acclimatise gradually, get used to thinking about a story. No time for any of that now.

Chapter 5

Heading back to his desk, Henning expects the worst. Heidi Kjus appears not to have noticed him, and yet she twirls around on her chair to face him the instant he gets there. She stands up, smiles her brightest Colgate smile and holds out her hand.

'Hi, Henning.'

Business. Courtesy. False smiles. He decides to play along. He shakes her hand.

'Hi, Heidi.'

'Good to have you back.'

'It's good to be back.'

'That's – eh, that's good.'

Henning studies her. As always, her eyes radiate earnestness. She is ambitious for herself and for others. He prepares for the speech she has undoubtedly rehearsed:

Henning, you were my boss once. Times have changed. I'm your boss now. And I expect that you blahblahblah.

He is taken aback when it fails to materialise. Instead she surprises him for the second time.

'I was sorry to hear about – to hear about what

happened. I just want to say that if there's anything you need, if you need more time off, just let me know. Okay?'

Her voice is warm like a rock face on a sunny afternoon. He thanks her for her concern, but for the first time in a long time, he feels an urge to get stuck in.

'So Iver is going to the press conference?' he says.

'Yes, he worked late last night, so he'll be going straight there.'

'Who's Iver?'

Heidi looks at him as if he has just suggested that the earth really is flat.

'Is this a joke?'

He shakes his head.

'Iver Gundersen? You don't know who Iver Gundersen is?'

'No.'

Heidi suppresses the urge to laugh out loud. She controls herself as if she has just realised that she is talking to a child.

'We hired Iver from *VG Nett* last summer.'

'Aha?'

'He delivered big stories for them and he has continued to do that here. I know that TV2 are desperate to get him, but so far Iver has been loyal to us.'

'I see. So you pay him well.'

Heidi looks at him as if he has sworn in church.

'Eh, that's not my area, but –'

Henning nods and pretends to listen to the arguments which follow. He has heard them before. Loyalty. A concept that has worn thin in journalism. If he were being charitable, he might be able to name two reporters he would describe as loyal. The rest are careerists, ready to jump ship every time a fatter pay package is offered, or they are so useless that they couldn't get a job anywhere else. When a relatively undistinguished *VG Nett* reporter is poached by a rival on-line publication, and later declines an offer from TV2, it's bound to be about the money. It's always about the money.

He registers Heidi expressing the hope that he and Iver will get along. Henning nods and says 'mm'. He is good at saying 'mm'.

'You'll get to meet each other at the press conference and then you can decide who will be doing what on this story. It's a frenzied murder.'

'What happened?'

'My source tells me the victim was found inside a tent, half buried and stoned to death. I imagine the police have all sorts of theories. It's obvious to consider foreign cultures.'

Henning nods, but he doesn't like obvious thoughts.

'Keep me informed about what you do, please?' she

34

says. He nods again and looks at the notebook on his desk, still in its wrapper. Brusquely, he rips off the wrapper and tries one of the four pens lying next to it. It doesn't work. He tries the other three.

Damn.

Chapter 6

It's not far from Urtegata to Grønland police station, where the press conference is being held. Henning takes his time and strolls through an area which Sture Skipsrud, his editor-in-chief, described as 'a press Mecca' when *123news* relocated here. Henning thought it was very apt. *Nettavisen* is there, *Dagens Næringsliv* has an ultra-modern office block close by and Mecca features in most flats in the neighbourhood. If you ignore the tarmac and the temperature, you might just as well be in Mogadishu. The aroma of different spices greets him at every corner.

Henning is reminded of the last time he was heading the same way. A man he had interviewed decided to kill himself a few hours later, and both the police and the man's relatives wanted to know if Henning had said something or had opened old wounds which might have pushed the man over the edge.

Henning remembers him well. Paul Erik Holmen, forty-something. Two million kroner mysteriously went missing from a company Holmen was working for and Henning had more than suggested that the extravagant vacation Holmen had just taken, combined with the renovation of the family's holiday cabin in Eggedal, might explain the whereabouts of the missing money. His sources were reliable, obviously. Holmen's guilty conscience and the fear of being locked up got too much for him and consequently Henning found himself in one of the many interview rooms at the police station.

They soon released him, but a couple of jealous reporters thought it was worth a paragraph or two. Fair enough, Henning could appreciate it was newsworthy to some extent even though Holmen would probably have topped himself anyway, but stories like that can be hard to shake off.

Human memory is selective, at best, and plain wrong at worst. When suspicions are raised or planted, it doesn't take much for speculation to turn into fact and suspicion into a verdict. He has covered many murders where a suspect is brought in for questioning (i.e., arrested), usually from the victim's close family (i.e., the husband), and all the evidence points to him. Later, the police find the real killer. In the meantime, the media circus has done its utmost to drag up anything in the husband's past which might cast aspersions on his character. Trial by media.

In the short term, truth is a good friend, but the doubt never goes away. Not among people you don't know. People remember what they want to remember. Henning suspects someone out there hasn't forgotten his role in Paul Erik Holmen's last act, but it doesn't bother him. He has no problem living with what he did, even though the police gave him a bollocking for trying to do their job.

He is used to that.

Or, at least, he was.

Chapter 7

It feels odd to be back inside the grey building at number 44 Grønlandsleiret again. Once upon a time the police station was practically his second home; even the cleaners used to greet him. Now he tries to make himself as inconspicuous as possible, but is hampered by the burn scars on his face. He is aware that the other reporters are looking at him, but he ignores them. His plan is just to attend, listen to what the police have to say and then go back to the office to write – if, indeed, there is anything to write about.

He freezes the moment he enters the foyer. Nothing could have prepared him for the sight of the woman leaning towards a man who shows every sign of being a reporter. Dark corduroy jacket, suitably arrogant presence, the 'did-everyone-see-the-scoop-I-pulled-off-yesterday' expression. He sports designer stubble which makes his face look more sallow than it is. His thinning hair is gelled and swept back. But it's the woman. Henning had never imagined he would see her, here, on his first day back.

Nora Klemetsen. Henning's ex-wife. Jonas's mother.

He hasn't spoken to her since she visited him at Sunnaas Rehabilitation Centre. He forgets when it was. Perhaps he has suppressed it. But he'll never forget her face. She couldn't bear to look at him. He didn't blame her. She had every right. He had been looking after Jonas, and he had failed to save him.

Their son.

Their lovely, lovely son.

They had already separated at that point. She only visited him at the hospital to finalise the divorce, to get his signature. She got it. No ulterior motives, no questions, no conditions. In a way, he was relieved. He couldn't have coped with her in his life – a constant reminder of his own shortcomings. Every glance, every conversation would have been tarred with that brush.

They hadn't said much to each other. He was desperate to tell her everything, tell her what he had done or failed to do, what he remembered of that night, but every time he breathed in and got ready to speak, his mouth dried up and he couldn't utter a single word. Later, when he closed his eyes and daydreamed, he talked like a machine gun; Nora nodded, she understood, and afterwards she came to him and let him cry himself out in her lap while she ran her fingers through his hair.

He has been thinking he should try again, the next time he saw her, but now is clearly not the time. He is working. She is working. She is standing very close to some reporter – and she is laughing.

Bollocks.

Henning met Nora Klemetsen while he worked for *Kapital* and she was a rookie business journalist on *Aftenposten*. They ran into each other at a press conference. It was a run of the mill event, no drama, merely the announcement of some company's annual results with so little headline-grabbing potential that they only warranted a paragraph in *Dagens Næringsliv* and a right-hand column on page 17 in *Finansavisen* the next day. He happened to sit down next to Nora. He was there to profile one of the senior executives who would be retiring shortly. They yawned their way through the presentation, started giggling at their respective and increasingly hopeless attempts at disguising their boredom, and decided to go for a drink afterwards to recover.

They were both in relationships; she was living – semi-seriously – with a stockbroker, while he had an on-off thing going with a stuck-up corporate lawyer. But that first evening was so enjoyable, so free from awkwardness that they went for another drink the next time they found themselves covering the same story. He had had many girlfriends, but he had never known someone who was so easy to be with. Their tastes were compatible in so many ways, it bordered on scary.

They both liked grainy mustard with their sausages, not the usual bottled Idun rubbish. Neither of them liked tomatoes all that much, but they both loved ketchup. They liked the same type of films, and never had protracted arguments in the video store or outside the cinema. Neither of them liked spending the summer in hot foreign places when Norway offered rock faces and fresh prawns. Friday was Taco day. Eating anything else on a Friday was simply unthinkable.

And, gradually, they both realised they couldn't live without each other.

Three and half years later they were married, exactly nine months afterwards Jonas arrived and they were as happy as two sleep-deprived career people in their late twenties can be, when their life is a plank full of splinters. Not enough sleep, too few breaks, minimum understanding of each other's needs – both at home and at work – more and more rows, less and less time and energy to be together. In the end, neither of them could take any more.

Parents. The best and the worst human beings can become.

And now her arm is entwined with another man's. Unprofessional, he thinks, flirting at a press conference. And Nora spots him halfway through a fit of laughter. She stops immediately, as though something is stuck in her throat. They look at each other for what seems like forever.

He blinks first. Vidar Larsen, who works for NTB, touches his shoulder and says 'hi, so you're back, Henning?' He nods and decides to follow Vidar; he says nothing, but he makes sure he get as far away from Nora as he can, looking no one in the eye, following feet and footsteps through doors he could find blindfolded. He takes a seat at the back of the press room where he can watch the back of other people's heads rather than vice versa. The room fills up quickly. He sees Nora and Corduroy enter together. They sit next to each other, quite a long way forward.

So, Nora, we meet again.

And, once again, we meet at a press conference.

Chapter 8

Three uniformed officers enter, two men and a woman. Henning instantly recognises the two men: Chief Inspector Arild Gjerstad and Detective Inspector Bjarne Brogeland.

Bjarne and Henning went to school together in Kløfta. They were never best friends, even though they were in the same year. That might have been enough to start a friendship back then. But it takes more. Chemistry and compatibility, for example.

Later, Henning also discovered that Bjarne was a Romeo whose ambition was to sleep with as many girls as possible, and when he started turning up at the Juuls', it wasn't hard to decipher Bjarne's true intentions. Luckily, Henning's sister, Trine, was on to him and Henning avoided having to play the part of Protective Older Brother, but his loathing of Bjarne stayed with him throughout their adolescence.

And now Bjarne is a policeman.

Not that this is news to Henning. Both of them applied to the police academy in the 1990s. Bjarne was accepted.

Henning wasn't. He was rejected long before the admission process even started, because he suffered from every allergy known to man, and had had asthma as a child. Bjarne, however, was the physically robust type. Twenty-twenty vision and great stamina. He had been an athlete when he was younger, and performed quite well in heptathlons. Henning seems to recall that Bjarne pole-vaulted over 4.50 metres.

What Henning didn't know was that Bjarne had started working in the Violent and Sexual Crimes Unit. He thought Bjarne was a plain-clothes officer, but everyone needs a change now and again. Now he is up there on the platform, gazing across the assembly. His face is grave, professional, and he looks imposing in the tight-fitting uniform. Henning reckons he can still pull. Short, dark hair, hint of grey above the ears, cleft chin, white teeth. Tanned and clean-shaven.

Vain Bjarne, Henning thinks.

And a potential source.

The other man, Chief Inspector Gjerstad, is tall and slim. He has a neatly trimmed moustache which he strokes repeatedly. Gjerstad was with the murder squad when Henning started covering crime, and he seems to have stayed there. Gjerstad despises reporters who think they are smarter than the police and, to be fair, Henning thinks, I'm probably one of them.

The woman in the middle, Assistant Commissioner

Pia Nøkleby, checks if the microphone is working, then she clears her throat. The reporters raise their pens in expectation. Henning waits. He knows the first minutes will offer nothing but introductions and reiteration of information already available, but he intends to listen carefully all the same.

Then something takes him by surprise. He feels a tingle of anticipation. To him, who has felt only rage, self-loathing and self-pity in the last two years, this tingling, this excitement prompted by work is something Dr Helge would undoubtedly classify as a breakthrough.

He listens to the woman's high voice:

'Good morning and thank you for coming. Today's press conference follows the discovery of a body at Ekeberg Common this morning. I'm Assistant Commissioner Pia Nøkleby, and with me I have Chief Inspector Arild Gjerstad, who is heading the investigation, and Detective Inspector Bjarne Brogeland.'

Gjerstad and Brogeland nod briefly to the reporters. Nøkleby covers her mouth and coughs, before she continues:

'As you're all aware, a woman was found dead in a tent on Ekeberg Common. We received a call at 6.09 a.m. The body was discovered by an elderly man out walking his dog. The victim is a 23-year-old woman from Slemdal and her name is Henriette Hagerup.'

Pens scratch against paper. Nøkleby nods to Gjerstad who moves closer to the table and the microphone. He coughs.

'We're treating her death as murder. No arrests have been made yet. At this point in the investigation there's very little we can tell you about what was found at the crime scene and any leads we may be following up, but we can say that this murder was particularly brutal.'

Henning notes down the word 'brutal'. In media and police speak 'brutal' means there is information the press shouldn't report. It's to do with protecting the public against knowing what the crackpots out there are capable of. And fair enough: why should relatives have every detail of how their child, brother, sister or parents were killed splashed across the papers for all to see? But that doesn't mean the press can't be told.

Apart from that, the press conference has little to offer. Not that Henning had expected much. There can be no suspects while the motive for the killing is unknown, and the police are still securing evidence at the crime scene. It's too early in the investigation to say if the evidence will give the police something to go on.

And blah-blah-blah.

Chief Inspector Gjerstad's briefing, if you can call it that, is over in ten minutes. As usual, there is time allowed for questions afterwards and, as usual, reporters compete to get their question in first. Henning shakes his head at this every time. The First Question is a constant source of envious looks and congratulatory slaps on the back in editorial offices everywhere. A reporter is regarded as one hell of a guy, by himself and by others, if he can make his voice heard first.

Henning has never seen the point of this and assumes it's about penis envy. TV2's Guri Palme wins this time. She doesn't have a penis, but she is a pretty blonde girl who has turned all the disadvantages that that entails to her benefit. She has surprised everyone by being ambitious and clever, and is successfully climbing the journalistic ladder.

'What can you tell us of the circumstances surrounding the killing? In your introduction, Chief Inspector Gjerstad, you mentioned that the murder was unusually brutal. What do you mean?'

Take your places: ready, steady –

'I can't comment at this time, nor would I want to,' Gjerstad says.

'Can you tell us anything about the victim?'

'We know that the victim was a student at Westerdal School of Communication. She had nearly completed her second year, and she was regarded as highly talented.'

'What did she study?'

'Film and television. She wanted to be a screenwriter.'

Three questions are all that Guri Palme gets and

NRK takes over the baton. Henning detects disappoint-
ment in the journalist's eye at coming second, though
he can only see him from the back. But it is Jørn
Bendiksen from NRK who takes them all by surprise.

'It's rumoured to be an honour killing?'

Journalists. Always ready with a statement that
sounds like a question. Assistant Commissioner
Nøkleby shakes her head.

'No comment.'

'Can you confirm that the victim had been flogged?'

Nøkleby looks at Bendiksen before glancing at
Gjerstad. Henning smiles to himself. There's a leak, he
concludes. And the police know it. Still, Nøkleby
remains professional.

'No comment.'

No comment.

You will hear that ten times, at least, during a police
press conference, especially at the early stages of the
investigation. It is known as 'tactical considerations'.
The strategy is to give everyone, the killer included, as
little information as possible about any leads the police
are pursuing or any evidence they may have found, so
they have time to gather all the evidence needed to
build a case.

Nøkleby and Gjerstad know they are playing a game
now. NRK has picked up two important pieces in The
Great Jigsaw: honour killing and flogging. Bendiksen

would never have made such allegations at the press conference without knowing that they are true, or pretty close. Nøkleby straightens her glasses. Gjerstad looks more uncomfortable now. Brogeland, who so far hasn't uttered a single word, shifts in his chair to find a more comfortable position.

It happens all the time. Reporters know more, much more, than the police would like them to, and, in many cases, they hinder the investigation. It is a complex dance for two; each partner depending on the other for results. Plus, on the journalists' side there is rivalry, gruelling competition with everyone covering the same case. On-line newspapers publish at a speed that limits the lifespan of the story and it's always about finding the Next Big Thing. It puts increasing pressure on the police and forces them to spend more time dealing with the press than doing the job they are meant to do.

Nøkleby ends the questions once P4, *VG* and *Aftenposten* have had their fill, but she can't get back to work yet. TV and radio stations need their own interviews to give their viewers or listeners the illusion of exclusivity; the questions are repeated and Nøkleby has another chance to say –

Exactly.

It is the same performance every time. Everyone knows that proper journalistic work starts after the press conference.

Henning decides to find Iver Gundersen and agree the best way to cover this story.

After all, he is supposed to be working again.

And the very idea of that strikes him as bizarre.

Chapter 9

The reporters try to squeeze in more questions, but are brusquely dismissed by the uniformed trio and the reporters file out. Henning is hemmed in by people he doesn't want to be near, someone shoves him in the back, he bumps into a woman in front of him, he mutters an apology and desperately longs for more space and greater distances.

They spill out into the foyer and he looks for Iver Gundersen. This would have been easier, if he knew what Gundersen looked like; there are at least fifty journalists present. Henning decides to find Vidar from NTB and ask him, but he doesn't have time to do anything before Nora appears in his field of vision. And he in hers.

He stops. They can't avoid talking to each other now.

He takes a tentative step towards her, she mimics him. They stop a few metres apart. Eyes meet eyes. All he can see is a face which contains a multitude of sentences that have never been uttered.

'Hi, Henning.'

Her voice is like a blast of icy wind. The 'hi' rises in pitch and the 'Henning' drops. He senses she is speaking to a creature that has done her a severe injustice, but to whom she is forced to relate. He says 'hi' to her. She hasn't changed, but he spots her grief just behind her eyelids, from where it could erupt at any moment.

Nora is shorter than most women and she tries to compensate for this by wearing high heels. She has short hair. Not like a boy, it is not ultra-short at the back, but her fringe is high up her forehead. She used to have long hair, but the short style suits her. The last time he saw her, she was ashen. Now her skin and her face glow. He suspects it might have something to do with Corduroy. The glow suits her.

Christ, how it suits her.

Many expressions inhabit Nora's face. When she is frightened, she opens her mouth, her teeth show and she closes her eyes slightly. When she is angry, she raises her eyebrows, she frowns and her lips narrow. And when she smiles, her whole face explodes, it widens, and you have to smile with her. Change is weird, he thinks. Once, he couldn't imagine life without her. Now, it would be hard to live with her.

'You're here?' he says, failing to disguise his nerves which choke him.

Nora simply replies: 'Yes.'

'Had enough of business?'

She tilts her head to the left, then to the right.

'I needed a change after –'

She breaks off. He is relieved that she doesn't finish the sentence. He has an overwhelming urge to go to her, to embrace her, but turning thought into action is out of the question. There is an invisible wall between them and only Nora can break it down.

'So – so you're back then?' she says.

'My first day today,' he says and tries to smile. She studies his face. It's as if she focuses on the areas where the flames did their worst, but doesn't think it's bad enough. He sees Corduroy behind her. He is watching them. I hope you're jealous, you tosser.

'How are you, Nora,' Henning says, though he doesn't actually want to know. He doesn't want to hear that she is happy again, that – at last – she can face the future with hope. He knows he can never win her back; That Which He Doesn't Think About will never go away. All the same, he doesn't want her to be lost to him.

'I'm good,' she says.

'You still living in Sagene?'

She hesitates. Then she says: 'Yes.'

He nods, sensing she is trying to protect him against something. He doesn't want to know what it is, though he has an inkling. And then it comes.

'You might as well know now, and it's best that you hear it from me,' she starts. He takes a deep breath, puts up a steel barrier which melts the moment she says:

'I'm seeing someone.'

He looks at her and nods. He thinks that it ought not to hurt, but he can feel his stomach lurch.

'We've been together for six months now.'

'Mm.'

She looks at him again. For the first time in a long time, there is warmth in her eyes. But it's the wrong kind. It's the warmth of pity.

'We're thinking of moving in together.'

He says 'mm' again.

'I hope you're okay,' he then adds.

She doesn't reply; all she gives him is a cautious nod. It's good to see her smile, but he realises he can't take much more of this, so he employs the only defence mechanism he has and changes the subject.

'You wouldn't happen to know who Iver Gundersen is?' he says. 'I've never met the man, but I think we'll be working together.'

Nora looks away.

He should have guessed it when he saw how awkward it was for her to tell him she had met a new man. But why should it? She has moved on, slammed the lid on their shared past. The future is where it's happening.

55

She sighs and he realises why, when she turns to Corduroy.

'Iver Gundersen is my new boyfriend.'

Chapter 10

He glares at Corduroy, whose eyes flicker around the room during an absent-minded conversation with a fellow reporter. Henning imagines Nora's fingers running though Corduroy's revolting hair, gently caressing his stubble, tender lips against lips.

He remembers how she used to snuggle up to him at night, when they had turned off the light, how she put her arms around him, eager to spoon. And now it's Corduroy who enjoys her small, loving hands.

'Right,' Henning says, and instantly hears how defeated he must sound. This was the moment he should have flown into a rage, scolded her, left her with the certain knowledge of having trampled on his heart, torpedoed it, chewed it up and spat it out again. You should have called her a heartless bitch, insensitive, the definition of selfishness, but you didn't. All you said was:

'*Right.*'

Pathetic. Utterly pathetic.

He can't bear to look at her. And now he has to work with Iver.

A cruel twist of fate, he thinks, it has to be.

He goes over to Gundersen. He hears Nora asking him not to, 'Please don't –', but he ignores her. He stops a metre from Gundersen and looks at him. Gundersen is halfway through a sentence, but he stops and turns.

He knows who I am, Henning thinks. I can see it in his eyes. And I can see that it makes him nervous.

'Hi,' Gundersen says. Henning sticks out his hand.

'Henning Juul.'

Reluctantly, Gundersen takes his hand. Henning presses it hard.

'Iver G—'

'I understand we're both covering this story. How do you think we should go about?'

He knows he has put Gundersen on the spot, but he doesn't care.

'I'm not entirely sure.'

Gundersen swallows, then he recovers.

'I suggest updating the story we've already published, with quotes from the press conference,' he begins, and looks over Henning's shoulder at Nora, who is observing their first meeting.

'I thought about following up this honour killing theory,' Gundersen continues. 'See if there's something in it. In which case, the list of suspects will be fairly

58

short and it won't be long before the police arrest someone.'

Henning nods. 'Has anyone talked to her friends?'

Gundersen shakes his head.

'Then I'll visit her college and do a story about her life and who she was.'

'Human interest.'

'Mm.'

Henning makes eye contact with Gundersen, who nods.

'All right, sounds good. I could try contacting the man who found the victim, but I've heard that he doesn't want to talk to the press. So –' Gundersen shrugs.

Henning nods, he sees that Gundersen is still uncomfortable, that there is something he feels the urge to say. He inhales, but Henning beats him to it.

'Great,' he says and leaves. He walks as fast as his damaged legs can carry him, straight past Nora, without looking at her.

Well done, Henning, he tells himself. You had the shit kicked out of you in round one, but you got back on your feet and you won round two. That's the inherent problem with boxing. Winning a round gets you nowhere, unless you also win the next one. And the one after that. And the one after that. And most important of all, the last one.

The battle has already been lost, Henning thinks. The judges have already decided. But, at least, he can try for a personal best.

He can avoid being knocked out again.

Chapter 11

It takes several minutes before his heart rate returns to normal. He crosses Borggata, trying to forget what he has just seen and heard, but is haunted by Nora's eyes and icy breath. He imagines the conversation between Nora and Iver, after his exit:

Iver: Well, that went all right.

Nora: Had you expected anything else?

Iver: I don't know. Poor guy.

Nora: It's not easy for him, Iver. Please don't make it harder for him than it already is.

Iver: What do you mean?

Nora: Exactly what I've just said. Do you think it was easy for him to see me here? See me with you? I think it was very brave of him to go up to you the way he did.

Stop it, Henning. You know that wasn't what she said. More likely, it went:

Nora: Ignore him, Iver. That's just the way he is. He has always done his own thing. Sod him. I'm starving. Let's have some lunch.

Yep, that's it. Much more authentic.

He decides he needs to clear his head. Forget Nora

and concentrate on the job in hand. As he waits for the lights to change at the junction with Tøyengata, it occurs to him that he will need his camera.

He goes home to get it.

Detective Inspector Brogeland slows down. The car, one of the many new Passats the police have purchased, comes to a smooth halt outside 37 Oslogate. He puts the selector into 'P' and looks at his colleague, Sergeant Ella Sandland.

Jesus, she's hot, he thinks, taking in the masculine uniform and everything it conceals. He fantasises about her constantly, pictures her without the leather jacket, the light blue shirt, the tie, stripped of everything except her handcuffs. Countless times, he has imagined her shameless, lascivious, giving herself completely to him.

Women think men in uniform are sexy. It's a well-known fact. Brogeland, however, thinks that's nothing compared to the other way round: women in clothes that radiate authority.

Damn, that's hot.

Ella Sandland is 1.75 metres tall. She is extremely fit, her stomach is flatter than a pancake, her bottom stretches her trousers perfectly when she walks; she is a little under-endowed in the breast department, a touch rough and masculine in an 'are-you-bi-or-straight' way, but it turns him on. He looks at her hair. Her fringe just brushes her eyebrows. Her skin fits snugly under her chin, over her cheekbones; it is smooth, with no blemishes or marks and not a hint of facial hair – thank God. She moves gracefully, she has one of the straightest backs Brogeland has ever seen; and she pushes her chest slightly forward, even when she is sitting, like women tend to do to create the illusion that their breasts are bigger than they really are. But when Sandland does it, it's just so sexy.

Damn, that's so sexy.

And she is from West Norway. Ulsteinvik, he thinks, though she has lost her accent over the years.

He tries to suppress the images that increasingly clutter his head these days. They are outside the home of Mahmoud Marhoni, Henriette Hagerup's boyfriend.

It is a standard home visit. In 2007, out of thirty-two murders thirty were committed by someone the victim knew or was in a relationship with. Statistically, the killer is likely to be someone close. A rejected spouse, a relative. Or a boyfriend. This makes the visit Brogeland and Sandland are about to make of the utmost importance.

'Ready?' he says. Sandland nods. They open their car doors simultaneously and get out.

Christ, just look at the way she gets out.

*

Brogeland has been to Oslogate before. Mahmoud Marhoni has even appeared on his radar earlier, in connection with a case Brogeland worked on when he was a plain-clothes detective. As far as they could establish at the time, Marhoni wasn't mixed up in anything illegal.

Brogeland has been a cop long enough to know that means nothing. That's why he experiences a heightened sense of excitement as they walk towards number 37, locate the doorbells and find the name of Henriette Hagerup's boyfriend to the left.

There is no sound when Sandland presses the button. At that moment, a teenage girl in a hijab opens the door to the backyard. She looks at them; she isn't startled as Brogeland had expected, but holds the door open for them. Sandland thanks her and smiles at the girl. Brogeland nods briefly by way of a thank you. He makes sure he enters last, so he can gorge himself on the sight of his female colleague's backside.

I bet she knows, Brogeland thinks. She knows that men love to stare at her. And the uniform doubles her power. She appears unobtainable because she is a policewoman, and because she is so desirable, she can take her pick of anyone she wants – from both sides of the fence, probably. She is in control. And that's irresistible, a huge turn-on.

They find themselves in a backyard which shows

every sign of neglect. There are weeds between the paving slabs, bushes have been left to grow wild and tangled. The flowerbeds, if they can still be called that, are a jungle of compacted soil and dusty roots. The black paint on the bicycle stand is peeling and the few bicycles parked there have rusty chains and flat tyres.

There are three stairwells to choose from. Brogeland knows that Marhoni lives in stairwell B. Sandland gets there first, finds the button in the square box on the wall and presses it. No sound.

Brogeland forces himself to take his eyes off Sandland's rear and looks up at the sky. Clouds are gathering over Gamlebyen. There will be rain soon. A swallow shrieks as it flies from one rooftop to another. He hears a jet plane pass, but he can't see it through the clouds.

Marhoni lives in the upper ground floor flat, but the window is too high for Brogeland to be able to look in. Sandland rings the bell again. This time she gets a response.

'Hello?'

'Hello. This is the police. Open the door, please.'

Brogeland relishes Sandland's juicy accent.

'Police?'

Brogeland registers a hint of reluctance and fear in the voice. That's not Marhoni, he thinks, Marhoni is a tough nut.

'Yes, the police.'

Sandland's sexy voice is more authoritative now.

'W-why?'

'Police? Don't let them in.'

The voice in the background is loud enough for Brogeland and Sandland to hear it.

'Open up.'

Sandland raises her voice. Brogeland snaps out of his fantasy and pushes down the door handle. He has noticed that the lock has been vandalised, and he stomps inside with Sandland right behind him. They race up the stairs to the elevated ground floor. Brogeland can hear someone fiddling with the lock, but he gets there first, his superb physical fitness pays off, and he tears open the door.

A man he instantly guesses must be Marhoni's brother gives him a frightened look; Brogeland ignores him, thinking that at any moment, he could be staring straight into the mouth of a pistol. He moves swiftly and noiselessly, he checks the flat, there is a smell of herbs, of cannabis, he opens a door, a kitchen, it's empty, he continues, a bedroom, no, no one there either, he is in the living room, and that's when he sees it, the fireplace, someone has lit a fire; however, it's not the flames that disconcert him, but what the flames are consuming with such greed, and he is taken aback for a moment, it's a computer, a laptop, he calls out to

Sandland to save it and he will go after Marhoni, he hears how his voice is rich with power, with experience, knowledge, guts, authority, everything you need to make on-the-spot decisions. Sandland responds just as Brogeland spots Marhoni trying to escape out of a window in one of the rooms accessible through the living room. Marhoni gets ready, then he jumps. Brogeland soon reaches the window, looks down before he climbs up, realises the drop is less than two metres, jumps, lands softly and looks around, spots Marhoni and chases after him. You'll be sorry you did that, he thinks, you prat, absconding from your flat the very day your girlfriend is found murdered, how do you think it's going to look, you moron?

Brogeland knows it will be an easy race to win. Marhoni keeps looking over his shoulder and every time Brogeland gains a few metres on him. Marhoni runs across the junction where Bispegata crosses Oslovei, without waiting for a green light. A car brakes right in front of him and sounds its horn. Brogeland pursues him. In the background, he can hear the tram, dring-dring; there are cars in the street, people behind windows following the chase with interest, probably wondering what on earth is going on, is someone making a film or is it the real thing? Marhoni turns around, then he runs straight ahead. Brogeland thinks Marhoni must want an audience or he would have fled in the direction of Aker Church. Brogeland is only ten metres behind Marhoni now and he is constantly gaining on him. He catches up with him and throws himself at him. They land on the tarmac outside Ruinen Bar & Café.

Marhoni breaks his fall and Brogeland is unhurt. There is a man sitting outside the café, smoking. He watches as Brogeland sits on Marhoni's back, pinning back his arms, before he calls in for assistance.

'19, this is Fox 43 Bravo, over.'

He gets his breath back, while he waits for a response.

'19 responding, over.'

'This is Fox 43 Bravo, I'm in St Hallvard's Square, I've arrested a suspect and I require assistance. Over.'

He breathes out, looks at Marhoni who is gasping for air. Brogeland shakes his head.

'Bloody idiot,' he mutters to himself.

Chapter 12

Westerdal School of Communication is situated on Fredensborgvei, close to St Hanshaugen. As always, when he finds himself in this part of Oslo, he thinks someone made a complete hash of urban planning: 1950s tenements painted a shade of grey that can best be described as concrete, and tiny, charming houses in vibrant colours, lie a hair's breadth from each other. The incline of Damstredet reminds him of the narrow lanes of Bergen, while the buildings along the road leading to the city centre evoke local government. There is a constant buzz and a permanent cloud of dust and pollution in the streets and the neighbourhood's few gardens.

But right now, Henning couldn't care less.

It is packed with people under the big tree outside the entrance to the college. Friends huddle together, hugging each other. There is crying. And sobbing. He walks nearer, sees others plying the same trade as him, but ignores them. He knows what tomorrow's news-papers will show. Photos of mourners, plenty of photos, but not very much text. Now is the time to wallow in grief, let the readers have their share of evil, the bereavement, the emotions; get to know the victim and her friends.

It is a standard package he is putting together. He could almost have written the story before coming here, but it has been a while since he wrote anything, so he decides to start from scratch and think of some questions that might make the package a little less predictable.

He opts for a slow and soft approach, quietly observing before identifying someone to interview. He has an eye for such people. Soon, he is caught up in a river of tears and finds himself overcome by an unexpected reaction:

Anger. Anger, because only a few people here know what real grief is, know how much it hurts to lose someone you care about, someone you love, someone you would willingly throw yourself in front of a bus for. He sees that many of the bystanders don't grieve properly, they exaggerate, they pose, relishing the opportunity to show how sensitive they are. But it's all fake.

He tries to shake off his rage. He takes out his camera and shoots some pictures, moves around, focussing on faces, on eyes. He likes eyes. They are said to be the mirror of the soul, but Henning likes eyes because they reveal the truth.

He zooms in on the impromptu shrine the victim's

friends have built under the huge tree to the right of the entrance. Three thick trunks have intertwined and created an enormous broccoli-shaped growth. The branches sag with the weight of the leaves. The roots of the tree are encircled by a low cobblestone wall.

A framed photograph of Henriette Hagerup is leaning against one of the tree trunks. The photograph is surrounded by flowers, handwritten cards and messages. Tea lights flicker in the gentle wind which has found its way here. There are photographs of her with her fellow students, with friends, at parties, on location, behind a camera. It's grief. It's condensed grief, but it's still fake. A textbook example, no doubt about it.

He looks up from the camera and concludes that Henriette Hagerup was a strikingly attractive woman. Or perhaps a mere child. There was something innocent about her: blonde curly hair, not too long, a brilliant broad smile and fair skin. He sees charm. And something more important, something better. Intelligence. He sees that Henriette Hagerup was an intelligent young woman.

Who could have hated you so much?

He reads some of the cards:

We will never forget you, Henriette
Rest in peace
Johanne, Turid and Susanne.

Missing you, Henry.
Missing you loads.
Tore.

There are between ten and twenty cards or notes about absence and grief, and all the messages have similar wording. He is scanning them absent-mindedly, when his mobile starts to vibrate in his pocket. He takes it out, but doesn't recognise the caller's number. He is supposed to be working, but decides to answer it nevertheless.

'Hello?'

He moves away from the crowd.

'Hi, Henning, it's Iver. Iver Gundersen.'

Before he has time to say anything, a blast of jealousy hits him right in the solar plexus. Mister Super Fucking Corduroy. He manages a flustered 'hi'.

'Where are you?' Gundersen asks.

Henning clears his throat: 'At the victim's college.'

'Okay. I'm calling to let you know the police have already made an arrest.'

For a moment, he forgets that he is having a conversation with his ex-wife's new lover. He actually detects a flicker of curiosity.

'That was quick. Who is it?'

'According to my sources, it's the boyfriend. I don't

know his name yet. But perhaps one of her friends could tell you?'

Henning can hear Iver's voice, but he barely registers what is being said. Among the myriad notes, candles and red eyes, he has spotted a message which stands out.

'You still there?'

'Eh, yeah. Her friends. Great.'

'It's a home run, I reckon.'

'They have evidence?'

'I think so. I'll start work on the story and expand on it later as more info becomes available.'

'Okay.'

Gundersen hangs up. Henning returns his mobile to his jacket pocket without taking his eyes off the card. He holds up his camera and snaps a picture, zooming in on the text:

I'll carry on your work
See you in eternity
Anette

He lowers the camera and lets it dangle around his neck. He re-reads the words before looking around the students.

Where are you, Anette, he wonders? And what's the work you intend to complete?

Chapter 13

Detective Inspector Brogeland takes off his jacket and hangs it on a coat stand in his office. He walks down the corridor and knocks on Sergeant Sandland's door. Secretly hoping to catch her in an erotic fantasy about him, he doesn't wait for her to reply before he opens it. Sadly, she has so far failed to respond to his numerous advances with even so much as a glance. *Perhaps I've been too direct. Or maybe it's because I'm married,* Brogeland thinks and enters.

Sandland is in front of her computer, typing. She doesn't look up when Brogeland appears.

'Are you ready?' he says. She holds up one finger, before resuming her race across the keyboard with a speed a Thai masseuse would have been impressed by.

Brogeland looks around. *Typical girly office,* he thinks. Neat and tidy, documents in organised piles, a pencil pot with two blue pens and one red, a stapler and a hole punch, Post-it notes next to them, a diary open on today's date, but no appointments, ring binders – all black – on the shelves behind her desk, work-related journals and reference books on a shelf of their own. There is a yucca palm on the floor, green and verdant. The roses in the glass vase on her desk are long-stemmed and fresh, there are apples and pears – perfectly ripe, of course – in a wooden bowl, next to a cactus, free from dust.

You're prickly, Sandland, Brogeland thinks, as he studies the look of concentration on her face. You're always prickly, but in such an enticing way. He tries to inhale her smell without her noticing. She doesn't wear perfume. Or perhaps she does, in which case it is very discreet.

Many of the women he has slept with have reeked of something so sweet, so cloying, that he has had to take long showers afterwards. His urge to screw them again evaporates the second he remembers their perfume.

It wouldn't be like that with Sandland. Oh, no. He imagines lying next to her, sweaty, his body happily exhausted after a prolonged wrestling match of sensual and rough sex. None of the usual post-coital unease and thoughts about how soon his cab can get there.

She must be a lesbian, he concludes, if she doesn't want to screw me.

Sandland hits 'enter' slightly harder than necessary and sheets of paper start spilling out of the printer. She gets up, goes over to the printer and picks up the small pile that has been spat out.

'Ready,' she says, without smiling.

Damn. Brogeland opens the door for her. Sandland exits and they go to the interview room where Mahmoud Marhoni and his lawyer are waiting for them.

Too many kebabs and not enough exercise is Brogeland's first impression when he takes a closer look at Mahmoud Marhoni. He has gained some weight since he last saw him and yet he wears a tight-fitting T-shirt. A spare tyre of puppy fat hangs around his waist. If I ever wanted to turn women off, Brogeland thinks, then that's precisely how I would go about it.

Marhoni's face is round. Brogeland estimates his stubble to be a week old, but Marhoni has shaved under his chin in a neat edge. His skin is chestnut brown. He is just under 1.70 metres, but he has a presence which suggests he is oblivious to his lack of height or the excess kilos.

Marhoni looks tough and displays the 'what are you looking at, pig' attitude. Brogeland has seen it before, he has seen it all before. He already knows what kind of interview it is going to be.

Marhoni's lawyer, Lars Indrehaug, is a creep who has defended vermin all his life. The prosecution service loathes him and regards him as a jackal who exploits loopholes in the law to put rapists, drug dealers and other scum back on the street. He is tall, thin and gangly. His hair flops into his eyes. He brushes it away with his fingers.

Brogeland and Sandland sit down opposite Indrehaug and his client. Brogeland takes the lead, goes through the formalities and fixes his eyes on Marhoni.

'Why did you run when we came to talk to you?'

Marhoni shrugs. You just carry on playing that game, Brogeland thinks, and continues:

'Why did you burn your laptop?'

Same response.

'What was on it?'

Still no reply.

'You know we're going to find out sooner or later, don't you? You can make it easier for yourself by saving us some time.'

Marhoni gives Brogeland a look loaded with contempt. Brogeland sighs.

'What can you tell me about your relationship with Henriette Hagerup?'

Marhoni barely looks up. Indrehaug leans towards him, whispers something neither Brogeland nor Sandland can hear, before straightening up again.

'She was my girlfriend,' Marhoni replies in broken Norwegian.

'How long had you been together?'

'About a year.'

'How did you meet?'

'At a concert.'

'What kind of concert?'

'Surely the nature of the concert is irrelevant to the investigation?' Indrehaug interjects.

Brogeland glares at Indrehaug who looks indignant on his client's behalf.

'We're trying to establish what kind of relationship your client had with the victim,' Sandland cuts in. For once, Brogeland decides not to look at her. He torpedoes Indrehaug with his eyes, though Indrehaug isn't impressed in the slightest.

'What kind of concert was it?' Brogeland repeats.

'Noori.'

'Noori?'

'At the Mela Festival.'

'Noori is a fairly well-known Pakistani rock band,' Sandland says. This time Brogeland looks at her, but tries to conceal how impressed he is, because he is also annoyed at her interruption.

'It's made up of two brothers from –'

'Yes, I get it.'

For the first time during the interview, something other than contempt emerges in Marhoni's eyes. He looks at Sandland, slightly more vigilant now. Brogeland registers this and signals that she should take over. Sandland moves closer to the table.

'When did you last see Henriette?'

Marhoni thinks about it. 'Yesterday afternoon.'

'Can you be more specific?'

'She was at my place until *Hotel Caesar* finished.'

'You watched *Hotel Caesar*?'

'Really –'

Indrehaug's cheeks have acquired a flame-red hue, which reveals his fondness for red wine. Sandland holds up her hands by way of apology.

'What did you talk about?'

'This and that.'

'Such as?'

Again, Indrehaug leans towards Marhoni.

'That's none of your business.'

Sandland smiles. She leans towards Brogeland, mimicking the performance across the table, but Brogeland stops listening once he realises that she isn't saying 'come home with me once this mind-numbing interview is over' – words he has dreamt of hearing from her lips for so long.

'Where was she going after *Hotel Caesar* had ended?'

'Don't know.'

'You don't know? Didn't you ask?'

'No.'

'She spends the night at your place sometimes, doesn't she?'

'Yes, sometimes.'

'But you didn't ask why she didn't stay over yesterday?'

'No.'

Sandland sighs. Marhoni's hard-boiled mask remains intact.

'Have you heard of Ekeberg Common?' she asks next.

'No.'

'Ever been up there?'

'Not that I remember.'

'Not been up there for the Norway Cup?'

'I don't like football.'

'No brothers or nephews who play? You haven't been up there to support them when they played?'

He shakes his head and twinkles arrogantly at her.

'Have you ever played cricket up there?'

He is about to say 'no' on autopilot, but he hesitates half a second too long. Brogeland notes down 'has been to Ekeberg, but is lying about it'. Sandberg reads it, and carries on:

'Do you own a stun gun, Mr Marhoni?'

His reaction suggests she has just asked him the stupidest question in the world.

'A what?'

'Don't give me that. You know what a stun gun is. Don't you ever go to the movies? Watch cop shows?'

He shakes his head again and adds a smirk.

'I don't like cops.'

'Inspector, what's the point of these questions?'

'We're getting to it, Mr Indrehaug,' Brogeland says with forced restraint in his voice. Sandland is about to attack. She pulls out a sheet.

'The victim was found with marks on her neck. They match those caused by a stun gun. Also known as an electroshock weapon, if you know what that is.'

She slides the sheet across the table and turns it over, so they can see it. It is a close-up of the victim's neck. Two rust-coloured, irregular burns can clearly be seen. Indrehaug picks up the photograph and studies it.

'There are many different models, but a stun gun is used when you want to paralyse rather than injure your victim. Render them helpless. So that you can put them in a hole and bury them.' Sandland looks at Marhoni, but he remains unimpressed and unaffected by her questions.

'For someone whose girlfriend has just been killed in a very brutal way, you don't seem terribly upset or sad,' she carries on. It is a question rather than a statement. Marhoni shrugs again.

'Didn't you care about her?'

A tiny twitch flits across his face.

'Didn't you love her?'

Marhoni blushes faintly.

'Did she meet with you yesterday to end it? Was that why you killed her?'

He is getting angry now.

'Had she met someone else? Bored with you, was she?'

Marhoni moves to get up. Indrehaug places his hand on Marhoni's arm.

'Sergeant –'

'Was that why you killed her?'

Marhoni stares at Sandland as if he wants to tear her apart.

'Did you look at Henriette like that when you picked up the rock and crushed her head?'

'Sergeant, that's enough.'

'Tell your client to answer the question.'

Brogeland coughs and gestures to Sandland to calm down. The room falls silent. Brogeland can see the pulse beat on Marhoni's throat. He decides to strike while the iron is hot.

'Mr Marhoni, preliminary examinations carried out at the crime scene and on the victim show she had very rough sex not long before she was killed. Would you know anything about that? What can you tell us about it?'

Marhoni is still glaring at Sandland with the same thunder in his eyes, then he quietly turns to Brogeland. He says nothing.

'Even though you don't watch cop shows, you probably know that semen is one of the best things a killer can leave behind? For the police, that is. DNA. You've heard of that?'

Still no reply. Cold-blooded bastard, Brogeland thinks.

'Last night, at 21.17, you received a text message from Henriette Hagerup.'

Marhoni's pupils contract slightly. Brogeland notices this.

'Do you recall what it said?'

Brogeland can see that Marhoni is thinking about it. Brogeland looks at a sheet, which Sandland has passed to him. He raises a fist to his mouth and coughs again.

'*Sorry. It means nothing. HE means nothing. You're the one I love. Can we talk about it? Please?*'

Brogeland looks at Marhoni and at Indrehaug, in turn. He lets the implications of the text message sink in, before he continues.

'Do you want me to read the next text she sent you?'

Marhoni looks at his lawyer. For the first time during the interview, the rock-hard surface is starting to crack.

'It would appear that Henriette was killed sometime between midnight and 2 a.m., that's only a few hours after sending you three text messages. If I were you, I

83

would start talking about what happened between the two of you last night.'

Marhoni shows no signs of wanting to talk. Brogeland sighs and looks at his sheet again.

'*I promise to make it up to you. Give me another chance, please?*'

Marhoni is shaking his head now.

'Inspector, I think –'

'You called her after the second text, but you got no reply. Is that right?'

Brogeland is getting annoyed with the silent bastard.

'*Please respond? Please? I'll never do it again. I promise.*' That was the third text, sent ten minutes later.'

Marhoni stares at the floor.

'What was it she promised never to do again, Mr Marhoni? What had she done that was so bad that you can't look me in the eye and tell me?'

No change.

'Who is "he"?'

Marhoni looks up, but not at Brogeland.

'Who is "he" who means nothing to her?'

Marhoni's lips are pursed. Brogeland sighs.

'Okay. It's not up to me, but I guarantee that you'll go before a judge and be remanded in custody later today. If I were your lawyer, I would start preparing you to spend the next fifteen to twenty years indoors.'

'I didn't kill her.'

His voice is faint, but Brogeland has already got up from his chair. He leans across the table and presses a button.

'Interview terminated at 15.21.'

Chapter 14

It starts to rain gently. Henning likes the rain. He likes getting wet when he is outdoors, likes looking up at the sky, closing his eyes and feeling the raindrops fall on his face. Too many people ruin a good shower by putting up their umbrellas.

A little rain is appropriate now. It provides a golden opportunity for the bystanders to show that they don't care about personal comfort in their hour of grief; they might be within range of a camera, they could even be on the news later today, so they cluster together. The rain is like tears from above, as if God himself grieves at the loss of one of his children.

Henning snaps away. His Canon takes three pictures per second. He imagines a fine photo montage in the paper later. But he isn't looking for people who are crying. He is looking for anyone standing quietly, alone, reflecting.

He approaches a lad with short hair, no sign of a beard yet, with the Björn Borg logo on his underpants showing above the waistband of his trousers. He is being interviewed by Petter Stanghelle from *VG*. *VG* loves a good sob story.

The tearful boy talks about Henriette Hagerup, how clever she was, what a huge loss it is to the Norwegian film industry etc. Henning carries on walking, making sure he keeps well away from the camera lenses, as he takes in the hysteria that surrounds him.

And that's when he sees her. Quickly, he takes her picture. She stands in front of the tree, she wasn't there a few minutes ago; she alternates between reading the messages and staring at the ground, shaking her head imperceptibly before looking up again. More Canon shots. Though he doubts he'll use a single one of them.

The young woman has dark, shoulder-length hair. He takes more pictures. She has an expression on her face he can't quite decipher. She just stands there, in a world of her own. But there is something about her eyes. He moves closer and closer, until he is practically standing next to her. He pretends to be reading the mawkish cards.

'Sad,' he says, just loud enough for her to hear. It could be a statement or an invitation to a conversation. The young woman doesn't reply. Without her noticing, he moves a step nearer. He stands there for a long time. His hair is starting to feel wet. He shields the camera to prevent it getting wet, too.

'Did you know her well?' Henning asks, addressing her directly for the first time. She nods briefly.

'Were you on the same course?'

At last, she looks at him. He expects her to flinch at the sight of his face, but she doesn't. She merely says:

'Yes.'

He lets more time pass. He can see that she isn't ready to talk, but she isn't crying, either.

'Are you Anette?' he asks, eventually.

She is startled. 'Do I know you?'

'No.'

He pauses, giving her time to assess the situation. He doesn't want to frighten her, he wants to arouse her curiosity. He can see she is studying him. A shiver of fear goes through her, as if she is bracing herself for what he might say.

'How do you know my name?'

Her voice is anxious. He turns to her. For the first time, she sees his whole face, scars and all. Yet, she still doesn't seem to really *see* him. He decides to put his cards on the table, before her fear gets the better of her.

'My name's Henning Juul.'

Her face remains unchanged.

'I work for *123news*.'

Her open face hardens instantly.

88

'Can I ask you some questions, please? Not intrusive, nosy, insensitive ones, just a few questions about Henriette?'

The apathetic stare she gave the flickering tea lights is gone.

'How do you know my name?' she repeats, folding her arms defensively.

'I guessed it.'

She stares at him with growing impatience.

'There are a hundred people here and you just guessed that my name is Anette?'

'Yes.'

She sniffs.

'I've nothing to say to you.'

'Just a few questions, then I'll leave you alone.'

'You reporters only ever have a few questions, but you end up asking hundreds.'

'One, then. I'll leave you alone if you answer this one question. Okay?'

He looks at her for a long time. She lets him stand there in the silence, before she tenses and relaxes her shoulders. He attempts a smile, but senses that his charm, which works on most interviewees, is lost on her. She tosses her head and sighs. Henning interprets the movement as consent and says:

'What was the work Henriette had started and which you intend to complete?'

She looks at him.

'That's your question?'

'Yes.'

'Not "how will you remember Henriette?" or "can you tell me something about Henriette that will make my readers sob?" or some crap like that?'

She makes her voice sound like that of a pestering child. He shakes his head. She snorts. Her eyes bore into his.

Then she tosses her head again, turns on her heel and walks off.

Great, Henning, he chastises himself. Well done.

And he thinks that the only interesting person in this landscape of mourners has just left. She is no great beauty. He bets she doesn't sit in the front row in the lecture hall or pose for pictures. He imagines her looking in the mirror and sighing, resigned; sees her giving herself to guys with beer goggles, late at night, and going home before daybreak.

But Anette, he says to himself. You're interesting. He feels like shouting it after her.

Then he realises what he saw in her eyes. He checks the camera as she disappears around the corner of a building. He scrolls to one of the first pictures he took of her, looks into her eyes. And he knows that he was right.

Eureka! He recognises the feeling when he grasps or

stumbles across something important. As he zooms in on the picture and studies her again, he wonders what Anette was so scared of.

Chapter 15

'He reeks of guilt.'

Detective Inspector Brogeland doesn't elaborate on his statement. He looks at Chief Inspector Gjerstad, the head of the investigation, who sits opposite him in the meeting room. He is flicking through the print-out of the interview. Sergeant Sandland sits at the end. She leans forwards and rests her elbow on the table. Her hands are folded.

Two other officers, Fredrik Stang and Emil Hagen, are present, in addition to Assistant Commissioner Nøkleby. She is officially in charge of the investigation, but she always works closely with Gjerstad. Everyone's eyes turn to Gjerstad, expecting him to say something. As always, when he is thinking, he strokes his moustache with his thumb and index finger.

'There's no doubt he has a problem explaining his situation,' Gjerstad says in a deep, growling bass. 'All the same . . .'

Gjerstad puts down the print-out. He takes off his glasses, places them on the table and rubs his face. Then he fixes his eyes on Brogeland.

'You should have carried on with the interview when he finally said he didn't do it.'

'But . . .'

'I know why you stopped at that point. You wanted to give him something to think about. But the way I read it, he was just starting to open up. He might have told us a lot more, if you had been prepared to give him a bit more time.'

'We don't know that,' Brogeland replies.

'Were you in a hurry?'

'In a hurry?'

Brogeland's face feels warm. Gjerstad looks at him.

'When you next interview him, give him a bit more time.'

Brogeland squirms in his chair. He wants to defend himself, but not in front of the team; he doesn't want to risk further humiliation.

Gjerstad looks up to the right, as if he is staring at something on the wall.

'There's circumstantial evidence that implicates Marhoni and it's tempting to treat this as an honour killing. If his girlfriend was unfaithful, he might have killed her to restore his honour.'

Sandland clears her throat.

'There is actually very little that suggests it might be an honour killing,' she says. Gjerstad turns to her.

93

'In a few countries, infidelity means a death sentence. In Sudan, for example, in 2007 . . .'

'Marhoni's from Pakistan.'

'I know, but they stone people to death in Pakistan, too. And, as far as the honour killing theory goes, several elements are missing,' Sandland continues. Gjerstad looks at her, indicates that she should go on. Nøkleby nudges her glasses further up the bridge of her nose and leans closer to the table. Her dark fringe falls over her eyes, but not to the extent that it irritates her.

'Honour killings are often carried out *after* the shame has become public knowledge,' Sandland begins. 'As far as we've been able to establish, all anyone knew about Hagerup and Marhoni was that they were an item. Secondly, honour killings are often planned. The decision is usually made by the family. As far as I know, Marhoni has no family in Norway, apart from his brother, who lives with him. And last, but not least: you own up to what you've done. Marhoni denies that he did it.'

Gjerstad digests the short lecture and nods with approval.

'What do we know about stoning?' Emil Hagen asks.

Hagen is a short man who has recently graduated from the police academy. Brogeland recognises the type: bursting with enthusiasm, keen to get stuck in and nurturing a vision of making a difference to society, one villain at a time. You just keep thinking that, Brogeland muses. You'll be brought down to earth soon enough, just like the rest of us. Emil has blond hair and looks like an adult version of the eponymous Astrid Lindgren character. He even has a big gap between his front teeth.

'Only Iran officially uses the method today,' Sandland explains. 'However, it's also used in other countries, as a form of vigilantism. It's mainly adultery, indecency and blasphemy which are punishable by stoning. In 2007, Jafar Keyani was stoned to death in Iran. It was the first time since 2002 that Iran officially admitted to using this form of punishment.'

'What had he done?' Nøkleby asks.

'You mean what had *she* done?'

Nøkleby bows her head, embarrassed at her ignorance.

'She had an extra-marital affair.'

The rest of the team looks at Sandland. Fredrik Stang puts down his water glass.

'I don't follow, didn't we just make an arrest?' he says. Stang has dark hair, cut short to the point of a crew cut and a face that always oozes earnestness. He likes to wear tight-fitting clothes, so people can see he spent much of his youth in the gym.

'Indeed we did, but he denies the murder and it's far too early not to pursue other leads. Besides, we're trying to establish a motive,' Nøkleby points out.

'Hagerup had screwed around,' Stang protests. 'The texts suggest she had. And Marhoni is a Muslim, isn't he. To me, it sounds like a straightforward home win.'

Sandland raises a bottle of Cola Zero to her lips and takes a swig.

'Sure, I agree that it might look that way. But I still think we need to ignore the honour killing theory. It's more obvious to take a closer look at sharia.'

'Sharia?' Gjerstad frowns.

'Yes. You do know what it is, don't you?'

She looks around the team. Most people nod, but not very convincingly. Emil Hagen shifts in his chair.

'Extreme rules telling you how to live or something?'

Sandland smiles briefly.

'That's one way of putting it. Most people who've heard about sharia immediately think "mad mullahs and fundamentalists". But sharia is a complex concept. Those who call themselves learned, as far as sharia is concerned, have studied the legal principles of sharia for years. They study the Koran, the sayings and doings of the Prophet Mohammed, Muslim history, how different legal schools have interpreted the law and so on. In Muslim countries today, sharia primarily applies to aspects of family law such as divorce and inheritance.'

'But what has this got to do with the murder of Henriette Hagerup?' Gjerstad asks impatiently.

'I'm getting to that. There's no such thing as one Islamic law, and only a few countries enforce a penal code based on Islamic law. The countries that do, have something they call hudud punishments.'

'Hu-what?' Hagen asks.

'Hudud punishments. It's a penal code in the Koran. It prescribes specific punishments for certain crimes. Flogging, for example. Or chopping off someone's hand.'

Brogeland nods quietly to himself. He has instantly grasped the implications of Sandland's information.

'So what crimes warrant these punishments?' Nøkleby asks, folding her hands in front of her. Sandland looks at her, while she explains.

'Adultery, for example. You can get one hundred lashes for that. If you're caught stealing, you might lose your hand. But the degree of enforcement of hudud punishments varies from country to country and, in some cases, people take the law into their own hands and justify their sick acts by referring to the law of Allah. The symbolic value of having such punishments is probably more important, because it proves that you respect the edicts of the Koran and Islamic law.'

'Even if it's only in theory?' Nøkleby continues.

'Even if it's only in theory,' Sandland says and nods.

'However, some countries do actually enforce the laws. In November 2008, a thirteen-year-old Somali girl was stoned to death for trying to report a rape. She was taken to a football stadium, buried in a hole which was filled with earth up to her neck. Then fifty people started stoning her and a thousand people watched.'

'Bloody hell,' Hagen gasps. Brogeland gazes dreamily at Sandland. You can lecture to me anytime, he thinks. With a cane and handcuffs within easy reach, for when I give the wrong answers.

Stang shakes his head.

'How come you know all this?'

'I did Religious Studies for A-level.'

'This is all very well,' Gjerstad interjects, 'but we're still no closer to knowing to *why* this happened.'

'No, or who did it.'

'You don't think Marhoni did?' Nøkleby asks.

'I don't know what I think yet. But Marhoni didn't strike me as a hardcore Muslim, to be flippant, or as someone who is up to date on hudud punishments. And I think it's important to bear in mind that this isn't normal Muslim behaviour. Someone with extreme views – and I mean *really extreme* views – and a twisted mind probably did this. And I don't think that description fits Marhoni.'

'Don't you have to be a Muslim to warrant the punishment?' Brogeland asks.

'Yes, that's correct, you do.'

'But Hagerup is white, like us?'

'Precisely. So lots of things don't add up.'

'She could have converted?' Hagen suggests.

Sandland pulls a face.

'But as she was white and Norwegian, this might not have anything to do with sharia or hudud,' Gjerstad objects.

'No, it's . . .'

'Perhaps someone just felt like stoning her to death. Hell of a way to kill someone. It takes forever, I imagine, especially if the stones are small.'

'Yes, but we should be looking for someone who knows about hudud punishments.'

'That could be anyone, surely?'

'Anyone can *read* up on it, that's true, whether you're Norwegian or Muslim. However, this killing is highly ritualistic. Flogging her, stoning her and chopping off one of her hands – it all means something.'

'So it would appear,' Nøkleby remarks.

'Was Hagerup unfaithful?' Hagen asks. 'Or did she steal something?'

Sandland shrugs.

'No idea. Could be both. Or neither. We don't know yet.'

'Okay,' Gjerstad says in a voice designed to bring the meeting to a close. He gets up. 'We need to carry out a more detailed background check on both Marhoni and Hagerup, find out who they were and what she did or didn't do, what she knew, what she studied, people she knew, friends, family situation and so on. Secondly, we need to talk to the Muslim communities, find out if anyone there approves of flogging and that kind of punishment and see if there's a link to Hagerup or Marhoni. Emil, you're an IT whiz. Check the chat rooms, homepages, blogs and more, look up everything you can on sharia and hudud, and report back if you come across any names we should take a closer look at.'

Emil nods.

'And one more thing,' Gjerstad says and looks at Nøkleby, before he continues. 'It shouldn't need saying, but NRK was remarkably well informed at today's press conference. This investigation ticks so many boxes that we'll only make it worse for ourselves if the press gets a hint of what we're looking into. Anything said here stays within these four walls. Understood?'

Nobody says anything. But everyone nods.

Chapter 16

It doesn't take him long to finish at Westerdal. He interviews some people, gets the information he knows the newspaper wants him to get, takes more pictures and heads home. He is outside Jimmy's Sushi Bar in Fredensborgvei when his mobile rings.

'Henning,' he answers.

'Hi, it's Heidi.'

He pulls a face and says 'hi' back without a flicker of enthusiasm.

'Where are you?'

'On my way home to write up the story. I'll e-mail it to you tonight.'

'*Dagbladet* already has a story about grieving students at the college. Why don't we? Why is it taking so long?'

'Long?'

'Why didn't you call in with what you had?'

'Surely I have to write the story before I can call it in?'

'Four lines about the mood, two quotes from a distraught bystander and we could have put together a story and padded it out with photos and some more quotes later. Now we're waaaaay late.'

He is tempted to say that the expression isn't 'waaaaay late' but either 'way behind' or 'running late', but he doesn't. Heidi sighs heavily.

'Why would anyone want to read our human interest story, when they've already read it elsewhere?'

'Because mine will be better.'

'Hah! I hope so. And next time: call in your story.'

He has no time to reply before Heidi hangs up. He grimaces at his mobile. And takes his time going home.

He changes the batteries in the smoke alarms in his flat and settles down on the sofa with his laptop. On his way home, he thought about possible angles. It shouldn't take him too long to write the story. He might even have time for a walk to Dælenenga and watch some training sessions, before it gets dark.

The most time-consuming task is uploading and editing the pictures, before he can send them to the news desk. He doesn't want to risk the news desk ruining them.

Six or seven years ago, he doesn't remember precisely, a woman was brutally murdered in Grorud. Her body was found in a skip. He had taken dozens of photos and sent them all to the news desk at *Aftenposten*, just as they were, because The Old Lady goes to press early. He stated explicitly which photos could be used and which ones couldn't, at least not before consent from her relatives has been obtained, as several of them had been present behind the police tape. He also stressed to the news desk that they must check with him before going to print.

He never heard anything back that evening and he never chased it. The following morning, the story was published with not only the wrong photos, but also the wrong captions. Humble pie time. He tried to apologise to the victim's relatives, but they refused to talk to him. 'Yeah right, blame the news desk,' they sneered.

But journalism is like any other profession. You learn from your mistakes. One of the first things a friend of his was told when he started his medical degree was that you won't become a good doctor until you have filled up a cemetery. You learn on the job, acquire knowledge, master new technology, adapt, get to know your colleagues and their skills, and learn to work with them. It is a continuous process.

He opens Photoshop and uploads the pictures. Grief, fake grief and more fake grief. And then, Anette. He double-clicks on the photos, his shot of her. Even on his 15.6 inch screen, every detail is visible. When he views the photos as a slideshow, it becomes even more obvious. Anette looks around, as though she is being watched, but then she steals a moment with Henriette. It is over in seconds, but he caught it on camera.

Anette, he thinks again. What are you scared of?

Writing the story and sending it to the news desk takes him longer than he had expected. The sentences don't come to him as easily as he had hoped. But he decides that even an old dog can learn new tricks. And he hopes Heidi is at home, foaming at the mouth because he kept her waiting.

He looks at the clock. 8.30 p.m. Too late to go to Dælenenga.

He sighs and leans back in the sofa. I should have gone to see Mum, he thinks. It has been days now. She is probably hurt. On reflection, he can't recall the last time she wasn't feeling sorry for herself.

Christine Juul lives in a simple two-bedroom flat in Helgesensgate. She has lived there for four years; it is one of those new developments, which cost a fortune to buy initially, but lose value over time. There are some of them in Grünerløkka as well.

Before Helgesensgate, she lived in Kløfta, where Henning grew up, but it proved to be too great a distance to him and Trine. She wanted to be closer to her children, purely so that they could take care of her. She spent nearly all her money on a flat devoid of character; she has nothing on her walls, only plain once-white surfaces, discoloured from all the smoke she blows out into the room every day. But he doesn't think that's why she is hurt.

Henning believes Christine Juul was quite content with her lot in life until her husband died. She had a good job as a care assistant, an apparently happy marriage, apparently happy and thriving children; not many friends, but she valued the ones she had, she was involved with the local choir and wine-tasting club, but when Jakob Juul died unexpectedly, she fell to pieces. Overnight.

Even though Henning and Trine were only teenagers when it happened, they soon discovered they had to fend for themselves. They had to shop, cook, cut the grass, trim the hedge, wash the clothes, clean the house, take themselves to football training and matches, to school and to their holiday cabin by the sea. If they had any questions about their education, they had to ask the neighbours. Or leave them unanswered.

All because Christine Juul got herself a new best friend.

St Hallvard is a sweet herb liqueur made from potatoes and it contains just enough alcohol to numb an anxious mind. Now, not a week goes by without Henning visiting to re-fill her drinks cabinet. Two bottles, at least. She sulks if she only gets one.

He has given it plenty of thought and come to the conclusion that if she wants to drink herself to death, then far be it from him to stop her. She seemed only mildly interested when he got married, attended Jonas's christening for less than an hour. She didn't even cry when Jonas died, though she turned up for his funeral. She was one of the last mourners to arrive and she didn't sit at the front with the rest of the family; she stood at the back and left the church as soon as the service had ended. Not even when Henning was a patient at Haukeland Hospital, in the Burns Unit, did she visit him or call to ask how he was. When he was transferred to Sunnaas Rehabilitation Centre, she visited only twice and never stayed for more than thirty minutes. She barely looked at him, hardly said a word.

Liqueur, Marlboro Lights and gossip magazines.

He feels he can't deny her these pleasures, the only three she has left, at the age of sixty-two. She barely eats, though he stocks up her fridge at regular intervals. He tries to vary her diet, get her to eat some protein, calcium, essential nutrients, but she has very little appetite.

Every now and then, he cooks for her and sits at the small kitchen table while they have dinner. They don't speak. They just eat and listen to the radio. Henning likes listening to the radio. Especially when he is with his mother.

He doesn't know why she is so angry with him, but it's probably because he hasn't *made something of himself*, unlike his sister – Trine Juul-Osmundsen, who is Norway's Minister for Justice. She seems to be making quite a name for herself. She is well liked, even by the police. But he only knows that because his mother told him.

He isn't in touch with his sister. That's how she wants it. He stopped trying long ago. He isn't sure how they ended up like this, but at some point in their lives, Trine stopped talking to him. She left home when she turned eighteen and never came back, not even for Christmas. But she wrote; to her mother, never to him. He wasn't even invited to her wedding.

The Juul family. Not exactly a happy one. But it's the only one he has.

Chapter 17

He looks at the piano. It stands up against the wall. He used to love playing it, but he doesn't know if he still can. It has nothing to do with his hands. His fingers work fine, despite the scars.

He recalls the night Nora told him she was pregnant. It was shortly after their wedding and it was a planned pregnancy, but they had heard about many couples who had tried for years without success. Henning and Nora, however, fell pregnant at their first attempt. Bull's-eye.

He was working on a story when Nora came into his study. He could tell from her face that something had happened. She was nervous, but excited. Brimming with fear and awe of what they had started, the responsibility they were taking on.

I'm pregnant, Henning.

He recalls her voice. Cautious, trembling. The smile, which soon spread across her face before giving way to an uncertainty he couldn't help but love. He got up, embraced her, kissed her.

Christ, how he had kissed her.

Nora was just over seven weeks pregnant that evening. He remembers her going to bed early because she felt nauseous. He sat alone for a long time, thinking, listening to the silence in the flat. Then he sat down at the piano. At the time, he was working very hard and he hadn't played for ages. But it is always the same when he sits down at the keyboard after a long break. Everything he plays sounds fine.

That evening, he composed possibly the finest song he has ever written. He woke Nora up and dragged her out of bed to play it to her. Nauseous and magnificent, she stood behind him as his fingers caressed the black and white keys. The tune was soft and melancholic.

Nora rested her hands on his shoulders, bent down and hugged him from behind. Henning called the song 'Little Friend'. Once Jonas was born, he often played it to him. Jonas liked to hear it in the evening, before going to bed. Henning wrote the lyrics too, but he is bad at writing lyrics, so he tended to hum along, mostly.

He should have played 'Little Friend' at the funeral, but he was in a wheelchair, encased in plaster and bandages. A friend could have played it, obviously, but it wouldn't have been the same. It should have been him.

Henning hummed while the vicar spoke. He hasn't hummed since.

*

Something has been bugging him all day. All good crime reporters have sources. Henning has a great one. Or he used to. This source came into Henning's life when he was surfing for child porn for a story one evening. He wanted to discover how easy it was to find child porn on the Internet, how many clicks it would take, and he soon reached a flagged page. Fortunately, the police already knew about it. But because Henning had visited it, they knew about him, too. He had been aware that this might happen, but that was also a part of his story. Establish how well informed the police were, how far he could go before he was stopped. He couldn't quite recall how he got the idea, but he thought it had come to him after learning he was going to be a dad. Perhaps it had been an attempt to meet trouble halfway?

After visiting several different child porn sites, he was befriended on-line by a woman calling herself Chicketita. She promised to give him some child porn DVDs if he met her in Vaterlands Park at 11 p.m. that night. He never went.

The day after, he was brought in for questioning, his laptop was seized and sent to Forensics to check if he had surfed for child porn before. Which he obviously hadn't. He was quickly released, once he had explained his actions to officers from the Sexual Crimes Unit. Chicketita, who turned out to be a female police officer called Elisa, was sympathetic. He was given permission to carry on with his project. She was in favour of the press highlighting the issue.

Some days later, he was contacted by *6tiermes7*. At first, he thought it was another police officer hunting paedophiles, but he eventually decided that it couldn't be. *6tiermes7* had a completely different agenda.

He didn't know if *6tiermes7* knew about his child porn story, but he suspected that he or she had followed his work for a while or, at least, checked him out to know that he was sound. At that time, he often worked undercover; he had exposed several scandals, which led to the police starting new investigations or solving cold cases. He got results. *6tiermes7* was willing to help him on the non-negotiable premise that he never revealed his source.

Via an e-mail account, which couldn't be traced to *6tiermes7*'s real name, Henning was sent a file containing a program called FireCracker 2.0 which he was told to install. Henning later searched the Internet for the program, but never found anything which suggested it might be for sale anywhere. He assumed that *6tiermes7* had written it, but he never asked. The program, once opened, connected to a server so they could chat safely. Or, in relative safety.

They used an encryption algorithm that made any keystrokes they sent to each other incomprehensible to outsiders – unless they had the key. This security feature obviously depended on their keystrokes not being recorded before they were encrypted. After all, it is possible to monitor a keyboard. *6tiermes7* could be risking his/her own life, but Henning had no wish to question the morals and ethical dilemmas faced by his source.

6tiermes7 soon turned out to be the best source he had ever had. Everything in journalism is about contacts. Having a reliable source, who brings the stories to you, not the other way round, someone who will regularly feed you information that helps you in interviews, insider knowledge that may not be useful at the time, but which turns out to be worth knowing, nonetheless. As leverage, for example. Or new developments in an investigation, what the police have discovered, which leads they are pursuing, names of people brought in for questioning – that kind of information.

6tiermes7 gave him all of that. He or she was Deep Throat, the deepest of them all. In the three years before That Which He Doesn't Think About, Henning had published several stories as a result of his partnership with *6tiermes7*. *6tiermes7* helped him, he in turn helped the police by breaking stories that threw fresh light on their investigations, new and old, and together they got results. *Quid pro quo*, as Hannibal Lecter would have put it.

But *6tiermes7* has never told him why or how. And Henning has never tried to uncover the identity of *6tiermes7*. Nor has he any plans to do so. Some things are best left alone.

Before he went back to work, he hadn't thought about *6tiermes7* for almost two years. He has no idea whether *6tiermes7* is still available to him as a source, if he or she has started working with other people, or if *6tiermes7* has simply vanished from cyberspace.

But he is about to find out.

Chapter 18

The steam rises and condenses under the roof. A high pressure hose is systematically swept across a dark red Audi A8 with shiny 19-inch chrome rims. Encrusted bird pooh, grit, gravel and pebbles are quickly washed off the paintwork. The car is drenched in seconds.

Yasser Shah puts down the high pressure hose and gestures to two men to get to work. A third man opens the doors and starts hoovering the interior. Soapy sponges squeak against the luxury car. The quartet works fast and efficiently. Mats are removed and hosed down. The boot is cleared of bark, grass and rubbish. Strips are wiped and soon the interior, steering wheel, dashboard, gears, sound system and windows all gleam. It takes them less than ten minutes.

And all for 150 kroner.

The car's owner, a man in a grey suit with a matching tie, waits outside. At regular intervals, he peers inside to check on progress. Zaheerullah Hassan Mintroza sits in his glass booth, aware of the owner's scepticism. It's probably because we're Pakistanis, he thinks. But we're cheap, so the guy's prepared to take a chance.

Wanker. If only you knew who is washing your car.

Hassan lets the quartet finish, then he presses a button which opens the door. The owner isn't sure if he is expected to go inside. Hassan gets up, comes outside and gestures to the four men to finish off the car in daylight. Yasser Shah gets in and starts the car, which roars aggressively in the acoustically perfect space, and backs out. The others follow with chamois leathers.

Hassan goes over to the owner and accepts the cash.

'Looks very good,' the owner remarks. Hassan nods, counts the eight 20-kroner notes and omits to mention there is 10 kroner too much. Quite right, he thinks, since he got the express-while-u-wait service.

Shah gets out of the car and hands the owner the keys. The other three wipe off the remaining moisture on the Audi's roof, doors and rims.

'Thank you so much,' the owner says and gets in. He drives off at a leisurely pace. Hassan looks at the others and signals that they should go back inside. They obey his command and step inside Hassan's glass cage office. It is the size of a bedroom. There are three chairs and a television in the corner, Al-Jazeera with the sound off. There is a mug of coffee, a computer and piles of documents and newspapers on Hassan's desk. An old nude picture of Nereida Gallardo Alvarez decorates the wall behind Hassan's squeaking chair.

'Close the door,' Hassan orders Yasser Shah. Hassan presses a button. A red light goes on outside the car wash.

The others wait. Hassan looks at them. His hair is longish, shining with Brylcreem and combed back. He doesn't have a ponytail, though his hair is long enough for one. He has strips of beard, carefully combed, around his mouth and on his cheeks. He wears a thick gold chain around his neck and earrings that match. He is wearing worn, stonewashed jeans and a white vest which stretches tightly across his stomach and chest. Hassan is thin, but not gangly. The muscles in his arms are noticeable. He has a tattoo of a green frog on one arm and a black scorpion on the other.

'We've got a problem,' he says, looking gravely at them in turn. 'We've talked about this before, what to do should such a situation arise, and especially if this particular situation should arise.'

The others nod silently. Yasser Shah opens his mouth slightly. Hassan registers it.

'Yasser – over to you now,' he says firmly. Yasser's about to speak, but Hassan interrupts him.

'We need to send him a message. This is your chance to prove that you're one of us, that you're serious about being here.'

Shah looks down. He is short and of heavy build. There is a square of dense beard around his mouth, his skin is smooth, and he has sideburns. His nose is crooked from a fist fight in Gujrat in 1994. His lip was split in the same fight, and he has a scar on his upper lip, to the left. The stud in his left ear looks like a diamond.

'Do you want to go to jail?'

Shah looks up again.

'No,' he mutters.

'Do you want the rest of us to end up in jail?'

'No.'

His voice is firmer this time.

'This way of life demands that we sacrifice ourselves for each other,' Hassan continues. 'We can't take risks.'

The others look at Hassan and then at Shah. Hassan waits a long time before opening a drawer and taking out black box. He opens it, takes out a pistol and a silencer and gives both to Shah.

'Nice and easy. No mistakes.'

Shah nods reluctantly.

'As for the rest of you. As soon as this hits the headlines – make sure you're near a CCTV camera and have plenty of witnesses who can vouch for you. The cops mightn't call, but if they do, it'll be to find out where you were.'

Everyone, apart from Yasser Shah, nods. He stares at the floor.

Chapter 19

Henning opens his laptop again and locates FireCracker 2.0 on the program menu. He hesitates for a few seconds before he double-clicks the icon of a miniature firecracker. Perhaps *6tiermes7* uses a different version now, a more recent one, new applications might have been added which require upgrades, but he clicks anyway. It's worth a try.

The program takes forever to load. I must get a new computer, he thinks, as the fan starts to whirr. While the machine hums into action, he goes to the homepage of *123news* to check if his story has been published.

It has. A quick glance tells him the news desk has made very few changes. It is their lead story. Iver Gundersen's story about the arrest is accessible via a link in the introduction. Just looking at Gundersen's words makes Henning feel sick.

So he concentrates on his own headline: '*We'll never forget you*'. The accompanying photograph is of the shrine and the cards and messages for Henriette Hagerup. A standard package. But a good one, a good start. It's not proper news as such, but it's a good start.

Someone stomps up and down the communal stairs. Henning tries to ignore it and checks if FireCracker 2.0 is up and running. It is. But *6tiermes7* isn't there. He leaves it for a few more minutes. In the meantime, he forces himself to read Iver Gundersen's story, telling himself that it might contain useful information. He remembers that Nora's new loverboy asked him to find out the name of Hagerup's boyfriend, something which completely slipped his mind.

He curses his useless grey cells, before he clicks on the story and begins to read.

STONING: MAN ARRESTED

A man in his twenties has been arrested in connection with the brutal murder of Henriette Hagerup.

There is a photograph of the crime scene – the right one, this time – next to the introduction. He can see the large white tent in the background. Some onlookers are standing behind the police tape. He reads on.

The man was arrested following a routine police visit to his flat. The man attempted to escape when officers knocked on his door, but he was quickly apprehended.

123news has learned that incriminating evidence was discovered in the suspect's flat. He will be brought before a judge and remanded in custody later today. Lars Indrehaug, the suspect's solicitor, denies that his client is guilty.

Gundersen then reviews the story, explains what has happened, when it happened and how the story has developed in the course of the day. He also includes a quote from Chief Inspector Gjerstad, a quote Henning recognises from the press conference.

Noise continues to come from the stairwell. He checks FireCracker 2.0 again. He is still the only user to be logged on. He decides not to log out in case *6tiermes7* logs on during the evening or overnight. But he has a sinking feeling that's not going to happen.

He sighs and stares blankly at the wall. His first day back at work is over and done with. He thinks about the people he met: Kåre, Heidi, Nora, Iver, Anette. After just one day at work, he has acquired knowledge and formed relationships he could, quite happily, have done without. Memories are returning, memories he had hoped would remain in the darkness.

He thinks about Nora, what she is doing now, if she is with Gundersen. Of course she is. Mister Super Fucking Corduroy. They are probably having dinner. In a restaurant. Swapping stories about their day, what they will do when they get home, under the duvet, or on top of it, possibly.

He decides not to think about it and hopes that the evening and the night will come quickly.

The stomping still hasn't ended. Henning gets up to investigate. An elderly man is on his way up the stairs when Henning peers out. The man is wheezing. He is dressed in shorts only, nothing on his upper body. Despite his age – Henning reckons he is well in excess of seventy – he still has plenty of muscles. They look at each other. The man is about to carry on, but stops and takes another look at Henning.

'Have you just moved in?' he asks.

'No,' Henning replies. 'I've lived here for six months.'

'Oh, have you? I live just below you.'

'Right.'

He walks down to Henning and holds out his hand.

'Gunnar Goma. I've had bypass surgery. Four veins.'

He points to a huge scar on his chest. Henning nods and shakes his hand.

'That's why I'm out of breath. I've getting back in shape. So I can satisfy the ladies, he-he.'

'Henning Juul.'

'And I go commando.'

'Thanks for sharing that with me.'

'Fancy a coffee some day?'

Henning nods again. He likes coffee, but he thinks it is unlikely that he will ever be drinking coffee with

Gunnar Goma. Though, on second thoughts, the invitation isn't entirely unwelcome.

He hears a ping from his laptop as he goes inside. He remembers that ping. Ding-dong, like a doorbell. It means someone has sent him a message via FireCracker.

6tiermes7. It has to be.

He quickly sits down, moves the mouse and wakes up the screen. He closes all other windows so only FireCracker is open. He looks at the screen. A small square window has popped up. Inside it says:

6tiermes7: Judge.

To be absolutely sure that no one else can use the program, they have agreed numerous code words. The person making contact writes the first part of the word. If the person responding gives the correct continuation, they are safe.

He smiles and replies:

MakkaPakka: Devil.

He is rewarded by a smiley.

6tiermes7 and Henning have chatted about much besides evidence and cases under investigation. He got his nickname, MakkaPakka, because *6tiermes7* knows Henning loathes *In the Night Garden*, a half-hour children's television programme which NRK broadcasts every afternoon before television for older children begins. The characters in *In the Night Garden* never say very much, instead they make sounds which correspond to their names. Igglepiggle, Upsy Daisy, Makka Pakka, the Tombliboos and the Ninky Nonk.

He is convinced that *6tiermes7* enjoys teasing him whenever they chat, no matter what motivates him or her.

MakkaPakka: I wasn't sure that you still existed.

6tiermes7: Or that you did. We've missed you.

MakkaPakka: Thank you.

6tiermes7: So you're back? I heard you came to the press conference today.

MakkaPakka: Who told you that?

6tiermes7: The Prime Minister. What do you take me for?

Henning sends a smiley.

6tiermes7: What's up?

MakkaPakka: Henriette Hagerup. What do you take me for?

More smileys.

6tiermes7: What do you want?

MakkaPakka: Everything you have – or haven't got.

6tiermes7: You certainly don't waste time.

MakkaPakka: Haven't got time to waste. Have they got
    something worthwhile on – what's his name?

He doesn't get an immediate response. Perhaps I
was too rash or pushy, he thinks. A minute passes. And
another. He slumps. Finally, a message pops up.

6tiermes7: Sorry. Loo break.

More smileys.

6tiermes7: His name is Mahmoud Marhoni. Her
    boyfriend. Fled when Sergeant Sandland and
    Inspector Brogeland turned up at his flat. Set fire to
    his laptop. Looks like he argued with HH the night
    she was killed. Compromising text messages from her
    to him.

MakkaPakka: Did you manage to save his laptop?

6tiermes7: Don't know yet.

MakkaPakka: Okay. Was Hagerup stoned to death?

6tiermes7: Stoned, flogged, hand chopped off. She had stun gun marks on her neck.

MakkaPakka: A stun gun? Like a cattle prod?

6tiermes7: Yes.

This doesn't sound anything like an honour killing, Henning thinks. More like sharia and hudud. Something doesn't add up.

MakkaPakka: Does MM have form?

6tiermes7: No.

MakkaPakka: What does Gjerstad think?

6tiermes7: Not much yet. Think he is glad to see some progress.

MakkaPakka: Does MM have any family?

6tiermes7: A brother. Tariq. They share a flat.

MakkaPakka: You said something about compromising text messages. Compromising how?

6tiermes7: Think she has been unfaithful.

MakkaPakka: And that's why she was killed? Is that why you're thinking honour killing?

6tiermes7: Don't know.

I bet Iver Gundersen doesn't know about this, Henning thinks and nods to himself. A plan is taking shape. He likes plans. But he doesn't like shortcuts.

And he has a feeling that the police are taking that route.

Chapter 20

Dreams. Henning wishes there was a button he could press to shut off access to his subconscious at night. He has just woken up, his eyes adjust to the darkness while he gasps for air. He is burning hot. It isn't morning yet, but he is wide awake. And he has been dreaming again.

He dreamt they had gone to the playground in Sofienberg Park, Jonas and he. It was winter, it was cold. He cleared a bench of snow and frost and sat drinking lovely hot coffee from a plastic cup, while he watched Jonas's grinning face, flushed cheeks and cloudy breath underneath the pale blue woolly hat which was pushed too far down his head, his eyes seeking out Henning's, all the time. And he saw Jonas climb to the highest point of the climbing frame. All his concentration went into looking at his dad so he didn't look where he was going, he stepped between the ropes, lost his grip, fell forwards and sideways and smashed his face and mouth into a post. Henning leapt up, ran over to him, turned the boy's head to examine the extent of the damage, but all he could see was a black, sooty face. Jonas's mouth was gone. No teeth.

The only things that weren't black were his burning eyes.

He wakes up and finds himself blowing, blowing desperately on Jonas's burning eyes to put out the flames. But they never go out. Jonas's eyes are like those birthday candles which re-ignite themselves; you can try, but you'll never succeed in blowing them out.

The dream knocks him for six, every time. When he wakes up, his pulse is racing and he closes his eyes to block out the image which makes him nauseous. He visualises the ocean. Dr Helge has taught him to do that, concentrate on a favourite place or activity, whenever he gets flashbacks.

Henning likes the sea. He has happy memories of saltwater. And the sea helps him open his eyes again. He rolls on to his side, sees, from the clock on his mobile, that he has slept for nearly three hours. Not bad, for him. And he decides that will have to do.

At least for today.

There isn't much he can do in the middle of the night. He ignores the matches and gets up. He goes into the living room, glances at his piano, but keeps on walking. His hip aches, but it is a little early for pills.

He sits down in the kitchen. He listens to the fridge. It hums and whirrs noisily. He thinks it is on its last legs. Just like him.

He hasn't been there for many, many years, but the groaning from the fridge reminds him of the family's summer cabin. It is just outside Stavern, by Anvikstranda Camping. It is plain, simple and small, probably no more 30 square metres. Fantastic view of the sea. Loads of adders.

His grandfather built the cabin as cheaply as he could, just after the war, and to Henning's knowledge, the fridge is still the original one. It moans and carries on almost like the fridge in Henning's flat.

He hasn't been to the cabin since he was a child. He thinks Trine goes there sometimes, but he doesn't know for sure. Perhaps the fridge is still there. It was only a half-size and they always had to kick the bottom of the door after closing it. If they didn't, the door would swing open again. The flap to the freezer compartment was missing. The shelves in the door were loose and cracked, which meant heavy items such as milk and bottles had to lie inside the main body of the fridge.

But the fridge worked. He can still recall how cold the milk would be. And he decides it's all right to grow old and still be in working order. He has never tasted milk so cold, never experienced brain freezes like the ones he used to get on summer holidays in their tiny cabin. But it was fun. It was cosy. They went crabbing, played football on the large plain at the camping site, climbed rock faces, learned to swim in the sea, bar-becued sausages on the beach in the evenings.

The age of innocence. Why couldn't it have stayed that way?

He wonders if Trine remembers those summers.

He thinks about sharia again. Allah-u-akbar. And he recalls what Zahid Mukhtar, the head of the Islamic Council in Oslo, said in 2004:

As a Muslim, you're subject to Islamic law and, to Muslims, sharia takes precedent over all other laws. No other interpretation of Islam is possible.

Henning interviewed a social anthropologist at the Christian Michaelsen Institute shortly afterwards, and she explained that most people in the West have a distorted image of sharia. Though there are traditions going back a thousand years and a certain consensus exists on how to interpret the laws of Allah, sharia isn't a single unambiguous set of written laws. Religious scholars, who interpret the Koran and Hadith texts, decide what is right and wrong, and their reading is influenced by whatever culture affects them. In Norway, most people associate sharia with the death penalty in Muslim countries. And this ignorance is deliberately exploited.

The social anthropologist, whose name he can't remember, showed him a website in Norwegian that listed sharia law in bullet points and the punishments for breaking them. 'This is very simplistic,' she said, pointing to the screen. 'Few people will understand what sharia is really about from this. It's people who *aren't* scholars who might post a page like this. They use a fluid concept to gain power and influence. Most people don't realise that hudud punishments are quite low key in the Koran. A few scholars even think they should be ignored completely.'

The interview made an impression on Henning because it challenged his own prejudices against Muslims in general and sharia in particular. And now, when he thinks about hudud punishments and links them to the murder of Henriette Hagerup, a number of things fail to add up. She wasn't a Muslim. Nor was she married to one and, as far as he knows, she hadn't stolen anything, either, and yet her hand had been chopped off.

He shakes his head. A few years ago, he might have been able to come up with a credible explanation, but now he is increasingly convinced that it makes no sense. And that's the problem. It *always* makes sense. It has to. He just needs to find the common denominator.

Chapter 21

Henning's flat reminds him of a garage sale. He doesn't like garages. He doesn't know why, but they make him think of cars, idle engines, closed doors and screaming families.

Back in Kløfta, the Juuls' garage contained tyres that should have been thrown out long ago, ancient and unusable bicycles, rusty gardening tools, leaking hoses, bags of shingle, skis no one ever used, tins of paint, paintbrushes, logs stacked against the wall. Even though Henning's father never tinkered with any of the cars he owned, the place always smelled like a garage. It smelled of oil.

The smell of oil will always remind him of his father. He doesn't remember all that much about him, but he remembers his smell. Henning was fifteen years old when his father died suddenly. One morning, he simply failed to wake up. Henning had got up early; he had an English test later that day. His plan was to do some last-minute revision before the rest of his family stirred, but Trine was already awake. She was sitting on the bathroom floor, her legs pulled up to her chest. She said:

He's dead.

She pointed to the wall, the wall to their parents' bedroom. She wasn't crying, she merely kept saying:

He's dead.

He remembers knocking on the door, even though it was ajar. The door to his parents' bedroom was always closed. Now it swung open. His father lay there with his hands on the duvet. His eyes were shut. He looked at peace. His mother was still asleep. Henning went over to his father's side of the bed and looked at him. He looked like he was sleeping. When Henning shook him, he didn't move. Henning shook him again, harder this time.

His mother woke up. At first, she was startled, wondering what on earth Henning was up to. Then she looked at her husband – and screamed.

Henning doesn't remember much of what happened next. He only recalls the smell of oil. Even in death, Jakob Juul smelled of oil.

After a breakfast consisting of two cups of coffee with three sugars, Henning decides to go to work. It is only 5.30 a.m., but he thinks there is no point in hanging around the flat.

He visualises the sea as he turns into Urtegata. He

should be feeling tired, but the coffee has woken him up. Sølvi isn't there yet, but he visualises her, too, as he swipes his card.

There is only one other person in the office when he arrives. The night duty editor is hunched over his keyboard, sipping a cup of coffee. Henning nods briefly to him as they make eye contact, but the duty editor soon returns to his screen.

Henning lets himself sink into his squeaking chair. He catches himself wondering when Iver Gundersen gets to work, if he is post-coital and glowing, if it's plain for all to see that Nora gave him a good start to the day.

By the time Henning snaps out of his self-flagellating fantasy, he could have sworn he could detect Nora's scent. A hint of coconut against warm skin. He doesn't recall the name of the lotion, the one she loved and which he loved that she wore. But he can smell coconut all around him. He turns, gets halfway up from his chair and looks around. The duty editor and he are the only two people there. And yet he can smell coconut. Sniff, sniff. Why can't he recall the name of that lotion?

The scent disappears as quickly as it came. He falls back into his chair.

The sea, Henning, he tells himself. Focus on the sea.

Chapter 22

Research is a fine word. It's even a profession. *A researcher*. Every TV series has one. Every TV news desk has one, sometimes many.

Henning spends his time doing a little research while the rest of the newspaper wakes up. Research matters, it is possibly a journalist's most important task when there isn't much else to do. Dig, dig dig. The oddest but ultimately crucial snippets of information can be found in the strangest texts or public records.

He remembers a story he worked on years ago. He was relatively inexperienced at the time, probably hadn't covered more than ten murders when a vicar, Olav Jørstad disappeared in the sea, off the coast of Sørland. Everyone knew how much Jørstad liked fishing, but he was familiar with the sea and would never have gone out if bad weather had been forecast.

Eventually, his boat was found, bottom up. Jørstad himself was never found and everything pointed to a tragic accident. The current had very likely carried his body out into the wide, blue sea.

Henning covered the story for *Aftenposten*, and put

together a standard package, which meant interviewing family, neighbours, friends, Jørstad's congregation, the whole Norwegian Bible belt, practically. After discussing the story with his editor, Henning decided to stay on because he had a hunch that something was missing from the picture of Jørstad that everyone was painting. In the eyes of his parishioners, Jørstad was an outstanding vicar, a brilliant spiritual leader, who had the gift of the gab; some even claimed that he had healed them, but Henning never reported such claims in his articles. He suspected some of them of actively courting publicity.

However, Jørstad's role as a choir master and conductor received very little attention. Every church has a choir. Vicars are trained in choral song. The Reverend Mr Jørstad was a man who liked discipline and consequently, it was a fine choir. Some days after Jørstad's disappearance, after the media novelty had faded, Henning was chatting to Jørstad's son, Lukas. They happened to talk about the choir and Henning asked if Lukas had been a member. Lukas replied no.

A few weeks later, Henning was trying to contact a member of the choir, a woman called Susanne Opseth, who was supposedly one of the last people to see Jørstad alive. Henning did his research and found several newspaper cuttings in which she was featured. And in one of them, from the early 1990s, before the Internet, he spotted her in a photo, singing in the choir with Mr Jørstad conducting. What Henning didn't notice at first, but discovered when he examined the picture in detail, was that Lukas was lined up in the back row.

Lukas had lied when he told Henning he had never sung in the choir. Why he would lie about something so trivial? The answer was obvious. There was something about the choir that Lukas didn't want Henning to know or find out about.

So Henning started digging, interviewing the rest of the choir and it didn't take long before he discovered that Lukas had left the choir as an act of rebellion against his father, to humiliate him publicly. The choir wasn't the only place where Mr Jørstad demanded discipline. It found expression in strict routines, the reciting of Bible verses, a stern upbringing devoid of affection. And it ruined Lukas's budding relationship with a girl his own age, Agnes. Mr Jørstad didn't approve of her and he didn't want Lukas wasting his time with her.

Lukas released, as police interviews later revealed, years of frustration and oppression one night when his father took him fishing. Lukas hit his father over the head with an oar, sending him over the railing. Afterwards, Lukas overturned the boat and swam ashore.

Lukas was a strong swimmer and he was willing to

face the consequences of his actions. Anything to rid himself of his father's hold on him. But Lukas had an unexpected stroke of luck: his father's body was never found.

Henning worked with the local police force and was able to break the story the day they arrested Lukas. He hasn't checked, but as far as he knows, Lukas is still in jail. And all because of a single picture printed in a local paper many, many years ago.

Research. Even the slightest gust of wind can upset a house of cards.

Henning likes research, likes finding out information about people. Especially if those people interest him or have done something he finds fascinating. The Internet is brilliant for research. He didn't like the Internet to begin with; in fact, he was opposed to it, but now he can't imagine life without it. Once you have driven a Mercedes, you never go back to your pushbike.

The research he is doing now gives him no obvious clues for how to spend the rest of the day. He hasn't come up with a plan when Heidi Kjus and Iver Gundersen enter together. Henning can't hear what they are talking about, but his ears prick up. Gundersen smiles and looks suitably pleased – with himself, Henning reckons – but Heidi is serious as always. She reeks of 'let's get this show on the road' attitude.

Heidi rarely allows herself to smile: she regards it as

a sign of weakness. When she started working at *Nettavisen*, she would often join them for a beer on Fridays. She would be chatty and sociable, but never visibly drunk. Today, he can't imagine Heidi in the pub. Now she is the Boss. And bosses are always in charge. If she is tired, she never lets on. She suppresses her laughter if someone cracks a joke. It is inappropriate to allow oneself to be seduced by humour during business hours: it dulls her focus.

Heidi looks at Henning while she talks to Gundersen. She is excited about something and gesticulates enthusiastically. Gundersen nods. Henning notices that Gundersen's facial expression changes when he sees Henning is already at his desk. It is as if the self-assured, arrogant and smug cosmopolitan develops teenage acne and regresses fifteen years.

'You're in early?' Gundersen remarks and looks at Henning. Henning nods, but doesn't reply and glances at Heidi who sits down without saying anything.

'How did it go yesterday?' Gundersen asks. Henning glares at him. Tosser, he thinks. Haven't you read my story?

'All right.'

'People keen to talk?'

Gundersen sits down and switches on his PC.

'Enough.'

Gundersen smiles a crooked smile and looks at Heidi.

Henning knows she is listening, though she pretends she isn't. He turns his attention back to the screen.

Salty waves, Henning.

Oh, what fun this is going to be.

A little later Heidi says, in her Boss voice, that it is time to have a meeting. Neither Gundersen nor Henning says anything, but they get up and trundle after her. Gundersen slips to the front of the queue and waits for twenty-nine seconds so he can take a fresh cup of coffee with him. This creates a moment alone for Henning and his Boss. He steels himself for another bollocking, but Heidi says:

'That was a good story, Henning.'

He already knew that. But he didn't know that Heidi was big enough to admit it. He feels like saying that he will be quicker next time, but he doesn't. She might be like one of those Death Eaters in *Harry Potter*. Perhaps she will be different tomorrow or change when it is a full moon? For Christ's sake – the last time he had a meeting with Heidi, *he* was evaluating *her* stories. Not the other way around. Imagine Cristiano Ronaldo teaching an eight-year-old kid to play football and then getting a pat on the back from the same boy a few years later for a good insider pass.

Okay, wrong metaphor, but really. He is sure that Heidi can read his mind, but Gundersen comes to his rescue by entering the meeting room.

'Just the three of us?' he asks.

'Yes.'

'What about Jørgen and Rita?'

'Jørgen is manning the desk today, and Rita is on duty tonight.'

Gundersen nods. Heidi sits down at the end of the table and takes out a sheet of paper. She reviews today's stories. And she does it quickly. Henning knows that is because the news desk or the team who monitor the news and publish stories on an ongoing basis can handle most things. Heidi has an ulterior motive: she wants to show them that she is the Boss, that she is in charge.

Then they get to the real reason:

'Where are we with the stoning? Any good follow-ups today?'

Henning looks at Gundersen. Gundersen looks at Henning. He is back in his role as the rookie, so he awaits Gundersen's star turn. Gundersen takes a sip of his coffee and leans forward.

'The police seem fairly certain that Marhoni did it. I've a reliable source at the station who might give me some info from their interviews with him.'

Heidi nods and makes a quick note on her sheet.

'Anything else?'

'Not at the moment. I'll check my sources and see if anything else comes up.'

Heidi nods again. Then she looks at Henning.

'Henning, what have you got today?'

Heidi has her pen ready. He isn't used to reporting to a superior, so he hesitates for a second before clearing his throat.

'Not sure yet.'

Heidi is about to write something, but stops.

'You're not sure yet?'

'No. I've got some ideas, but I don't know if they'll lead to anything.'

The truth is he doesn't know if he can get hold of the people he wants to talk to or if they will tell him anything useful, and he doesn't want to promise something at the meeting he later finds he can't deliver. Best not to say anything.

'What kind of ideas, Henning?' she probes. He can hear the doubt in her voice. And he sees her sneaking in a quick sideways peek at Gundersen.

'I want to talk to a few more people at Hagerup's college – if they're there today.'

'We've done human interest.'

'This isn't human interest. This is different.'

'What is it?'

He hesitates again, he wants to tell her about Anette's eyes, about how the hudud punishments don't make sense, but he doesn't trust Heidi or Gundersen. Not yet. He knows they are his colleagues and that he needs

142

to work with them, but they have to earn his trust first. It has nothing to do with professional rivalry or ego.

'I think there's more to Hagerup's background and life, something which matters to this story,' he says. 'I'm hoping people at her college can shed some light on who she was and why someone chose to knock her out with a stun gun and throw rocks at her head until she died.'

He is pleased with his own reply until he realises what he has just said.

'A stun gun?'

Gundersen looks at him. Henning curses himself. He says.

'Eh?'

A pathetic attempt to buy time.

'I don't recall reading anything about a stun gun?'

Henning says nothing; he feels two pairs of eyes sticking into him like pins. His cheeks redden.

'Who told you that, Henning?' Heidi asks.

'I thought I had heard somewhere that a stun gun was used,' he says, instantly hearing how feeble his explanation sounds. He can tell from their faces that they don't believe him. But they say nothing. They just stare at him.

Crested, salty waves won't help you now, Henning. He can hear his own laboured breathing. Then he says.

'Are we done?'

He doesn't look at them, but he gets up and avoids meeting their eyes as he goes to the door, half expecting to hear Heidi's sharp voice order him back, Henning the Labrador, sit, but he grabs the handle without anything happening, he pushes it down, pulls the door open and leaves.

The silence he leaves behind is like a plane crash in his head. He can only imagine what Gundersen and Heidi say about him in his absence. Not that it matters.

He is just grateful to be out of there.

Chapter 23

Henning hits the streets of Grønland before Heidi and Gundersen finish their meeting. The temperature has risen by several degrees since he got to work and the air is humid. He looks up. Clouds, white and grey, rush across the sky. It is almost nine o'clock. Tariq Marhoni probably isn't up yet.

Henning found little of interest about him on the Internet: Tariq came to Norway from Islamabad in the mid 1990s, his brother had arrived a few years earlier, and they have shared three different addresses. While Mahmoud couldn't be found in any newspaper articles, chat rooms, web pages or tax registers, Tariq featured in a *VG* survey a couple of years ago where he was asked if he was for or against the EU.

Tariq placed himself in the 'don't know' category. And that was all Henning had learned. In other words, the Marhoni brothers have kept a low profile, but Henning has been around long enough to know that means nothing. Tariq is still best placed to tell him about Mahmoud, the police's only suspect, and he has

145

been branded guilty already. That's why Henning needs to find out as much about him as he can.

It has only just gone nine, but he decides to go to Tariq's flat anyway. If he doesn't reply because he is asleep or out, Henning can go to a nearby café and grab some breakfast. God knows, he needs some.

On his way to Oslogate, he passes the police station where a man in a reflective vest is cutting the grass outside. Cars rush past. He heads for Middelalderparken. The area has had a facelift in the last few years, façades have been re-plastered, new residential housing developments have been completed and made the district more attractive. Bjørvika seafront is only a few hundred metres away. You can walk to the new Opera House in ten minutes without getting out of breath.

Before he gets to number 37, he switches his mobile to silent. Too many interviews are ruined or lose their momentum due to intrusive bleeping from a laptop or a jacket pocket.

The door to the backyard is open, so Henning just walks in. The corridor is dark and empty. Middle Eastern music flows from a window. Someone is having a loud discussion in the same flat. He can smell something sweet.

He heads for stairwell B where the Marhoni brothers live. He is about to press a button saying 'Marhoni' when the door in front of him is opened. A man with a ginger beard comes out. He takes no notice of Henning and doesn't close the door behind him, so Henning grabs the handle before the door slams shut.

There is a powerful aroma of spices in the stairwell. His hip protests as he walks up the stairs. He curses himself for not taking his pills this morning, but forgets all about his discomfort when he sees the name MARHONI on a plate on the door of an upper ground floor flat. He stops, gets his breath back. His first home visit. You were rusty yesterday, Henning. Perhaps you're a little less so today?

He rings the doorbell. He waits and listens. The bell seems to be faulty. He decides to knock. He clenches his fist and knocks hard three times in quick succession. His knuckles hurt.

Was there movement from inside? It sounded like it. Like someone turning over in bed. He knocks again. The sound of feet on floor. He takes a step back. The door opens. A bleary-eyed Tariq Marhoni stands on the threshold. Henning thinks he looks like he is still asleep. His eyes are narrow and he sways. He is dressed only in underpants and a filthy vest. His face is drawn, he has huge bags under his eyes and his stubble suggests he is trying desperately to grow a beard. Tariq is chubby with curly, bushy hair. He looks like he hasn't showered for days.

Tariq supports himself against the wall.

'Hi, I'm Henning Juul.'

Tariq says nothing.

'I work for *123news*, and –'

Tariq takes a step back and slams the door. And he double-locks it.

Great, Henning. Well played.

'All I need is two minutes, Tariq.'

The sound of footsteps fading away. Henning fumes, but knocks again. He plays his last card.

'I'm here because I think your brother is innocent.'

He shouts a little louder than he had intended. The sound reverberates. He waits. And waits. No noise from the flat. He curses to himself.

This used to be straightforward.

He lets a minute pass, maybe two, before he decides to leave. He is about to open the front door when he hears a creak. He turns around. The door opens. Tariq looks at him. The apathy in his eyes has gone. Henning seizes his chance and holds up his hands.

'I'm not here to dig up dirt on your brother.'

His voice is soft, filled with compassion. Tariq seems to buy his explanation.

'You think he's innocent?'

He speaks broken Norwegian in a high-pitched voice. Henning nods. Tariq hesitates, debates with himself. His stomach bulges behind the vest.

'If you write some shit about my brother –'

He pulls an aggressive face, but doesn't finish his threat. Henning holds up his hands again. His eyes alone should convince Tariq that he is serious. Tariq goes back inside, but leaves the door open. Henning follows him.

Good, Henning. You're catching up fast.

Henning closes the door behind him and checks the ceiling. And finds what he is looking for.

'I need to get dressed,' Tariq calls out.

Henning explores the flat which surprises him by being clean and tidy. There are two doors to the right off the hallway where shoes are lined up neatly against the skirting board. A door to his left is open. He sneaks a peek. The toilet seat is up. The faint scent of Cif lemon wafts into the hallway.

He passes the kitchen. There is a plate with a few crumbs and a glass with traces of milk in the sink. He heads for the living room, sits down in a chair so soft he wonders if his backside is touching the floor. He can see the hallway, past the shoes, to the front door. Everywhere is clean.

He looks around, as he always does when he visits someone. *Details*, his old mentor, Jarle Høgseth used to say. The first thing that strikes him is the surprising number of plants and flowers in a flat inhabited by two brothers. An impressive large pelargonium with pink flowers sits on the windowsill. Orchids in a vase on a corner table. Pink roses. The brothers clearly have a thing about pink. Two candleholders with white candles. A large television, 45 inches, at least, he reckons, stands up against the wall. Home cinema – of course – from Pioneer, with tall speakers either side of the television and two behind. Henning looks for the subwoofer and assumes it must be hidden under the dark brown sofa. If he had been in a home in Oslo's West End, he would have guessed the sofa was designed by Bolia.

The coffee table is low and inspired by oriental style, with curved legs and a square top. The table was black once, but has now been painted white. A clean glass ashtray sits in the middle. More flowers. Another candlestick. A photo of a large Pakistani family, the family in Islamabad, he guesses, hangs on the vanilla-coloured wall. There is a fireplace in one corner.

But no photos of Henriette Hagerup.

The flat is starting to affect him. He had imagined a dump, dust everywhere, mess and rubbish. This flat, however, is tidier than his own has been for the last six months, longer, perhaps.

He knows he is prejudiced. But he likes prejudices, likes having to review or change his opinion when he learns something about a subject, which overturns a preconceived notion. The knowledge he has gained from studying the Marhoni brothers' flat is like one of those boiled sweets that doesn't look very tasty, but tastes delicious when you unwrap it and pop it in your mouth.

He smiles as Tariq appears in the hallway. Tariq has put on a pair of black jeans and a black linen shirt. He goes to the kitchen. Henning hears him open and shut the fridge quickly, then he opens a cupboard and takes out a glass.

'Do you want a glass of milk?' he calls out.

'Eh, no thanks.'

Milk, Henning muses. He has made numerous home visits, but no one has ever offered him milk before. He hears a firm glass-hitting-kitchen-counter slam followed by a grunt of satisfaction. Tariq enters the living room and sits down opposite him on a wooden stool. He takes out a packet of cigarettes and offers Henning a white friend. Henning declines, muttering something about having quit.

'What happened to your face?'

The unexpected question takes Henning by surprise. He replies without thinking.

'My flat burned down two years ago. My son died.'

He doesn't know if it is the brutal truth or the unsentimental way in which he said it that makes Tariq uncomfortable. He tries to say something, but stops.

Tariq fumbles with the cigarette, lights it and tosses the lighter on the coffee table. Henning follows the rectangular tool from hell with his eyes, watches it skid to a halt by the ashtray.

Tariq looks at him. For a long time. Henning says nothing; he knows that he has stirred Tariq's curiosity, but he has no plans to bombard him with questions. Not yet.

'So you don't think my brother did it?' Tariq asks and takes a deep drag on his cigarette. He pulls a face, as if it tastes of stinking feet.

'No.'

'Why not?'

He answers frankly.

'I don't know.'

Tariq snorts.

'And yet you don't think he did it?'

'That's right.'

They look at each other. Henning doesn't capitulate; he isn't scared of what his eyes might reveal.

'So what do you want to know?'

'Do you mind if I use this?'

He takes out his Dictaphone and places it on the table between them. Tariq shrugs.

Far too few reporters use a Dictaphone. When he first started out, he would scribble like a maniac while listening to what his subjects said and thinking about the next question to ask them. Needless to say that was a hopeless way of conducting an interview. You don't catch everything that's being said and your follow-up questions aren't logical either, because you're concentrating on two things, at least, at the same time. Dictaphones are brilliant.

He presses '*record*' and leans back in the chair. He puts his notebook in his lap. Pen poised. A Dictaphone should never replace pen and paper. If the recording fails, you will be grateful you made some notes, ideas to follow up later.

He looks at Tariq and can see he is upset by the arrest of his brother. A murder suspect. He has probably been wondering how to break it to the family back home. What will their friends say?

'What can you tell me about your brother?'

Tariq glares at him.

'My brother is a good man. He has always taken care of me. He was the one who got me up here, away from Islamabad, away from the slums and the crime there. He said life in Norway was good. He paid for my ticket, gave me a place to stay.'

'What does he do for a living?'

Tariq looks at him, but doesn't reply. Too soon, Henning thinks. Let the man talk.

'It was tough to begin with. Couldn't speak the language. Our only friends were other Pakistanis. But my brother got me in to Norwegian classes. We met people from other countries. Norwegian women –'

He sings the last word slightly and smiles. His smile promptly disappears. Henning says nothing.

'My brother didn't kill anyone. He's a good guy. And he loved her.'

'Henriette?'

Tariq nods.

'Had they been together for a long time?'

'No. A year, that was all.'

'What was their relationship like?'

'Good, I think. A lot of action.'

'They had a lot of sex, you mean?'

Tariq smiles. Henning can tell that Tariq has a memory, perhaps several, in his head. He nods.

'Were they faithful to each other?'

'Why do you ask that?'

'You think the police haven't asked your brother that question already?'

Tariq doesn't reply, but Henning can see he is debating it.

'It was a bit on and off.'

'What do you mean?'

'I think they broke up many times, but they always got back together again. And they were at it yesterday afternoon, well, I don't know anyone who does that.'

'So they –'

Tariq nods.

'Henriette made a lot of noise. She always does, but it was extra loud yesterday.'

The smile fades. He hasn't smoked for a minute, but now he takes a deep drag of stinking feet again before stubbing out the cigarette in the ashtray.

'They met at the Mela Festival. Nothing happened at the time, later they ran into each other at a film audition. Then it was –'

Tariq's mobile rings from what Henning assumes to be a bedroom. He has heard the ring tone before, but he can't place it. Tariq is momentarily distracted, but he ignores the call. He reaches out for the lighter, picks it up and studies it.

'It's a bad thing that's happened,' he says without raising his head.

'Do you have any idea who might have done it?'

Tariq shakes his head.

'Did Henriette and your brother have mutual friends they hung out with?'

Tariq presses the lighter wheel hard. A proud flame shoots out. Henning feels his chest tighten.

'We're from Pakistan. We've lots of friends.'

'Any ethnic Norwegian friends?'

'Many.'

'Were some of them married?'

155

'Married?'

'Yes. Wedding bells, rings on their fingers?'

'I don't understand the question.'

'Had any of them been to church and –'

'Hello – I know what marriage is. I just don't understand why you ask.'

Tariq carries on fidgeting with the lighter, while he looks at Henning. He doesn't quite know how to phrase his next question without revealing too much or saying something which might be offensive.

'Were either of them unfaithful?'

Tariq hesitates for a second. He holds Henning's gaze before he averts his eyes and looks at the floor.

'I don't know.'

His voice is quieter now. Henning thinks there is something Tariq isn't telling him. He makes a note 'both unfaithful?' on his pad.

'What does your brother do for a living?'

Tariq looks up again.

'Why's that so important to you?'

Henning shrugs.

'It mightn't be important at all. Or perhaps it's the most important thing of all. I don't know. That's why I'm asking, to get closer to understanding who your brother is. For most of us, we are what we do. We live through our work.'

'Do you?'

Henning wants to carry on while the going is good, but the question stops him in his tracks. He tries to come up with a sensible answer, but he can't.

'No.'

Tariq nods. Henning thinks he can read empathy in Tariq's eyes, but he can't be sure.

'My brother drives a minicab.'

'Does he work for himself?'

'No.'

'Who does he work for?'

'Omar.'

'Who's he?'

'A friend.'

'What's he called apart from Omar?'

Tariq sighs.

'Omar Rabia Rashid.'

'And what do you do for a living?'

Tariq gives Henning a weary look.

'I'm a photographer.'

'Freelance or employed?'

'Freelance.'

Henning tries to sit upright in the soft chair, but he sinks back into it.

'You brother refused to let the police in yesterday and he set fire to his computer. Do you know why he would do that?'

Henning notices that Tariq's eyes look worried now.

Tariq takes out a new cigarette and lights it. Then he shakes his head.

'You've got no idea?'

He shakes his head again.

'My brother was the only one who used it. I've my own computer.'

'You never saw what he used it for?'

'No, but it was probably the usual stuff. Surfing. E-mail. Are we done? I'm meeting a friend.'

Henning nods.

'Just a few more questions, then I'll go.'

At that moment, someone knocks on the door. Three short knocks. Tariq appears surprised.

'Your friend?'

Tariq doesn't reply, but he gets up.

'If it's another reporter, then I suggest you slam the door in his face,' Henning jokes. Tariq goes to the door. Henning can see him from where he is sitting. Tariq opens the door with a swift movement.

Henning leans forward, turns off the Dictaphone and gets ready to leave. He has just slipped it into his pocket, when he hears Tariq say:

'What the –'

Then Tariq is hit by two bullets to his chest.

Chapter 24

The shots are silent, but powerful enough to throw Tariq Marhoni against the wall. Henning registers two red spurts from Tariq's chest and has no time to react before the mouth of the pistol appears inside the door. A man enters. He sees Tariq slumped against the wall and fires another bullet straight into his head.

Jesus Christ.

Henning tries to get up as quietly as he can, but he is so deep into the soft chair that it is impossible without the killer noticing him. Henning watches the gun turn 90 degrees towards him and just manages to roll out of the way before the back of the chair receives a hole the size of an eye, right where his head was a second ago. The stuffing bursts out, foam and fabric whirl in the air. Henning hears footsteps and thinks that this is the end, bloody hell, this is it, it's over before it has even begun; panicking, he looks around, he sees a door in the living room, a door leading to another room, he has no choice, he has to go that way, he stands up and runs as fast as someone with his legs can. He can feel pain in his hip, his legs don't want to obey him, but he aims for the door and throws it open.

He hears another swift plop, a hole is ripped in the door behind him, but the bullet doesn't touch him; he is in another room, a small living room with a large window, he reaches for the catch, pushes it down, but it's the wrong way, he pushes it outwards instead, but it only opens a few centimetres, before it refuses to budge. He pushes it again, harder this time, but it stops in the same place. He turns around; the killer hasn't caught up with him yet. Henning looks at the window, discovers a child lock which he can override and opens the window in one movement. He climbs out on the windowsill, looks down, sees that the drop is only two metres and has a flashback to the balcony where he stood with Jonas, ready to jump. At that moment, he hears the killer enter the room. He expects to feel the sharp, paralysing pain from a bullet in his back, but before he has time to think, he is in the air, he feels nothing underneath him, he waves his arms, scared to look around, all he knows is that the ground is underneath him. Suddenly it's there, his knees buckle, he tumbles forwards, breaks the fall with his hands, pushes himself up on his palms, rolls around and nearly ends up in the street, on the tram lines, but the danger from the window is far greater, he tells himself, all the killer needs to do is pull the trigger and it will all be over.

Henning stands up, he hears a car coming towards him and gets out of the way. Forget the pain in your legs and hips, he commands himself, just keep running. He doesn't know which direction he is going, there is tarmac and litter all around, he sees a house, a yellow one. He has no idea where he is, he just carries on running. He corners the building as two bullets hit the wall in quick succession, but he is unhurt.

He finds himself in a small street, a one-way street, it must be St Hallvardsgate, he thinks, what a stroke of dramatic irony that would be, if he were to die here. He doesn't want to think about his mother now, all that matters is that he is out of the killer's range, and he keeps on running. He feels his heart pumping, adrenaline is released straight into his bloodstream. He runs past parked cars, sees people in the street, flashes of colour, the street bends, he follows it, running as fast as he can, he can't feel his legs; it is as if his legs and his hips are oddly out of sync and can't decide which of them should do what, but he doesn't give a damn about it, he knows he must put as much distance between him and the killer as possible, because the killer is fleeing, too.

Henning knows he ought to call the police, but his own safety takes priority. He must get himself to a place where he can catch his breath and talk without wheezing. He spots an open space: *GAMLEBYEN SPORT AND LEISURE PARK* it says in curved black letters on a sign above the entrance and Henning runs inside, past a red Mitsubishi Estate. There is no one around; rubbish bags slump against a derelict hut, the walls are covered with graffiti. His shoes pound the smooth concrete. He can see a ramp, a skateboard and an old plastic chair; it is not a large area. It says *WELCOME EVERYONE*, in clumsy italics on a sign on a blue wall. The graffiti letters and flames are intertwined in a way Henning doesn't understand. He reads: *We look out for each other because nobody else is bloody going to* below on the same sign. He looks around, the area is fenced in, Jesus Christ, he is trapped. There are trees all around, but he sees a gap in the fence, a hole, he aims for that hole and creeps through it. His jacket catches on something, but he yanks it free and hears it rip. He crawls between trees and shrubs, dense like a jungle, and skids past a rusty old fridge. He sees a house on the slope opposite and knows where he is.

He walks down to the train tracks, looking over his shoulder to see if he is being followed, but there is no sign of the killer. He hides behind a large tree, sits down and pants.

Breathe, Henning. For God's sake, man, breathe.

He finds his mobile, calls the police and inhales deeply while he waits for a reply. His call is answered quickly. He identifies himself and says:

'Get me Detective Inspector Bjarne Brogeland. Now.'

Chapter 25

When Henning turned thirteen, he was allowed to rent *Witness*, the film starring Harrison Ford and Kelly McGillis, where Danny Glover makes a rare appearance as the killer. After seeing it, Henning didn't use a public toilet for a long time.

Even though it is twenty-two years ago, he has never forgotten the scene in the gents where the terrified Amish boy is crying and Danny Glover opens one door after another to check if there were any witnesses to the murder. Henning must admit that Danny sprang to mind as he sat in the clearing, watching the trains speed by and listening out for approaching killers.

Now he is in a waiting room. He knows why they are called that. This is where you are meant to wait. And Henning waits. He has been given a glass of water. Nothing to read. That's because he needs to think. When the officers who will be questioning him finally arrive, his memory needs to be as organised, as detailed and as accurate as possible.

He is usually very accurate, but he feels out of practice. He thinks about Iver Gundersen and Heidi

Kjus – perhaps he should have called them as well, but before he has time to think it through, the door to the waiting room is opened. A tall female officer with short hair enters. She looks at him.

'Sergeant Ella Sandland,' she introduces herself and holds out her hand. Henning gets up, shakes her hand and nods briefly. Bjarne Brogeland, who follows just behind her, eats her up with his eyes, before he sees his old schoolfriend and grins broadly.

'Hallo, Henning.'

And there it is, the feeling he always used to get when he was around Bjarne. Aversion. These days, it is unlikely to have anything to do with Trine. Certain things just don't change.

Ella Sandland sits down on the other side of the table. Brogeland comes up to Henning and offers him his hand, too. Brogeland must have interviewed hundreds of suspects, Henning thinks, met all kinds of people, but despite his training, it is still there, the slight change in his expression that Henning has seen so many times, usually much more obvious. It is only a fraction of a second and Brogeland tries to be cool about it, tries to be professional, but Henning sees him recoiling at the scars.

They shake hands. A firm squeeze.

'Holy cow, Henning,' Brogeland says and sits down. 'It's been a long time. How many years is it?'

His tone is jovial, cosy, chummy. They applied to the police academy at the same time, but they had nothing in common then, either. Henning replies:

'Fifteen – twenty years, perhaps?'

'Yes, it must be, at least.'

Silence. He usually likes silence, but now the walls cry out for sound.

'Good to see you again, Henning.'

He can't quite say the same thing about Bjarne, but he replies:

'Likewise.'

'I only wish the circumstances were different. We've a lot to talk about.'

Do we? Henning wonders. Perhaps we do. But he looks at Brogeland without replying.

'Perhaps we should start?' Ella Sandland suggests. Her voice is firm. Brogeland looks at her as though she is lunch, dinner and a midnight snack rolled into one. Sandland goes through the formalities. Henning listens to her, reckons that she comes from Sunnmøre or somewhere close by, Hareid, possibly?

'Have you got the guy?' he asks, as she is about to ask her first question. The officers look at each other.

'No,' Brogeland replies.

'Do you know which way he escaped?'

'We're actually here to interview you, not the other way round,' Sandland says.

166

'It's fine,' Brogeland interjects, placing his hand on her arm. 'Of course he wants to know. No, we don't know where the killer is. But we hope you can help us find him.'

'So can you tell us what happened?' Sandland completes the sentence. Henning inhales and tells them about the interview with Tariq Marhoni, the shots, his escape. He speaks quietly and with composure, even though his insides are churning. It feels weird to relive it, articulate it, to know that he was a millimetre or two from death.

'What were you doing at Marhoni's?' Sandland asks.

'I interviewed him.'

'Why?'

'Why not? His brother's in custody for a murder he didn't do. Tariq knows, or knew, his brother best. I would be worried if that thought hadn't already occurred to you.'

'Of course it has,' Sandland says, offended. 'We just haven't got that far yet.'

'Is that right?'

'What did you talk about?'

'His brother.'

'Can you be a bit more specific?'

He breathes in, theatrically, while he tries to remember. He has everything on the Dictaphone in his pocket, but he has no plans to hand it over.

'I asked him to tell me about his brother, what he did for a living, what his relationship with Henriette Hagerup was like – the sort of questions you ask people you want to know a little more about.'

'What did he reply?'

'Not very much of interest. We never got that far.'

'You said his brother's in custody for a murder he didn't do. What do you mean by that? What makes you say that?'

'Because I seriously doubt that he did it.'

'Why?'

'There's little in his background to suggest that he's a fervent supporter of hudud punishments, and the murder has – as far as I understand it – links to that.'

Sandland sits immobile and looks at him for a long time, before she exchanges glances with Brogeland.

'How do you know that?'

'I just do.'

Sandland and Brogeland look at each other again. Henning can guess what they are thinking.

Do we have a leak?

Sandland fixes her blue eyes on him. He feels the urge for a gin and tonic.

'You seem to know quite a lot.'

Sandland says it like a question. Henning shrugs.

'Or you used to. *Kapital, Aftenposten, Nettavisen,*

123news. How many front-page stories have you had, Juul? How many scoops? That's what you journalists call it, isn't it?'

Henning's shoulders rise in preparation of another deep breath.

'If it will help your investigation, then I can find things out.'

Sandland smiles. It is the first time he sees her smile. Perfect teeth. A red, inviting tongue. He guesses Brogeland has tasted it.

No, on second thoughts, no. She is not that stupid.

'And, once again, you're at the centre of an investigation, but this time you're a witness. How does that feel?'

'Are you fishing for a second career with NRK Sport, by any chance?'

'I think this interview will go better and quicker if we avoid sarcasm, Henning,' Brogeland says and gives him an amicable look. Henning nods and concedes that, for once, Brogeland has a point.

'It's more like a new experience, you could say,' he starts, a tad more polite now. 'I've witnessed a few things in my time, robberies and stabbings, two own goals by the same player in the same match, but it's a strange feeling to see someone I've just been speaking to, who has just offered me a glass of milk, be shot twice in the chest and once in the head.'

'Milk?'

'Skimmed.'

Brogeland nods and smiles briefly.

'Did you catch a glimpse of the killer?'

He hesitates.

'It happened so quickly.'

'But even in brief flashes, the brain can register a great deal of information. Think about it again. Think hard.'

He thinks hard. And, suddenly, the shell cracks. He sees something. A face. An oval face. A beard. Not covering the whole face, only around the mouth, in a square. Thick sideburns.

He tells them. And he describes something else: his lips. A little crooked to the left. Brogeland was right, he thinks. Bloody hell, Bjarne Brogeland, that prize wanker, was right.

'Did you see what kind of weapon he used?'

'No.'

'Sure?'

'A hand gun. A pistol? I don't know a lot about weapons.'

'Silencer?'

'Yes. Haven't you found bullet cases on the crime scene?'

Sandland looks at Brogeland again. Yes, of course they have, Henning thinks, and then he feels his mobile vibrate in his pocket. He tries to ignore the call, but it refuses to be silenced.

'Sorry,' he mutters, pointing to his pocket.

'Turn off your mobile,' Sandland orders him. He takes it out and has time to see that Iver Gundersen is trying to get hold of him. He presses extra hard on the '*off*' button and holds it down for a long time.

'Did you see what the killer was wearing?'

Think. Think.

'Dark trousers. I think his jacket was black. No, it wasn't. It was beige.'

'Black or beige?'

'Beige.'

'What colour was his hair?'

'Don't remember, but I think it was dark, too. The guy was dark.'

Sandland sends him a dubious look.

'Apart from his beige jacket,' he adds, quickly.

'Immigrant?' Brogeland asks.

'Yes, I would guess so.'

'Pakistani? Like the victim?'

'Yes, that's possible.'

Brogeland and Sandland both make notes. Henning can't see them, but he knows what they say.

The killer knew the victim.

He exploits the short pause that has arisen.

'So, what do you think, did you arrest the wrong Marhoni?'

He takes out his notepad. Sandland and Brogeland look at each other again.

'I thought I had made it clear to you that –'

Brogeland coughs. His hand goes back on Sandland's arm. She reddens.

'It's too soon to say.'

'So you don't rule out revenge as the motive?'

'We rule out nothing.'

'On which theory are you basing the investigation, then? Mahmoud is arrested, suspected of murder and less than twenty-four hours later, his brother is killed.'

'Inspector –' Sandland objects.

'No comments. And the interview's over,' Brogeland announces.

'Would you recognise the killer if you saw him again?' Sandland continues. Henning thinks about it, replays the scene in Marhoni's flat in his head, and says:

'I don't know.'

'Could you try?'

He sees what she means.

'Have you got some pictures for me to look at?'

She nods gravely.

'I could always give it a try,' he says.

Chapter 26

'Are you always like that?' Brogeland asks as he sits down at a table and opens up a laptop. They have relocated to a smaller room. Henning sits on the other side of the table and watches Brogeland clicking and typing on the tiny keyboard.

'Like what?' Henning replies.

'Disrespectful and arrogant?'

Brogeland turns the laptop towards him and smiles. The question takes Henning by surprise. He turns down the corners of his mouth and tilts his head, first to the left and then to the right. If he hopes to turn the officer in front of him into a potential source, arrogant and disrespectful behaviour isn't the recommended approach in *Journalism for Dummies*. So he says:

'Sorry, I didn't mean to.'

He holds up his hands.

'I'm not quite myself after what happened. It's not every day I witness a murder. I'm not usually like this. It's probably a defence mechanism or something.'

Brogeland nods.

'I understand.'

It's not a bull's-eye, but he hits the target, at least. Brogeland pushes the computer a little closer.

'Use the arrows to go forwards and backwards. If you want to have a closer look at one of the pictures, you just click on it.'

'These people all have form?'

'Yes. I've selected offenders with an immigrant background. I've add a couple of other criteria as well.'

Henning nods and starts scrolling through the pictures.

'So, Bjarne, what have you been up to since you left school?' he asks while he looks at the screen.

'A bit of this and that, like most people. After A-levels, I joined the Army, I was abroad for one year, Kosovo, and then I did a three-year degree course at the Sports College. After that, I applied to the police. And I've been here ever since.'

'Family?'

Henning despises himself right now.

'Wife and child.'

'Your wife – is she someone I know or would know of?'

'I doubt it. I met her at Sports College. Anita's from Hamar.'

Henning nods while he carries on looking. He does

recognise some of the faces, but only because he has written about them previously, or seen them in the papers.

'Do you enjoy being a police officer?' he fawns and wants to puke.

'Very much so, though it's a tough job. I don't get to see as much of my daughter as I would like. Antisocial working hours. There's always an investigation going on.'

'How old is your daughter?'

'Three. Three and a half,' Brogeland adds quickly.

'Lovely age,' Henning says and regrets going down this route immediately. He hopes Brogeland will refrain from asking the question which would traditionally follow his, and says:

'What's her name?'

'Alisha.'

'Nice name.'

Henning feels the bile rise in his throat with yesterday's coffee.

'My wife wanted an international name. So our kid can live abroad without having to spell her name all the time.'

Bjarne laughs briefly. Henning tries to laugh too, but it sounds forced, so he stops and concentrates on the laptop. Faces, faces, and more faces. They reek of crime. Angry eyes, embittered mouths. But no killer.

He must have been pressing arrows for around fifteen minutes, when Brogeland says:

'Do you think the killer got a look at you?'

Henning lifts his eyes from the screen and stares at the Inspector. Funny how that never occurred to me, he thinks.

'I don't know,' he replies and visualises his own flight. The killer mostly saw his back, but there was a moment when their eyes met. And it's not easy to forget Henning's face.

Yes, he saw me, he concludes. He must have.

He looks at Brogeland and knows what he is thinking. If Forensics don't find any evidence that proves the killer was at the crime scene, then *only* Henning can place him there. In a subsequent trial, Henning's testimony makes it a penalty kick into an open goal.

Only one thing is required.

That Henning stays alive.

Chapter 27

Forty-five minutes later, he taps the screen eagerly with his index finger. Brogeland gets up and comes round to his side of the table.

'Are you sure?'

Henning looks at the man's crooked upper lip.

'Yes.'

Brogeland's eyes light up. He takes over the computer, turns it away from Henning, sits down, types and clicks.

'Who is he?' Henning asks. Brogeland looks up over the screen, his eyes flickering slightly.

'His name's Yasser Shah,' he says reluctantly. 'But don't you dare put that in your paper.'

Henning holds up his hands.

'What's he done?'

'Nothing much. He has a couple of convictions for possession. Petty crime, small stuff, really.'

'So he has gone from small-time dealing to hired killer?'

'Looks like it.'

'Hm.'

'He belongs to a gang that calls itself BBB. Bad Boys Burning.'

Henning wrinkles his nose.

'What kind of gang is that? I've never heard of them.'

'One which has come to our attention in the last year. It's involved in a range of criminal activities. Smuggling, drugs, debt collection using fists and weapons such as – eh – well, weapons. Colleagues working directly with organised crime know a lot about them, I believe.'

'Did the Marhoni brothers have anything to do with BBB?'

Brogeland is about to reply, but he stops and looks at Henning. And, again, he knows exactly what Brogeland is thinking.

Henning, you're probably a decent guy, but I don't know you well enough yet.

'This is really good,' Brogeland says instead. 'Thank you so much. You've been a great help.'

They get up. Brogeland holds out his hand. Another firm handshake. Henning leaves the police station with a feeling that the person he helped the most was probably himself.

Outside in the street, the headline comes to him. *Tariq's last words.* It will be a great story, he thinks. Tourette Kåre will click. Literally.

He switches on his mobile as he turns into Grønlandsleiret. Thirty seconds later, the text messages flood in. Several people have left messages on his voicemail. Iver Gundersen is one of them. Henning knows why they are calling, obviously, of course he does, but he hasn't got the energy to respond and he is about to hit the delete button when Gundersen calls again. Henning sighs and replies with a curt 'hi'.

'Where are you?'

'At the police station.'

'Why haven't you called us? It's a huge story and we would have been the first to break it.'

'I was a bit busy saving my life. What's left of it.'

'For God's sake, I've been trying to get hold of you for three and a half hours.'

'Three and a half hours?'

'Yes.'

'You timed it?'

Gundersen takes a deep breath and exhales so hard that it roars in Henning's ear.

'It's totally unacceptable that NRK gets to break the news that a *123news* reporter witnessed a murder and was shot at himself.'

'Is that Jørn Bendiksen again?'

'Yes.'

'His sources must be very good.'

Henning says it in a way which can't be

misinterpreted. He knows that Gundersen will regard it as a personal insult.

'At the very least, I need an interview with you now, so you can tell me what happened. We have omitted quoting NRK and given our readers the impression that we have spoken to you, but I feel sick to my stomach. An eyewitness report from you would put a lot of things right.'

'You haven't faked any quotes, have you?'

'No, no. You can check for yourself when you get in, or you can read it on your mobile. Do you want to do it in the office, or over the phone?'

'No.'

'What do you mean, no?'

'No, no,' Henning says, mimicking Gundersen's voice. 'There'll be no interview.'

Total silence.

'Is this a joke?'

'No, no.'

'Why the hell not?'

'Because a couple of bullets whizzed past my ears roughly three and a half hours ago. I've no intention of making it easy for the killer to find me, in case he fancies having another go. He knows that I saw him. Or, if he doesn't, he soon will.'

Gundersen heaves a sigh.

'I'm going home now to write up the interview with

Tariq. When that's done, that's me out of the picture for a couple of days,' Henning continues. He just manages to complete the last sentence, before Gundersen hangs up on him. Henning gloats.

He is about to stop off at Meny supermarket when his mobile rings again. He doesn't recognise the number. Perhaps it's Gundersen pretending to sell subscriptions? He switches off his mobile and dreams of one, maybe two, three or four warm fish cakes.

Yum.

Chapter 28

His supply of batteries is starting to run out, but he has enough to replace the batteries in all eight smoke alarms as he gets home. He goes into his living room. No killers lying in wait for him. He hadn't really thought so, either, but you never know.

He takes a shower while his computer boots up at a snail's pace. Fifteen minutes later, he is cleaner than a Johnson's baby and he loads FireCracker 2.0. He has a question for *6tiermes7*. This time Deep Throat is already logged on:

MakkaPakka: Turbo.

6tiermes7: Negro.
  It didn't take you long to become a target?

MakkaPakka: In that particular respect, I'm not out of
  practice.

6tiermes7: Still in one piece?

MakkaPakka: Oh, yes. Just as well I don't need to sleep
  at night.

6tiermes7: Count sheep. Have a wank.

MakkaPakka: Too much effort.

6tiermes7: :-)

MakkaPakka: I'm thinking of taking a couple of days off, but I'm curious about something.

6tiermes7: Time off? You?

MakkaPakka: Do the Marhoni brothers have anything to do with BBB? Are they members?

6tiermes7: No. We are struggling to find the link.

MakkaPakka: But there is one?

6tiermes7: Don't you think so?

MakkaPakka: I don't know. They may just have known each other socially.

6tiermes7: Yeah, right.

MakkaPakka: Will you be carrying out a raid against them soon?

6tiermes7: I don't know anything about that yet. But I'm guessing they'll try Yasser Shah's home first.

MakkaPakka: He has probably gone underground.

6tiermes7: You don't think he'll have another go at you?

MakkaPakka: Would you? When all eyes are on him?

6tiermes7: No. Did they offer you protection?

MakkaPakka: Yes.

6tiermes7: Good. But you never know, someone else might want to finish the job.

MakkaPakka: I declined.

6tiermes7: Oh. Did you?

MakkaPakka: Very funny.

6tiermes7: So what happens now?

MakkaPakka: I'm thinking of lying low for a couple of days.

6tiermes7: At least.

MakkaPakka: Okay. I might work from home. I'll see what happens.

6tiermes7: Okay.

MakkaPakka: Any developments in the investigation?

6tiermes7: A few. They're hunting high and low for links and clues. Many interviews.

MakkaPakka: Any details you can feed to me?

6tiermes7: Well, they've given up on the honour killing theory.

MakkaPakka: Any other excitement?

6tiermes7: Not quite sure. I don't know if this means anything, but a film company had taken out an option on a screenplay written by Hagerup.

MakkaPakka: How recently?

6tiermes7: A while ago, I think.

MakkaPakka: Student rivalry, perhaps?

6tiermes7: No idea. But they're talking to all her friends and tutors.

MakkaPakka: Did Hagerup have a tutor?

6tiermes7: Yes. A chap called Yngve Foldvik.

MakkaPakka: That name sounds familiar.

6tiermes7: Means nothing to me.

MakkaPakka: Do you know anything about the tent on Ekeberg Common?

6tiermes7: The college had put it up. They were in the middle of filming.

MakkaPakka: Do you suspect any of her fellow students?

6tiermes7: Not at the moment. I think Mahmoud

Marhoni is their prime suspect. They've evidence
which implicates him.

MakkaPakka: Has he been questioned following the
murder of his brother?

6tiermes7: No. His lawyer threw his weight around.

MakkaPakka: Okay. Thank you. See you later.

6tiermes7: Stay healthy.

Stay healthy.

The quote is from the film *Heat* with Robert De
Niro and Al Pacino. Jon Voight's character sits in the
car with De Niro, planning a break-in, and as De Niro
gets out of the car, Voight tells him to stay healthy.

6tiermes7 likes *Heat*. And Voight is on to something.
It's important to stay healthy. And it's good to know
that someone cares about you, even if Henning doesn't
know who that someone is.

Chapter 29

6tiermes7 was right. It won't be easy to lie low. Too many questions are buzzing around his head and the more he thinks about it, the more convinced he is that Henriette Hagerup's college and its students hold many of the answers.

He visits Westerdal's homepage and switches on his mobile again. Just like the last time, the messages pile up. And just like the last time, he deletes them without checking them first. He clicks on the college's film section, finds a staff list and localises Yngve Foldvik after some quick scrolling and clicking. A photograph with a CV and contact details pop up. Henning studies him.

Where does he know him from? Dark hair, side parting to the left. Narrow nose. Sallow skin, not brown, the kind which tans easily. Light stubble with streaks of grey. He looks to be in his late forties, but he is still a handsome man. Henning suspects some of the students have secret crushes on him.

He checks the time. 5.30 p.m. Tariq's last words will have to wait. He rings Foldvik's mobile instead. Three rings later, he strikes lucky. Henning introduces himself. Foldvik says 'hi' in a voice that Henning instantly recognises as the 'oh shit' tone.

'I don't have much to say to you,' he begins. His voice is high.

'I don't want you to, either,' Henning counters. Silence follows. He knows that Foldvik hasn't quite understood what he meant. And that's the idea. He lets Foldvik wait until he grows sufficiently curious and simply has to ask:

'What do you mean?'

'If I could meet you tomorrow morning, at a time convenient to you, then I can explain what I want to talk to you about. But I would be lying if I said it didn't have anything to do with your late student.'

'I don't know if I have –'

'It'll only take a few minutes.'

'Like I said, then –'

'I want people who read about Henriette to get as accurate a picture of her as possible. I think you might be the most suitable person to paint that. You knew her in a different way to her fellow students, and – to be honest – they have a tendency to say some strange stuff.'

Another silence. He can hear Foldvik mull it over. And that's part of the technique. Massage the ego of those you want to interview to such an extent that it becomes harder and harder for them to say no.

'Okay, two minutes. Ten o'clock tomorrow?'

A broad smile forms around his lips.

'Ten o'clock would be fine.'

It is a straightforward matter to write out an interview when he has everything on tape. To begin with, he decides to use everything Tariq said, word for word, since they were the man's last, but he abandons that idea as soon as the interview takes shape on his computer. Too much irrelevant information. And he doesn't want people to know everything Tariq said about his brother. After all, Mahmoud is still in custody and it very much remains an open investigation.

It takes him half an hour to type up everything Tariq Marhoni said. He starts to edit and decides to focus on the fine description Tariq gave of his brother.

My brother is a good man.

It borders on the dull, but it's a start. He types on:

Tariq Marhoni spent his last moments praising his brother, who is suspected of murder. Read the exclusive interview here.

He knows that people will read this story, even though it is not very exciting. There is something about a man's last words. They appeal, no matter what he said. And when it is as exclusive as this, everyone with even a vague interest in the story will click on it. Other media will trawl the story for quotes they can use. This means '. . ., *said Tariq Marhoni to 123news, only minutes before he died.'*

Quotes. Apart from advertising revenue and profit, being quoted in rival media is what matters to many newspapers. At the same time, it is possibly also the greatest source of irritation, especially among smaller publications, when the big fish use a quote from someone else's story and fail to credit them.

This happens every day. The big fish are so afraid of the little fish growing bigger that they sacrifice both good manners and press ethics in the process. If it isn't a case of downright theft, they will often contact the source to obtain the same quotes which enables them to insist – often with a large portion of indignation – that 'we just happened to have the same idea'. NRK, for example, has a standard policy that if a story appears in two media, at least, there is no reason to credit either of them.

He doesn't know if this policy has changed during the two years he has been out of the game, but it's impossible not to quote the Tariq story. He guesses that Heidi Kjus will be particularly pleased about it. Possibly Iver Gundersen, too.

No, on second thoughts, no. Not Gundersen.

He thinks about BBB. Bad Boys Burning. What a name for a gang. Some gangs have a great need to send out warnings. Bandidos. Hell's Angels. And yet,

Henning can feel himself growing curious about BBB. He googles the full name and gets thousands of hits, many of which are irrelevant and inaccurate. Reviews of the film *Bad Boys*, articles about a Swedish crooner who had a hit with a song called 'Burning' a couple of years ago, people who are described as 'bad boys' and a gang from the Furuset area of Oslo, who also call themselves that. Little of relevance.

However, he finds an article from *Aftenposten* from six months ago about a gang confrontation in Furuset, coincidentally. The Google text doesn't mention BBB in the link, but he clicks on it anyway.

He gasps for air. Nora wrote this story. She has ventured into dangerous territory. Gangs are usually associated with drugs and debt collecting. Its members are wannabe criminals, people searching for an identity, usually. That's one of the reasons they become hooligans. To have a place to belong.

Nora's headline is 'BRUTAL GANG CLASH IN FURUSET'. He looks at the story. No photos from the crime scene. Only an archive photo of an axe against a baseball bat. He guesses that Nora worked the night shift and that *Aftenposten* wasn't prepared to fork out on a new picture from Scanpix. Or that Scanpix has had to make cuts, too.

Nevertheless, he can see that Nora did a good job. She interviewed the officer in charge of the investigation, the head of Oslo's Operation Gangbuster, got hold of two eyewitnesses, spoke to a high-profile ex-gang member who knows what this kind of confrontation is about and delivered fifty lines on a subject which normally gets only a mention in most newspapers.

People don't usually care about gang fights. They think: 'great, let them kill each other, get a few idiots off our streets'. He isn't sure why he does it, but he decides to call her. It is possible she has fresh information about these morons, but he suspects he might have an ulterior motive.

He wants to know where she is.

He knows that it is stupid and beyond all reason, but he can't help it. He wants to know if she is with Gundersen, if her voice is happy or sad, if there is a hint of longing when she hears him speak. They haven't spoken on the telephone since the day Jonas died. She called to ask him if he could pick up Jonas from nursery and look after him until the following morning, even though it was actually her week to have him. She wasn't feeling very well. He replied: *yes, of course, don't worry about it.*

And he knows it is not the fire itself, or that Jonas died, which is eating Nora. She will never forgive herself for falling ill that day and asking him to swap. If she hadn't felt unwell, Jonas wouldn't have been with Henning. And their son would still be alive.

He is convinced that whenever Nora feels a touch of 'flu or a twinge somewhere, she dismisses it as unimportant. She will be fine. I'm all right, I'm going to work. And every time, the same thought haunts her: why didn't I just pull myself together and pick him up? How ill was I *really*?

Thoughts like that can drive you mad. As for him, he thinks about the three generous brandies he drank after Jonas had gone to sleep that night. Perhaps he would have been able to save him if he had only had two? Or how about one? What if he had gone to bed earlier the night before, then he wouldn't have been overtired and nodded off in front of the television before the fire started?

What if.

Chapter 30

He lets it ring a long time. Perhaps her display informs her that it is him? Or she might have got a new mobile and not transferred the numbers from the old one? Or maybe she has quite simply deleted him? Or she is busy doing something? Like having a life.

He is surprised when she finally picks up. He could and probably should have hung up after the tenth ring, but he couldn't bring himself to do it. Her voice is awake when she says 'hi, Henning'. He replies:

'Hi, Nora.'

Christ, how it hurts to say her name out loud.

'How are you?' she says. 'I heard what happened.'

'I'm good.'

'You must have been terrified?'

'More angry, really.'

That's actually true. He isn't trying to come across as some macho action hero. He *did* get angry, mainly because he didn't want his life to end like that, in a crescendo, in the middle of something unresolved.

They fall silent. They used to be very good at silence,

both of them, but now it is merely uncomfortable. She asks no follow-up questions. He starts a conversation before it gets too awkward. He imagines that she doesn't want to seem overly concerned about his welfare if Gundersen is in the room with her.

'Listen, I'm working on a story and I came across an article you wrote about a gang, Bad Boys Burning, about six months ago. Do you remember?'

A few seconds of silence follow.

'Yes. They had a bust-up with another gang, if I remember rightly. Hemo Raiders, or someone like that.'

They sound like a nice, friendly bunch, he thinks.

'That's right.'

'Four or five of them ended up in hospital. Stab wounds and broken bones.'

'Right again.'

'Why are you writing about them?'

He debates whether to tell her, but remembers that they work for rival newspapers and that trust is a closed chapter in their joint book of memories. Or, partly closed, at any rate.

'I'm not writing about them. Or, at least, I don't think so.'

'BBB is no joke, Henning.'

'I never joke.'

'No, I mean it. Some of those boys are psychopaths.

195

They don't give a toss about anyone. Do you think that they're behind the murder of Tariq Marhoni?'

Oh, Nora. She knows him far too well.

'I don't know. It's early days yet.'

'If you decide to go after them, Henning, then be careful. Okay? They're not nice people.'

'It'll probably be all right,' he says, thinking how weird it is to discuss stories and sources with Nora again. Journalists inevitably end up talking shop. When you live together as well, it just becomes more shop. Until the whole thing topples.

He worked too much for a while. When he finally got home, Nora was so tired that she didn't want to hear another word about newspapers. It all got too much. It was his fault, obviously. That, too. It is becoming the pattern of my life. I manage to destroy even the finest things, he thinks.

He thanks her for her help and hangs up. He stays on the sofa, staring at the telephone as though she is still down the other end. He presses the telephone against his ear again. Nothing but silence.

He is reminded of a double murder in Bodø he covered some years ago. Before Nora went to bed, one of the first nights they were apart, he called her. They spoke for half an hour, longer possibly. When he heard her yawn, he told her to put the handset on her pillow but not hang up. He wanted to hear her sleep. He sat in his hotel room, listening to her breathing which was rapid to begin with. Then deeper and deeper. Then he lay down, too. He doesn't remember if he hung up. But he remembers how well he slept that night.

Chapter 31

Zaheerullah Hassan Mintroza leans forwards on the squeaky chair in his glass cage. He is counting money. Cash. It's only ever cash in the car wash. He does have a till and it is plugged in, but he never uses it.

Nothing beats cash in hand.

He is very pleased with today's takings so far. 12 passenger cars × 150 kroner each = 1,800 kroner. Plus 2 polishes @ 800 kroner. And 36 mini cabs × 100 kroner each. 7,000 in total. Not bad. And it's two hours till closing time.

Offering cabbies a discount was a good move.

He is about to go and greet a new customer, when two other cars pull up behind the filthy Mercedes parked outside. Two police cars.

Damn, Hassan thinks. The officers, three in total, get out. Hassan goes to meet them. He has seen one of them before.

'Are you the owner of this car wash?' asks Detective Inspector Brogeland. He raises his voice to drown out the sound of the high pressure hosing-down in progress inside the car wash. Hassan nods.

'Do you employ a man called Yasser Shah?'

Damn, Hassan thinks again.

'Yes.'

'Where is he? We would like to talk to him.'

'Why?' Hassan asks.

'Is he here?'

'No.'

'Do you know where he is?'

Hassan shakes his head.

'Isn't he supposed to be at work today?'

'No.'

'Do you mind if we take a look inside the car wash?'

Hassan shrugs and remains outside while the officers enter the car wash. The filthy Mercedes drives off.

Hassan thinks about Yasser. Bloody amateur. Didn't he tell him 'no mistakes'?

Work inside stops. An Avensis minicab is nearly ready. The officers talk to the men, but Hassan can't hear what they are saying. He sees Mohammed shake his head. Omar too.

The officers search every room, look around the glass cage, check in front of and behind the car wash. Brogeland says something to the other officers, before he comes over to Hassan again.

'We need to talk to Yasser Shah urgently. If you do see him, you must tell him to contact me or the police as soon as possible.'

Brogeland hands him a card. Hassan accepts reluctantly, but he doesn't look at it. In your dreams, pig.

'We know what you're doing here, Hassan.'

Hassan tries not to show unease, but he can feel it in his cheeks. He waits for the threat which never comes and realises that is because it has already been made.

Brogeland says nothing else. Hassan understands that the police will keep the car wash under surveillance from now on to get hold of Yasser Shah and to monitor his other activities.

He glares at Brogeland and the other officers as they get in their cars. Perhaps I ought to offer the police a discount, Hassan thinks, and watches them drive off. Free car wash in return for their bodies at the bottom of Oslo Fjord.

He goes back in and gestures for the others to come over. They assemble inside the glass cage. Hassan doesn't sit down. He looks at each of them in turn.

'They know Yasser did it,' he says.

'How can they?' Mohammed asks.

'Are you thick? Yasser told us there was a man there. He must have seen Yasser and identified him to the police. He can ruin everything for us.'

'Who? Yasser?'

Hassan sighs and shakes his head.

'The witness, you moron.'

Mohammed shrinks.

'I don't care how you do it, but I want you to find him.'

Hassan looked at them, one by one.

'Find out everything you can from the papers, speak to people you know, in case one of them can name the witness. Yasser said the man's face was scarred. Burn scars. That should make your job easier. If the police don't find any evidence that Yasser was in the flat, that witness is the only person who can ruin it for him and for us. When you find the guy, then you let me know.'

'Why, what are you going to do?' one of the men asks. Hassan breathes deeply.

'What am I going to do? What the hell do you think?'

Henning finishes typing out the interview with Tariq and e-mails it to the news desk. He writes – in capital letters – that his name and photo must under no circumstances be displayed when the article is published. He has no intention of going underground, but nor does he want to advertise his whereabouts.

He looks at the clock. Damn. The off-licence is closed. And he isn't going to his mother's without St Hallvard. He decides to go for a walk instead. There might be a match practice that I can watch, he thinks, and unwind a little.

The sun over the Old Sail Loft hits his back as he gets outside. A table and two chairs have been put outside Mr Tang's Restaurant. A dog under the table closes its eyes. He thinks it is an Irish setter.

He loved dogs when he was little. And dogs loved him. His grandparents had a dog called Bianca. Bianca worshipped him. Even more so after he became allergic to her.

A yellow Opel Corsa zooms down Markvei, just as Henning is about to cross. Yellow cars always remind him of Jonas. Once, when he picked up his son from nursery, Jonas pointed out every single yellow car he saw on his way home. The game was to be the first person to spot them. They played it again the next day. And the day after. The whole summer, in fact. Not a day goes by without Henning looking for yellow cars. And every time, he hears his own voice cry out: *Yellow car!* And Jonas protests: *I saw it first. It wasn't proper yellow. Anyway, it doesn't count, we hadn't started yet.*

Kids. They can turn anything into a game.

There is hardly an empty spot in the stand. Football players, parents, balls, buggies. He sits in his usual place, among the bitter nightshade. He watches them practise and he watches them play; he recognises most of the children on the pitch. Boys huddle together. One of them holds a bag of crisps in his hands. A blond boy wearing goalkeeper gloves tries to do a headstand.

The coach's voice sounds stern, he tells the boys to get ready, the game is about to begin.

The boys are wearing purple oversized Grüner football shirts. Jonas always looked good in those big shirts. White shorts and white socks. Henning closes his eyes and tries to imagine Jonas, two years older. Perhaps his hair would have been longer. He used to like it long. It might be possible to make out the features of an older boy, the beginnings of a young man. Perhaps he would have started looking at girls, but denied it vehemently.

Perhaps.

What if.

He opens his eyes. The crisps have all been eaten. Sated, the boy tosses aside the packet and gulps down a mouthful of Coke.

Chapter 32

That night he dreams about pistols. Huge pistols spewing bullets. The bullets are coming his way, but he wakes up every time, right before they hit him.

How he hates sleeping.

He can't bear to be inside the flat, so at dawn the next morning, he goes up to Ekeberg Common. He rides on his Vespa, his rusty, pale blue Vespa, zooming through a city which has yet to wake up.

It was something he often used to do, return to the scenes of the murders he covered. It was his old mentor, Jarle Høgseth, who told him to do it. Get a feel for the surroundings, ideally at the time when the murder was committed. There might be information which hasn't emerged from interviews, police reports and witness statements. Jarle Høgseth was a smart man. Except when it came to smoking.

Henning parks next to the tarmac path that runs across the Common, right by Ekeberg School. The tent is still there, surrounded by police tape. It is just past 6 a.m.

He looks around. A solitary horse is grazing near

Ekeberg Farm. A woman, with blonde hair in a ponytail, is out jogging. He sees a dog running around on the grass where the huge birches appear to have grown into one tree. The dog has a stick in its mouth.

He heads for the tent and tries to visualise what happened. Henriette Hagerup in the hole in the ground, knocked out by a stun gun. A man throwing heavy rocks at her, flogging her, chopping off her hand. Perhaps she didn't start screaming until it was too late. No one saw or heard her.

She must have been killed in the middle of the night or very early in the morning. And she must have come here of her free will. No one could have carried an unconscious person across Ekeberg Common without being seen. Not even at night. There would still be traffic around. This makes him think she must have been meeting someone she knew. Could the filming have something to do with it?

His thoughts are interrupted by the dog jumping up at him. He just manages to raise his hands in defence as the dog tries to take a chunk out of his arm. He shakes and pushes the dog away. It doesn't hurt him, but it growls. Its owner comes over.

'Sit.'

The man's voice is firm. The dog scampers around Henning's feet before it returns to its master, reluctantly.

'I'm sorry,' the older man says. 'He just wants to

play. He's very frisky, you see. Are you all right? He didn't bite you?'

Henning doesn't mind frisky, but he draws the line at attempted murder. He wants to shout at this bloody idiot of a dog owner who lets a lethal weapon run free in a public space. But he doesn't. Because he remembers Assistant Commissioner Nøkleby saying at the press conference that:

The body was discovered by an older man out walking his dog. He called the police at 06.09.

He checks his watch. It is almost ten past. He inhales deeply and looks at the dog owner.

'I'm fine,' he says, brushing off invisible dog hairs. With Henning's usual luck, some of them will have got stuck in his nostrils and he will have a fun couple of days of sneezing and wheezing to look forward to.

'Lively animal,' he says, forcing a smile.

'Yes, he's a bundle of energy. His name is Kama Sutra.'

Henning stares at the man.

'Kama Sutra?'

The man nods proudly. Henning decides not to ask the obvious question.

'You're out early?'

'We're out early every day. I'm an early bird, always have been. Kama Sutra loves to start his day up here. And so do I. When it's all quiet and the air is fresh.'

'Yes, I see what you mean,' Henning says, and looks around again.

'Thorbjørn Skagestad,' the man introduces himself before Henning has time to ask. He holds out his hand. Henning shakes it.

'Henning Juul.'

Skagestad wears a Norwegian army cap, though it is summer. The cap sits loosely on his head. His wellies are army green, too. His combat trousers have pockets on the front, on the back and on the legs, and are reinforced with leather patches on the knees. His jacket matches the trousers, both in colour and in style. Skagestad would look at home on the cover of *Hunting and Fishing*. His skin is lined and his teeth show his love of coffee and tobacco. Yet, he has an amiable face. It looks like it could break into a smile at any time.

'Are you a police officer?' he asks and throws the stick as far as he can. Kama Sutra shoots off. Henning sees its small paws dart across the soft grass.

'I'm a reporter. I work for the on-line newspaper, *123news*.'

'*123news*?'

'Yes.'

'What kind of name is that?'

Henning holds up his hands.

'Don't ask me. I didn't pick it.'

'But what are you doing out here at this hour? There's no one around.'

'You're here. It was you who found her, wasn't it?'

Skagestad becomes defensive. Most people do, when they realise they are about to be interviewed. But Skagestad has no choice but to answer every single one of Henning's questions. After all, his dog has just attacked him, so Henning doesn't feel bad in the slightest for imposing on Skagestad.

'I don't want to get in the paper.'

'You won't have to.'

Kama Sutra returns with the stick in its mouth. Skagestad takes one end and pulls as hard as he can. The dog growls again, no way will it let go and it doesn't until Skagestad overpowers it. The dog pants, its tongue dangles out of the corner of its mouth. Kama Sutra sits down, its eyes filled with anticipation. Skagestad hurls the stick again.

'I've never seen anything like it.'

Henning can quite believe that.

'What has happened to this country?' Skagestad continues. 'A stoning in Norway?'

He shakes his head.

'I bet it's those bloody immigrants.'

Henning wants to say something, but stops himself. As Jarle Høgseth used to say: *When people want to get something off their chest, then you let them talk. Let them*

208

talk themselves dry. Even if you don't like what they are saying.

'There are far too many of them here.'

Skagestad shakes his head again.

'I've got nothing against helping people who've had a rough time where they came from, but if they're going to live here, they should jolly well abide by Norwegian laws, respect our culture and our way of life, do things like we've always done them.'

'We can't be sure that an immigrant did this,' Henning says.

'Is that right? We've never had a stoning in Norway before.'

It's too early in the morning to have the immigration debate, so he says:

'Why did you go inside the tent?'

'That's the thing. I'm not really sure. But the tent wasn't there the day before, I'm here every day, you see, and I was curious.'

'Did you see anyone?'

'I usually do, but not near the tent. Nothing caught my eye as I walked up here. I live in Samvirkevei.'

'Can you describe the crime scene?'

'The crime scene?'

'Yes. What did it look like inside the tent, did you notice anything?'

Skagestad takes a deep breath.

'I have already done this with the police.'

'Yes, but you may not have remembered everything. The brain is remarkable. We rarely remember every detail of a traumatic experience at the time. However, things may surface later, things you didn't consider important, but which turn out to matter.'

I sound like a policeman, Henning thinks. But it works. He can see that Skagestad is trawling through his memories.

'It could be anything. A sound, a smell, a colour,' Henning continues. Something causes Skagestad's facial expression to change. He grows more alert.

'Actually, there is one thing I remember now,' he says and looks at Henning. Kama Sutra returns. Skagestad ignores the dog.

'I noticed it when I entered the tent, but then I forgot all about it.'

'What was it?' Henning says.

'The smell,' says Skagestad, remembering it. 'It smelt stuffy, as it usually does inside a tent. But there was something else.'

Then he starts to laugh. Henning is puzzled.

'It's a bit embarrassing,' he says.

Henning is sorely tempted to thump the old man.

'What is?' he asks, patiently.

Skagestad shakes his head, still smiling. Then he looks straight at him.

'I could smell aftershave.'

'Aftershave?'

'Yes.'

'Not perfume?'

'No. Aftershave.'

'Are you absolutely sure?'

He nods.

'How can you be?'

Skagestad smiles again.

'That's what's embarrassing,' he says, but he doesn't elaborate. Henning thinks the man would make an excellent torturer at Guantanamo.

'Romance,' he says. By now, Henning is completely lost.

'From Ralph Lauren,' Skagestad continues.

'How –?'

'I use it myself, you see. It was a present from my grandchild. That's why I recognised it.'

'Was it very noticeable?'

'No. Very faint. But I've a strong sense of smell. And like I said, I use it myself sometimes, when I'm going out to – eh – meet someone.'

Kama Sutra growls again. Skagestad throws the stick. Run, drool, chew, run.

'And I think the ladies like it.'

He smiles briefly. This time Henning really doesn't want Skagestad to elaborate. Skagestad grows serious.

'Poor girl.'

'Did you notice anything else inside the tent?'

'You don't think that was enough?'

'Yes, yes. But anything could be important.'

'True. No, I don't think there was anything else.'

They stand in silence.

'You won't write anything about this in your newspaper – what was it called again?'

'*123news*. And, no, I won't.'

Skagestad nods and thanks him. Then he makes to leave.

'Nice talking to you. Time for me to go home, have a coffee and a cigarette,' he says. Henning waves and thinks that Thorbjørn Skagestad, embarrassed or not, might just have contributed an important piece to the jigsaw.

Jarle Høgseth must be smiling in his grave.

Chapter 33

He has some hours to kill before meeting Yngve Foldvik, so he goes down to the newspaper. He does so with a feeling that today has got off to a good start. It's a rare sensation.

He had said he wouldn't show his face for a couple of days, but he can't be bothered to go home now. The tired duty editor is at his desk when Henning arrives. A young woman sits with her back to him. The duty editor sees him and straightens up, but says nothing. Henning imagines that he has been told what has happened in the last twenty-four hours. He is probably surprised to see him at work, so soon.

Henning is surprised, too. Surprised that he doesn't feel in need of some time off. It must be about having a sense of purpose, something that fills up your days, something that takes away the focus from That Which He Doesn't Think About. And he has always been like this, when he gets the bit between his teeth. He can't let go.

Dr Helge would probably be concerned, if he could see me now, he thinks.

Don't take on too much, Henning, take it easy for the first couple of weeks.

Take it easy, that's a good one. I'm really taking it easy now.

He presses the button to get a cup of coffee, waits 29 seconds, lets the machine finish dripping and goes over to his desk. He switches on his computer. The place is quiet. The only sounds are sporadic clattering from a keyboard and voices from a television near the duty editor. It sounds like CNN. Lots of breaking news.

A minute later, he is on the Internet. It doesn't take him long to establish that little has happened overnight. His story about Tariq Marhoni is still *123news*'s main story. The right-hand column on the front page tells him that his story is the most read in the last twenty-four hours.

He clicks to check that everything is as it should be. He has taken his first sip of coffee and only just manages not to spit it out again. He stares at the screen. He has a by-line and a by-line photo. The body text, too, has been broken up by a photograph of him.

He shoots up and stomps over to the duty editor who is startled when Henning appears. The duty editor says nothing, but straightens up in his chair.

'Did you upload my story?' Henning thunders.

'Your story?'

'Yes, the one about Tariq Marhoni.'

'When did you submit it?'

'Last night.'

'I started my shift at midnight, so it can't have been me.'

Henning shakes his head and swears silently to himself.

'Is anything wrong?'

'You bet your life something's wrong. I wasn't supposed to have a by-line and now my face is plastered all over the story.'

The duty editor says nothing. The young woman sitting opposite carries on typing as if nothing has happened. Henning snorts.

'Is there any way I can find out who uploaded the story?'

'Yes, hold on a moment.'

The duty editor clicks. Henning paces up and down, and then stops behind him. The publishing tool, Escenic Content Studio, is open. The duty editor opens the article log and clears his throat.

'It was entered by Jørgen last night at 20.03, edited by Jørgen at 20.06 and 20.08, before Heidi opened it at 21.39 and 21.42.'

'Heidi Kjus?'

'Yes.'

His cheeks feel hot. He returns to his desk without

saying thank you. Heidi ought to thank her lucky stars that she isn't here yet.

She arrives half an hour later. She goes straight to Henning's desk. She looks angry. That makes two of us, Henning fumes.

'Why don't you answer when I call you?' she says, dumping her bag on his desk. He is temporarily flummoxed.

'I –'

'When I call you, you pick up. I don't care what time it is. Is that clear?'

'No.'

'What did you say?'

She plants her hands on her hips.

'I said no. When I'm off duty, then I'm off duty. I don't have to report to you then. And why the hell did you insert my by-line photo, when I expressly said I didn't want a by-line on the Tariq story?'

Now it's Heidi's turn to be taken aback.

'I –'

'You realise how easy it'll be for the killer to find me now, if he wants to?'

She digests this.

'On this paper, everyone who writes a story gets a by-line,' she begins cautiously, then gets into her stride.

'If we don't have the balls to stand by what we write

and put our name and photograph to it, then we shouldn't publish it.'

He is unsure if he has heard her correctly, so he says 'hm' and looks at her.

'Besides, your name and photograph are in every paper today, so if we don't include it, it just looks weird.'

He looks at her, but can't think of anything to say. Because she has a point. Bloody hell, he thinks, she's actually right.

Heidi sits down and begins her morning rituals. She switches on her computer, takes her mobile out of her bag, opens her diary. She has won. The bitch was right.

And he was just thinking that today had got off to a good start.

Chapter 34

Heidi walks quietly up and down, while Henning drinks his coffee in silence. She probably has important meetings today, he imagines. Every time she sits down, she glances at him, before her eyes become managerial again.

The clock turns eight without Lord Corduroy deigning to make an appearance. He probably worked late last night. Perhaps he is doing something? Or he has already filed a story? Henning decides to give him a call, even though their last conversation wasn't particularly amicable. Sometimes you have to offer your hand in friendship, swallow a camel and all that. This has rarely been Henning's strongest point.

Gundersen answers quickly, but his voice sounds sleepy.

'Hi, it's Henning.'

'Good morning.'

No background noises. Good.

'Where are you?' he asks, even though he doesn't want to know.

'At home. I'll be in a little later. I've already spoken to Heidi about it.'

'That's not why I'm calling.'

'Oh?'

Gundersen is slightly more awake now, but a pause arises and gives Henning the feeling that they both have something they want to say, but that neither of them wants to go first. Like two awkward teenagers.

'Are you busy?' Henning asks at last. 'Any plans for today?'

He hears Gundersen sit up. His voice sounds distant. He lights a cigarette and blows the smoke hard into the handset.

'I had a brief chat to Emil Hagen,' he says, inhaling deeply.

'Who is he?'

'A police officer from the investigation. Seems quite new. He bridled a little when I mentioned the stun gun.'

Henning gulps.

'What did he say?'

'He didn't want to comment on it. Mahmoud still denies having done anything wrong, but he hasn't said anything to prove his innocence, either, so the police aren't really getting anywhere. He doesn't have an alibi for the evening. You met the only person who could provide him with one, yesterday.'

'Do you think that's why Tariq was killed?'

He asks on impulse. But now that the question has been aired, he decides it was actually a good one.

'That's hard to know. Might have been.'

He nods to himself. It might very well have been. In which case, someone doesn't mind if Mahmoud Marhoni stays where he is. But why doesn't Marhoni say something?

'And you? Are you at work since you ask?'

Henning looks at Heidi.

'Yes, I'm at the paper.'

'I thought you were meant to take it easy for a couple of days?'

'So did I.'

He is in no mood to discuss his mental health with Gundersen, so he carries on:

'Did Emil Hagen say anything about the hunt for Yasser Shah?'

'Yasser who?'

'The man who shot at me yesterday. I picked him out on a police database.'

'I asked how far they had got in the hunt for the killer, but Hagen didn't know. Didn't seem like the sharpest knife in the drawer. Hagen, I mean.'

Henning nods to himself and wonders if the Operation Gangbuster team is now in charge of the hunt for Shah, seeing that he was a member of BBB.

'I've an appointment with the first victim's supervisor today. I don't know if he has anything useful to tell us, and I'll try to speak to more of her friends. There's something wrong at that college.'

'Sounds good. I might see you later,' Gundersen says and inflects it as a question. Henning has no idea what will happen after his meeting with Foldvik, but he still says:

'Yeah, you probably will.'

Then he hangs up. He is left with a strange feeling that this was possibly their first civilised conversation. Or it was their first conversation which lasted more than two sentences.

'Don't forget we have a staff meeting today at two o'clock.'

Heidi's voice is frosty. She doesn't look at him.

'A staff meeting?'

'Yes. Sture will be giving us a general update. Business is bad at the moment.'

Isn't it always?

'I only mention it because I overheard you saying you have an appointment later today. Attendance is compulsory.'

Henning thinks *yes, I bet it is*, but refrains from saying it out loud.

Sture Skipsrud. Founder and editor-in-chief of *123news*. Sture and Henning worked together at *Kapital* for a couple of years. The advantage of working on a specialist journal, which isn't published daily, is that you have time to investigate a story in depth. Interview several sources, form a proper and balanced impression of the issue. Good stories are born in that atmosphere. Stories that need a little more time.

Sture was a great investigative journalist. He received the profession's self-congratulatory award, The SKUP, at the start of the nineties for an exposé of the Trade Minister which led to the minister's resignation. It made his career and Sture used his superstar status to negotiate better contracts; he worked for *Dagens Næringsliv* for a while, wrote a couple of books about some finance wizards, joined TV2 before he left to start *123news* in the late nineties. Many have wondered why a man who had made his name in investigative journalism would suddenly want to promote its absolute opposite.

But Henning has always believed in the simplest explanation, which was that Sture wanted a reaction. Things weren't happening fast enough for him. He wanted results. And preferably 1 – 2 – 3.

'I'm off now,' Henning says. He needs some breakfast before he talks to Yngve Foldvik.

'Aren't you coming to the morning meeting?'

'You already know what I'm doing today.'

'Yes, but –'

'I'll try to make the staff meeting.'

'You must.'

'I'll remember that when I've a gun to my head.'

Okay, so that parting shot was a tad melodramatic, but it worked. Heidi says nothing and lets him go.

1 – 1, he thinks.

Chapter 35

He stops off at Deli de Luca in Thorvald Meyersgate and buys a pesto chicken calzone. He also gets a couple of tabloids and a cup of coffee and sits down on a bench opposite Deichmanske Public Library. The worst of the morning rush-hour is over, but there are still cars, trams and people late for work around. He takes careful sips of his coffee and starts reading *VG*. Their front-page story is a scaremongering tale about a new lethal bacteria terrifying Denmark, and which the Norwegian Institute of Public Health fears will reach the country by the autumn. There is a small photo of him in the top right-hand corner with the caption 'Tried to kill journalist' underneath it.

He swears under his breath, doubly annoyed because not only is there actually a photograph of him, but also because Heidi Kjus was right. He finds the story on page four. Petter Stanghelle gets the by-line. Henning skims through the text until he reaches a quote:

'Juul was lucky to escape the killer. Besides the three shots which killed Tariq Marhoni, another four were fired. None of them hit the reporter,' says Chief Inspector Arild Gjerstad, who is heading the investigation, to *VG*.

Four shots, Henning thinks. He doesn't remember there being four. He reads on:

VG has been unable to contact Henning Juul, but Juul's editor, Heidi Kjus, made the following comment on the dramatic situation: 'We're obviously deeply grateful that Henning is all right. I dread to think what might have happened.'

Henning smiles to himself.

You can always rely on Heidi.

Stanghelle goes on to speculate whether there is a link between the murder of Marhoni and the murder of Henriette Hagerup, but no one from the police will comment on it.

No surprise there.

Dagbladet also leads with the murder of Tariq Marhoni, but doesn't mention Henning. Their angle is that it was a straightforward execution, carried out by a professional, it would seem. Except that Henning escaped.

He is about to get up and leave, when a silver Mercedes minicab slows down as it drives past Deli de

Luca. The car stops for a red light. There are two men inside, both in the front. Henning's eyes are drawn to them, because they are looking at him. And they carry on looking at him, even though the lights have now changed to green.

The tram behind the minicab beeps its horn and the Mercedes slowly accelerates. Henning's eyes follow the minicab as it turns right into Nordregate and disappears behind the library. Of course, it could be nothing, he thinks. But it could also be the exact opposite. He swallows the rest of his coffee, tosses the paper cup into an already overflowing bin and heads for the junction. He looks for the Mercedes, which has turned left into Toftesgate, but fails to get the car's registration number or its licence number on the roof.

Henning tries to dismiss the incident, but it's not easy. He only had time to see that the two men in the car looked similar. Both dark, with black hair, dark beards. Brothers possibly? And they were immigrants.

Coincidence?

Perhaps he should get a move on, before the silver Mercedes returns? He aims for the steep incline between Markvei and Fredensborgvei, where the sleepy current of the River Aker flows under the bridge, but decides on a whim to go to the off-licence. For once, it has nothing to do with his mother.

He stands at the window in the off-licence, hiding

behind the customers and flicking through a leaflet while he checks the road. Many Mercedes, many of them silver, but none containing two dark men.

A good while later, he goes back outside, glances to the left and the right, before marching briskly in the direction of Westerdal School of Communication. His breathing is faster than normal. And he keeps looking over his shoulder.

When he finally puts the traffic behind him and is back on college premises, his breathing starts to relax. He decides that if the minicab duo was keeping him under surveillance, they were pretty useless at it, given that he managed to lose them so easily. Either that or they were doing a brilliant job, since he couldn't see them any more. They might just have slowed down to stare at his face. He decides to forget all about it. It is nearly ten o'clock. Time for a chat with Henriette Hagerup's supervisor.

Chapter 36

The area around the college has changed in the last two days. The cameras have gone and with them the fake mourners. Hagerup's shrine is still there, but no tea lights are burning. He notices more cards, a couple of bouquets of flowers and roses which are already wilting, but no sobbing students in front of her photo. The few people who are outside chat with no trace of sadness in their eyes. Two students, one male, one female, are smoking at the college entrance.

Perhaps it's the end of term, Henning thinks, perhaps they are taking their last exams? Or they might already have broken up? This could make the story considerably more difficult to investigate or, indeed, solve.

He becomes aware that the smokers are staring at him as he enters the main building. As soon as he gets inside, he sees a reception area to his left with a semi-circular counter with two people behind it. They are wrapped around each other, kissing. He makes a point of coughing slightly, as he puts his hands on the counter.

They jump, giggle and look up at him, before exchanging 'why-don't-we-get-a-room' looks. Oh, to be twenty again, Henning muses.

'I've an appointment with Yngve Foldvik,' he says. The young man, who has long dreadlocks and an untrimmed beard, points towards a staircase.

'Take the stairs up to the first floor, turn right and right again, and you're there. That'll take you straight to his office.'

Henning thanks Dreadlocks for his help. He is about to leave when he remembers something.

'You wouldn't happen to know who Anette is?'

'Anette?'

You idiot, he tells himself, there's bound to be at least fifteen Anettes here.

'I only know her first name. She was a friend of Henriette Hagerup. They were on the same course.'

'Ah, her. Yes, Anette Skoppum.'

'Have you seen her today, by any chance?'

'No, I don't think so. Have you?' Dreadlocks says, looking at his girlfriend who is fiddling with her mobile. She shakes her head and doesn't look up.

'Sorry,' he says.

'Not to worry,' Henning says and leaves.

Suddenly he is engulfed by students. He passes some on the stairs, too. It's like turning back the clock, twelve or thirteen years. He recalls his time at Blindern, student life, an age of few responsibilities, parties, exam stress, coffee breaks, alert eyes in the lecture hall. He liked the eyes in the lecture hall, liked being a student, liked absorbing all the knowledge he could.

Foldvik's office is easy to locate. Henning knocks on the door. No reply. He knocks again and checks his watch. It is one minute to ten. He knocks a third time and pushes down the door handle. The door is locked.

He looks around. The place is deserted now. He can see doors. A whole corridor of them. It says 'Editing Suite' or 'Rehearsal Room' on most. He notices a black backdrop and a film poster with the wording *To Elise*.

The sound of footsteps on the stairs makes him turn around. A man comes round the corner, straight towards him. Yngve Foldvik looks exactly like his photograph, same side parting. Again, Henning has a strong feeling of knowing the man, but he can't place him.

He decides to forget about it and goes to meet Foldvik. Foldvik holds out his hand.

'You must be Henning Juul.'

Henning nods.

'Yngve Foldvik. Nice to meet you.'

Henning nods in return. From time to time, when he meets new people, he is struck by how they speak, the phrases they tend to use. First and surname, followed by a 'nice to meet you', for example. Nothing unusual about that. But what's the point of saying that it's nice to meet him, before knowing if it is? His mere existence surely isn't automatically nice?

Nora used to say '*hi, Nora calling*' when she rang him. It irritated him every single time, but he never mentioned it. He thought it was bleeding obvious she was *calling* him, given he was holding the telephone and talking to her.

Phrases, he thinks. We surround ourselves with phrases, never contemplating what they suggest, how superfluous they are and how little meaning they convey. Of course he hopes that the meeting with Yngve Foldvik will be nice, but strictly speaking that isn't why he has come.

'I hope I haven't kept you waiting,' Foldvik says in a *nice* voice.

'I've just arrived,' Henning says and follows him into the office. It is a small study. There is a huge computer monitor on a desk, two television screens mounted on the wall, a couple of chairs, and a display of film posters. The bookshelves are packed with reference books and biographies which he instantly sees are all about films. He also notices that Foldvik has the screenplay for *Pulp Fiction* in book form. Foldvik takes a seat and offers him the other chair. He rolls his chair to the window and opens it.

'Yuk! It's stuffy in here,' he says. Henning has a view

of the car park. His eyes stop at a car waiting for the lights to change at the junction of Fredensborgvei and Rostedsgate. It's a silver Mercedes. A silver Mercedes minicab. This time, he manages to read the licence number on the roof:

A2052.

He decides to check the number as soon as he gets a chance.

'So how can I help you?' Foldvik asks. Henning takes out his Dictaphone and makes a point of showing it to Foldvik, who nods by way of consent.

'Henriette Hagerup,' Henning says.

'Yes, I guessed as much.'

Foldvik smiles. Everything is still nice.

'What can you tell me about her?'

Foldvik breathes in deeply and sifts through his memories. He becomes wistful and he shakes his head.

'It's –'

He shakes his head again. Henning lets him.

'Henriette was remarkably talented. She was highly intelligent and she wrote exceptionally well. I've taught many students here in my time, but I can't honestly remember anyone with greater potential than her.'

'In what way?'

'She was utterly fearless. She wanted to provoke and she did, but her provocations had substance, if you know what I mean.'

Henning nods.

'Was she well liked among the other students?'

'Henriette, yes. She was very popular.'

'Social, extroverted?'

'Very much so. I don't think she ever said no to a party.'

'What's the atmosphere like at the college?'

'Good. Very good, I think. Henriette's year had bonded particularly well. It's a part of our teaching philosophy that everything is permitted in the creative process. Let go, drop your inhibitions, give it your all. If you're scared of being judged by those around you, you can't do that. That's alpha and omega, if you're to create anything. At first, you must overcome your shyness.'

Henning is close to applying for a place himself, but he snaps out of it and gets back to reality.

'So no jealousy here, in other words?'

'Not that I know of. Though teachers don't know everything,' he says and laughs. Then the implication in Henning's question dawns on Foldvik.

'Do you think that's why she was killed?' Foldvik asks. 'Jealousy, I mean?'

'At the moment I think nothing.'

I sound like a copper, Henning thinks. Again.

'I thought they had already arrested her boyfriend for the murder?'

'He's only a suspect.'

'Yes, but surely he did it? Who else could it be?'

Henning feels like saying 'why do you think I'm here?' but he drops it. He wants to have a nice time for as long as possible. But he is aware that Foldvik has become defensive.

'I won't deny that there might be friction among the students, but that's not unusual among creative people who have different visions of the same projects.'

'Do some of your students have sharper elbows than others?'

'No, I wouldn't say that.'

'You don't want to say it or you don't know?'

'I don't know. And I'm not sure that I would tell you if I knew.'

Henning smiles to himself. He isn't ruffled by the slightly less nice atmosphere that has developed in the last few minutes.

'A film company had bought an option on a screenplay she had written, is that right?'

'Yes, that's correct.'

'Which company was it?'

'They call themselves Spot the Difference Productions. A good company. Serious.'

Henning makes a note of it.

'Do students normally sell projects to serious film companies before they graduate?'

234

'It happens. There are many desperate producers out there looking for new exciting voices. But, to be honest, many of those scripts have been rather poor.'

'You're saying some of your students try to learn the profession and practise it at the same time?'

'That's right. And I would be lying if I didn't tell you that several of them don't believe they should be here at all, they should be out in the real world, making films, producing, writing.'

'So we're talking about people with big egos?'

'Ambitious people often have. It's funny, but the most talented usually have the biggest egos.'

Henning nods. A pause ensues. A framed newspaper article on the wall catches Henning's attention. It's a story from *Dagsavisen*. There is a photograph of a young lad. Foldvik's son, it has to be, he thinks. Same mouth, same nose. The boy looks to be in his teens. *Da Vinci Code Lite*, is the headline. The article explains that Stefan Foldvik has recently won a scriptwriting competition.

'The interest in films runs in the family, I see,' Henning says, pointing to the article. He often does this during an interview, introduces an unrelated subject, preferably something personal, an object he sees, for example, as a quick way in. It's hard to get a good interview if you only talk shop. It can be done, of course, but it's easier if you can break through people's defences, find something they can discuss freely, preferably something you can relate to. And it's always a good idea to volunteer information from your own life, it makes the conversation feel like a chat. It's about getting the subject to forget that he or she is being interviewed. Often, the best information comes from what is said spontaneously.

And that's what he hopes will happen to Foldvik. Foldvik looks at the article and smiles.

'Yes, that's often the case. Stefan won the competition when he was sixteen years old.'

'Wow.'

'Yes, he's not untalented.'

'Like Henriette Hagerup?'

Foldvik contemplates this.

'No, Henriette's talent was greater. Or, so it would seem.'

'What do you mean?'

Foldvik looks uncomfortable.

'Well, Stefan doesn't seem so committed to his writing now. You know. Teenagers.'

'Girls, beers and student life.'

'Precisely. I hardly ever see him these days. Do you have kids?'

Henning is taken aback by the question. Because he has and he hasn't. And he has failed to prepare a suitable reply, never *thought* about one, even though he knew that the question would be asked sooner or later.

He gives the simplest answer he can.

'No.'

But his heart aches as he says it.

'Children can be a real pain sometimes.'

'Mm.'

Henning's gaze stops at a 4 × 6 photograph, also framed, sitting on Foldvik's desk. It is a photo of a woman. Long, black hair that has started to go grey. She isn't smiling. He estimates her to be in her mid-forties. Foldvik's wife.

And that's when Henning remembers where he first saw Yngve Foldvik.

Yngve Foldvik's wife is called Ingvild. Henning re-members everything now. Ingvild Foldvik was brutally raped, not far from Cuba Bro some years ago. He knows this because he was at the trial, reporting on the story. Yngve Foldvik sat in the courtroom day in day out, listening to every grotesque detail as it was laid bare.

Henning remembers Ingvild Foldvik in the witness stand, how she shook, how she had been traumatised by the man who beat her up and raped her. Had it not been for a brave and very strong man out walking his dog that night, she would probably have been killed. She was horribly mutilated with a knife. All over. Her rapist got five years. Ingvild got life. And Henning can see it now, that the wounds have yet to heal. The nightmares. And possibly the screams, too.

He shelves the memory after the fleeting satisfaction of finally putting a name to a face.

'What did Henriette write?'

'Short films, mostly.'

'About what? You said that she liked being provocative?'

'Henriette managed to make two short films while she . . . while she was here. One was called *When the Devil Knocks* – it was about incest; the other one was called *Snow White*. The story of a girl who gets hooked on cocaine. Rather clever films. She was about to make a third.'

'The one they were going to shoot on Ekeberg Common?'

'Yes.'

'But why now? So close to the summer holidays?'

'I believe it takes place in early summer. It's important that every detail is as authentic as possible; it adds to the film's credibility.'

'What was it about?'

'The third film?'

'Yes?'

'I don't know the details, we only discussed it briefly.'

'But what do you remember?'

Foldvik heaves a sigh.

'I think she wanted to do something about sharia.'

Henning stops in his tracks.

'Sharia?'

'Yes.'

He clears his throat, tries to organise the thoughts which are bombarding him. The first to become clear is the message Anette wrote to Henriette.

'Did Anette Skoppum work with Henriette Hagerup on this film?'

Foldvik nods.

'Henriette wrote the script and Anette was meant to direct it. But, knowing Anette, she probably had a lot of say in the script, too.'

Anette, Henning thinks. I have to find you. And if there is one thing he is 100 per cent sure about, it's that the film they were going to make has something to do with the murder.

'Do you know if she's still here or if she has gone home for the summer?'

'I think she's still here. I saw her yesterday. And I'm meeting with her in a couple of days, if I remember rightly, so she's unlikely to have left.'

'You wouldn't happen to have a telephone number I can reach her on?'

'I do, but I'm not allowed to give it to you. And I'm not sure that I want you pestering my students. Everyone's really upset.'

Yes, I know, Henning thinks. He lets it pass.

'The script for the short film, do you have a copy of it?'

Foldvik sighs.

'Like I said, Henriette and I only ever talked about it. She told me she would e-mail it to me once it was finished, but I never saw it.'

'What happens to the film now?'

'We haven't decided yet. Is there anything else? I have another appointment.'

Foldvik gets up.

'No, I don't think so,' Henning replies.

Chapter 37

Dreadlocks is still at it when Henning returns to the ground floor. Good God, he thinks, the guy is trying to resuscitate that poor girl. Henning clears his throat. Dreadlocks looks up. The bashfulness of youth, which Yngve Foldvik eulogised, has definitely gone out of the window.

'Thank you very much for your help,' Henning begins. 'It was really easy to find Foldvik's office.'

'No problem.'

Dreadlocks licks his lips.

'I was wondering if I could ask you for another favour. I'm a reporter and I'm working on a story about Henriette Hagerup and students in her year, how they manage to carry on after the dreadful thing that has happened. It's not going to be an intrusive article, a more abstract one based on the silence which follows, how a trauma like this affects a group of students.'

If there is an award for laying it on thick, Henning's nomination is in no doubt. Dreadlocks nods sympathetically.

'What can I do for you?'

'I'd like a list of her fellow students. You wouldn't happen to have that on your computer, would you?'

'Yes, I think I might. Hang on,' he says and grabs the mouse. He clicks and presses a few keys. The glare from the screen reflects in his eyes.

'Would you like a print-out?' Dreadlocks asks.

Henning smiles.

'Yes, please. I'd like that very much.'

Clicking, typing. Next to them, a printer warms up. A sheet slides out. Dreadlocks picks it up and hands it to Henning with a service-minded smile.

'Super. Thanks so much,' Henning says and takes the sheet. He quickly skims the names, twenty-two in all. One of the cards he read the first day he visited the college pops into his head. *Missing you, Henry. Missing you loads. Tore.*

Tore Benjaminsen.

'Excuse me,' he says to his good Samaritan on the other side of the counter. Dreadlocks is just about to resume devouring what is left of his girlfriend, but he turns around at the sound of Henning's voice.

'Yes?'

'Do you know Tore Benjaminsen?'

'Tore, yes. Sure do. I know him. Everybody knows Tore, he-he.'

'Is he here today? Have you seen him?'

'I saw him outside somewhere.'

Henning turns towards the exit.

'What does he look like?'

'Short hair, small, skinny. I think he was wearing a dark blue jacket. He usually does.'

'Thanks so much for your help.' Henning says, and smiles. Dreadlocks raises his hand and bows his head slightly. Henning goes outside and looks around. It takes only a second to spot Tore Benjaminsen. He is having a cigarette; he was one of the smokers Henning passed on his way in nearly an hour ago.

Tore and the young woman, who is also smoking, notice him before he reaches them. They realise that he wants something and stop talking.

'Are you Tore?' Henning asks. Tore Benjaminsen nods. Henning recognises him now. Tore was interviewed by Petter Stanghelle a couple of days ago, in the light rain outside the college. Henning didn't read what Tore said about his late friend, but he remembers the Björn Borg underpants.

'Henning Juul,' he says. 'I work for *123news*. I was wondering if we could have a chat?'

Tore looks at the girl.

'I'll see you later,' he announces grandly. It won't be difficult to massage Tore's ego.

Tore's hand feels like a child's when Henning presses it, and they sit down on a nearby bench. Tore takes out his cigarettes, pulls out a white friend and offers

Henning one. Henning declines politely, but his eyes linger on his old acquaintance.

'I thought Henriette was yesterday's news?'

'In a way, yes. In another, no.'

'I don't suppose murder ever is,' Tore says and lights up.

'No.'

Tore returns his lighter to his jacket pocket and inhales deeply. Henning looks at him.

'Henry was a great girl. In many ways. Very fond of people. Perhaps a little too fond of them.'

'What do you mean?' Henning asks, just as it occurs to him that he ought to have switched on his Dictaphone. Too late now.

'She was extremely extroverted and – how shall I put it – almost excessively fond of people, if you know what I mean.'

Tore takes another drag and blows out the smoke, then he looks around. He nods to a girl who is passing them.

'Was she a flirt?'

He nods.

'I don't think there was anyone here with something between his legs who didn't, at one point or another, fancy –'

He stops and shakes his head.

'It's really bad,' he continues. 'That she is dead, like.'

244

Henning nods silently.

'Did you ever meet her boyfriend?'

'Mahmoud Marhoni?'

Tore spits out the name and hawks extra long on the 'h' sound.

'Yes?'

'No idea what Henry saw in that wanker.'

'Was he a wanker?'

'He was a total wanker. Drove around in a massive BMW and thought he was a big shot. Always throwing money around.'

'So he was a big spender.'

'Yes, but in a totally failed way. He left his credit card behind the bar and told Henry's friends that drinks were on him. Like he was desperately trying to prove he was one hell of a guy. It wouldn't surprise me if –'

He breaks off again.

'What wouldn't surprise you?'

'I was about to say that it wouldn't surprise me if he turned out to be a drug dealer, but I know that sounds racist.'

'Perhaps, but what if it's true?'

'I don't know anything about that. And just because I said it, doesn't mean I'm a racist.'

'I don't think you are.'

'But he didn't deserve her. He really was a tosser.'

Tore has finished his cigarette and throws the stub

245

on the ground without stepping on it. The small white friend lies there, gasping blue-grey smoke, right next to a puddle.

'What was their relationship like?'

'Stormy, I think we can say.'

'How?'

'It was very much on and off. And Mahmoud was the jealous type. Though given how Henry carried on, you could see why.'

Henning thinks about sharia again.

'Was she ever unfaithful?'

'Not that I know of, but it wouldn't surprise me. She acted out a lot, enjoyed being the centre of attention on the dance floor, to put it one way. Wore provocative clothes.'

He looks away with a sad expression in his eyes.

'Was there someone she flirted with more than others?'

'Many. There were, eh, lots.'

'Were you smitten, too?'

Henning looks up from his notepad and meets Tore's eyes. Tore smiles and looks down. He sighs.

'There was never an empty seat at Henriette's table. Practically everyone on the course wanted to work with her, too. I made friends with her early on. We had an awesome time together, Henry and I. We were always flirting. I had just ended a relationship when we got to know each other and we discussed it a lot. She was very supportive, compassionate and warm. She was one of those people who know how to listen. And whenever I opened up to her, she always gave me a hug. A very long hug. I opened up quite a lot over those six months,' he says, laughing.

Henning can imagine it, can imagine her. Beautiful, gentle, open, social, flirtatious. Who wouldn't want to be around such a ray of sunshine?

'It was easy to mistake her warmth for something else, as an invitation and one day I went too far. I tried to kiss her and –'

He shakes his head again.

'Well, it turned out I had misread the signals. At first, I was furious, I felt she had led me on, trapped me in her net, only to reject me. As though that was her game, like. Cat and mouse, a prick teaser. And I spent a couple of weeks being angry with her, but I got over it. One night, when we had gone out, a group of us, we talked about it. She wanted to be my friend, she said, but nothing more. I decided I would much rather be her friend than waste a lot of energy feeling rejected and, from then on, we were great friends.'

'Did you feel bad when she got together with Mahmoud?'

'No, not really. I knew she didn't fancy me. But – there's no law against envy, is there?'

Henning nods. Tore takes a big, greedy drag of his next cigarette.

'Do you have any idea who might have killed her?'

Tore stares at him.

'You don't think Mahmoud did it?'

Henning stops for a moment, unsure of how frank he should be; something tells him Tore is a bit of a gossip. So he says:

'Well, he has been arrested, but you never know.'

'If it wasn't Mahmoud, then I don't know who might have done it.'

'Do you know if she had other Muslim friends, apart from Mahmoud?'

'Plenty. Henriette was everyone's friend. And everyone wanted to be friends with her.'

'What about Anette Skoppum?'

'What about her?'

'She worked with Henriette sometimes – from what I've been told?'

Tore nods.

'Do you know her well?'

'No, hardly at all. She's the total opposite of Henriette. Never says very much. I've heard she suffers from epilepsy but I've never seen her have a seizure. Rarely puts herself about. At least, not while she's sober. But when she's drunk –'

'Then she loosens up?'

'Well, that's one way of putting it. Do you know what she always says when she's pissed?'

'No?'

'What's the point of being a genius if nobody knows?' Tore mimics her voice and smiles.

'If anyone ever had a good reason for low self-esteem, then it's her. She's not particularly talented. And I know at least three guys who got into her knickers when she was drunk. I think she must be a lesbian.'

'What makes you say that?'

'I'm probably being stupid. It's just a gut feeling I have. Hasn't that ever happened to you? You feel you intuitively know things about people?'

'Happens all the time,' Henning replies and flashes a smile.

'She was certainly a big fan of Henriette, that was plain to see. But then everyone was. What a waste,' Tore says and shakes his head again.

'I would like to talk to Anette as well. Would you happen to have her mobile number, by any chance?'

Tore takes out his mobile. It is a shiny dark blue Sony Ericsson.

'I think so.'

He presses some buttons and turns the mobile to Henning, who reads the eight digits and notes them down.

'Thank you,' he says. 'I don't have any more questions. Anything you would like to add?'

Tore gets up from the bench.

'No. But I hope the police have got the right guy. I would like to –'

He stops.

'You would like to what?'

'Forget it. It's too late now, anyway.'

Tore Benjaminsen holds up a hand to Henning and starts walking towards the entrance.

'Thanks for the chat.'

'Likewise.'

Henning sits there and looks after him. Tore tries to act tough as he walks with his trousers hanging low. Björn Borg is in place today as well.

Chapter 38

He sits on the bench for a while after Tore has gone. He spends a lot of time hanging around, wearing benches out these days. And that's fine. Very nice. No deadly nightshade here. He can't see Anette. People come and go. Every time, Henning's eyes seek out the red entrance steps. And every time, he is disappointed.

He decides to call her. Before he types in the number, he registers that the time is 1.30 p.m. already. He wonders what reprisals might await him if he fails to show for the fabled staff meeting, but he bets that Sture, for old times' sake, will give him the abbreviated version later. Besides, Henning has a pretty good idea of what his boss is going to say:

Due to unforeseen fluctuations in the advertising market, we are forced to reduce costs. In the short term, this won't impact on staff, but it might well do in the long term, if we don't produce more pages. The more pages are read, the faster we can re-sell the space to new advertisers. However, as we have sold all available advertising space, we need to generate more pages. This means we need to make decisions about the stories we write. We need to be more critical in our selection of material. And blah blah blah –

Some people are bound to make noises about integrity, and 'how about importance and relevance', and Henning knows that Sture will declare that he agrees with most of it, and yet demand a tighter ship. And a tighter ship for on-line newspapers that want to survive means more sex, more tits and more porn. That's what most people want. They may say that they don't, but they still click on it when they have a minute or two to spare, wanting to get a closer look at the tits or the arse used as bait. On-line newspapers know this, they have the figures and statistics which prove that such stories generate hits and based on that criterion, the choice is simple.

It'll probably vex Heidi, Henning thinks, but she is middle management and has no choice other than to carry out executive orders. And she will never say anything negative in public about the top management or the mindless decisions they take. She learnt that at her middle management course.

Henning rings Anette and waits for her to reply. Her mobile rings eleven times before she picks up.

'Hello?'

Anette's voice is frail and guarded.

'Anette, my name's Henning Juul. I work for *123news*. We met briefly last Monday.'

'I've nothing to say to you.'

'Wait, don't hang –'

The phone goes dead. He swears to himself, looks around. A man in a boiler suit arrives. He is carrying a bucket.

I'm going to do it, Henning tells himself. I'll call her again, even though it's a high-risk strategy. I might alienate her even further. Pestering people rarely pays off, but she hasn't given me anything yet.

At first, he gets a ring tone, but is then invited to leave a message. Damn, she is blocking my call, he thinks, and sees another man in a boiler suit. He decides to send her a text instead:

I know you don't want to talk to me, but I'm not looking for an interview. I think Henriette was killed because of the film you were making. I would like to talk to you about it. Can we meet?

He presses '*send*' and waits. He waits. And he waits. No reply. He swears again. Now what?

No, he thinks. No bloody way. He writes her another text message:

I know you're scared, Anette. I can tell. But I think I can help you. Please let me help you?

'*Send*' again. He knows that he is starting to sound desperate and it isn't far from the truth. He jumps when his mobile bleeps a few seconds later. He opens the text.

No one can help me.

His blood tingles. Things are getting seriously interesting. He replies:

You don't know that, Anette. If you let me see the script, perhaps we can take it from there? I promise to be discreet. If you don't want to meet – perhaps you can e-mail it to me? My e-mail address is hjuul@123news.no.

'Send.'

Eternity compressed in seconds. He hears them tick.

No, he thinks. It's no use. Anette is gone. She doesn't want to, doesn't want to be a source, not even a confidential one. He derives some consolation from the fact that he made a serious attempt. But he has no room for cold comfort. He gets up and starts to walk.

His mobile bleeps again. Four quick beeps.

The Gode Café. In an hour.

Chapter 39

Bjarne Brogeland sighs. He is reading a document on his screen, but having to squint for so long is giving him a headache. I need a break, he says to himself. A long one. Perhaps I should ask Sandland if she fancies a late lunch somewhere, talk a little shop, discuss the case, a little sex. Bloody little prick teaser. I'll have to tie a knot in it soon, if I don't get to . . .

Brogeland's thoughts are interrupted by a window popping open on his screen. The face of Ann-Mari Sara, a forensic scientist, fills the screen via a webcam. Brogeland leans forward and turns up the volume.

'We've made some progress with the laptop,' she says.

'Marhoni's laptop?'

'No. Mahatma Gandhi's. Who else?'

'Have you found anything?'

'Oh, I think we can safely say that.'

'Okay, hold on. I just want to get Sandland.'

'No need. I'll e-mail my findings to you. I just wanted to check if you were around.'

'Okay.'

Brogeland gets up and goes out into the corridor. Any excuse for knocking on Sandland's door must be exploited. He opens it. She is on the telephone. All the same, Brogeland whispers with exaggerated diction:

'Marhoni's laptop.'

He gestures towards his own office, even though there is no need. She will get her own copy of the e-mail. Sandland mimes that she will come down to his office shortly.

Oh, how I want you to *come*, Brogeland thinks as he closes the door behind him. He returns to his own office and lets himself fall into his chair. He opens his inbox and sees that an e-mail has arrived from Ann-Mari Sara. He clicks on it and downloads the attachment.

At that very moment, Sandland enters the room.

'Perfect timing,' Brogeland says. Sandland stands right behind him and leans over his shoulder. Brogeland can barely control himself. She has never been this close to him. He can smell her, her –

No. Don't even think about it.

He reads the message from Ann-Mari Sara aloud:

The hard disk was severely damaged and there is a lot of information, we have yet to retrieve. However, I think we may already have got the most important stuff. Click on the attachment and you will know what I mean.

Brogeland clicks on the attachment and watches the

screen with excitement. When the image appears, he turns and looks up at Sandland. They both smile. Brogeland turns his attention back on the computer, clicks '*reply*' and writes:

Good job, AMS. But carry on working on the hard drive. There may be more information which we might need.

Brogeland rubs his hands and thinks he is moving into the final lap.

The lap of honour.

Chapter 40

Coffee usually does the trick, but not when he is tense. Not when he is waiting for someone. Not when the hour Anette suggested passed long ago.

He has chosen a window table in the Gode Café, where he can keep an eye on passing traffic and people walking along the pavement, just an arm's length away. Another reason for sitting here is that it is near the exit. Should anything happen.

What's keeping you, Anette? He frets and thinks that if this had been a film, then Anette never would arrive. Someone would get to her, take whatever Henning is looking for, and make sure that her body was never found. Or perhaps they wouldn't even bother hiding it?

He shakes his head at himself, but it is tempting to entertain such thoughts given she is now more than thirty minutes late. He tries to imagine what could have happened. She might have had an unexpected visitor, maybe her mother called, or she was waiting for the washing machine to finish or that delivery guy from Peppe's Pizza was a fashionable half-hour late?

No. Unlikely, at this time of day. Perhaps she is quite simply unreliable? There are people like that, but he didn't get the impression that Anette was one of them. She is one of those who try; try to make something of themselves, do something with their lives, realise their ambitions.

Too much, possibly, to draw such conclusions after one brief meeting, but he is good at reading people: who is grumpy, who is a soft touch, who is real and not a fake, who beats up his wife, who might be tempted to drink a glass or three too many when the occasion presents itself, who couldn't care less and who tries. He is quite sure that Anette tries, and he thinks she has been trying for a long time. That's why he is starting to feel a little anxious.

But then the door to the Gode Café is opened. He jumps when he realises that it is Anette. She looks different from two days ago. The fear is still there, in her eyes, but she is even more introverted now. She has pulled her hood over her head. She isn't wearing make-up and she looks scruffy. She stoops a little. She carries a backpack. A small grey backpack with no label, but many stickers.

She spots him, looks around the room and heads towards him. In nine out of ten cases, he would have got a bollocking. Bloody journalists, who can't leave decent people alone, who have no sense of shame. He has heard it all before. And it has hit home in the past, but not now.

Anette stops at the table. She doesn't sit down. She looks at him while she takes off her backpack. Judging from the stickers, she has travelled widely. He sees names of exotic cities from faraway countries. Assab (Eritrea), Nzerekore (Guinea), Osh (Kyrgyzstan), Blantyre (Malawi). She plonks the backpack on the chair.

'Can I get you something to drink?'

'I'm not staying.'

She takes a pile of paper from her backpack, throws it in front of him and closes the bag with a swift movement. She puts the backpack back on, spins on her heel and is about to leave.

'Anette, wait.'

His voice is louder than he intended. People stare. Anette stops and turns around again. I hope she sees the urgency in my eyes, Henning thinks, the kindness, the sincerity.

'Please, have a coffee with me.'

Anette does nothing, she just looks at him.

'Okay, not coffee, it tastes like shit, but a latte? A cup of tea? Chai? Eins, zwei, chai?'

Anette takes a step towards him.

'Comedian, aren't we?'

He feels like a twelve-year-old who has been caught cheating in a test.

'Like I said: I've got nothing to say to you.'

'So why give me this?' he asks, pointing to the pile of paper in front of him. On the front page, it says:

A SHARIA CASTE

WRITTEN BY HENRIETTE HAGERUP

DIRECTED BY ANETTE SKOPPUM

He struggles to control himself. He wants to read it right there and then.

'So you'll understand.'

'But –'

'Please – don't try to help me.'

'But, Anette –'

She has already begun to leave. He is about to get up, but realises the hopelessness and the desperation of such an act. Instead he calls out after her:

'Who are you scared of, Anette?'

She pushes down the door handle without looking at him or replying. She just leaves. He looks in the direction he thinks she might be walking, alone, with her backpack. He catches himself wondering if there was something else in it. An extra item of clothing? A film or book?

Or a stun gun perhaps?

The thought appears out of nowhere. But he tastes it, now that it is here. It's a rather interesting thought. After all: who knows the script better than Anette?

No, he says to himself. If Anette had anything to do with her friend's murder, why would she let me read the script? Why would she help me to understand? He dismisses the idea. A stupid notion. I need to read the script, see if it gives me any clues.

There has to be something.

Chapter 41

Lars Indrehaug, the solicitor, runs his fingers through his fringe and sweeps it across his temples, away from his eyes. Tosser, Brogeland thinks. What I wouldn't like to do to you in a soundproof room one day, when the cameras are turned off.

Dreams and reality. Two completely different concepts, sadly. The thought grows even more frustrating because Sergeant Sandland is sitting next to him. Brogeland looks at the papers on the table, flicks a switch and then another. They have prepared the interview carefully, gone through the evidence and agreed how to present it. Even though Sandland still doubts that Marhoni is guilty, he needs to come up with some convincing answers to the questions they are about to ask.

Brogeland loves talking shop to Sandland, gets off on seeing her lips when she is serious, dogged, consumed by indignation on society's behalf. He looks forward to seeing the satisfaction in her eyes when she crosses the finishing line. If only she would take out that satisfaction on *him*.

Wrong switch, Bjarne.

Mahmoud Marhoni sits next to Indrehaug. Marhoni is upset, Brogeland thinks. Distraught at the murder of his brother, rattled by being remanded in custody. There are definite cracks in his tough shell. He looks scruffier. A couple of days without a razor and a ruler do that to a face accustomed to warm flannels every night.

They aren't the only things you'll have to get used to now, Mahmoud, Brogeland thinks. He signals to Sandland to begin the formal part of the interview: the introduction of those present and the reasons for their presence. Then she looks at Marhoni.

'My condolences,' she says, her voice all creamy. Marhoni gives his lawyer a quizzical look.

'I'm sorry about your brother,' she adds. Marhoni nods.

'Thank you,' he says.

'We're doing everything we can to find out who did it. But perhaps you already know?'

Marhoni looks at her.

'I don't know what you're talking about.'

'Are you involved with Bad Boys Burning, Mahmoud?'

'No.'

'Yasser Shah?'

Marhoni shakes his head.

'Answer the question.'

'No.'

'Did your brother know any of them?'

'If I don't know who they are, then how can I know if my brother had anything to do with them?'

Well done, Marhoni, Brogeland thinks. You avoided the trap.

'We've managed to save the contents of your laptop,' Brogeland continues and waits for a reply. Marhoni tries to appear unconcerned, but Brogeland can see that he is boiling on the inside. Though we don't have *everything*, Brogeland remembers. Not yet, anyway.

But Marhoni doesn't know that.

'Are you sure you don't want to change the replies that you just gave my colleague?' Brogeland asks.

'Why would I want to do that?'

'To avoid lying.'

'I never lie.'

'Oh no?' Brogeland quips.

'Perhaps you would like to confront my client directly rather than pussyfoot around?' Indrehaug says. Brogeland sends him an evil stare before he addresses Marhoni again.

'How many people, apart from you, use your laptop, Mahmoud?'

'No one.'

'You haven't ever lent it to anyone?'

265

'No.'

'Not with you watching, either?'

'No.'

'And you're quite sure about that?'

'Yes.'

'Inspector –'

Indrehaug throws up his hands and sighs wearily. Brogeland smiles and nods to himself.

'What were you were doing on Henriette Hagerup's e-mail account on the day that she was killed?'

Marhoni looks up.

'What?'

'Why were you reading your girlfriend's e-mails?'

Brogeland registers that Marhoni looks surprised.

'Was it to sneak a peek at this?'

Brogeland pushes a sheet of paper across the table. It's a photograph of Henriette Hagerup draped around a man. The man's face can't be seen, only the back of his head. His hair is dark and thin. Marhoni looks at the picture.

'Who is this, Mahmoud?'

He doesn't reply.

'This picture was found in your late girlfriend's e-mail account, which was read from your laptop on the day she died. Do you want to comment on that?'

Marhoni looks at the photograph again.

'Who sent the e-mail?' he asks.

266

'Let us worry about that. I'm asking you again, do you know the man in the picture?'

He shakes his head.

'You understand that this doesn't look good for you, Mahmoud?'

Marhoni still has nothing to tell them. Brogeland sighs. Indrehaug looks at his client. Marhoni rubs his thumb against the palm of his other hand. Neither Sandland nor Brogeland says anything for a while; they wait for him to crack.

'I didn't do it,' he suddenly whispers.

'What did you say?'

'I didn't check her e-mails.'

Brogeland rolls his eyes as if he has just suffered the world's greatest injustice.

'You've just said that you're the only one to use your laptop. Is that no longer the case?'

Marhoni shakes his head.

'It can't be.'

'So someone else used your laptop – without your knowledge – to look at a photograph of your girlfriend in the arms of another man? Is that what you're telling us?'

Marhoni nods cautiously.

'Who could have done it? Your brother? Henriette?'

'I don't know.'

'Is that why they're both dead, Mahmoud?'

'I don't know.'

'No, you don't know.'

Brogeland sighs and looks at Sandland. She scans Marhoni's face for any giveaway signs or expressions.

'What do you think about sharia?' Brogeland continues.

'Sharia?'

'Yes. Pakistani band. Played at the Mela Festival about a year ago.'

'Inspector –'

'Bad joke, I know. But answer the question, what do you think about sharia? Sharia laws. Do sharia laws represent a view of women which you agree with, Mahmoud?'

'No.'

'You don't think that stoning a woman – for example – is a suitable punishment for infidelity? Or chopping off someone's hands for stealing?'

Brogeland doesn't wait for a reply. Marhoni looks baffled.

'Who did Henriette have an affair with, Mahmoud?'

'If you're innocent and want to help yourself, I strongly recommend that you start talking now.'

'Who's the man in the photograph?'

Brogeland and Sandland speak simultaneously. Marhoni sighs.

'The longer you drag this out, the worse it will look.'

'Who was the man she had an affair with?'

'Was that why you killed her?'

'Who are you protecting?'

Marhoni raises a hand.

'You don't understand anything.'

He looks down, shaking his head.

'Then help us.' Brogeland says. He looks at Marhoni, waiting for him to explain.

'Henriette was never unfaithful,' Marhoni says, having thought about it for a long time.

'What did you say?'

'Henriette was never unfaithful to me.'

'Then how do you explain these text messages? *Sorry. It means nothing. HE means nothing. You're the one I love. Can we talk about it? Please?*'

Brogeland stares hard at Marhoni.

'And you're telling me she was never unfaithful?'

'Yes, or, I don't know.'

'No, you don't. If you can't come up with a better answer than this, then –'

'She never mentioned anyone else to me.'

'So the contents of the text messages make no sense to you?'

'No.'

'You've never discussed anything like this before?'

'No.'

'Sorry, but you're going to have a big problem

convincing a jury of this. And you know it, Mr Indrehaug.'

Brogeland eyeballs the lawyer. Indrehaug gulps. Then he runs his fingers through his hair, one more time.

Chapter 42

Before Henning starts to read it, he spends a little time staring at the first page of the screenplay. He feels apprehensive. A little nervous, too, when he thinks about it, though he can't quite explain why. Perhaps because the answer to why and how Henriette Hagerup was killed is lying right in front of him?

He takes a deep breath and begins:

1. INT — A TENT ON EKEBERG COMMON — EVENING:

A woman, MERETE WIIK *(21), stands with her back to the camera. The light reflects off the spade she holds in her hand. She is breathing heavily, she is exhausted. She wipes the sweat off her brow. Then she sinks the spade into the ground.*

2. EXT — OUTSIDE THE TENT ON EKEBERG COMMON — EVENING:

A car drives up beside the tent. The driver turns off the engine. We see the boot open. MONA KALVIG *(23) gets out. She goes to the boot.*

3. INT – A TENT ON EKEBERG COMMON –
EVENING:

MONA KALVIG *opens the tent and enters. She is carrying
a heavy bag. She stops in front of a hole in the ground.*

> MONA:
> You've done a lot of digging.

Merete wipes away sweat and smiles.

> MERETE:
> It's good exercise.

> MONA:
> Have you tried it?

> MERETE:
> No, it's your hole, so I thought you should
> do the honours.

4. INT – A TENT ON EKEBERG COMMON –
EVENING:

*Close-up of the hole. Mona jumps into it and checks it
out. It comes up to her waist.*

> MONA:
> It's perfect.

> MERETE:
> Great. Did you bring your mobile?

MONA:

Yep.

MERETE:

Time to send the first one?

Mona climbs out of the hole and brushes off moist sand.
She takes a mobile out of her pocket and checks the time.
Then she flashes Merete a conspiratorial smile.

5. INT — A FLAT IN GALGENBERG:

A man, YASHID IQBAL *(28), is watching* Hotel Caesar
on TV2. His mobile beeps. He picks it up and checks his
messages. He frowns as he reads it. The sender is 'Mona
mobile'. We see what it says:

'Sorry. It means nothing. HE means nothing.
You're the one I love. Can we talk about it?
Please?'

6. INT — A TENT ON EKEBERG COMMON — EARLY
EVENING:

The women are sitting next to each other. They share a
cup from a flask. Steam is coming from the cup.

MERETE:

Was it good?

Mona slurps the hot tea.

273

MONA:

Mm.

MERETE:

I didn't mean the tea.

MONA:

Then what did you –

Mona realises what Merete was referring to. Mona smiles.

MONA:

It was especially good today. I like it when he's rough.

MERETE:

Perhaps it was extra good because you knew it was the last time.

MONA:

Perhaps.

MERETE:

Will you miss it?

Mona shrugs. She passes the cup to Merete. They are quiet for a while.

MERETE:

Time to send the next one?

MONA:

MONA:

We'll wait. Give him a little more time.

MERETE:

Okay.

End of credit sequence and logo.

So far it reads like the introduction to a snuff movie, Henning thinks. He reads on:

7. INT — A FLAT IN GALGENBERG — EVENING:

Yashid Iqbal is in his kitchen. He opens the fridge and takes out a carton of skimmed milk. He is about to get a glass from a cupboard when his mobile beeps again. He takes his mobile out of his pocket. It is another message from 'Mona mobile'. He reads it:

   'I promise to make it up to you. Please — give me another chance?'

Yashid Iqbal shakes his head, mutters 'what the hell is she —?' then he presses 'call sender'. He is irritated as he walks around the kitchen. But he doesn't get a reply. He tosses his mobile aside in anger.

8. INT — A TENT ON EKEBERG COMMON–
    EVENING:

Mona and Merete are still sitting beside the hole.

MERETE:

Do you think it's going to work?

MONA:

It has to.

Mona's mobile vibrates. The display says YASHID.

MERETE:

That's him calling.

MERETE:

Aren't you going to answer it?

MONA:

No.

Merete looks at Mona. It is clear that Mona is the boss.

9. INT — A FLAT IN ST HANSHAUGEN — EVENING:

The GAARDER family is having dinner. The mood is tense. The son, GUSTAV, is sullen and picking at his food. The wife, CAROLINE, looks at her husband, HARALD. He is eating, but he is uncomfortable.

GUSTAV:

Please may I leave the table?

CAROLINE:

But you've hardly eaten a thing.

GUSTAV:

Not hungry. Please may I leave?

Caroline sighs, nods to her son and watches him leave the room. She looks at her husband.

CAROLINE:

We are pushing him away. You are pushing him away.

Harald looks up from his plate.

HARALD:

Me?

CAROLINE:

Yes, who else?

Harald sighs.

HARALD:

Are you going to bring that up again? I thought we were done with all that?

CAROLINE:

Easy for you to say. Oh, it's so easy for you to be 'done with all that'.

Caroline mimics him. Harald flares up.

HARALD:

I don't know what else you want me to do.

I've told you that I won't be seeing her again.
What more do you expect?

CAROLINE:

That you actually mean it, possibly? That
you stop thinking about her day in and day
out, like you are now?

Harald looks away, realises that he cannot bluff.

HARALD:

I can't help it.

CAROLINE:

(*mimics her husband*)

'I can't help it.'

*Caroline sighs. Harald doesn't reply. A long pause
ensues.*

CAROLINE:

I think we should get a divorce.

HARALD:

What?

CAROLINE:

Why not? It's not like we've a life together.

HARALD:

You don't mean that, Caroline. What about
Gustav?

CAROLINE:

So now you suddenly care about him? You
weren't worried when you −

*Caroline cannot bear to complete the sentence. She breaks
down and sobs. Harald puts down his knife and fork,
resigned.*

10. INT − A TENT ON EKEBERG COMMON −
    EVENING:

*Close-up of the display on Mona's mobile. We watch her
text. 'Please reply? Please? I'll never do it again. I
promise.' She presses 'send'.*

11. INT − A FLAT IN GALGENBERG − EVENING:

*Yashid wanders restlessly around the flat. He talks to his
brother, FAROUK IQBAL, who is in the living room,
drinking milk. They speak in broken Norwegian.*

YASHID:

Whore.

FAROUK:

I tried telling you.

YASHID:

Fucking whore.

*Yashid's mobile beeps again. The brothers look at each
other.*

279

FAROUK:

Is that her?

YASHID:

Don't know, you moron. I haven't checked it
yet.

FAROUK:

Then do it, you moron.

*Yashid glares at his brother. Then he opens the text and
reads it. He tosses the mobile on to the sofa.*

YASHID:

Fucking whore.

It's tempting think the characters in the script are
based on real people, Henning thinks. But it's also a
little too convenient.

The desire for coffee resurges. He orders one from
the waiter behind the bar, who looks like he minds
very much that Henning has bought just the one coffee
in all the time he has been there. There are only two
other people in the café. They are eating their salad in
silence.

His coffee arrives just as he is about to start reading
again.

12. INT — A TENT ON EKEBERG COMMON — LATE EVENING:

Close-up of the hole in the ground. Mona has jumped into it again. Merete is filling up the hole with earth.

MERETE:

You managed to sort out his computer?

MONA:

Oh yes. It was easy. He took a shower after we had had sex, not a problem.

MERETE:

Have we remembered everything?

MONA:

I think so. Wait a moment — let me get my arms out.

MERETE:

Okay.

Mona pulls her arms out of the sandy soil.

MONA:

Right. Carry on.

Merete carries on filling the hole. Soon the sand reaches all the way up to Mona's armpits. Merete puts down the spade, she is panting.

Anything you want to say before we begin?

Mona considers this. She clears her throat.

MONA:
(*in a solemn voice*):
This is for all the women in the world. But
especially for us in Norway.

*Merete smiles. The camera moves slowly from Merete's
face to the ground behind her. We see the spade. We see
the bag Mona brought with her. It is open. Next to it
lies a large heavy stone.*

Henriette can't possibly have subjected herself to
this, Henning thinks, and looks up. She can't possibly
have acted out a role, used her own script and let herself
be stoned to death to promote a political message?

It's only a movie, Henning. He hears his mother's
voice and remembers how he used to climb up on her
lap when Detective Derrick solved murder mysteries
every Friday evening. Someone must have used
Henriette's script against her. To mock her? To point
the finger at someone?

He reads on:

Caption against a black background: Two weeks later

13. INT — AN INTERVIEW ROOM AT THE POLICE STATION — LATE MORNING:

Yashid Iqbal sits at a table. Police officers sit opposite. The officers look grave.

OFFICER 1:

What did you do after you received the text messages, Yashid? Did you go over to confront her?

Yashid doesn't reply.

OFFICER 2:

We know that you tried to call her. We also know that you left your flat just after eight o'clock that night.

OFFICER 1:

There's evidence of a brutal sexual assault, Yashid.

OFFICER 2:

And we have your laptop. You checked her e-mail that afternoon. Why did you do that?

OFFICER 1:

We get it, Yashid. You got angry. It's understandable. She was screwing around, you got angry and you taught her a lesson.

OFFICER 2:

You can make it much easier for yourself by
talking, Yashid. Tell us what happened.
You'll feel better for it.

Yashid says nothing.

OFFICER 1:

After you got the text messages, you went to
the place where she was filming. You raped
her and buried her in a hole in the ground.
Afterwards, you picked up some heavy stones
and threw them at her until she died. That's
the appropriate punishment, isn't it? For
being unfaithful?

*Yashid looks at the police officers. Yashid's lawyer leans
towards him and whispers into his ear. Yashid leans
forward.*

YASHID:

I love Mona. I'm innocent.

The police officers look at each other and sigh.

*Caption against a black background: Five
months later*

14. INT — OSLO COURTHOUSE — NOON:

Yashid sits next to his lawyer. Harald Gaarder sits some

284

rows behind him. He looks depressed and gloomy.
Farouk Iqbal is there, too. He looks anxious. The judge
enters. Everyone stands up.

>JUDGE:

Sit down, please.

Everyone sits down. The judge looks at the jury.

>JUDGE:

Has the jury reached a verdict?

>FOREMAN OF THE JURY:

We have.

15. INT — OSLO COURTHOUSE — NOON:

Close-up of Yashid. He looks down. He is visibly
nervous. The camera zooms out. Merete sits at the back
of the courtroom. The picture of her grows sharper. She
remains in focus while the foreman of the jury reads out
the verdict.

>FOREMAN OF THE JURY:

In the case against Yashid Iqbal we, the jury,
find the defendant guilty of all charges.

The courtroom erupts with jubilation. Merete looks at
Harald Gaarder. She smiles to him. Gaarder looks away
and leaves. Merete takes out a mobile. She writes a text
message. We see what she writes.

'One down. Plenty more to go.'

She scrolls through her contacts, finds Mona, and presses 'send'.

THE END

He puts down the script, slightly disappointed, and rubs his eyes. The trailer promised a blood-dripping thriller and all he got was a mediocre drama. The script was supposed to be his Pandora's Box, but there was no mention of stun guns, floggings or severed hands. He begins to wonder if other, more brutal, versions of the script exist.

The initial premise was fine: Two women stage a 'murder' and make sure that one woman's boyfriend is arrested and convicted of the murder, even though he is innocent. It is only a flight of fancy, Henning reasons, wishful thinking. Translated into real life, Mona and Merete will respectively be Henriette and Anette, while Mahmoud Marhoni is Yashid Iqbal. And Tariq is Farouk.

So far so good. And, so far, most of it matches Henning's own theories. Mahmoud Marhoni is innocent, and someone is trying to set him up. Text messages, hinted infidelity, a last rough fuck which borders on rape. It won't be easy for a suspect to distance

286

himself from that kind of evidence, especially not if the suspect stays silent during interview.

But who is Harald Gaarder? His family and its fate were given so much space in the script that they must be important. But are they important in real life, too? As his mother said, it's only a film. Not everything has to mirror reality.

He explores the possibility, anyway. Harald Gaarder had an affair with Mona – who else could it have been – and the infidelity is punished by stoning. But then why do Gaarder and Merete look at each other at the end? Why was she smiling?

The real life Gaarder character must know Anette. The man who had an affair with Henriette must be known to both women. The only one Henning can think of, based on the people he has met so far, is Yngve Foldvik. But Foldvik hasn't read the script, so it can't be him. Unless Foldvik is lying? But why would he lie about that? He must be aware that this kind of allegation is easy to check, if the police can be bothered. Evidence on his computer, copies of the script somewhere, in his office, at home. If he is caught out in such a simple lie, it's handcuffs straight away and welcome to Ullersmo Prison. There must be other adults, he thinks, another family. Anette's, perhaps? Or Henriette's?

He thinks about Henriette. Beautiful, gentle, extrovert Henriette. What sort of person were you really?

Foldvik described your work as 'provocations with substance'. Henning can see what he meant, even though the issue of sharia is examined in a narrow and very simplistic manner. The message seems to be that idiots who promote sharia need to be got rid of, and that we – for our own sake – mustn't shy away from any means in the fight to protect ourselves and our culture; women the world over – unite – and don't put up with it.

But where is the gunpowder? When is the *explosion*? Where are the incriminating lines, the ammunition, which caused someone to act out what was a fantasy? Hagerup isn't exactly Theo van Gogh, the Dutch director who made films critical of Islam and who was killed with eight pistol shots in Amsterdam in 2004. The killer went on to cut van Gogh's throat, insert two knives into his chest and attach a long threatening letter to them. As far as Henning knows, Hagerup wasn't Islamophobic. And her boyfriend was a Muslim.

The more Henning thinks about it, the more convinced he is that someone close to Anette and Henriette must be behind this. I have to find out who was involved in the filming, he thinks, who had access to the script and if any outsiders read it. The killer, or the killers, must be among them.

Chapter 43

He fights the urge to call Anette. It's too soon. She made it clear that he mustn't try to help her, and besides, he wants more control over the story before he contacts her again.

Instead he calls Bjarne Brogeland. Henning got his mobile number after his interview at the police station. Brogeland replies almost instantly.

'Hi, Bjarne, it's Henning.'

'Hi, Henning. How are you?'

'Eh, all right. Listen – can we meet?'

A few seconds of silence follow.

'Now?'

'Yes. Straight away, if you can, and some place neutral, preferably. There's something I need to talk to you about.'

'In your capacity as a journalist?'

'Of that I'm not entirely sure.'

'Does this have anything to do with Tariq Marhoni?'

'No. His brother. And Henriette Hagerup. In the light of that, it might have something to do with Tariq. Like I said, I'm not sure.'

'You're not sure?'

'No. But I guarantee that you'll want to hear what I've got to say and see what I've found. I just don't want to do it over the telephone.'

A thinking pause follows.

'Okay. Where do you want to meet?'

'Lompa.'

'Good. I can be there in fifteen minutes.'

'Great. See you there.'

He decides to take a cab from the Gode Café, no matter how risky it might be. He waits in Fredensborgvei until he sees a free taxi, which isn't silver. It isn't made in Germany and doesn't have the number 'A2052' on its roof, either. The driver is an older man with grey hair, steel spectacles and he smells of Old Spice. He doesn't say much during the trip.

This suits Henning fine. It means he can think in peace while they drive past buildings, people and cars. He always feels a sense of calm when he is on his way somewhere and he isn't responsible for the transport. It's like pressing the pause button on yourself while the rest of the world carries on moving.

He wonders what must have gone through Henriette Hagerup's head when it dawned on her that her own script was about to be played out for real and she had the starring role. Perhaps you never saw it coming, he thinks. Perhaps she didn't have time to react before she was stunned by the gun, and the stoning began before she regained consciousness.

He hopes so. And he hopes that Anette lies low. If Henriette was killed because of the script, Anette is likely to be the next victim.

Chapter 44

Lompa, or The Olympen Restaurant, to give it its proper name, was closed at the start of October 2006 for refurbishment and reopened the following year. Henning was a regular at Lompa before That Which He Doesn't Think About. It was a great place to grab a bite to eat and a beer; unpretentious clientele and a friendly service.

The moment he enters, he realises that the atmosphere has changed. It is missing the magic ingredient that creates the buzz, the charming chaos, the relaxed crowd. If you remove that one ingredient from the recipe, the sauce will never be the same again. The place looks great after the renovation, but it's not the same.

He finds Brogeland in the bar. He isn't in uniform now. Bubbles sparkle in a shiny glass next to him. They shake hands.

'Do you mind if we sit down?' Henning says. 'Preferably near the exit?'

He doesn't feel like explaining why, so he makes up an excuse:

'Standing up gives me backache.'

'Of course.'

They go to an empty table by the window. They have a view of Grønlandsleiret. Cars zoom past. All of them appear to be silver. An effusive woman in a waitress's uniform comes over to them.

'Would you like to see the menu?'

'No thank you. Just coffee, please.'

Brogeland gestures to indicate that he is happy with his effervescent drink. He follows the waitress with his eyes as she leaves and disappears behind the bar. When he turns around, the expression in his eyes has changed. He doesn't say anything, he just gives Henning the 'start talking' look. Henning takes it as a sign that Brogeland has no interest in swapping life stories since the vacuum that arose between school and work.

He takes out the script and slams it on the table.

'The text messages which Henriette Hagerup sent to Mahmoud Marhoni the night she was killed, they wouldn't happen to look like these?'

He shows him the page with the first text message and studies Brogeland's reaction. It's not a difficult task. Brogeland recoils.

'What the –'

'This screenplay was written by Henriette Hagerup and one of her fellow students.'

Henning shows him the next two text messages. Brogeland skims them.

'But these are word for word. How did you get hold of them?'

'Anette Skoppum,' Henning says, pointing to her name on the cover. Brogeland leans forward. Henning continues: 'The script tells the story of a woman who is stoned to death in a hole in the ground, in a tent on Ekeberg Common. At the end, an innocent man is jailed for her murder.'

'Marhoni,' Brogeland says, softly. Henning nods. He decides to share most of his thoughts and findings from the last few days. He holds a monologue that lasts almost five minutes. It is a deliberate strategy. Firstly, it is always good to discuss your ideas with someone. Your thoughts and opinions may change when you voice them. Writing sentences is similar: it may look fine on paper, but you never really know if a sentence works until you say it out loud.

Secondly, he wants Brogeland to owe him. Now that he is absolutely sure that Brogeland didn't know about the script when he entered Lompa, Henning is owed at least one favour in return. It is the ultimate way to foster a relationship with a source.

'Where is Anette now?' Brogeland asks when Henning has finished.

'Don't know.'

'We need to find her.'

'I don't think that's going to be very easy.'

'What do you mean?'

'She knows Henriette was killed because of the script and, if I were Anette, I would be terrified of being the next person buried in that hole.'

'You think she has gone into hiding?'

'Wouldn't you?'

Brogeland doesn't reply, but Henning can see that he agrees with him.

'I'll need to take that script with me.'

Henning is about to refuse, but he knows that would be obstructing an ongoing investigation. And that's a criminal offence.

He would prefer not to have a criminal record.

'If you could make me a copy, that would be great,' he says.

'I'll do that. Bloody hell, Henning. This is –'

He shakes his head.

'I know. I bet Gjerstad's eyes will pop out, when you pull this out at the next meeting.'

Brogeland smiles. Most people harbour negative feelings about their boss. It could be body odour, dress sense, accent or eating habits – trivial things, or simply the way they do their job. There are a lot of bad managers out there.

And a joke at the expense of Brogeland's boss is an effective weapon for someone like Henning who is trying to build a relationship with a source – if the source responds to it, that is. The source might like his boss or might even be having an affair with the person in question. In other words, tread softly, take your time. But Henning is good at taking his time. And he can see that Brogeland gets an image of Gjerstad in his head.

Brogeland takes a sip of mineral water and coughs.

'The day Henriette was killed,' he says, putting his glass down, 'Marhoni saw a photo that had been e-mailed to Henriette.'

Henning looks up at him.

'A photo?'

'Yes.'

'What of?'

'Of Hagerup and an unidentified man. They're embracing each other.'

'One of those "hi-great-to-see-you" hugs, or something more incriminating?'

'A little more incriminating. It looks like she's throwing herself at him.'

'And you don't know who he is?'

'No. But he looks mature. Over forty.'

'And this picture was e-mailed to Henriette?'

'Yes.'

'Who sent it?'

'We don't know. Not yet, anyway. The sender is an anonymous e-mail account. The computer it was sent from has an IP address belonging to an Internet café in Mozambique.'

Brogeland throws up his hands.

'But Marhoni had a look at Henriette's e-mails and he saw the picture?'

'Yes. He denies it, but he has also stated that he's the only person who uses his computer.'

'And that was the only thing he looked at?'

Brogeland shakes his head.

'He checked his own e-mails as well and he visited a couple of other websites that day. Nothing special or compromising.'

'In the script, Merete asks Mona if she has "sorted out his computer". Here, do you see?'

Brogeland can see it.

'Yashid took a shower after they had had sex and that's obviously when Mona did it. Sorted out his laptop.'

Brogeland nods and swallows the last of his mineral water. He puts the glass down with a bang and suppresses a burp discreetly.

'Henriette might have done the same,' he says eagerly. 'She was with Marhoni the day she was killed. And there were clear signs that she had been given a good seeing to.'

'I don't know,' Henning hesitates.

'What is it?'

'This would suggest that Henriette is doing this with her eyes open. That she deliberately goes to see Mahmoud, has it off with him, makes sure she fiddles with his computer while he's not looking and goes out later that night to be stoned to death. That doesn't make sense.'

Brogeland hesitates, then he nods.

'No one willingly lets themselves be stoned to death, no matter how messed up they might be,' Henning continues. 'I can't imagine that Henriette would do something like this to get a message across. The film was supposed to be her message. It might be a coincidence that she checked her mail that very day. At Marhoni's. Or, somebody wanted her to do it, to make it look bad for Marhoni. What do her phone records show around the time in question?'

'We haven't managed to cross-reference the records yet, but she probably made some calls.'

Henning explains there is no mention of a flogging, a stun gun and a severed hand in the script. Brogeland digests it all.

'How do you know all that? That information hasn't been released to the press yet.'

Henning smiles.

'Oh, come on, Bjarne.'

'Gjerstad is furious because someone's leaking to NRK.'

'And it wasn't you?'

'Dear Lord, no.'

'And it wasn't that blonde you can't keep your eyes off?'

'Out of the question.'

Then Brogeland realises what Henning has said.

'What do you –'

'We never reveal our sources,' Henning says. 'You know that. I'll never disclose your identity, either. Likewise, I expect you to keep my name out of this.'

'I can't promise that.'

'Is that right? I've no intention of wasting the next few days in an interview room at the police station. If you want my continued co-operation, I'm prepared to talk to you and no one else. Okay?'

Brogeland debates this. Up until now, Henning has viewed him with the same suspicious eyes as when he was a child. This might be about to change.

'Okay.'

'Good. Tariq, incidentally, also features in the script,' Henning continues. 'But he plays only a minor role.'

'He doesn't get killed?'

'No.'

'So someone is taking liberties with the script.'

'Yes, or they're adapting it. Or making sure that anyone who knows what happened is removed.'

'I'm not sure.'

'What do you mean?'

'I think there must be more than one killer.'

'Why?'

'You think Yasser Shah killed Henriette Hagerup *and* Tariq Marhoni? That doesn't sound likely.'

'He might have killed them both to hurt Mahmoud?'

'Possibly, but I'm not buying it. Why go to so much trouble to kill Henriette, when two shots to the chest and one to the head does exactly the same job for Tariq?'

'Perhaps Tariq knew who the killer was? What if he was killed as part of a clean-up operation?'

'In which case, Tariq knew a lot more than we first assumed. It also means that both he and his brother were mixed up in something nasty.'

'Tariq didn't strike me as the type. He took photographs. Besides, he seemed like a decent guy.'

'Well, you would know better than I. After all, you interviewed him just before he was killed.'

'Yes, and I don't remember him saying anything which might suggest that someone would want to silence him. But he was reluctant to tell me what his brother did for a living and that struck me as a little odd.'

'Precisely.'

'And you haven't found Yasser Shah yet?'

'No. He's not at home, not at work or in any of the

places he usually hangs out, nor has there been any activity on his credit card in the last few days. He hasn't crossed any borders, either.'

'Do you think he's still alive?'

'Are you saying someone might have killed him?'

'Yes. It's not improbable, given that I identified him and you're looking for him. Yasser Shah was, as far as I could tell from his criminal record, a small fish. He only had petty crime convictions. His disappearance suggests he was paid for the hit or that someone ordered him to do it. And if that someone is trying to cover their tracks, then Shah is potentially a huge problem. He knows too much. He might even know why Hagerup and Tariq were killed.'

'Yes, but gangs look after their members. They're prepared to keep their people hidden, if they get into trouble.'

'Perhaps. But do you think they're ready to run that big a risk? We're talking about a murder here.'

'Possibly. I don't know a lot about BBB. They came to our attention after I finished working as a plain-clothes officer, after Operation Gangbuster was set up.'

Henning ponders this for a while. The more he bats the arguments back and forth, the more he agrees with Brogeland. The murder of Tariq is unrelated to the murder of Henriette Hagerup. Tariq was collateral damage. He was no player. All he did was take photographs.

Then a thought occurs to him. And after that first one, the ideas start to flood in: Tariq Marhoni was killed to send a message to Mahmoud. That's why Mahmoud isn't talking, that's why he set fire to his laptop. There is something on his computer which implicates other people. People who are prepared to kill to keep that information hidden. And Henning doesn't think for one moment that information is a picture of Henriette hugging an unidentified man.

He shares his thoughts with Brogeland, who is silent for a long time. When he does start talking again, he does so quietly. And he is very serious:

'If what you're saying is true, we need to put the pressure on BBB. And this will have consequences for you, Henning,' he says, boring his eyes into him. 'You'll need to tread carefully from now on.'

'What do you mean?'

'If these guys are anything like the other gangs operating in Oslo, then we're talking about hardcore bastards. They've no conscience. If you're the only person who can put Yasser Shah on the crime scene, you are – in their eyes – a dead man. Like I said, they look out for each other. But worse, you have helped aim a spotlight on them and their activities, which could ruin their source of income. Or reduce it significantly.

These guys are very concerned about profit. Mix it all together and you have a lethal cocktail.'

'You're saying they want me dead?'

Brogeland looks at him gravely.

'There's a good chance, certainly.'

'Perhaps,' Henning says and looks out of the window. A man is smoking across the street. Henning looks at him. The man looks at Henning. For a long time.

He considers what Brogeland has said. Henning's face is plastered all over today's newspapers. It won't take long to find out where he works, where he lives or get to his relatives.

Damn, he says to himself.

Mum.

Chapter 45

Henning can no longer see the man across the street. He didn't get a proper look at him, but he noticed that the man was short and compact. He was bald, too, and he wasn't an ethnic Norwegian, he was a little more dark-skinned. He wore shorts and a white, open-necked, short-sleeved shirt with some sort of print on it, but it was hard to take everything in during the brief moment he looked at him. And now, the man has gone.

Henning calls his mother as he walks. Her telephone rings. It rings for a long time. He starts to worry. He tells himself that her mobility isn't that bad, only that she needs time to move from one point to another if she gets a coughing fit.

He lets the telephone ring and ring. Perhaps she is cross and is leaving it to ring deliberately because she wants him to feel bad. That usually works. And it's working now. For God's sake, Mum, he says to himself. Pick up, please.

He crosses the road at the top of Tøyengata. He stares at the pavement, trying to look inconspicuous.

He can feel his heart beat faster and faster under his shirt. For God's sake, Mum, he thinks again and speeds up. His legs protest, but he has already made up his mind to visit her. If she isn't answering her telephone, he needs to hurry up. He looks around as he walks, but it is chaos, there are people everywhere, cars, taxis; he sees them, but he doesn't *see* them. He has a constant feeling that someone is watching him, following him, He smells something sharp and spicy. He passes a video shop at the entrance to Grønland Underground Station and just as he is about to hang up, the telephone is answered. But there is no reply.

'Mum?' he whispers. He doubts that his voice can be heard through the noise from the station, but he can hear her breathing, or her attempts to breathe.

Nothing is wrong. No new disasters, at any rate. He can hear that she is angry – without her saying anything. That's the strange thing about her. She can give a whole lecture without uttering a single word. A glance, a sigh, a grunt or a turn of her head is enough. Christine Juul has a whole arsenal of feelings or opinions which are never spoken. She is like Streken, the children's television character whose background changes colour depending on what mood he is in.

Nothing good ever happens to Streken.

'Are you there?' he continues.

A snort.

Precisely.

'How are you, Mum?' he says, realising the point-lessness of his question immediately.

'Why are you calling?' she grunts.

'I just wanted to –'

'I'm out of milk.'

'Eh –'

'And I need more cigarettes.'

He doesn't know why he waits for her to tell him that he needs to go to the off-licence as well, because she never does, she just lets it hang like an invisible bridge between his telephone and hers, as if she expects him to understand without the need for her to say so. And he does. Perhaps that's why.

'Okay,' he says. 'I'll come and see you soon. I don't know if I can manage it today, because I've a lot on, but it won't be long. And another thing, Mum. Don't open your door to strangers. Okay?'

'Why would I want to open the door? I never get any visitors.'

'But if someone were to ring the bell, and it isn't me or Trine, then don't open the door.'

'You both have keys.'

'Yes, but you –'

'And I need a new magazine.'

'I –'

'And some sugar. I'm out of sugar.'
'Okay. See you soon.'
Click.

Chapter 46

Zaheerullah Hassan Mintroza is having dinner. Today, as yesterday, it is chicken biryani with chapatti, but it doesn't taste like it does in Karachi. It rarely does. Hassan doesn't know why, because the ingredients are the same, they are flown to Oslo almost daily and the food is cooked in Norway by Pakistanis. Perhaps it is to do with the cooking utensils, the air temperature, the humidity, the love with which the food is prepared?

Hassan remembers when Julie, the finest mistress he had some years ago, surprised him by cooking Pakistani lamb casserole with mint chutney and naan when he visited her one evening. She had got the recipe from Wenche Andersen on *Good Morning, Norway*. She had even tried to bake naan from scratch.

It tasted good, but that was all. Real naan is baked in a tandoori oven, at the far end, and it must cook for no more than fifteen to twenty seconds. The lamb casserole contained far too much coriander and ginger, and not enough chilli.

He dumped her a month later. None of his other mistresses has ever been allowed to cook for him. They know what he expects from them, and dinner on the table when he visits isn't the reason he pays their rent.

In Pakistan all chefs are men. Women don't measure up. That's just the way it is.

Hassan is watching an episode of *MacGyver* when his mobile, which is lying next to his plate, starts to vibrate. He swallows a large chunk of chicken, slightly too large, and has to force it down. He washes it down with Coke before he answers the call. When he finally does, it is with a brusque 'yes' and still with food somewhere in his throat.

'It's Mohammed. We've found him.'

Hassan swallows again.

'Good. Where is he?'

More Coke.

'Walking down the street. He's in Grønlandsleiret right now. Do you want us to take him out right away?'

Hassan prods the food on his plate with his fork.

'In the middle of the afternoon? Are you stupid or something? We've attracted enough attention as it is.'

'Okay.'

Hassan takes another bite.

'By the way, I want a word with him before he dies. I want to know how he got those horrendous scars,' he says, still eating. He puts down his fork and wipes his mouth.

'Okay.'

'I want to know where he spends the rest of the day. Don't do anything until you've spoken to me.'

Another okay.

'And put a car outside his place of work and his flat.'

'Will do, boss.'

Hassan hangs up and finishes his dinner. Definitely not chicken biryani tomorrow. No, he fancies dhal, perhaps a kebab of grilled tandoori king prawns with onion and paprika. Yes. Definitely king prawns. A royal meal fit for a king.

Chapter 47

It is almost four o'clock, but Henning decides to stop by the office anyway. He has no articles to file, because he hasn't found out anything he feels he can write about yet, but he is working. And he hasn't shown his face since this morning. I ought to report to Heidi or Tourette Kåre, he thinks. Have a chat with Gundersen, perhaps, if he is around.

He takes a risk and crosses the street at Vaterlands Park. He is dragging his legs across the road, some distance away from the pedestrian crossing, dodging the worst of the rush-hour traffic, when he becomes aware of a car on the far side of the lights. It's not a silver Mercedes, it's a Volvo too far away for him to make out the model, but it accelerates as the lights change from green to amber. It is forced to brake when the car in front blocks it. Tyres screech. Horns beep. Horns beep all over Oslo. All day long.

The Volvo gets a response from the car in front. Henning is half expecting a confrontation, that the Volvo driver will get out and have a go at the driver of the car in front, but it doesn't happen. Instead the man in the passenger seat rolls down his window and sticks his head out. Henning can't make out his face properly, all he can see is a pair of gleaming, gold-framed sunglasses, even though there isn't a single ray of sunshine for miles around.

He registers this because he instantly gets the feeling that the man is looking for him. If they are all like Ray-Ban Man, Henning thinks, perhaps he doesn't have much to fear. But some idiots carry guns and if you give a moron a gun, you can get him to do almost anything.

The thought makes him speed up and he decides to make a detour on his way to the office. The area between Grønlandsleiret and Urtegata can seem a little inhospitable, regardless of the time of day, so he walks up Brugata, mingles with people at the bus station and jumps on the number 17 tram when it arrives a few minutes later. He rides it up Trondheimsvei and gets off at the Rimi supermarket, follows Herslebsgate until the large yellow building at the top of Urtegata is once more in sight. Cars zoom past him in both directions; it is the height of the rush-hour, and if anyone wants to kill him or kidnap him, it would be impossible to do it here. With one million witnesses and no clear escape routes, Henning can feel safe. Or relatively safe.

Perhaps I'm just paranoid, he thinks, perhaps I've been out of the game too long to know that this is completely normal, that nothing is going to happen? But there was something about the way Brogeland spoke which got his attention. Brogeland was worried. He knows about this gang. And as Nora said: they're not nice people.

He catches himself wondering how this is all going to end. If they are trying to kill him – as Brogeland hinted – because he can place Yasser Shah in Tariq Marhoni's flat, they won't stop until they have succeeded.

Chapter 48

Henning needs to check a couple of things. When he arrives at the office, he is thinking about them and practically collides with Kåre Hjeltland at the coffee machine. Kåre is about to step aside, when he sees who it is.

'Henning.'

'Hi, Kåre,' Henning replies. Kåre gazes at him as if he were Elvis.

'How are you? Bloody hell. Bloody hell, you must have been scared shitless?'

Henning reluctantly agrees that he was a little scared, yes, he probably was.

'What the hell happened?'

Henning takes a step back and hopes that Kåre won't notice. While he gives him the abbreviated version, he checks the room. Gundersen isn't there. But he spots Heidi. And he can see that Heidi has spotted him.

'Listen, I didn't manage to get back to the staff meeting,' he says. 'I heard Sture was going to say a few words?'

'Yes, a lot of fun that was, he-he. Same old story. You were lucky, you had a good reason for getting away, away, AWAY!'

Kåre grins from ear to ear, once his tic has died down.

'What did he say?'

'Nothing we haven't heard before. Bad times, you lot need to generate more pages and do it faster, if we're to avoid cuts and boo fucking hoo.'

Kåre laughs and smiles – for a long time. Heidi would probably enjoy cutting me right now, Henning thinks. But he'll cross that bridge when he gets to it.

He excuses himself by saying he needs a word with Heidi before he goes home for the day. Kåre understands and slaps him hard on the shoulder, three times. Then he is off again. Henning decides to strike first.

'Hello, Heidi,' he says. She turns her head.

'Why the hell –'

'Bad times, slowdown in the advertising market, we need to deliver more pages, cuts.'

He sits down without looking at her. He feels her eyes on him and is reminded of the North Pole.

'That's right, isn't it?'

He turns on his computer. Heidi clears her throat.

'Where have you been?'

'Working. Is Iver around?'

Heidi doesn't reply immediately.

315

'Er, no. He has gone home.'

He is still not making eye contact with her and tries to remain unaffected by the unpleasant silence which envelops them. Heidi doesn't move. When Henning finally looks up, he is surprised by the expression in her eyes. She looks like she has had a puncture and there is no sight of a bus stop for miles.

'I'm close to breaking a really good story,' he says in a milder voice and tells her about his meetings with Yngve Foldvik and Tore Benjaminsen, tells her that the police will soon eliminate Mahmoud Marhoni as a suspect, and that from now on, the focus of the investigation will be on Henriette Hagerup's closest circle of friends. He doesn't mention his sources, but Heidi nods all the same and doesn't pressure him.

'Sounds very good,' she says. 'Will it be an exclusive?'

'Yes.'

'Great.'

The sting in her voice has gone. Perhaps I've finally broken her, Henning thinks. Perhaps I have won The Battle. Or perhaps she is like Anette Skoppum. Perhaps she is one of those people who keep trying, only to get deeply upset when they fail.

Ten minutes later, Heidi goes home. She even calls out 'take care!' He says 'you too'. Then his thoughts return to the three things he has come to check. He starts with Spot the Difference Productions.

Neat name. He guesses that whoever set up the company was fed up with continuity errors in films and their manifesto is never to make such howlers themselves. He looks forward to the newspaper headlines the day Spot the Difference Productions actually make some. They must be tempting fate.

He reads everything he can find about the company on the Internet. They have produced a couple of films, which he hasn't seen yet and has no intention of ever seeing. They have a website, whose homepage is a collage of continuity errors from different Hollywood productions. He recognises photos from *Gladiator*, *Ocean's 11*, *Pirates of the Caribbean*, *Spider-Man*, *Titanic*, *Lord of the Rings* and *Jurassic Park*. There are more, but he can't place them off the top of his head. It says *'Make visible what, without you, might perhaps never have been seen'* in a small font at the bottom of the page, and the quote is attributed to Robert Bresson.

He clicks away and finds the page with contact details. Spot the Difference Productions have two producers and a director on their staff. He decides to call the first person on the list, for no reason other than he has such a fine first name. He rings Henning Enoksen's mobile. The call is answered after several long rings.

'Hello, Enok here.'

The voice is dark and deep, but welcoming.

'Hi, my name is Henning Juul.'

317

'Hello, Henning,' Enoksen says, greeting Henning like an old friend.

'I work for the on-line newspaper, *123news*. I'm working on a story about Henriette Hagerup.'

A moment of silence follows.

'I see. How can I help you?'

Henning quickly explains that he is curious about the screenplay written by Henriette Hagerup, which Spot the Difference Productions had taken out an option on.

'Hagerup, yes,' Enoksen sighs. 'A tragedy.'

'Yes, it is,' Henning says and waits for Enoksen to add something. He doesn't. Henning clears his throat.

'Can you tell me anything about the script?'

'Will you be writing about this?'

'No, I doubt it.'

'Then why do you want to know? Didn't you just say you were a reporter?'

Enoksen's powers of deduction are impressive.

'I've a hunch that the script might be important.'

'Why?'

Something tells him that Enoksen was a right pain at school.

'To find out what happened, to find out who killed her.'

'Right.'

'So, please, would you tell me about the script, which

you must have liked, since you took out an option on it?'

He hears mouse clicking in the background, fingers skating across a keyboard.

'Well, to be honest, it was mostly my co-producer, Truls, who was in touch with her.'

'So you've never read the script?'

'Ah, well, obviously –'

'What's it about?'

More clicking.

'It's about –'

He pauses to cough.

'It's about, eh, I don't actually know what it's about. Like I said, it was Truls who dealt with Henriette and Yngve, and –'

'Yngve?'

'Yes?'

'Yngve Foldvik?'

'Correct. Do you know him?'

'Was Yngve Foldvik involved with the script?'

'He was her supervisor, I think.'

'Yes, but I thought she'd written the script in her own time? Not as part of her coursework?'

Enoksen hesitates.

'I don't really know anything about that.'

Henning decides he needs another chat with Yngve Foldvik.

'Do you and Truls normally buy options on scripts you haven't discussed?'

'No, this was a special case.'

'How?'

'Truls and Yngve used to work together, Yngve tipped us off about Hagerup's script.'

'I see.'

'But remember, it was only an option.'

'What does that mean?'

'It means we think the script has potential and we want to develop the idea, see if we can turn it into a decent film.'

'You're not obliged to do anything more?'

'That's right.'

That question came automatically while Henning's brain was busy absorbing the information he had just been given. Yngve Foldvik was actively involved in a project that Henriette Hagerup hoped would launch her career. Henning wonders if Foldvik's interest extends to all his students, or if his enthusiasm is reserved for pretty young women with an outgoing personality and a flirtatious streak.

'Do you think I could have a quick word with Truls?' Henning asks, while he checks the company's contact details and reads that Truls's surname is Leirvåg.

'Er, he's a bit busy right now,' Enoksen says, quickly.

'Okay.'

He deliberately waits a few seconds. But Enoksen doesn't elaborate.

'I'll try him on his mobile later. If you could tell him that I would like a word, that would be great.'

'I'll try to remember that.'

'Thank you.'

Henning hangs up, wondering what was on the tip of Enoksen's tongue.

Chapter 49

A couple of quick Internet searches inform him that Henriette's parents are called Vebjørn and Linda, and that she has an older brother, Ole Petter. He looks up Anette Skoppum. Her parents, Ulf Vidar and Frøydis, are both over seventy, so Anette is most definitely an afterthought. She has three older sisters, Kirsten (thirty-eight), Silje (forty-one) and Torill (forty-four). In a matter of minutes, Henning has established that neither the Hagerups nor the Skoppums are a good match for the Gaarder family in the script.

He drops the idea and visits a public register of licences. Here, you can search for information from three different categories: 1) Business Type and Named Licence Holder. 2) Licences. 3) Applications for Cross-county Routes. The page is produced by the Department of Transport in collaboration with Hordeland County Council, which might explain the convoluted language.

Henning moves the cursor to box 2, selects 'Oslo' and 'Taxi Licences' and types in the serial number '2052'. Then he hits *'enter'*. The answer pops up instantly. And his heart skips a beat.

Omar Rabia Rashid.

He knows where he has heard that name before. Omar Rabia Rashid is the man Mahmoud Marhoni was driving a minicab for. It wasn't a coincidence. Why else would Omar's taxi be there, in that very place? Why else would those two men be staring at him?

Omar is registered as having three minicabs in Oslo. The number three is blue and when he clicks on it, a page entitled 'Information about the Licence Holder' appears. It sounds a dead end, he thinks, but is pleasantly surprised at the text which fills the screen a few seconds later. He skims through it and smiles. Omar, he thinks.

I know where you live.

He decides to go home. The urge to sit down, have a think and work out what to do next is impossible to ignore. He waits until some of his colleagues, two women, get up and he follows them. They exit the office building. The black gate is open. He leaves some space between him and the women, walks down the pavement and checks the street. Two large stones divide Urtegata in half, making it impossible to drive in the direction of Grønland.

A Honda and a Ford are parked behind the stones. Both are empty. There is a man with a mangy-looking dog lying at his feet outside the Salvation Army building. If he were to suddenly jump up and pull out a Kalashnikov, Henning is prepared for that. He is surrounded by open spaces, the River Aker flows quickly down the hill, and it would be easy to point the mouth of a gun out of a car window and start firing.

No. That's enough. He has to stop looking for assassins. He has only been back at work for a few days, and already he has managed to convince himself that hardened criminals are trying to kill him. Enough. I don't want to live like this, he tells himself.

He decides to stroll along, take his time and enjoy the afternoon sun, which has broken through the dense layer of clouds over Oslo Plaza. He approaches Grünerløkka with a growing sense of composure. And when he lets himself into his flat, he decides to take no notice of the smoke alarms. He is about to go into the kitchen, when he stops in his tracks.

Damn, he thinks. There is no way I can ignore them.

Chapter 50

I'm so looking forward to this, Brogeland tells himself, when he knocks on Gjerstad's door. Gjerstad's deep voice shouts out 'come in.' Brogeland enters. Gjerstad has his telephone pressed against his ear, but he gestures towards the chair in front of his desk. Brogeland sits down. If only Sandland could be here now, he thinks, then maybe –

Gjerstad is listening and making 'hm' noises. He listens for a long time, before he finally nods and says:

'Okay. Then that's how we'll do it. Keep me posted.'

He hangs up and looks at Brogeland.

'Yes,' he says with a sigh. There is a hint of weariness in his voice, but Brogeland pays no attention to it. This is his moment. He places Hagerup's script on the desk and looks expectantly at Gjerstad, who picks it up and starts flicking through it.

Brogeland spends the next few minutes summarising. When he has finished, Gjerstad isn't looking at him with satisfaction. Quite the opposite.

'And you got this from Henning Juul?'

'Yes. Juul is –'

'Let me tell you something about Henning Juul,' Gjerstad snarls and stands up. He starts pacing to and fro.

'Some years ago, a man was killing prostitutes in Oslo. He was no Jack the Ripper, far from it, but he murdered some girls from Nigeria and threatened to kill some more unless we took them off the streets. He contacted us directly to announce his intentions.'

'I remember the case. If –'

'There was obviously no way we could do that, even if we wanted to. Firstly, we never give in to threats of that type, and secondly, the girls move around all the time and their pimps protect them.'

Gjerstad strokes his moustache and stops right in front of Brogeland.

'Henning Juul found out that the killer was talking to us and had warned of further attacks. When the next Nigerian girl turned up with forty-seven stab wounds to her back, stomach, chest and face, Juul launched a major campaign. Hung us out to dry as the Big Bad Wolf because we hadn't responded to the killer's threats. To top it all, Juul tracked down the killer himself and interviewed him – without letting us know, so we could arrest him. Bottom line, Juul cared more about making us look like idiots than catching a killer. What does that tell you about Henning Juul?'

Brogeland stares at the floor, looking for an answer, but finding none.

'Why do you think he came to you with this?' Gjerstad says, pointing to the script. 'Do you think he did it because he wanted to help the police or because he wanted to help himself?'

Brogeland remembers that Gjerstad is well known for his rhetorical powers. And he can think of nothing to say by way of reply.

'Juul may very well have stumbled across something important, but don't think for a minute that he's doing this to benefit society. He's using you, Bjarne. I think that what happened to him, however tragic it was, it did something to him. Given what I know of Henning Juul, my guess is it has only served to make him more cynical and manipulative.'

Brogeland doesn't know what to say, so he says nothing.

'Have you done anything about it yet?' Gjerstad asks, referring to the script.

'I've tried to get hold of Anette Skoppum, but no luck so far. She doesn't answer her mobile and she isn't in her flat, either. I sent Emil to talk to her, but when she wasn't there, I placed a unit outside.'

'Where does she live?'

'Bislett.'

'Okay.'

'She also withdrew 5,000 kroner from a cashpoint in Akersgate, a couple of hours ago.'

'Five grand? That's a lot. Well, at least she is still alive.'

'Most probably. But it also suggests she isn't planning on withdrawing cash for a while. I've sent Emil to Westerdal to look for her and to talk to her friends, but I haven't heard anything from him.'

Gjerstad nods and waits, but Brogeland has nothing more for him. He has a feeling of emptiness. Just as well that Sandland didn't come with him, after all.

Could Henning Juul really have been that ruthless? Let a killer go free in return for a good story? Of course he could. And might Juul screw him, too, one day? But they know each other. A little.

Brogeland looks at Gjerstad, who has sat down behind his desk again and started to leaf through some documents. If Brogeland has learned anything during the seventeen months he has been working for Gjerstad, it is that once his boss has formed an opinion about someone, it takes a lot to change it. Perhaps that's why he is such a good police officer, Brogeland thinks. Or perhaps that's why he'll never be a great one.

Brogeland gets up; he waits for Gjerstad to say something. But he doesn't. Brogeland closes the door behind him on his way out.

Chapter 51

Jonas's burning eyes rip Henning out of his sleep. He curses, sits up, finds himself on the sofa in front of the television and realises he must have dozed off during an episode of *That 70s Show*.

The television is still on. The screen is filled by a man with blond hair who is eating cheese while a multitude of women of different colours and shapes and one man swap seats. Henning leans back and imagines himself riding a wave. Keep breathing, he says to himself. Keep breathing.

He is reminded of *Finding Nemo*, the animated film, where Nemo's father searches for his missing son and meets Dory, a fish who can barely remember her own name, but who loves to sing. Henning can hear her voice in his head: '*Just keep swimming, just keep swimming.*'

They must have watched *Finding Nemo* at least thirty times, most of them the summer they visited an idyllic Danish island called Tunø. It rained the whole time. They hardly left the charming cottage they had rented on the car-free island. But Jonas loved Nemo.

He wonders what that holiday would have been like without Nemo.

His mobile vibrates on the coffee table. The noise startles him. He looks at the display: caller unknown.

'Henning Juul,' he says and clears his voice of sleep.

'Hi, it's Truls Leirvåg. I hear you've been trying to get hold of me?'

The voice is dark and coarse. As he gets up, Henning places Truls's dialect somewhere near Bergen. Perhaps even in Bergen.

'Oh, hi. Yes. Great. Thanks for calling.'

No response.

'Er, yes. I wanted to ask you about this screenplay you've taken out an option on. Henriette Hagerup's script.'

More silence.

'Can you tell me a little about her script, please? Why did you decide to option it?'

'For the same reason we usually option scripts, I suppose. We liked it. We think we can turn it into a good film – eventually.'

'What's it about?'

'It's called *Control+Alt+Delete*. It's about a young woman who achieves fame and fortune, but dreams about pressing Control+Alt+Delete on her keyboard – and starting her life over. She doesn't like the person she has become. And using a very special keyboard, she gets the chance to relive her life. Now the question is: will she make the right choices this time or will she make the same mistakes again?'

'I see.'

'The script needs some work, if I can put it like that, but the story has great potential.'

Henning nods to himself.

'And Yngve Foldvik came to you with this script?'

A pause follows.

'Yes.'

'Is that common?'

'What?'

'Supervisors tipping off former colleagues about a script written by a student?'

'I don't know, but why not? I don't see anything wrong with it. If you're planning on writing some crap suggesting that, you can –'

'Oh, no, I'm not going to write about it. I'm merely curious. It was my understanding that your co-producer, Henning Enoksen, wasn't party to the discussions which ended up with you buying the option. Why wasn't he?'

'Because we trust one another's judgement. Have you any idea how many scripts are sent to us, Juul? Every day. How many meetings we hold, how much paperwork we have to plough through in order to make the films we want to, how hard –'

'I know,' he interrupts. 'What was your impression of Hagerup?'

Henning hears Leirvåg take a deep breath.

'She was a really attractive girl. I can't believe what has happened to her. She had such a zest for life. So open and hungry, so trusting. Not arrogant or pretentious.'

'I presume that you had meetings with both Foldvik and Hagerup, given that he introduced her to you?'

'Yes, of course.'

'What was the chemistry like between them?'

'What do you mean? Chemistry?'

'You know, chemistry. The way they looked at each other. Did you pick up any sexual tension between them?'

Another silence. A long one.

'If you're saying what I think you're saying, then you can fuck off,' Leirvåg says in a rising, braying Bergen accent. 'Yngve is a decent man. One of the very, very best. He tried to help one of his students. What's wrong with that?'

'Nothing.'

'Do you ever go window-shopping, Juul?'

'Yes.'

'Do you always buy the things you like?'

'No.'

'No. Precisely.'

Henning isn't put off by the irritation in Leirvåg's voice.

'What happens to the script now?'

Leirvåg sighs.

'I don't know yet.'

'But you still have your option, even though the writer is dead?'

'Yes. I think it would be sad if we didn't complete something she started. She would have wanted the film to go ahead.'

Nice PR point Henning thinks.

'What does Yngve think?'

'Yngve? He agrees with me.'

'So you've already discussed it, then?'

'No, I, eh, we –'

Henning smiles to himself and wonders if this might have been what was on the tip of Henning Enoksen's tongue. That Leirvåg was busy planning the film's future life without Henriette – and with Yngve.

'Thanks for talking to me, Truls. I don't have any more questions.'

'Listen, you're not going to write about this, are you?'

'About what?'

'About Yngve and the film and all that?'

'I don't know yet.'

'Okay. But if you do, I want copy approval. You know, check quotes and so on.'

'I don't know if I'll be quoting you at all, but if I do, I'll be in touch before it goes to print.'

'Great.'

Leirvåg gives him his e-mail address. Henning pretends to be writing it down, but is in fact standing in front of his piano, wishing he could play it again. Leirvåg hangs up without saying goodbye.

Chapter 52

His legs hurt. He has walked a lot in the last two days, much more than he usually does. I should start taking my Vespa to work, he thinks, then I won't need to take a taxi if I have to go from one place to another.

He is amazed at how quickly the time has gone. Before he went back to work, he was grateful when only an hour had passed. Now he feels he is losing track of time.

He looks at the clock and wonders what to do with the rest of his evening. Now that he has had a nap, there is no point in going to bed. He might as well do something productive before night comes, before Jonas's eyes bore into him again.

I could always go to Dælenenga, he thinks, but knows he won't be able to sit still tonight. What can he do? Seek out the lion in his den by paying a visit to Omar Rabia Rashid? Or perhaps it's time to call on the very obliging Yngve Foldvik?

Henning strangles a yawn and hears that Gunnar Goma is stomping up and down the stairs again. Henning pads across the filthy parquet floor and opens

335

his front door. Goma is at the bottom of the stairwell, panting. More footsteps. He sounds like an elephant as he tramples upstairs at a slow but steady pace. He comes round the banister and catches sight of Henning.

'Oh, hello,' he says and stops. He is gasping and rests his hands on his knees to breathe more deeply.

'Hi,' Henning says, trying quickly to remember the number of the emergency ambulance. Is it 110, 112 or 113? He can never remember.

'You gave me a fright,' Goma says, exhaling. He is growing a moustache.

'I'm sorry, I didn't mean to,' Henning says and studies his neighbour. Goma takes a few more steps. Bare-chested as always. The smell of acrid sweat is strong, even from a distance. He is wearing his usual red shorts.

'I was wondering about something,' Henning begins. He waits for Goma to stop, but he doesn't.

'You carry on talking,' Goma says, and walks on. 'I can hear you. Bloody good acoustics in here. I could screw one of my girlfriends and entertain the whole neighbourhood, ha-ha.'

Henning isn't sure how to phrase his next question without giving away too much or sounding weird. And it's not easy to concentrate with a frisky 75-year-old elephant disappearing higher and higher up the stairs.

He opts for the direct approach.

'You've a spyhole in your door, don't you?'

He already knows the answer, but asks nevertheless.

'Bet your life I do, ha-ha.'

Goma stops again and wheezes.

'Arne on the third floor, HI ARNE,' Goma shouts, before he continues: 'Arne on the third floor gets so many lady visitors at night. Sometimes, I watch them through the hole in the door, ha-ha.'

Arne? Arne Halldis?

'Why do you want to know?'

'I'm not going to be at home much tonight, but it's possible I might get a visitor. I was wondering, if you're in anyway and if you hear someone, please would you have a peek through your spyhole and take a good look at them?'

Henning closes his eyes while he waits for Goma to reply; he must sound like a teenager taking the girl of his dreams to the cinema for the first time. Goma is clearly questioning Henning's sanity.

'What on earth do you want to know that for? If you're not in, they'll just come back another time, won't they?'

'Yes, but I'm not entirely sure that I'll enjoy this visit.'

Silence. Even the acoustically perfect stairwell is quiet.

'Lovesick woman, is it?'

337

'Something like that.'

'Not a problem. I'll keep my eyes peeled.'

Stomp, stomp.

'Thank you.'

The old man would have made a brilliant interview subject, Henning thinks. The only question is what would I interview him about? He also thinks, for some inexplicable reason, that the story would be subject to fairly heavy censoring by the news desk. Nevertheless, he leaves his flat certain in the knowledge that the stairwell is safely guarded for the rest of the evening.

He has a hunch that something might happen.

Chapter 53

As he is wearing a helmet, it will be hard for anyone to recognise him, especially since he has lowered the visor. He makes sure to pull his jacket high up under his chin.

The Vespa starts without problems and Henning feels like a sixteen-year-old on his way to a secret date, as he zooms up Steenstrupsgata and passes the School of Art and Foss College, still making good progress. The great thing about the small scooter is that he can go everywhere and, if a car were to chase him, he can always drive on the pavement, down a path or an alleyway.

It doesn't take him long to reach Alexander Kiellands Square, where people are eating outside and he can see the gushing fountains on Telthusbakken. He crosses Uelandsgate and watches the homeless and druggies huddle up outside Café Trappa. It feels good to be back in on the road. It has been a long time.

The Vespa is one of the few of his father's possessions he has kept. It would be wrong to say that he has taken particularly good care of it. He tends to leave it exposed to the elements in the backyard all year round, and it surprises him by starting contentedly every time.

He parks outside the Rema 1000 supermarket at the bottom of Bjerregaardsgate, hangs his helmet on the handlebars and looks to both sides, before walking up the right-hand side of the street. He passes number 20. Yngve Foldvik lives at 24B.

He stops outside the red-painted door to Foldvik's building and looks at the doorbells. The middle one says FOLDVIK. He presses it and waits for a reply. While he is waiting, he thinks about the questions he will ask and how to phrase them. He is starting to believe that Yngve Foldvik might be Harald Gaarder in the script, after all. In which case, he plays an important part, but not one that makes a lot of sense. And that's why Henning needs to talk to him.

He rings the bell again. Perhaps it doesn't work, he thinks? Or they are simply not in? He presses it again, but soon realises it is a waste of time. He swears, tries another bell that says STEEN, just to make sure that it isn't the bell or the cables that are faulty. Soon he hears a crackling voice say: 'Hello?'

'Hi, I'm from Mester Grønn. I've got a delivery for Foldvik. They're not answering. Please would you let me in?'

He closes his eyes, knowing he is about to do something stupid. A few seconds pass. Then there is a buzz.

340

He opens the door and enters. He doesn't know why, Yngve Foldvik is obviously not at home. I'll just take a quick look, he thinks, sniff around a bit, like Jarle Høgseth always told me to. *Use your senses, Henning. Use them to form an impression of the people you're interviewing.*

He finds himself in a smallish backyard. Leaves he presumes to be from last autumn still cling to the ground like obstinate stickers. There is a strange absence of greenery. A pot plant, whose name he doesn't know, is standing in the centre. An unlocked bicycle is tilted against the wall.

There are two doors, one directly in front of him and one to the right. He checks the one to the right first, because it is nearer. There are no doorbells with Foldvik or Steen. He tries the other door, quickly finds both names and presses the bell saying STEEN. Without him needing to identify himself again, the door buzzes and he opens it.

Stairwells. The first impression you get of how people live. A pram blocks a door which must lead to the basement. There is a broken umbrella behind the pram. A stepladder, stained with white and navy blue paint, is leaning against the wall. The letterboxes are green. It smells damp. The residents are undoubtedly plagued by dry rot.

Upstairs, a door is opened. Perhaps Mrs Steen wants

to double-check that there really is a delivery man downstairs? Damn, he says to himself. What do I do now? The door slams shut. He stays where he is. Footsteps approach. A woman's shoes. He can tell from the sound. Should he turn around and leave?

That same moment, another door is opened. Henning suppresses the urge to look up.

'Oh, hi,' he hears from upstairs. 'I'm just popping down to the shops, Mrs Steen.' He detects a certain fatigue in the voice. Friendly, but long-suffering.

'Hi.'

How on earth do I explain my presence, he wonders, if the woman coming down the stairs wants to know who I am?

'Do you need anything?' she asks Mrs Steen.

'Please would you get me a copy of *Her og Nå*? I've heard there's a story about Hallvard Flatland today. I do like him.'

'Yes, of course.'

'Wait a moment, let me get you some money.'

'It's all right, Mrs Steen. You can pay me later.'

The voices echo strangely off the walls.

'Thank you ever so much. That's very kind of you.'

Click, clack. Her footsteps sound like a drum roll to Henning's ears. He grabs the stepladder and starts walking up. The woman is on her way down. Henning holds the stepladder in front of him and keeps his head down. They are on the same floor now. She comes towards him, he can only see her feet, high heels, 'hello' he mutters and carries on walking. She says hello, too, and he is overwhelmed by her perfume, which is so heady that he nearly gasps. She doesn't stop and they both walk on. He hears her open the entrance door and leave. The door closes with a bang.

Henning stops and takes some deep breaths, letting the silence fill the space. Then he turns and walks softly down the stairs, praying that Mrs Steen won't hear him. Back on the ground floor, he spots a wooden sign saying FOLDVIK in a child's asymmetrical writing on a dark blue door. The letters are burned into the wood. He puts down the stepladder and knocks, twice. After all, the doorbell could have been faulty.

He waits, listens out for footsteps, which never come. He knocks twice more. No, they are not in.

He is about to leave when he notices that the door hasn't been shut properly. Hm, he thinks, that's strange. He looks over his shoulder, even though he knows there is no one around. Carefully, he prods the door. It swings open. Am I really about to do this, he thinks, should I go inside and have a look?

No. Why would he? He can think of no earthly reason why. And, as far as the law is concerned, it's the equivalent of breaking in. And how would he explain his presence in the flat, if anyone were to turn up? Like, for example, the people who live there?

Turn around, Henning. Turn around and go home, before it's too late. But he can't. He creeps in. It's dark inside. The only light is coming from the stairwell. He doesn't want to leave fingerprints, so he ignores the switch on his left, behind the front door. This is a really bad idea, he tells himself.

But he doesn't leave. He isn't sure what he is looking for. Is he hoping to find something that might implicate Foldvik? His computer? But he has no intention of touching it, unless he finds it already switched on and displaying incriminating documents.

He is in the hallway. Shoes, a shoe rack, coats on pegs, a wardrobe and a fuse box. Smoke alarms in the ceiling. They have smoke alarms in their ceiling, thank God. He pauses. The green lights reassure him. His own private all-clear signal.

He can smell cooking. Lasagne, would be his guess. Right in front of him, further down the hallway, is a door with a red felt heart. A door to the left leads to the kitchen. He sees a filthy white cooker. A saucepan with leftover spaghetti is resting on one of the hobs.

There are no boxes on the walls indicating that a burglar alarm has been installed, so he carries on. An arch leads him into a spacious living room. A television in the corner, a dining area. High-backed chairs and soft, embroidered cushions. He can see a large, square coffee table in front of a brown, distressed leather sofa further into the living room. There are three candle-holders on the coffee table with creamy white candle stubs. The white linen curtains behind the sofa are closed.

Closed? Why closed so early in the evening?

A dark brown woven rug covers the floor and hides a scratch in the parquet floor. He notices it, because the scratch is so long that it carries on either side of the rug. The dining table is clear of objects. Clean and recently wiped, perhaps?

The Foldviks had spaghetti for dinner before going out. They must have been in a hurry, since they forgot to close their front door properly. There is another open door. It leads to the master bedroom. It's dark. The curtains are closed there, too. A digital piano stands up against one wall. Henning nearly trips over some cables on the floor. A laptop with a mouse sits on the piano. There is another door in the room and very welcome light pours in from it.

An en-suite bathroom. Henning enters. It is small and has a floor of white tiles and a shower cabin in the corner. The sink is white, too. It is right in front of him and there is a mirror above it. The mirror is on the door of a wall-mounted cabinet. He can see the remains of toothpaste spit on the glass; tiny, white dots. He opens the cabinet and takes a peek inside. Toothbrushes, toothpaste, dental floss, mouthwash, face creams, several pill jars whose labels face away from him. He turns one of them around. The label reads 'Vival' and Ingvild Foldvik's name is printed on it. The jar is nearly empty. But that's not what catches his attention. Further inside the cabinet, to the far right, is a bottle of aftershave. And though the wording on the label has partly worn off, he can see that the aftershave is called *Romance.*

Henning gulps as he recalls Thorbjørn Skagestad outside the tent at Ekeberg Common, how Skagestad entered the tent and smelled death and the aftershave that he splashes on himself to attract the opposite sex. What are the chances of finding the same aftershave in Yngve Foldvik's bathroom cabinet?

I'm reasonably well informed, Henning thinks, but my knowledge is somewhat limited when it comes to aftershave in general and the popularity of Romance in particular. Did Yngve Foldvik kill his favourite student? Or could the aftershave belong to Stefan?

He closes the cabinet and decides to leave. He stops in the hallway when he notices a door to the left of the lavatory. A piece of paper saying STEFAN in black letters is attached with a pin. There is a sticker depicting a red skull on a black background underneath. He goes to the door. That too, is ajar. He pushes it open. And that's when he sees him.

Stefan.

He is lying under the duvet with his eyes open.

But his eyes are open because he is dead.

Chapter 54

Bjarne Brogeland is in his office, staring into space. His hands are folded behind his head. He is thinking. And, for once, he isn't thinking about Ella Sandland, stark-naked and free of inhibitions. He is thinking about Anette Skoppum, if she is in danger, who might be trying to hurt her and where she might be hiding. Brogeland jerks upright, picks up his telephone and calls Emil Hagen.

Hagen answers immediately.

'Where are you?' Brogeland barks. His voice is authoritarian. He feels he can speak like this to a junior officer.

'Westerdal School of Communication. No one has seen her. I'm thinking I might hang round anyway.'

'Is anyone still there this late in the evening?'

'Yes, quite a few people, would you believe it? Last-minute exam cramming. And I think there's a party later. There are posters on the notice board to that effect.'

'Okay. Stay where you are and see if you can find her.'

'That's what I thought.'

Brogeland hangs up without saying goodbye. He leans back and starts thinking about Henning Juul. Could I really have been wrong about him, he wonders? Am I the one being used here? Could I really have been that naive?

He doesn't have time to think about the Nigerian women before his mobile starts to vibrate on his desk. He looks at it. Talk of the devil, Brogeland thinks.

And ignores Juul's call.

It feels like his feet are nailed to the floor. He has seen dead bodies before and death tends to look peaceful. Not in Stefan's case. He looks tormented, as if he suffered right up until his final moment. Black rings around his eyes, bags under them, pallid skin; his face looks exhausted. One arm is on top of the duvet, stretching up towards his head. He is curled up against the wall as if he was trying to crawl inside it.

There is a glass on Stefan's bedside table with a few drops of liquid in it. A pill lies next to it, on top of a book with a black cover. Valium, he thinks. An overdose. He knows he shouldn't do it, but he goes over to the bedside table, leans forwards and sniffs the glass. It smells sharp. Alcohol. He steps closer to the bed. There is a crunching sound under his foot. He looks at the sole of his shoe and sees the remainder of something white and powdery. He mutters a curse, as he bends down and removes the blanket which overhangs the edge of bed.

He has stepped on a pill. A whole one is lying next to his shoe. Carefully, he picks it up, studies it and sniffs it. The pill and its smell remind him of something, but he can't place it. He curses a second time and returns the pill to the exact same spot he found it, and stands up. The powder on the sole of my shoe will leave a trail, he thinks. And if I don't boil my shoe, crime scene technicians will be able to place me here.

The room grows stuffy and humid. Henning feels the urge to run, but he doesn't give in to it. Something on the desk stops him. It's Henriette and Anette's script. 'A Sharia Caste' is lying there, open on scene 9, the scene where the Gaarder family is having dinner. And Henning thinks that something is terribly, terribly wrong.

He rings Brogeland's mobile. While he waits for him to reply, he tries to remember if he touched anything. The last thing he needs is the police to find his fingerprints in the Foldviks' home.

The bathroom cabinet. Damn. He opened the bathroom cabinet. He closed it with his right hand.

Damn.

He lets the phone ring, but Brogeland doesn't reply. He picked a great time to be busy, Henning fumes.

You bloody amateur, he berates himself. But how was he to know that there was a dead body in a flat he just happened to visit?

He leaves, making sure the front door is almost closed, like it was when he arrived, and he does the same with the door to the backyard. Back outside, he feels how wonderful it is to be surrounded by fresh air, and he looks up at the windows. No one is looking down. He lets his mobile ring twenty times, at least, before he gives up. Damn, he thinks. Damn, damn, DAMN. What do I do now? I have to get hold of Bjarne. I can't ring the police like I normally would and report this. If I do that, I'll have to wait here, tell them what I was doing and I know it won't look good. I won't be able to give a proper explanation, at least not one that puts me in the clear. First Tariq and now Stefan.

No, he says to himself, I have to get hold of Bjarne.

He tries calling him again. The telephone rings and rings. Arrghhh! Henning rings the switchboard and asks to be put through to him. A female voice says 'just a moment'. Too many long seconds pass before he is transferred.

The telephone rings again. But only twice. Then Brogeland picks up.

351

Chapter 55

Bjarne Brogeland never used to have a problem with dead bodies, but these days he can barely look at them. Especially not teenagers or children. I suppose it's because I'm a father myself now, he thinks. Every time he arrives at a crime scene or goes to a home where a child has died, or been killed, he always thinks about his daughter, beautiful, lovely Alisha, about what his life would be like without her.

Yngve and Ingvild Foldvik must be devastated.

Brogeland enters the family's flat. The atmosphere inside is one of professional detachment. The mask the police put on in order to do their job, the subdued voices, the quick glances, conveying the words none of them can bear to utter. No one moves quickly. There is no banter, no smart remarks like in detective series on television.

Brogeland goes into the bedroom. Ella Sandland is bent over the body. He called her on the way because she lives nearby. She turns to him.

'Suicide, most probably,' she says quietly. Brogeland looks around; he can't bear to look at Stefan.

'Traces of alcohol in the glass, possibly vodka.'

Brogeland goes over to the bedside table and sniffs the glass. He doesn't nod or shake his head.

'Suicide note?'

'Haven't seen one yet. So there probably isn't one.'

'He might have died from natural causes.'

Sandland nods, reluctantly. Brogeland turns around, taking in the whole room. He notices the script which Henning Juul told him about. Scene 9, just like the devious bastard said on the telephone. A poster for the film *Seven* hangs above Stefan's bed. An empty CD sleeve for the Danish band Mew lies open on his desk. Brogeland guesses that the CD itself is in the sound system on a stool next to the bed. Speakers have been mounted high up on either side of the wall, behind the desk. A battered skateboard is leaning against the wall behind a chair.

'Have we managed to get hold of his parents yet?' he asks.

'Yes. They're on their way home.'

'Where were they?'

'Don't know. Fredrik is dealing with that.'

Brogeland nods.

'Poor people, I feel so sorry for them,' Sandland begins.

'Yes, so do I.'

'However, a couple of things strike me as odd,' Sandland whispers. She comes closer.

'What?'

'Look at him.'

Brogeland looks. He sees nothing but a dead teenager, a dead boy.

'What is it?'

'He's naked.'

'Naked?'

'Yes.'

Sandland goes back to the bed and gently lifts up the blanket and duvet. Brogeland looks at Stefan, as naked as the day he was born.

'I've never heard of anyone who took their clothes off before killing themselves.'

'No, you're right, that's extremely rare.'

'And he's lying in a strange position.'

'How do you mean?'

'Look at him. He's pressed up against the wall.'

'Surely that's not unusual? Do you sleep in the middle of your bed?'

'No, but it looks like he has tried crawling into the wall.'

'My daughter sleeps like that. Most children, most grown-ups, in fact, like curling up to something. It's not necessarily significant. Besides, it might just have been his death throes.'

354

Sandland studies Stefan's dead body for a few more seconds, but she doesn't say anything. They walk around each other, absorbing more details from the room.

'We need to find out if he had a history of depression,' Brogeland continues, 'if he was seeing a psychologist or a psychiatrist. At first glance, I think it looks like suicide, but he might have had an aneurysm or a congenital heart defect. Nevertheless, we'll treat it as a suspicious death for the time being. Please would you get a court order? We need to seal the crime scene and get some technicians in here.'

Sandland nods, rips off the plastic gloves and takes out her mobile.

Chapter 56

The moment he walks through his front door, he knows someone has been there. He can smell it. Something sharp mixed with a faint trace of sweat. He moves quietly into the kitchen, then into the living room, without turning on the light. He stops, he listens. The tap in the bathroom is dripping. A car hits a puddle outside. Far away, someone shouts something he can't make out.

No, he thinks. There is no one here now. If there is, they are able to stand completely still and not make a sound. His belief that someone was there is confirmed when he returns to his living room. He looks at the coffee table where his laptop normally sits.

It's not there now.

He walks over to the coffee table, as if that would make it reappear. He swiftly reviews whether he had something valuable on his hard disk. No. Nothing but FireCracker 2.0. All essential research and documents have been printed out and filed. He doesn't have a spreadsheet with a list of his sources.

So why steal his computer? He stands in the middle

of the room, shaking his head. A long and eventful day, culminating in a break-in in his own flat. 'Okay, boys,' he says out loud, 'you're clever. You got into my flat, you got out again and you've sent me a message: we can get to you any time and we can take anything you care about.'

They are only trying to scare him. But it's working. When there is a hard knock on his door, his knees buckle. He is half expecting it to be the police, that Brogeland has been unable to keep Gjerstad at bay long enough for Henning to clear his head, but it's not Brogeland or Gjerstad or his recent uninvited guests.

It's Gunnar Goma.

'The door was open,' Goma says in a loud voice. Henning tries to breathe normally, but his chest tightens and he can feel a warm tingling sensation in his hands. Goma enters, without waiting to be asked. He is wearing the red shorts, but he has a white vest on his upper body this time.

'If this is about your Nancy boys, then it's the last time I'm doing you a favour,' Goma snorts.

'What do you mean?'

'Nancy boys. The people who came to your flat today. They look like Nancy boys, both of them. If that's what you're into, you're on your own.'

Henning takes a step forward, feeling an urgent

357

need to account for his sexual orientation, but his curiosity gets the better of him.

'You saw them?'

Goma nods.

'How many were there?'

'Two.'

'Can you describe them?'

'Do I have to?'

'No, you don't have to, but it would be really helpful.'

Goma sighs.

'They were dark, both of them. Dark-skinned, I mean. Muslims, I reckon. Their beards were too well groomed and fancy. One of them – it didn't look like he had proper hair. More like it was painted. Or drawn. Very complicated pattern. The other was as thin as a rake, but he walked like a Nancy boy.'

'Anything else?'

'The first guy walked in exactly the same way. Wriggling his bum, like, and swinging one arm slightly.'

Goma grimaces.

'Did you get a look at his face?'

'Same kind of beard. Sparse, but even, and shaved in straight lines. He was a little chubbier than the other immigrant poof. And he had a bandage on one finger. On his left hand, I think it was.'

'When was this?'

358

'An hour ago. It was a stroke of luck really, because I had just decided to have a nap, when I heard footsteps.'

'How long were they here?'

'At first, I thought you had come home, because it was quiet in the stairwell, but then I heard some more noise, now, when was it, ten minutes later, maybe? And so I had another look at them through the spyhole. But if they're your Nancy boys –'

'They're not.'

He doesn't elaborate. Goma appears to accept his brief denial.

'Thank you so much,' Henning says. 'You've been a great help.'

Goma grunts, turns around and makes to leave.

'By the way,' he says, grabbing the door handle. 'One of them was wearing a black leather jacket. With flames on the back.'

BBB. Bad Boys Burning. It has to be, Henning thinks. He nods and thanks Goma again. He looks at the clock. It is almost 1.15 a.m. He is wide awake. Too much has happened and his mind is buzzing.

Goma closes the door with a bang. The noise makes the flat feel frighteningly empty, as if Henning is in a vacuum. He fetches a mop and places it under the door handle. If anyone tries to come in, he will hear them. The mop will slow them down and give him time to escape.

359

He finds the escape rope coiled up under the bed and ties it around the TV stand. The television alone weighs 40 kg, and with various DVDs plus the stand itself, it should be enough to take his weight, he estimates. The last time he checked, he weighed 71 kg. He probably weighs even less now.

He sits down on the sofa and stares at the ceiling. He still hasn't switched on the light. If anyone is watching him from the street, he doesn't want to reveal that he is back.

Stefan's pale face pops into his head. Please don't let him haunt me as well, he prays. What on earth causes a seventeen-year-old boy to take his own life? If that is what he did?

The thought makes him sit up. What if he didn't? What if someone killed him and made it look like suicide?

No. So what about the script? It looked staged, somehow. As if someone wanted it to be noticed, to add the interpretation of the scene? It must have been a suicide, Henning tries to convince himself. Stefan must have got hold of the script and read it. Leaving the script in plain view was a message to his parents or, more likely, his father. Look what you made me do. I hope you can live with yourself.

Yes. That must have been what happened. But all the same. Henning has done this before, reasoned his way to a logical conclusion and yet been unable to shake off a feeling that a vague but ominous hook has anchored itself in his stomach. It yanks him, not constantly, but every now and then it wriggles, making him unpick the jigsaw puzzle and put the pieces back together again differently.

He doesn't know why. There is nothing to suggest that he is wrong, but his feeling of unease tells him that some of the pieces in Stefan's puzzle don't fit. Stefan's puzzle might not be complete yet.

Chapter 57

He nods off in the early morning hours and is woken up by a car beeping its horn. He is lying on the sofa, adjusting his eyes to the light. It is 5.30 a.m. He shuffles into the kitchen, gets a glass of water, fetches the medicine jars from his bedside table and swallows two tablets. The matchbox is where it always is, but he hasn't got the energy to challenge the soldiers from hell today.

He feels like he has been on a week-long bender. He knows he ought to eat something, but the thought of stale bread with dried-out ham is about as attractive as eating sawdust.

He thinks about the men who came to his flat. What would they have done if he had been there? Were they armed? Would they have tried to kill him?

He pushes the thought away. The point is that he wasn't there, that there was no confrontation. He decides to forget about breakfast and go straight to work, even though the day is just beginning.

An hour later, he rings Brogeland. A detective never sleeps more than a couple of hours when an investigation intensifies and Henning has questions he is dying to ask. Brogeland's voice sounds groggy when he finally picks up.

'Hi, Bjarne, it's me,' Henning says, suitably jovial and matey.

'Hi.'

'Are you awake?'

'No.'

'Well, are you up?'

'Define up.'

'How did it go yesterday?'

'That's also up for discussion.'

'What do you mean?'

Brogeland doesn't reply.

'Are you saying he didn't kill himself?'

Henning is on the edge of his seat.

'No. No, I didn't say that. It went well, in the sense that we did what we had to do at the crime scene. What do you want to talk about? Why are you calling me this early?'

Henning is wrong-footed by Brogeland's brusque tone.

'Well, I –'

'I'm about to go to a meeting and I've got work to do. So if it's not anything in particular, then –'

'Yes, it was.'

'Okay, spit it out.'

It takes Henning a moment to gather his thoughts.

'There's something I need to know.'

'Yes, I imagined as much.'

'Was there any e-mail correspondence between Henriette Hagerup and Yngve Foldvik in the time leading up to her murder?'

'Why do you ask? Why do you need to know?'

'I just do. Okay? I feel I've a certain right to know.'

'Right?'

'Yes. I've helped you quite a lot in this investigation.'

'I know.'

Brogeland sighs deeply.

'E-mails? I don't know. Don't remember. I'm too tired to remember things.'

'For God's sake, Bjarne, you can't be; the son of one of your potential suspects has just died. I don't know why you're suddenly being an arsehole after everything I've done for you, but that's fine. I don't need to talk to you anyway.'

He is about to hang up, when Brogeland yawns.

'Okay, sorry, I'm just so bloody tired. And Gjerstad, he –'

More yawning.

'What about Gjerstad?'

'Oh, forget it. Yes, Hagerup e-mailed Yngve Foldvik several times and he replied.' Brogeland says and exhales heavily.

'Were any of the e-mails about the script?'

'Yes, one of them. But not about the contents, only that she would send him the script when she had finished it.'

'Do you remember roughly when that was?'

'A while ago. I don't remember the exact date.'

'How about text messages? Have you found out who texted Henriette on the day she was killed? About the time she was with Marhoni?'

'She received two or three texts during that period. One of them said *"check your e-mail"*.'

'Who sent it?'

'We don't know. But we know that that text, like the e-mail with the photo, was also sent from Mozambique, from one of those anonymous sites.'

'Right. Okay. Thank you.'

'By the way, you need to come in for an interview today. Gjerstad lost his rag last night when I told him we had only spoken on the telephone.'

'When?'

'We'll be interviewing Mahmoud Marhoni again at ten o'clock. Sometime after that. Why don't we say 11 a.m., and see how the land lies around that time?'

'I'll try and make it.'

'You have to.'

'You said "the crime scene" a minute ago. Does that mean you're treating Stefan's death as suspicious?'

Brogeland groans.

'I haven't got time to talk to you. I've got to go. We can talk later.'

'So you *are* treating his death as suspicious.'

'I didn't say that. And don't you dare speculate about it in your newspaper either.'

'I never speculate about suicide.'

'No, okay. Talk to you later.'

Click. Henning stares into the distance. The police have found something, he thinks, or the absence of something is enough to make them suspicious. If not, Brogeland would have dismissed it categorically.

Chapter 58

Brogeland happens to meet Ella Sandland at the coffee machine.

'Good morning,' she says, without turning around.

Damn, she's hot.

'Good morning.'

Her hair looks as if she has just washed it. She smells discreetly of lavender. Or is it jasmine? He doesn't remember her smelling of creams or soaps before. Scents suit her. Damn, how they suit her. He feels like eating her up, savouring her, slowly, with a spoon and sugar and whipped cream.

Brogeland is reminded of something Henning Juul said, when they met at Lompa. *'And it wasn't that blonde you can't keep your eyes off?'*

Is he really that obvious? And if Juul can see it, then surely Sandland can, too? He hopes so and, at the same time, doesn't. Whether she has noticed or not, she is doing disappointingly little about it. Perhaps she's just waiting for me to make the first move, he thinks. Perhaps she's one of those.

'Sleep well?' she asks and pours herself a cup of coffee.

'No.'

'Me neither.'

She smiles briefly and offers him a cup. He nods.

'Are Gjerstad and Nøkleby here?'

'No, they'll be in later. Gjerstad said to start without him. The more theories we can examine before they get here, the better.'

'Okay.'

They take their coffee cups and go to the meeting room. Emil Hagen and Fredrik Stang are already there. Hagen is flicking through *Aftenposten*, while Stang is staring at a board displaying the names of the victims and the people connected to them. It looks like one big muddle of names, lines, times, dates, arrows, bold lines and more arrows going back and forth. There is a time-line beginning with the murder of Henriette Hagerup.

Sandland and Brogeland sit down.

'Good morning,' they say in unison. Hagen and Stang straighten up.

'So, where are we?' Brogeland says. There is a tacit agreement that Brogeland is boss when the boss isn't there.

'Anette Skoppum never showed up at the party yesterday,' Hagen begins and yawns. 'I was there till just after one o'clock this morning.'

Brogeland picks up a pen and makes a note.

'Any credit card or mobile activities?'

'No. None. Her mobile has been switched off since yesterday afternoon.'

Brogeland nods, but doesn't make a note.

'Fredrik, you're in touch with Operation Gangbuster. Any news about BBB?'

'They know what the leader and some of the members are up to, but there are a lot of them. Something may be happening further down the food chain.'

'Something always is.'

'Yes, unfortunately they don't have the resources to watch every gang member. Even the ones we know about. And there are other gangs in Oslo they need to keep an eye on as well. Nevertheless, I doubt that BBB would get up to anything now that they know we're watching them.'

'No trace of Yasser Shah?'

'No. He has gone underground. I spoke to an officer from Operation Gangbuster yesterday who said he thought Yasser could have gone back to Pakistan.'

'What about Hassan?'

'He goes to work and then he goes home. Or rather to his homes, he has several, so it depends on which girlfriend he wants to screw.'

Stang looks at Sandland and reddens. She looks back at him with no signs of embarrassment.

'Er, that's all, really.'

Brogeland sighs. The investigation is making slow progress. He is just about to start briefing them on Stefan Foldvik when Sandland's mobile vibrates. She apologises. Then Brogeland's own mobile buzzes. Beeps come from Hagen's. Stang looks at the others. His mobile stays silent.

'What's happening?' he says. Brogeland opens the text message he has just received. He types in a number and waits for a reply. It follows promptly.

'Hello, this is DI Brogeland.'

He looks at Sandland while he listens to the voice down the other end.

'Are you sure? You've checked everywhere, spoken to neighbours, friends, relatives, everyone?'

Brogeland listens, nods and hangs up.

'Damn,' he says and shoots out of his chair, as quick as lightning.

Chapter 59

Iver Gundersen manages to look even more tired than Henning feels. Henning crosses his fingers and hopes that Gundersen's lack of sleep is the result of a blazing row with Nora. Gundersen joins the national news crowd and says hi, his breath reeking of garlic and alcohol. He sets down his cup of coffee.

'Late night?' Henning asks.

'Later than I had planned,' Gundersen says, bending down to switch on his computer. He straightens up, pulls a face and starts to massage his temples with his fingertips.

'They cook bloody good food at Delicatessen,' he says. 'One beer soon leads to another, when you're enjoying yourself.'

Enjoying yourself, Henning fumes. Dammit. He was going to tell him about yesterday, but given that Iver is preoccupied with enjoying himself, he drops the idea.

'What's up?' Gundersen asks and takes a seat. His body wobbles on the chair. He runs his fingers through his hair. Henning suspects Gundersen didn't even shower before going to work, that it is all a part of his image: A rough diamond.

What does she see in him?

'Nothing much,' Henning says. 'Any excitement your end?'

'Maybe,' Gundersen says, moving the mouse. 'I've a twelve o'clock appointment with Mahmoud Marhoni's lawyer. The police are interviewing him again this morning, and I hope to get a detailed update of recent developments. I've got a good relationship with Indrehaug. Heidi mentioned that you thought the police were about to eliminate Marhoni?'

Henning swears silently, while Gundersen opens his browser.

'Yes, I think so.'

'Based on what?'

'Facts and evidence,' he snaps. It is clearly too early for a serious discussion, maybe Gundersen can only do one thing at a time: read the newspaper, drink coffee, then read the other newspapers, drink more coffee, gradually get his head in gear.

'And that means?' Gundersen says, slurping his scalding hot coffee. Henning exhales and wonders where to begin. He is saved when Gundersen's mobile beeps. Gundersen reads the message and frowns.

'Do you know who Foldvik is?' he asks.

'Foldvik?'

'Yes. Yngve and Ingvild Foldvik?'

'Yes, I know who they are,' Henning says, barely managing to control his breathing. 'They work at the college where Henriette Hagerup was a student. What's this about?'

'I've got a tip-off that the police are looking for them.'

'What do you mean "looking for them"? Have they disappeared?'

'Seems like it.'

'Are you sure?'

He has already risen from his chair. Gundersen snorts.

'I'm only reading what it says here.'

Henning squeezes past him as fast as his legs will allow him.

'What's wrong?' Gundersen calls out. The bewilderment in his voice is audible, but Henning ignores it. He doesn't have time. He rushes outside, gets on his Vespa and zooms off in the direction of Westerdal School of Communication.

Chapter 60

There might be a perfectly natural explanation, Henning thinks, as he drives down Urtegata. Perhaps the Foldviks needed to get away, just the two of them, process their grief in private. Create some distance from their tragedy, reduce the noise.

He pushes the Vespa hard, turns into Hausmannsgate and crosses the junction just as the lights change from green to amber. A dark-haired woman pushing a pram shakes her fist at him and shouts something he doesn't hear. He can see her outrage clearly in his wing mirror as he passes a dirty, oyster grey Opel Vectra.

And he spots something else, too. A minicab. Even in the small wing mirror, he can see a letter and four numbers.

A2052.

Omar Rabia Rashid, or someone driving for him, accelerates. The silver Mercedes receives the same angry hand gesture from the dark-haired woman, but the minicab crosses without anyone getting hurt.

On impulse, Henning turns left into Calmeyersgate, speeds up and passes a lorry left with its engine running outside a Thai supermarket. Henning ignores the Give Way sign as he comes up to the next street, but he can't turn into it, because it is one way and then he thinks why not, there are no cars around, so he does it, he turns right, someone on the pavement shouts after him, but he doesn't care. If the police happen to be in the vicinity and notice his careless or dangerous driving, they are welcome to pull him over. It would give him a chance to point out the guys who are following him.

He soon finds himself in Torggate where the cars are bumper-to-bumper. One of them is yellow; even now he can't ignore yellow cars. He sees that the bicycle lane is clear and pulls into it, speeds up again, nearly running over a seagull, which flaps up right in front of him. He checks his mirror to see if the Mercedes is following, but it isn't in his field of vision. Suddenly, he has to brake, bloody pedestrian crossing, why doesn't anyone look where they are going, he thinks, people just walk straight out into the road, he wants to beep his horn, but realises what a self-defeating gesture it would be. He presses the accelerator and gains speed before he has to stop again, this time for a red light.

He is tempted to jump the lights, which are pain-fully slow to change. He checks his mirror, no silver Mercedes; he looks up, cars are zooming back and forth in both directions, but then they start to slow down. The lights change from green to amber, he twists the throttle open full force, turns to the left and manages to get across the pedestrian crossing before the pedestrians are halfway across the road. Back in Hausmannsgate, he checks his mirror again: no sign of A2052, he drives on, aware that several cars are having to slow down, but he has no intention of letting them pass. Another pedestrian crossing, he sweeps across it, passes Elvebakken School to his right, some students are outside smoking. He soon reaches the bottom of Rostedsgate, another red light, damn. He positions himself as far ahead as he can, turns to see where the minicab is. He can see other minicabs, but not A2052, not yet, but it might be only seconds before it catches up with him, what will happen then? They're bound to know where I'm heading, he thinks, they know where Westerdal is, they're cabdrivers, for crying out loud! He drives on to the pedestrian crossing, registers that a pedestrian glares at him, but he doesn't give a toss, he pulls up on the pavement, speeds up, carries on driving down the pavement, until he can pull out into the street again. When he looks to the left, all he sees are buildings and concrete. The minicab can't possibly see him now. Oh, you lovely Vespa!

He accelerates down the street until he reaches Fredensborgvei and turns into the college car park. He sees a substation and parks his Vespa behind it, out of sight to anyone driving past. He removes his helmet and looks around. No A2052. Though they can't be far away. He hurries into the college grounds.

He spots Tore Benjaminsen straight away. He is tempted to go over to him, but there are too many people around. And what would he say? 'Have you seen Yngve Foldvik? Did you know that he has gone missing?' It occurs to him that he isn't entirely sure why he has come. What did I think I would see or understand, once I got here? he asks himself. It's not like the Foldviks might be hiding out at the college. Was he hoping that the students or the staff would know where the Foldviks go when they want a little time to themselves? He can't even be sure that anyone here knows what has happened.

He shakes his head at his own impetuousness. Then he turns around and jumps. He is looking right into the eyes of Anette Skoppum.

Chapter 61

Bjarne Brogeland is pacing up and down his office. The tired, Lapp face of Ann-Mari Sara, the crime scene technician, has just popped up on his screen again, to report on the most recent findings from Marhoni's laptop. Interrogating Marhoni will be more interesting now. But that's not where I want to be, Brogeland groans. What the hell is going on with Yngve and Ingvild Foldvik? Why can't anyone find them?

Brogeland is swearing silently when Sandland knocks on his door and asks him if he is ready. I'm ready, Brogeland thinks, I've never been more ready in my life.

As usual, Lars Indrehaug is indignant on his client's behalf when Sandland and Brogeland welcome them back to the interview room and go through the formalities.

'So what's today's theme?' Indrehaug snarls when Brogeland has finished. 'My client's favourite colour? Favourite car?'

Indrehaug nods to Marhoni. Brogeland smiles. He is anything but tired now, and the sight of the slimy lawyer makes his blood boil. He slides a sheet across the table, placing it halfway between them, so both can study it. Marhoni leans forward and glances at the sheet before looking away. He shakes his head, faintly. Brogeland registers it.

'What's this?' Indrehaug asks.

'I would have thought that was obvious,' Brogeland says. 'But perhaps you could explain it to us all the same, Mr Marhoni?'

Marhoni stares at the wall.

'Okay, then I'll do it for you,' Brogeland says, addressing Indrehaug. 'Your client has, believe it or not, a highly developed sense of order. He likes to know where everything is. Perhaps you've been to his flat? Neat and tidy. The document in front of you is a print-out of an Excel spreadsheet we found on your client's laptop, the one he tried to burn. Perhaps you can see why?'

Indrehaug studies the document closely. He sees names, telephone numbers and e-mail addresses.

'A quick check, not that you need to look very hard, will tell you that these are very bad people. Very bad indeed. People who make sure that our streets are flooded with drugs, which our children take, and which turn them into very bad people, too.'

Indrehaug shoves the document back to Brogeland and snorts.

'This proves nothing. There could be any number of legitimate reasons why my client might choose to keep this information on his computer. Just because you bookmark the homepage of Rema 1000, it doesn't follow that you shop there. The names you have found on my client's computer certainly don't prove that he killed someone.'

'No, you're right about that,' Brogeland replies, smiling. 'But how would you explain this?'

He slides another sheet towards Indrehaug and Marhoni.

'This photograph was also found on your client's computer. In fact, we found several very interesting pictures.'

Indrehaug pulls the sheet towards him. Marhoni doesn't look at the print-out which shows him with a man in a black leather jacket. The jacket has an emblem of flames on its back. The man's face is clearly visible.

'This is your client in the company of a man called Abdul Sebrani. If you check the list we've just shown you, you'll see that his name appears on it. The photograph was taken during the delivery of a batch of cocaine from BBB – Bad Boys Burning – to your client earlier this spring. It was taken down at Vippetangen. Can you see the water in the background?'

Indrehaug studies the photograph. The image is sharp and shot with a telephoto lens from some distance.

'Do you remember where you were supposed to take the drugs, Mr Marhoni?' Brogeland asks. There is no reply.

'We have more pictures like this. Your client – and I'm only guessing here – wanted some sort of insurance against his business associates, just in case they started to play hardball. Or perhaps they had already started threatening you, Mr Marhoni?'

Marhoni ignores Brogeland's hard stare.

'Your client kept his head down. But when his girlfriend was killed and we came knocking on his door, he realised that his laptop might incriminate him. And BBB. That's why he tried to burn it, to destroy the evidence.'

Brogeland looks at both Marhoni and Indrehaug. Indrehaug blanks him and leans towards Marhoni instead. Whisper, whisper.

Slam-dunk, Brogeland thinks. He looks at Sandland, hoping that she is thinking the same, but she is always difficult to read.

'Your brother was a photographer, wasn't he?' she asks. Marhoni turns to her, but doesn't reply.

'He took these pictures, didn't he? He uploaded them to your laptop.'

Marhoni still doesn't reply, but there is no need for him to say anything.

'Where's the rest of your family, Mahmoud?'

Marhoni keeps his eyes fixed on Sandland, before he averts them and whispers:

'Pakistan.'

'What will happen to them?'

'What do you mean?'

'Who is going to send them money now?'

Marhoni looks down.

'We know that you send them a lot of money every month. Your father has brain disease. The money buys the treatment he needs. The amounts vary slightly, but I presume that's to do with the exchange rate. You live on what you earn from minicabbing, while the money you're paid for transporting drugs and driving gang members around ends up in Pakistan. That's how it works, isn't it?'

Marhoni doesn't reply.

'Would you like to change your statement, Mahmoud?' Brogeland interjects. 'Would you like me to ask you, once more, if you know Zaheerullah Hassan Mintroza? Or Yasser Shah?'

Marhoni doesn't reply. Brogeland waits for him to crack.

'They're going to kill them,' Marhoni whispers after a long pause.

'Who are they, Mahmoud?'

'Hassan and his men.'

'Who are they going to kill?'

'My family. If I give them up. I've been wanting to quit, I've been looking to get out for a long time, but they started threatening me.'

'And you responded by taking photographs of the deals?'

Marhoni nods.

'And they found out?'

He nods twice.

'Answer the question.'

'Yes.'

'So the murder of your brother was a message? Keep your mouth shut or we'll kill the rest of your family?'

He nods three times.

'Answer the question, please.'

'Yes.'

'How long has this been going on, Mr Marhoni? When did it start?'

He sighs.

'Some time after I got my minicab licence. I started driving for Omar, we already knew each other and after a while he asked me if I wanted to earn some extra cash. I said yes, because my father was ill and, to begin with, all I had to do was a bit of driving and a few deliveries. But then they wanted more. In the end, I wanted out.'

'But you knew too much, so they couldn't risk it?'

'No.'

Brogeland looks at Indrehaug, who runs his fingers through his hair. He tries to sweep it away from his eyes, but it keeps flopping into them.

'What do you want?' Indrehaug says.

'What do we want? We want the big fish, we want to know who your client's supplier is and how the drugs get into this country. And that's just for starters. I'm sure you can imagine the rest.'

Indrehaug nods.

'You're presuming that my client will testify against BBB?'

'Of course.'

'Despite his family situation back in Pakistan?'

Brogeland looks at the lawyer and sighs. Then he fixes his gaze on Marhoni.

'We know that you didn't kill Henriette Hagerup.'

Marhoni looks up at Brogeland.

'There's a good chance that you can walk out of here very soon, if you co-operate.'

Marhoni looks more alert now. He turns to Indrehaug who turns to Brogeland.

'Are you offering my client a deal?'

Brogeland looks at Sandland, smiles, and looks back at Indrehaug.

'You bet we are.'

Chapter 62

Henning is so shocked at seeing Anette at the college that he is lost for words. He just stands there, gawping at her. He was convinced she had gone into hiding. Then he wonders whether Anette is like him. Perhaps she has also had enough of looking over her shoulder and prefers to confront her fears rather than give in to them.

She makes no attempt to get past him.

'Hi,' he says, at last.

'Hi.'

They look at each other, both waiting for the other to say something.

'I've read the script,' he says, even though he knows that she knows. She nods.

'I've also shown it to the police.'

'Yes, I imagined you would.'

'Have they spoken to you yet?'

'No. They've tried, but I haven't returned their calls.'

He frowns.

'Why not?'

'I don't feel like it.'

She says it without blushing and seemingly without a hint of guilt. He studies her.

'But I'm thinking of doing it now.'

'Aha? Why? Why now?'

'Because I think I know who killed Henriette.'

He can barely hear her. Intrigued, he takes a step closer.

'Who?'

He can hear the trembling in his own voice. Anette glances around to make sure they are alone. They aren't. But no one is close enough to hear what she says.

'Stefan Foldvik,' she whispers. Henning gasps. Anette watches his reaction.

'Why?'

'Haven't you read the script?' she asks.

'Yes.'

'Then it should be obvious.'

She offers no further explanation. Henning thinks about it.

'The Foldvik family is the Gaarder family. In the script.'

He is half asking, half stating it. Anette nods.

'Did Yngve have an affair with Henriette?'

Anette takes a quick look around again before she nods. Her eyes are grave.

'Stefan must have found out.'

'How?'

'I'm not sure. Perhaps he found a copy of the script at home or on his father's PC? I don't know.'

'Yngve hadn't seen the script,' Henning says.

Anette frowns. 'He told you that?'

'Yes,' he admits, guiltily, as it strikes him that something doesn't add up. 'Has anyone else from college read the script?'

'No.'

'No actors or extras?'

'We *were* the actors and we had only got as far as shooting the first scenes. We were going to film the rest later in the autumn, so we haven't shown the script to anyone else. Not yet.'

He nods, thinking Yngve must have been lying. He had the script, after all. It is the only logical explanation Henning can think of, since Stefan had a copy of it. Perhaps Yngve realised that the truth about his affair would come out eventually and chose to tell his family first? Later, Stefan finds the script among his father's things, or asks to see it.

Anette could be right about Stefan: he killed Henriette because she had destroyed his family and was about to compound the damage by making a film about it. But now Stefan is dead, either by his own hand or because someone killed him. And that changes everything, in Henning's view. But who would benefit from Stefan's death? Calm down, Henning, there might be other reasons why a young man chooses to end his life, reasons which have nothing to do with 'A Sharia Caste' or Henriette or Yngve. Besides, there is one option he hasn't allowed for: Stefan's death could be due to natural causes.

He is starting to feel a little dizzy. He knows he shouldn't be discussing this with Anette, but he has no one else, and he needs to test his theory on someone while the ideas are coming at him from all angles.

'Did you ever discuss the script with Yngve?'

'I imagine Henriette did, but I never went to any meetings about it, if that's what you're asking.'

'Do you think they discussed the Gaarder storyline?'

'No idea.'

'It's pretty rich to expose your own lover like that.'

Again he utters it like something halfway between a question and a statement.

Anette sniffs. 'Are you saying that Yngve did it?'

'No, not necessarily.'

'You don't know Yngve. He's a pussycat.'

'A pussycat who helped Henriette sell an option on her film.'

Anette smiles. It is the first time he has seen her smile.

'Yes, I imagine that's why Henriette slept with him.'

'So it only happened once? It wasn't a full-blown affair?'

She shakes her head and suppresses a laugh. 'Oh, no.'

She doesn't elaborate. He lets it lie. He isn't writing a gossip column.

'Did her boyfriend know about this?'

'Mahmoud? I don't think so.'

'How do you think he would have reacted to the film? Wouldn't he have assumed that Mona, Henriette that is, might have been unfaithful in real life? Given that most of the plot mirrored reality?'

'I don't know,' Anette responds. 'And anyway, it doesn't matter now.'

'But didn't Henriette consider this when she wrote the script? Wasn't it something you discussed?'

'Well, we –'

She ponders this, but doesn't expand on her reply.

'So Henriette had no problem using her boyfriend as the basis of a character who is set up? How would you like it, if your boyfriend did that to you?'

'I don't have a boyfriend.'

'No, no. But you understand what I'm saying?'

'Of course. Maybe Henriette had talked to Mahmoud about it, what do I know? Explained to him that we didn't mean it literally, that we don't believe he's an idiot who should be taken off our streets. I've no idea.'

She shrugs.

'Does he support sharia and hudud punishments? Do you know?'

'I can't imagine that he does.'

'So the Yashid character wasn't a fanatical, fundamentalist Muslim?'

'No.'

'Then why was Mona stoned to death? Don't you have to be a Muslim to be stoned to death in accordance with sharia and hudud?'

'Oh, for God's sake, you still haven't got it, have you?'

'Then explain it to me. From the start.'

Anette sighs.

'The point of the film is to highlight what's going on in the world, something that might, one day, be commonplace in Norway, if extreme Islamic beliefs gain a foothold and are allowed to flourish. Soon it won't matter whether we are Norwegians or Muslims. What do you think Oslo will look like in thirty or forty years? We'll probably all be Muslims, indoctrinated and well behaved. That's why Yashid is an ordinary Muslim and Mona is an ordinary Norwegian woman. To make people think.'

'Right.'

'Was that so difficult?'

She looks at him as if he is slow on the uptake.

'No. But there's nothing to suggest that might happen, Anette. Very few people believe that Norwegian law should give way to sharia.'

'And?'

He frowns.

'And? The premise for your film is wrong. It has no roots in reality. You're not about to tell me that you also have a sick wish to be killed by eight gunshots?'

Anette looks up at the dark grey, ominous clouds.

'I'm sure Henriette is up there with Theo van Gogh, as we speak. I didn't know you were on their side.'

Henning sighs and forces the air through his nostrils. He looks frustrated.

'There are aspects of Islam and sharia which I personally don't care very much for, but what you're doing only contributes to making matters worse. What about integration, multiculturalism and all that?'

'Save it for the speeches. Besides, this has nothing to do with Stefan.'

He presses his lips together. He wants to carry on the discussion, but now is not the time. Instead, he thinks about Stefan and Romance. He remembers, from his own teenage years, how the boys doused themselves with excessive quantities of aftershave to impress the girls. Some even applied it to their clothes. It stank, in the changing rooms, in the classrooms, even in the school playground. That might have been why the smell was still in the tent when Thorbjørn Skagestad discovered the body.

He becomes aware that Anette is looking at him. She coughs anxiously.

'I tried getting Henriette to drop the Gaarder storyline. I didn't think it was relevant to the film's message. But she wouldn't listen to me. I also thought it was a bit weird, surely everyone would know who it was based on? The Foldvik family had suffered enough.'

'How do you mean?'

'Stefan told me about his mother. That she had been raped and . . .'

'*Stefan* told you about that?'

'Yes.'

'How did *you* know Stefan?'

'Stefan won a script competition last year. I wanted to film his script for one of my projects. It was a good story.'

'Didn't he get a prize?'

'What do you mean?'

'I mean, didn't the organisers of the competition promise to film his script? That's the usual prize in such competitions, isn't it?'

'It depends, but it wasn't the case here. I think he got a few thousand kroner and an invitation to Zentropa in Denmark. Stefan was thrilled when I asked him.

Stefan's a nice guy, a smart guy. But dangerous, too. I got the feeling that he had some mental problems.'

'What do you mean? What made you think that?'

'I'm not really sure. It's a little hard to explain. You needed to spend time with him to notice. Sometimes, he was over the moon. Laughed at everything, hyper, almost. Other times you could barely get a word out of him. Like he had shut down completely.'

Henning nods and thinks that the description fits a boy who takes his own life after taking someone else's. What if the burden grew too heavy or the memories too powerful? Maybe he couldn't bear to close his eyes at night without seeing her dead, without reliving what he had done?

Perhaps there is nothing suspicious about his death, after all? But then why have his parents gone missing?

That moment, it starts to rain. The heavens open completely. Henning and Anette rush to the lobby. They aren't the only ones to seek shelter there, a bottle-neck is created, but it lasts less than a minute, then everyone is inside.

People smile at each other while they shake off the water. Anette runs her fingers through her wet hair. They find themselves by the reception counter. Dread-locks is there today, but there is no sign of his girlfriend. Dreadlocks meets Henning's eyes and they nod to each other.

'Have you seen Yngve today?' Henning asks Anette in a low voice. She shakes her head and replies 'no' at the same time. She is about to say something else.

'It's his day off today.'

They turn around and look at Dreadlocks.

'Yngve and his wife have both taken today off,' he says and holds up his hands. 'Sorry, I overheard you. I didn't mean to. Yngve called in this morning, he wanted to speak to the Principal, but he wasn't in, so I took a message. He said that neither he nor his wife would be coming to work.'

'That's weird,' Anette says. 'I was due to meet him today. Did he say why?'

Henning is on the verge of saying that their son has died, but remembers at the last moment that the death isn't public knowledge yet.

'He said something about going on a trip,' Dreadlocks replies.

'A trip?'

'Yes. A camping trip, I think he said.'

'Camping?'

Henning is aware that he is nearly shouting.

'Yes.'

His stomach lurches. The usual thing would be to tell the truth, that their son has died and they are taking some time off. Everyone would understand. So why say they are going *camping*?

'Why did he tell you that?'

'I just thought he wanted me to know. In case someone asked after him or them. I don't know. He sounded – how can I put it – a bit agitated. Or manic, I'm not really sure.'

'How? What do you mean?'

'If I didn't know him, I would have said that he was high. He spoke faster than he normally does.'

'Did he say where they were going?'

'No. Only that they were going camping. I did think it sounded weird, I've never really seen Yngve as one of those, you know, the outdoor type. But I thought – why not – camping is cool, so –'

He holds up his hands.

'When was this?'

'Just after eight o'clock this morning, I think. I can't be sure. I hadn't had my first coffee yet.'

'Sod it,' Henning mutters to himself, but Anette hears him.

'What is it?'

He shakes his head and whispers to her so that Dreadlocks can't hear.

'The police are looking for them, but no one knows where they are.'

'Why? Do you think that they –'

He gives her a sharp look. She understands him instantly, moves closer and whispers:

'Are you saying that *they* know that Stefan killed Henriette?'

He knows what he wants to say, but he shakes his head.

'I don't know.'

'And now they've gone? Disappeared?'

'It looks like it.'

They stand for a while without saying anything. Then it dawns on him. He turns to Dreadlocks again.

'Do you know if the tent on Ekeberg Common is still there?'

'The tent for the filming? Yes. The police finished with it yesterday, they said they had taken all the pictures and gathered all the evidence they needed. They called to say we could pick it up.'

That's where they must be. Henning looks out of the window. The rain will soak him. And a minicab is out of the question. He lifts up his helmet.

'Do you want me to drive?'

He looks at Anette, surprised. 'You have a car?'

'Yes. Why shouldn't I have?'

He thinks no, why shouldn't she?

'Don't you have a lecture or something?'

'Like I said, I was due to meet with Yngve, but as he's not here, then –'

She throws up her hands. 'And if he's somewhere else, and you know where and why, I'm happy to provide transport. It's no big deal. I can give you a lift up there.'

The prospect is too tantalising for him to resist it.

'Is your car close by?'

'It's just over there,' she says, pointing over his head.

'Okay. Let's go.'

Chapter 63

They manage to get soaked to the skin in the short distance from the lobby to the car park. Anette opens the door on the driver's side first, gets in, and unlocks the passenger door for him. He climbs inside a small dark blue Polo, which appears to be in good nick, even though it must be at least fifteen years old. The car is remarkably free from smells, given that it is a woman's car, but something tells him that Anette doesn't care much for perfume.

She starts the car, turns the wipers to maximum speed and reverses out. She is about to put the car in gear, when she stops and looks at him. The sound of the wipers brushing back and forth mixes with protests from the engine that has yet to warm up.

'What's going on?' she says. Henning groans. I can't tell her about Stefan, he thinks. It's not up to him to give out that sort of information.

'I need to speak to the Foldviks.'

'Both of them?'

'Yes.'

'Why? Does it have anything to do with Stefan? Or Henriette?'

He nods. 'But I don't know what. Or how.'

Suitably enigmatic, he thinks. It also happens to be true. He has no idea what is going on or what to say to them, if and when he finds them. But his instinct tells him he needs to find them, and he needs to find them fast.

'Please, Anette, just drive. Okay? I'll explain everything later. But right now, we haven't got time to talk.'

Anette looks at him, lets a few seconds go by. Then she puts the car into first and drives off. Henning says a silent prayer.

They go down Fredensborgvei. I ought to ring Brogeland, he thinks, tell him what I know, but I can't. Not yet.

They drive on in silence. That suits Henning fine, it gives him a chance to think. Anette drives cautiously, not nervously, but with care and without excessive stomping on the accelerator or the brakes. She forces the Polo up a long, winding road, past the old business school and Ekeberg Restaurant which nestles further up the hill. Henning can see Oslo Fjord stretch out between the islands, ferries in the port; a few private boats have gone out, despite the dreadful weather. They also pass some poor cyclist, who no longer cares about getting wet when Anette splashes him.

While the rain cascades down, he thinks about Stefan, he visualises him in the tent, holding the rock over his head, the rage which took over, so he couldn't stop until Henriette's body was lifeless, before he had flogged her and chopped off one of her hands. Where does such rage come from? And how do the hudud punishments fit in?

He is reminded of the photograph of Stefan and the newspaper cutting about him in Yngve Foldvik's office. And once he has compared recent events to the information in the article, everything falls into place.

Well, I'll be damned.

It takes them no more than eleven or twelve minutes to get from Westerdal to Ekeberg. He sees the white tent the moment they reach the Common. He asks her to pull into a bus stop. She does so.

'Thanks for the lift,' he says, as he opens the door.

'But –'

'This is no place for you now, Anette. Go home. Thanks for the lift.'

Anette is about to say something, but thinks better of it.

'I'll just have to read about it later,' she says and smiles briefly. Maybe, he thinks, and gets out. He slams the door shut behind him. The rain pelts down. Trying to escape it is pointless.

He watches Anette drive off and heads down the tarmac path that winds its way across the Common in the direction of Ekeberg School. There is nobody outside now, in the school playground, or the playing fields. Nor can he see any cars parked near the tent. Hm, he wonders, could I have been wrong? Perhaps they're not here, after all?

Sneaking around like this makes him feel like he is doing something illegal, an extreme form of apple scrumping. He is just about to open the tent, when he freezes. A sound. A voice? No. Through the intense drumming of the rain, he can hear someone groaning inside. He listens out. But it's the sound of one person only. Not two. He looks over his shoulder. There isn't a soul to be seen.

Damn, Henning, he thinks. What's your plan once you go in? 'Hi, I am Henning Juul from *123news*. I'd like to interview you, please.'

Damn. He turns around again. The Common is deserted. The rain hammers against the roof of the tent. He checks the time. It has just gone noon. He was supposed to be at the police station an hour ago. Perhaps Brogeland is waiting for him? No. He would have called. And with Marhoni's interrogation, Stefan's suspicious death and the disappearance of the Foldviks, Brogeland probably wouldn't have time to interview him, anyway.

I'm going in, he says to himself. I'll just have to take things as I find them.

He bends down, gets hold of the zip and pulls it up in one swift movement. He looks inside. At first, he wonders if there is something wrong with his eyesight. Slowly, the picture becomes clearer. Ingvild Foldvik is holding a spade. Rocks lie at her feet, big and small. She looks at him with terror in her eyes. He looks at *her* with terror in his eyes.

Then he sees the hole in the ground. Yngve is buried in it. And he has a red mark from a stun gun on his neck.

Chapter 64

Henning struggles to control his breathing. He holds out his hands. Raindrops trickle down his head. He wipes his face with one hand and steps inside the tent. The air is stuffy. The merciless rain bangs against the roof, which can't keep out all the water, so some seeps through and drips on to the grass. He looks into Ingvild Foldvik's eyes. They are wide open and fixed. There is a shiny, faraway expression in them he has only ever seen in people who are insane.

'Take it easy,' he says and realises immediately how stupid that sounds. She is holding a spade, there is a pile of rocks by her feet and it doesn't take a whole lot of imagination to work out what she intends to do with them.

She is much thinner than when he last saw her. She was slim when she gave evidence in court, but now she is practically a skeleton. Her clothes hang on her like rags. She has aged ten years, at least. Her skin sags. She is a zombie, he thinks. Her teeth are stained yellow from years of smoking and her hair has started to go grey. It is tied back into a hasty ponytail; strands of damp hair fall over her face, a pale, gaunt face with large bags under her eyes.

'W-who are you?' she stutters.

He looks at Yngve in the ground. His head has flopped. But he is breathing.

'My name's Henning Juul,' he says with as much control in his voice as he can muster. He can see that the name means nothing to her.

'I reported on your court case. Before this happened,' he says, pointing to his face, thinking that the scarring might earn him some sympathy points.

'What are you doing? Why are you here?'

Her voice is sharper now. He looks at Yngve.

'Don't do it, Ingvild,' he says. 'Deep down, you don't really want to do it.'

'Oh yes, I do,' she snarls. 'What have I got to live for? He has taken everything from me. EVERY-THING. My whole life. It's – it's –'

Her eyes narrow. She starts to cry without making a sound. The tears just fall from her eyes. Then they start to glow again and she looks at her husband with contempt. She turns to Henning. It is as if a veil has been placed over her face.

'Do you know what he made my son do? Do you know who my son is?'

Henning takes another step into the tent.

'Stefan,' he says, gently. 'And it was Stefan who killed Henriette Hagerup.'

She lets out a pitiful howl.

'H-how do you know that?' she sobs. He takes a deep breath and prepares himself.

'I read Henriette Hagerup's script.'

She sniffs, brushes away the hair from her face. He thinks about what to say, how to find an inroad to the sentient part of her brain. Brute force is no good. Throwing himself at her and dragging her outside is hopeless. Ingvild Foldvik may be reduced to skeleton, but she is a skeleton with a purpose. And, if you have enough of that, you can achieve most things. Besides, she has a stun gun.

'If you'll let me, Ingvild,' he says, as softly as he can, 'then I want to talk to you about the script.'

'Ingvild,' she says, mimicking his voice. 'So now you think you know all about me, eh? Stupid journalist.'

'Stefan killed Henriette because your husband slept with her. He might even have been in love with her. He destroyed your family. *She* destroyed your family and wrote a script which – in parts – dealt with what happened. But Stefan read something more into the script.'

'What do you mean?'

He glances at Yngve, who is still unconscious.

'Stefan was into symbolism. *The Da Vinci Code Lite*,

405

that's what the newspaper called his script, wasn't it? Henriette's hand was chopped off. There was nothing about that in her script. Hudud punishments in sharia law prescribe that thieves are punished by having their hand chopped off. Henriette stole your husband.'

Ingvild digs the spade into the ground. But she stops shovelling more sand and grass around her husband. She clasps her mouth with her other hand.

'And the flogging. There was nothing about flogging in the script, either. But the film would have ridiculed you and your family. And a woman isn't allowed to mock, either. The punishment for that is flogging –'

'Stop,' she shouts. It is deadly silent inside the tent. 'Please stop. I can't take any more. Please stop.'

The spade keels over and falls to the ground. Ingvild buries her face in her hands. Henning moves further inside the tent, without her noticing. Yngve's green shirt is soaked with sweat. Ingvild collapses. Henning does nothing, he just watches her cry into her hands. She sits like this for a while, then she dries her tears and looks up at him.

'You said you reported on my court case,' she starts in a rusty voice. She clears her throat, she sees him nod.

'So you know that the bastard raped me and cut me afterwards. I took a course in self-defence, learned all sorts of things, but I never felt safe. Wherever I went, I saw his shadow, felt the knife against my throat, the tip of the knife touching my stomach, touching my –'

She heaves a sigh.

'Yngve was understanding. Gave me time, never pressured me. But he got tired of waiting. Waiting for –'

She closes her eyes and starts to cry again. Henning steps further into the tent. The roof is a couple of metres above his head. It is a large tent, probably big enough for twenty people.

She opens her eyes again. They watch each other for a while, but Henning has an inkling that he is the only one actually seeing. Ingvild's eyes change from being remote to flashing when she registers colour or movement. Then she disappears into a world of her own again, or some other place where she has no contact with anybody.

'I got myself one of these,' she says and takes a mobile out of her pocket. It looks like an ordinary Nokia phone.

'You can't get these in Norway.'

She waves the mobile in the air.

'It's a combined mobile telephone and stun gun. Yes, such things are actually made. I got this in the US for less than $200. And everyone has a mobile these days, don't they? People are always fiddling with them. Ringing, texting, talking rubbish. This never leaves my hand, but no one ever asks why. And if anyone tries to attack me again, I'm ready. 800,000 volts, straight into the body, Zzzzzt. It'll knock you out, I promise.'

He looks at Yngve, though he needs no convincing.

'And Stefan knew that you had one? It was your stun gun he used, wasn't it?'

She nods reluctantly.

'Did he ask if he could borrow it?'

'No. He took it one evening – I mean – that night. I had already gone to bed. I realised that he had used it the following day, because the mobile wasn't where I had left it. I'm always meticulous about such things. I notice *everything*.'

'Did you confront him about it?'

'Not there and then. I woke up late and he had already left for college. But it came up yesterday afternoon, and – and –'

She starts to cry again, but she carries on talking.

'I asked him what he had done with my mobile, why he had borrowed it, but he wouldn't say. Then Yngve took over and it got –'

She shakes her head.

'Everything Stefan had been keeping back came out. He wanted Yngve to own up to what he had done, be honest with himself and us. Stefan almost went berserk, he wanted to fight Yngve and, in the heat of the moment, Stefan told us what he had done, why he had taken my mobile and it became –'

More shaking of the head.

'It was so ugly. So –'

She looks at her husband, whose head is still flopped to one side.

'It was bad. So very bad –'

She closes her eyes.

'What happened after Stefan confessed to the murder? Because he was alone when he died.'

Ingvild sighs deeply.

'I don't really remember. I think I ran out of the flat. I've a vague memory of Yngve shaking me, at the top of St Hanshaugen. He said he had been looking for me for hours. I think I must have walked up there. Or run, I don't know. I don't remember. And when we came back, then –'

She starts to cry again, silently. He sees her tremble, holding one hand over her mouth. Then her eyes cloud over. She looks straight ahead, into the wall of the tent. Then, abruptly, she regains lucidity.

'How did you know that we were here?'

'I spoke to someone at the college reception this morning.'

'Gorm?'

'Might have been.'

'How did –?'

He holds up his hands.

'He said that Yngve had rung to let the Principal know that you were going camping. The Principal wasn't there, so he took a message. I added two and two together and got 400. It was a fluke that I found you. I had a feeling that everything had something to do with this tent, this hole,' he says, pointing to the ground. 'And if everyone was looking for you, but hadn't been able to find you, I guessed that you might be here. Since you were going "camping", like Yngve had said.'

Ingvild looks at him for a long time, before she nods.

'I barely remember what happened yesterday. I had run out of pills, too, I guess they were the ones Stefan took, so I couldn't get to sleep, either. I doubt I would have slept anyway.'

Her eyes are red.

'Why did you come here?'

'So I could get my revenge. In my own way.'

'How did you persuade Yngve to come with you?'

'I told him I needed to be here, in the tent, to see if I could even begin to understand what my son had done. It wasn't just an excuse. I really *needed* to. Does that sound strange to you?'

He shakes his head.

'Now that I'm here, it feels a little weird. But I know how Stefan felt. I recognise the hatred. And, as his mother, that's a relationship that I'm grateful for.'

He is about to say something, but her face fills with contempt and anger. Before he has time to react, before he has time to grab her, she has picked up one of the rocks and thrown it at Yngve. She hits his shoulder, he jerks and wakes up; slowly his eyes open, he lifts his head slightly, but he is too deep in the hole to be able to move much. Finally, he sees Ingvild, then Henning, and understands what is about to happen. He tries to raise his arms in self-defence, but they are trapped in the ground. Ingvild picks up another rock.

'Wait. Ingvild, don't –'

Yngve screams, Henning takes a long step towards Ingvild to stop her, but she sees him, her eyes widen and she holds the mobile in front of her, waving it at him, pressing it; sparks fly, and he stops and retreats.

'What do you think you're doing?' Yngve howls.

'*You* killed that *whore*,' Ingvild hisses. 'Yes, you, Yngve. If only you had stayed away from her, none of this would have happened. You killed Stefan too, you drove him to take his own life –'

'Ingvild, it –'

'Oh, stop whining. It's only fair that you get a taste of your own medicine, the same rocks, and that it happens here, in the same place, so you can die in the same way as your mistress, that *whore* –'

'It wasn't –'

'Oh, shut up.'

411

Ingvild has picked up another rock, she is foaming at the mouth and her eyes shine with hatred. Henning doesn't know how to stop her; she waves her mobile maniacally, pointing it at him. Should I call for help, he thinks? No use, they won't get here in time. The rocks are so heavy that a single, well-aimed throw could be the end of Yngve. Henning tries to think of something clever to say, but he can't find the words, he finds nothing, so he shuffles his feet on the damp grass. Then he sees Ingvild raise the rock above her head and aim.

'It's because you fucked her, you bastard. I know I haven't been a wife to you for a long time, I have been a zombie ever since I was raped, but you should have helped me, you should have helped me, you shit, you shouldn't have raped my soul, and worst of all, worst of all, you shouldn't have driven our son insane. I know, I know how he felt when he stood here, like me, holding the stone over his head, when he aimed it at that whore who ruined everything.'

'But I never slept with Henriette.' Yngve yelps and squeezes his eyes shut. Henning raises his arms in an impotent effort to defend himself against her, even though she is standing several metres away from him and he, too, shuts his eyes, and waits for the thud and the scream.

It never comes.

He opens his eyes again. Ingvild is still holding the stone above her head. She is gasping for air.

'I swear I never slept with Henriette.'

Yngve's voice is pitiful, on the brink of tears. Then Henning hears movement behind him.

'No. But you did sleep with *me*.'

Henning spins around. And, for the second time in less than an hour, he is looking straight into the eyes of Anette Skoppum.

Chapter 65

If there is a God, then he has just pressed the pause button. Henning's jaw drops. Anette enters and looks at them all in turn.

'Sorry, Juul,' she says. 'My curiosity got the better of me.'

He looks at her without blinking.

'W-who are you?' Ingvild says.

'I'm the woman your husband had sex with.'

She says it straight out, no embarrassment, no anger, presents it as a purely factual matter. And Henning knows he isn't the only one who is dumbstruck.

'But –' Ingvild's voice is devoid of strength.

'I can see why Stefan thought it was Henriette. I mean, look at me, I'm not a patch on her. Her script, too, made it obvious, I would have thought.'

Anette looks at Yngve. He stares at the ground, shamefaced. A tear rolls down his cheek. His hair, what little he has, is bathed in sweat.

'And Henriette was a huge flirt, everyone knew that. She could charm the birds off the trees, if she put her mind to it.'

They all look at Yngve, who sighs and shakes his head.

'It wasn't very easy, for any of us, in the time after . . . after what happened to Ingvild. It hadn't been that good before, and afterwards, well, it was completely impossible to live together as man and wife. Every time I came near you, you would move away, you almost shuddered when I, your husband, came near you.'

Yngve looks at her.

'Physical contact was an unknown concept. And then I met Henriette . . .'

He shakes his head again.

'She was beautiful, full of life, clever, and yes, she flirted and I won't deny that she stirred feelings in me, which I thought were long dead. But I didn't want to destroy the trust between us. After all, I was her tutor, her supervisor, and I couldn't –'

Foldvik looks at them in turn. His eyes stop at Anette. Henning can see that Foldvik is consumed by remorse.

Anette takes another step inside. She, too, is soaked to the skin. Henning wonders what made her come back. He can understand her being curious, but why drop such a bombshell?

Of course. To put things into perspective. If Ingvild had killed her husband for having had an affair with Henriette, the truth – when it came out later – would

415

have destroyed Ingvild completely. How can you live with the knowledge that your own son killed the wrong woman and you killed your husband because he recklessly drove your son mad?

Ingvild looks like she has a puncture. Her shoulders sag, her back is hunched, her eyes are swollen. Henning looks at Anette. She is much smarter than he had assumed.

'I'm sorry, Ingvild,' Anette continues. 'I never meant for this to happen. It just did. I had been working on an idea for a long time, I had written quite a good storyline, too, which I wanted Yngve to take a look at. I knew that he had helped Henriette secure an option with Spot the Difference Productions, and thought he might be able to help me as well. Alcohol was involved, I won't deny it, but we chatted in his office, and –'

'Anette, don't –'

Yngve closes his eyes. Anette holds up her hands.

'No, I won't go on. I just want to apologise. For the harm I've caused you. If I had known what it would lead to, then –'

She is about to complete the sentence, but breaks off. She, too, is crying now. She steps towards Ingvild, bends down and places her hand on her back. At that moment, Ingvild's arm shoots out. Henning doesn't see it until it is too late, but Ingvild has got her mobile out and presses it against Anette's neck. Zzzzzzt. She gives Anette a shock which floors her. Henning is about to jump on Ingvild to prevent her from releasing more hatred, from taking it out on Anette, who lies unconscious on the grass, face down. But Ingvild holds out her hands as she gets up. She says nothing, she just looks straight ahead with that faraway expression and lets the mobile drop. It lands right next to Anette.

'You can call the police now,' Ingvild says to him, quietly. The look in her eyes is dull, vacant. Henning stares at her for a long time before he takes his mobile out of his wet jacket pocket, wipes the display and sees that he has a signal.

Then he calls Bjarne Brogeland.

Chapter 66

Brogeland arrives quickly with a team of police officers. Henning recognises Ella Sandland. He half expects to see the towering figure of Chief Inspector Gjerstad appear and scratch his moustache, but he isn't there. Nor is Assistant Commissioner Nøkleby.

The police start processing the tent and its contents. Sandland takes Ingvild away. Other officers start to dig out Yngve Foldvik. Two ambulance men attend to Anette. Brogeland comes over to him with his eyebrows raised.

'You've got good instincts, Juul, I'll grant you that,' he says, placing a hand on Henning's shoulder. Henning isn't used to being complimented, nor does he like praise, but he mutters a thank you. He becomes aware that his clothes are sticking to his body and loosens his shirt and trousers a little.

'Now don't you go running off again,' Brogeland smiles. 'We need to go through this properly, and we're not doing it by phone this time.'

'I'll be outside,' Henning says.

It has stopped raining when he goes outside and into

the fresh air. The wind is chilly. He hadn't realised that his cheeks were warm, but the icy breeze feels pleasant against his damp, burning hot face. I'm going to get a cold, he thinks. He is soaked to the skin. So what? It's not like it matters.

He takes out his mobile and rings Iver Gundersen. Gundersen answers immediately.

'Hi, Iver, it's me,' he says.

'Hi.'

Gundersen doesn't know yet, Henning thinks.

'Are you at work?'

'Yes.

'Are you in front of the computer?'

'Yep.'

'Do you fancy a scoop?'

Silence.

'A scoop?'

'Yep. A scoop. Yes or no. If not, I'll call someone else.'

Henning can hear Iver splutter.

'No, I, or I mean, yes. Yes, of course I want a scoop. Where the hell are you, eh, what's happening?'

Henning takes a deep breath of good solid north wind through his nostrils. Lovely.

'These are my terms. You can ask questions, but not why I want it done in this way. Is that clear?'

'Henning, I –'

'Is that clear?'

'Christ, Henning, yes, it's clear.'

Henning grins. He is allowed to have a bit of fun at Gundersen's expense.

'Okay, get ready,' he says.

And he starts with the headline.

Henning wanders up and down while he talks to Gundersen, sneaks a peek at Ingvild and Yngve while Brogeland and his team carry out preliminarily interviews outside the tent. Ingvild and Yngve Foldvik are each wrapped in a blanket. They don't make eye contact with the police officers who are talking to them.

They don't look at anyone.

By the time Brogeland beckons him over, it is early afternoon. Traffic has intensified on the Common, newspaper and TV vans have arrived, a crowd of onlookers have gathered, wondering what kind of evil has happened in the tent this time. He doesn't blame them. He would probably be curious, too. And they will be even more shocked when they read *123news* later today, if Gundersen has the brains to make sense of the facts and the chronology.

'Okay, let's walk,' Brogeland says. Henning follows him away from the others.

'What do you think about all this?' Brogeland asks him.

'What do you mean?'

'Is it the end of civilisation as we know it?'

'I don't know,' Henning says.

'Me neither. Jesus Christ,' Brogeland exclaims, shaking his head. 'Can you imagine what kind of future the two of them will have?'

'No.'

'Nor can I.'

'How is Anette doing?'

'She'll make a quick recovery.'

'Are you taking her to the hospital?'

'No need.'

They walk on. Above them, the clouds move swiftly. The temperature is dropping. His clothes no longer stick to his body.

'Have you found out what killed Stefan yet?' he asks. They are heading back to the tent now. Brogeland shakes his head.

'It's too early to say, but everything suggests an overdose of pills and alcohol.'

'So his death is no longer suspicious?'

'No, doesn't look like it.'

'Does that mean you haven't requested the full range of tests?'

'It's not my decision, but, yes, I imagine he'll go to the back of the queue.'

'Mm.'

Henning looks around. A cameraman from TV2

hoists his camera on to his shoulder. A reporter checks his notes before rehearsing his presentation, off-camera.

'It's a bit odd that Stefan was naked, don't you think?' Henning remarks, when the reporter has finished. Brogeland turns to him.

'Hm?'

'Why do you think Stefan was naked?'

'Not entirely sure. He had a thing about symbolism. Perhaps it was his way of saying that the cycle was complete.'

'Born naked, die naked, you mean?'

'Yes.'

A reasonable interpretation, Henning thinks.

'But how did Stefan know that Henriette would be in the tent that evening? Was there any mobile phone activity between them?'

'Not that I remember. Don't think so.'

'So how did he know?'

Brogeland ponders this for a while.

'Perhaps they had a verbal agreement?'

'About what? Stefan wasn't involved with Henriette's film.'

'No, I know. No idea. Anyway, somehow he knew. We'll never get the answer to that now.'

Henning nods, slowly. The question irks him. He doesn't like puzzles with missing pieces. He always ends up staring at the gaping hole.

'Quite a comeback for you,' Brogeland says, as they stroll on.

'What do you mean?'

'This case. But it's just up your street, isn't it? You like going it alone?'

Henning looks at Brogeland and wonders what has prompted this shift in tone.

'What are you saying?'

'Gjerstad told me about the Nigerian women,' Brogeland confronts Henning. His smile has gone. 'Gjerstad told me about the story you wrote, your interview with the killer.'

Henning nods and smiles. Oh, Gjerstad.

'Did Gjerstad tell you the whole story?'

He waits for Brogeland's reaction, but it never comes.

'Did he tell you that I did the interview and gave the guy the publicity he wanted on one condition?'

Henning pauses for effect.

'What condition was that?'

'That he would stop killing Nigerian women, or indeed killing anyone at all. It's a pipedream to believe the police can prevent prostitution in Oslo. It's the equivalent of telling kids to stop eating sweets. There is a reason why it's called the world's oldest profession. Did Gjerstad say anything about how many more women the man murdered?'

Brogeland doesn't reply.

'No, exactly. And I couldn't have handed him over to the police, either, because I never met him. We spoke on the telephone – twice – and both times, he called me. I never took the trouble to find out where he was calling from, because I knew it would be a waste of time. Besides, he was nicked a couple of months later. For something else.'

Henning visualises Arild Gjerstad, remembers some of the rows they have had, the blatant antipathy and contempt in his eyes. I may be prejudiced, he thinks, but I'm a tyro compared to Gjerstad.

'Okay, I –'

'Forget it.'

'But I –'

'Gjerstad doesn't like journalists, Bjarne, and I'm his least favourite person. That's just how it is.'

'No, but I –'

'Leave it. It's not important.'

Brogeland looks at him. Then he nods, quietly.

Chapter 67

When Henning arrives at the office an hour later, he senses immediately that the mood has changed. Yes, it's a Friday, and Fridays have their own momentum, but it's like Christmas has come early. He can tell from people's smiles, hear it in their carefree laughter, see it in the relaxed way a woman moves, as he passes her on the stairs.

He walks down the narrow corridor and into the kitchenette, where the coffee machine stands strangely abandoned. It is just after 3 p.m. There are still plenty of people around. Kåre Hjeltland is hovering behind a journalist at the news desk, as usual.

'Henning!' he shouts, when their eyes meet. He gives the journalist some instructions and races to the kitchenette. Henning takes a step back in anticipation of Kåre's impact, so as not to be knocked over. Heidi crosses behind Kåre. She sees them, but she doesn't join them.

'Have you seen Iver's story?' Kåre roars.

'Eh, no?'

'He has solved the Hagerup case. The stoning, all of

it. I believe there was a showdown in the tent at Ekeberg Common earlier today. Bloody hell. Our hits are GOING THROUGH THE ROOF! Fuck, FUCK!'

Kåre laughs out loud and slaps Henning on the shoulder, hard.

'Are you coming with us after work? We've got to celebrate this.'

Henning hesitates.

'It's Friday, for God's sake.'

'Is Iver coming?'

Not that it would make a difference either way, but he prefers to know.

'No. He's on *17.30* on Radio 4 later today. Got to stay sober. And he has a TV talk show afterwards, I don't remember which one, ha-ha.'

At that moment, Gundersen comes out from the lavatory. He wipes his wet hands on his worn, slightly mucky jeans, but stops mid-movement when he sees Henning. They look at each other. Kåre shouts something Henning fails to hear. He looks at Gundersen, who nods cautiously. There is gratitude in his eyes combined with a strange mix of respect and wonder.

'Some other time,' Henning says to Kåre. 'I'm meeting someone.'

'Oh, no,' Kåre exclaims. 'What a shame.'

Gundersen starts walking in their direction, but passes them without saying anything. His eyes flicker as he scratches his stubble. Henning smiles to himself.

'Got to go,' he says, looking at Kåre.

'Okay. See you on Monday.'

When he steps outside, the afternoon has turned colder, more merciless. He wraps his jacket tightly around his body. He is walking towards the black gate, wondering where the nearest off-licence is, when he hears a voice.

'Juul!'

He turns around. The voice belongs to a man Henning recognises. The sun reflects in his sunglasses. Now that Ray-Ban is close to him, he sees what Gunnar Goma saw when he peered out through his spyhole. The hair looks like it has been painted on to his skull. The pattern resembles corn circles. A thick, shiny chain dangles around his neck. He wears a black leather jacket, which undoubtedly has a flame motif on its back.

'Do you see that car over there?' the man says, indicating a black car outside the gate. 'Go over to it. If you scream or try anything, we'll kill your mum.'

He receives a persuasive nudge to his chest. Henning starts to move. He glances from side to side, looking for faces, but he sees no one he can wink or make a hidden gesture to. His pulse is throbbing in his neck. He is walking, but he can't feel the ground.

What the hell do I do now, he thinks?

The man in the driver's seat stares at him as Henning approaches the car. His left arm leans on the windowsill. One finger is bandaged. Gunnar Goma doesn't miss a trick, Henning thinks, although he hasn't picked up anything remotely camp about the men.

'Drive,' orders the man, who sits down next to Henning in the rear. The car accelerates. Henning is forced back into his seat. The car hums contentedly, but he is incapable of paying attention it, the people or the surroundings they pass. Again he thinks that he ought to alert someone, signal that he is being kidnapped, but what will happen to his mother then? And what's going to happen to him?

'We're on our way.'

The driver is talking into a small microphone. He wears an earpiece.

What do you do when you can see no future? Henning has asked himself that question many times in the last two years, standing in the shadow, feeling it was about to swallow him up. There are no comforting words like when he was little and his mum would kiss everything better and he would know it was all going to be all right; there is nothing. Calm down, it will pass. The fear is paralysing, like frost. Floating on the gentle sea won't help you now, Henning. The only one who can, is you.

But how? What do you do? What do you say?

They haven't been driving for long, but before he realises where they are the car has disappeared into a car wash. It grows dark around them. The car has stopped, but nobody gets out. Behind them, the door rolls down slowly.

Henning feels a pistol in his side. He hears himself gasp.

'Get out.'

He stares at the weapon, pressed against one of his ribs.

'Get out, I said.'

The voice is deep. Henning opens the door and steps out on to a wet concrete floor. It smells the way it always does in a car wash. A mixture of humidity and some indeterminate detergent. But there are no other cars around. And it isn't an automatic one, where you drive the car in yourself and the machine does all the work, apart from wash the car properly.

The door closes with a bang and the walls echo. Why didn't I say anything about this to Bjarne, he wonders, why didn't I say that I had unfinished business with Bad Boys Burning, that they had been to my flat and stolen my computer, that they've been following me? Brogeland had already mentioned it. That these guys were hardcore. Christ, even Nora warned me.

Nora, he thinks. Will I ever see you again?

A door opens. Henning sees a glass cage. A man comes out, smiling.

'Henning,' he says, as though he is greeting an old friend. Henning doesn't reply. He merely looks at the smiling man.

'I've many names, but everyone calls me Hassan,' he says, holding out his hand. Henning takes it and squeezes it. Hard. Hassan's smile reveals a gold tooth in the upper row of otherwise healthy teeth and gums. He wears a vest and has a gold chain around his neck. Henning stares at the tattoos on Hassan's arms. There is a green frog on one and a black scorpion on the other. Frogs live on land and in water. At night, they prefer to be on dry land. They hunt invertebrates there. During the day, they hide from predators in shaded and damp places. Scorpions are mainly nocturnal. And they have a vicious sting.

Hassan strokes his beard.

'So,' he says, circling Henning. 'Perhaps you know why you're here?'

Henning gestures towards his wet clothes.

'I don't suppose I'm here to have a shower.'

Hassan laughs out loud. The sound sets off a hollow echo around the walls. Hassan looks at his men while he carries on moving.

'You've been making things difficult for me,' Hassan

430

says, without looking at him. Henning stands motionless on the floor, concentrating on his breathing. He is only just holding it together; at any moment he could crumple, lose contact with the ground and collapse. His thoughts are all over the place, he tries to contain them, but he is paralysed by an overwhelming feeling of loneliness. Perhaps it's meant to be this way, he thinks, it's what he has coming. What he deserves. No one is on his side when push comes to shove.

Don't show your fear, he tells himself. Don't let them see you at your most pathetic, stripped of honour and dignity. If you're about to die, then go out with your head held high.

The thoughts are like a kick up the backside. And that's why he says:

'I've worked it out.'

Hassan stops

'You have?'

'Yes, it wasn't difficult. Yasser Shah, one of your thugs, is wanted by the police because he killed Tariq Marhoni. It's not easy being you right now with so much heat around. Have you seen *Heat*, Hassan? Al Pacino and Robert De Niro?'

Hassan smiles, but shakes his head. He starts circling him again.

'A classic. The point is, if you want to be a successful criminal, don't fill your life with anything you aren't willing to leave in thirty seconds, if it gets too hot. And you have no plans to leave, have you, Hassan?'

Hassan laughs briefly, but he doesn't reply.

'Then we have a problem.'

Hassan looks at Henning.

'We?'

'Surely you're not dumb enough to kill me, just because Yasser Shah didn't do his job properly?'

Hassan's steps shorten. Henning decides to keep talking while Hassan reviews his options.

'Yasser Shah is on the run from the police, who can link Tariq Marhoni's brother to you, and it doesn't take much imagination to work out that they'll turn the heat up on you from now on. You see, Mahmoud Marhoni is about to be released from custody. Detective Inspector Brogeland told me so an hour ago. Do you know what else he told me?'

Henning doesn't wait for a response.

'He said that Mahmoud has enough evidence to bring you down. In which case, is it a stupid or a smart move to kill a journalist, even though he witnessed a killing you ordered?'

'One killing more or less makes very little difference,' Hassan says brusquely and looks to the others for confirmation. 'Besides, no one will ever find you.'

'No, perhaps not. But if you think it's going to make your life easier, you're wrong. You drug dealers bumping

432

each other off is one thing. Most people don't have a problem with that. But murdering a journalist – now that's something else. We journalists aren't always popular, far from it, and many people would happily tell you that they loathe us, but deep down, I think they're glad that we exist. And, if anyone kills a reporter or makes him disappear because he was doing his job, there'll be hell to pay, believe you me. The police already know you've taken an interest in me and, if you think it's bad now, then wait and see what happens from tomorrow onwards, when they start looking for me. Brogeland offered me protection against you, but I declined. Do you know why? Because I've no intention of going into hiding or looking over my shoulder for the rest of my life and because I don't think you're stupid enough to make it worse for yourself by hurting me. But if you want to kill me, Hassan, then do it now, don't hesitate. You'll be doing me a huge favour.'

His voice sounds thick against the walls. His heart is pounding. He looks at Hassan, who is still prowling around. His shoes make soft, slurping noises against the wet floor. The rest of the gang are following their boss with their eyes.

'What happened to your face?' Hassan asks after a while.

Henning sighs. Perhaps it's right that Jonas is here now, he thinks. My lovely, lovely boy. He remembers

433

the leap through the flames, how he tried to shield his face with his hands and arms, his hair which caught fire, the burning and the stinging, Jonas's eyes when he saw him, how he helped extinguish the flames before they got to them.

He remembers them standing on the balcony, greedy flames chasing them from the living room, he remembers how Jonas looked to him for support and safety, the words he said to him, words he will never forget, *it'll be fine, don't be scared, I'll take care of you*, he remembers how they climbed up on the top rail of the balcony, he grabbed hold of his son's hand, looked into his eyes and said it was only a little jump and they would be safe, but it was so cold, it had been raining for days, the railing was slippery, he felt it as he climbed it, but he thought that it didn't matter what happened to him, as long as I save Jonas, I need to land first, so I can cushion his fall, Jonas can land anywhere on me, it doesn't matter as long as he survives, and Jonas resisted, he cried, he said he didn't want to, he was too scared, but Henning made him, his voice became strict, he said that they had to, or they would both die, he promised they would go fishing next weekend, just the two of them, once they were back on the ground, and finally Jonas nodded, shedding tears of bravery, he pulled himself together, he was a big boy. Henning's eyes were stinging and he struggled to find his way, but he had to make it, had to be in front and do all he could do to save his son. He climbed up on the railing, he balanced on the top, he grabbed hold of Jonas's trembling hands, lifted him up, reassured him once more, those damn words, but when he looked down, when he tried to look down, he got dizzy, everything started spinning, there was a smell of burning from the flat or perhaps it was coming from his own face, smoke was pouring from the balcony door, which they had left open, but it was now or never, they had to jump, he took a small step to steady himself, only to discover there was nothing under his feet, the railing was gone, so was his hold, so was the child in his arms, Jonas, where the hell is Jonas, he couldn't see anything, his eyes were stuck together, and he floated, he fell towards the ground, anticipated the impact, felt it even before it came; he was trapped by a wall of darkness, and he saw nothing, he felt nothing, he sensed nothing, everything was darkness, the darkness was total.

He had never seen darkness before. Never seen what the darkness could conceal.

But he saw it then.

Jonas was scared of the dark.

How he loved Jonas.

Jonas.

'My flat burned down,' he says, quietly. 'Do you have children, Hassan?'

435

Hassan shakes his head and scoffs.

'Not going to have any, either.'

Henning nods.

'Let's get it over with,' he says, filled with serenity. He is ready. It doesn't matter. Let eternity come. Hassan stops right in front of him. He takes out a pistol. He raises it, making sure that Henning has seen it, and presses it against his forehead.

And now the darkness returns, the darkness I've been waiting for, where dawn never breaks, where voices fall silent, dreams are still and the flames have gone. Come to me. Take me to the land of the dead, but please, let there be someone waiting for me.

He waits for a bang, or maybe just a puff or a pop, if Hassan uses a silencer. Henning wonders if he will hear anything before his head explodes in a mass of blood and brains. Death is terrible, but at least it takes away the pain.

The pressure against his forehead disappears. Henning opens his eyes and looks into Hassan's. Hassan has lowered his arm.

'Okay,' he says, taking a step closer and coming right up to him.

'But if they catch Yasser,' he hisses, 'and there's a trial and you're the prosecution's only witness, we'll come back for you. Understand? We may not even offer you a lift first.'

He takes a step backwards, makes a cutting movement across his throat with the pistol. Henning
swallows, hard. They stand there, looking at each
other. For a long time.

'Understand?'

Henning nods.

He understands.

'Open the door,' Hassan orders one of the men,
while still looking at Henning.

'But –'

'Just do it.'

The man shuffles along the concrete. He presses a
button. The door protests as it rolls open, but it only
sounds loud because of the silence in the hall. Henning
looks at Hassan as the space fills with light again. Still
tough. And Henning doesn't doubt for a second that
Hassan means what he says.

The door has rolled back completely and stops with
a bang.

'My computer,' Henning says. 'Can I have it back?'

Hassan jerks his head towards one of the men, who
obeys, but with disapproval in his eyes. A few seconds
later he comes back and shoves Henning's computer
into his arms.

When Henning is back outside and walking on dry
tarmac again, a smart Alfa Romeo sweeps past him.
He turns and looks at the car wash. The door slowly

closes again. What a strange sight. Bad Boys Burning, standing together, watching him. They look tough. Hardcore. They would make a good CD sleeve, he thinks, for a band about to release its final album. And it feels very quiet and empty, when the door has rolled all the way down and he can no longer see them.

Chapter 68

Someone is having sex. Just as he is about to stick his key in the lock in his mother's front door, Henning realises – to his considerable relief – that the noise is coming from a television. Thank God, it's from a television. And thank God, it's not coming from his mother's television, but from her neighbour's, from Karl's.

Karl is the building's caretaker. Karl likes porn. Henning has never said anything to his mother, but he thinks Karl fancies her. If she, against all expectation, were to discover this for herself one day, he hopes she won't bear him any further grudges for failing to steer her in the direction of Karl's arms in her old age. Something tells him such a set-up might be a little uncomfortable, though it isn't a thought he intends to pursue.

As always when he visits his mother, he is nearly suffocated by blue fug. The shade of her wallpaper is Marlboro. If anyone ever dared to wash her ceiling, the suds would be brown bubbles of ancient nicotine and tar. Henning realises how pleased he is that he no longer smokes. Because his flat would have looked exactly the same.

He picks up the shopping bags, all six of them, and goes into the living room. He can hear the radio, he can't avoid hearing it, it is always on. Christine Juul sits in the kitchen, as usual, smoking. She barely raises her eyes from the newspaper when she sees her son.

'Hi, Mum,' he calls out to drown the noise from the radio. The return of the prodigal son. But no tearful embraces await him. She looks at the bags he is holding. He deliberately shows her the brown bag from the off-licence first.

'About time too,' she barks. He ignores her remark, enters the kitchen and opens the fridge. The bottles clink. And he knows it's her favourite sound. He unpacks groceries, milk, cheese, sugar, bread and so on, while he steals a glance. She looks unchanged. She is wearing the smoke-stained trousers which were once white, a smoke-stained blouse, which was once pale yellow and a brown cardigan because it's cold. And it's cold, because she is airing the flat. Thank God, she has opened the windows.

'How are you?' he says.

'Bad.'

'Oh? Any news?'

'News?'

She grunts. It would have been quicker to check her

medical records before I came here, he thinks, and smiles to himself.

There is a debate on the radio. It takes him a minute, while he puts away the shopping, to work out that she is listening to *17.30*. He shouldn't be surprised when he hears Iver Gundersen's voice, and yet he feels a little bit excited. He listens to the presenter:

So, Iver Gundersen, it was you who solved this case earlier today, what do you think will happen now? Do you think Norway will pay more attention to sharia from now on?

No, Andreas, I don't think so. I think most people understand that this won't be something that happens every day in Norway, no matter how many Muslims come here. It might raise our awareness of what sharia actually is. I think we can all benefit from that.

Good boy, Henning thinks. He is about to ask his mother to turn down the volume, but he knows she won't, so he tries to block out the sound. He watches her try but fail to unscrew the top of a bottle of St Hallvard. He takes the bottle from her and removes the top in a nanosecond. He finds a shot glass from a cupboard above the kitchen counter and places it in front of her. You can pour your own drink, he thinks. And he sees how her hands tremble and she spills as she does so. Bloody hell, how she shakes.

He is consumed by a mixture of compassion and

anger. He sighs as he watches her swallow the first big mouthful. She closes her eyes, he sees the viscous liquid warm her from the roof of her mouth to her throat and down into her chest. And he is absolutely sure that this is her best moment today, perhaps for several days.

The radio presenter moves on to the next story.

Justice Minister, Trine Juul-Osmundsen, is courting controversy again.

His mother turns up the volume. Henning wants to scream.

She wants to limit the automatic right to appeal in cases where the defendant has been sentenced to more than two years imprisonment, allegedly as part of an efficiency drive. Her proposal has been met with considerable resistance from some members of the opposition. With us in the studio today, we have Karianne Larsåsen from Venstre, who believes that –

She turns down the volume. Thank God, he thinks.

'Bloody journalists,' she mutters. He stops in his tracks, he is about to say something, but changes his mind. What's the point? He shuts the fridge with an impotent gesture and looks around. Crumbs, mixed with cigarette ash, litter the floor. Everywhere. He can see the dust on the television from the kitchen. The living room, which consists of a brown three-seater sofa, a Stressless with a foot stool in front of it, a dark wooden dining table and Hessian wallpaper, appears tidy, but he knows what it really looks like under the table, in the pile of the red Persian carpet, under the three-seater and under the TV unit.

He starts by fetching the Hoover from a hallway cupboard and switches it on. He quickly hoovers the hallway, the small narrow bathroom, the bedroom and whirls his way through the living room. He is about to take the mouthpiece off the Hoover and suck up dust around the fireplace, when something on the marble mantelpiece catches his eye.

The mantelpiece is covered with pictures. He has seen them a hundred times before. Photographs of his mother, when she still was his mother, his parents on their wedding day, pictures of Trine, Trine and her husband, Pål Fredrik, when they got married, pictures of Trine and Henning together when they were kids, on the pebble beach by their cabin.

And he sees a photograph of Jonas.

He picks it up and studies it. Jonas smiles at the photographer. It is taken around Christmas. He knows this because there are Christmas cards on the wall behind Jonas's blond curls, on a green silk ribbon. Instead of lining all the cards up on the mantelpiece, they would hang them on a silk ribbon with paperclips and create a Christmas-tree shape of good wishes.

Jonas was three years old when the photograph was taken. Henning doesn't remember the occasion, but

Jonas's smile is filled with pre-Christmas anticipation. He looks at the picture for a long time while the Hoover hums next to him. He is unable to put it down.

He doesn't know how long he has been standing there, but it's a long time. He snaps out of his trance when his mother demonstratively turns up the volume on the radio to drown out the Hoover. That's enough, he thinks, and puts the picture back.

But not face down.

Chapter 69

After his one-hour visit to his mother, he buys an economy-sized box of batteries. As he leaves the shop, he sees how Sofienberg Park is filling up with happy people enjoying their Friday. His mobile beeps. He opens the message while he walks and sees, to his great surprise, that it is from Anette.

You still alive?

He smiles to himself and types a reply.

Just about. Am tempted to ask you the same question. How are you?

He strolls on, still holding his mobile, while he watches people spread picnic rugs, unpack barbecue trays and unfold deckchairs. Anette replies swiftly. His mobile simultaneously vibrates and beeps in the palm of his hand. Four short beeps.

A bit groggy, but all right.

He has never been zapped with a stun gun. He hopes he never will, either. And he is convinced that Anette will never forget it.

He sends another text:

I'm hungry. Do you fancy a bite to eat somewhere?

He presses 'send', and hopes that Anette won't misinterpret his message. He just feels the need to talk about what has happened. And he is genuinely hungry, he has barely eaten these last few days.

His mobile beeps again.

Yes, please. Am starving. Fontés in Løkka? They do good food.

He texts her straight away.

Great. See you there.

He snaps the mobile shut and speeds up. She's right, he says to himself. Their food is good. And decides he has also earned himself a beer.

After all, it is Friday.

He has managed to down his first beer before Anette arrives. He is sitting near the fireplace, where a log fire is blazing like a small furnace, despite the June evening, and where people walk up and down the stairs to get to the toilets. He has doubts about the fire, but it was the only vacant table.

He waves at her. Anette spots him immediately and smiles as she walks towards him. He gets up. She hugs him.

It has been a long time since anyone hugged him.

They sit down. The waiter, a tall dark guy with the whitest teeth Henning has ever seen, is quick off the mark and takes their order.

'A Fontés burger with bacon. And the biggest beer

you've got,' Anette says and smiles. Someone is breathing a sigh of relief, Henning thinks.

'And one for me, too,' he says. 'Both, I mean.'

The waiter nods and leaves. Clumsy, Henning groans inwardly, expressing myself like that. He feels awkward. Even though his intentions are strictly honourable, it's like they are on a date. And that's an uncomfortable scenario.

'So,' she says, looking at him. 'Did it make a good story?'

'It'll do,' he says. 'At least, I think so. I didn't write it myself. Didn't have the energy.'

'So you got some poor sod to do it for you?'

'Something like that.'

'It's much more fun to write yourself.'

'I thought you wanted to be a director?'

'Yes, but the best directors are often the best writers. Quentin Tarantino, for example. Oliver Stone. I was about to mention Clint Eastwood, but I don't believe he writes very much himself, now that I think about it. Did you know that Clint Eastwood composes practically all his own film scores?'

'No.'

'Now you do. And very good scores they are too. Very jazzy, a lot of piano.'

Henning likes jazzy. And a lot of piano. They look at each other without saying anything.

447

'What will happen to the film now?' he asks, and immediately kicks himself for bringing up the subject so soon.

'Which one of them?'

'Well, both.'

'Please can we not talk about that? My best friend is dead, she was killed by a lunatic I wish I had never met, and the last thing I want to think about is what happens to the film. Or films. Right now, all I want to do is eat my burger. I don't give a toss about anything else.'

He nods. Anette looks for the waiter. There. Eye contact. The waiter nods and makes an apologetic movement with his hands.

'Has Bjarne been grilling you?' Henning asks.

'I'm well done on both sides.'

'Was he okay? Did he treat you all right?'

'Oh, yes. Nice and easy. I should expect to be interviewed again, but that's fine. I understand.'

The waiter brings their much-needed drinks. Anette thanks him, swallows a large mouthful and licks off the foam which has settled on her upper lip.

'Ah, a life saver.'

Henning takes his own glass and twirls it around. He sits like this for a while.

'It was me who found him,' he suddenly says. He doesn't know where that sentence came from. He just blurted it out.

'Stefan?'

'Mm. I wasn't supposed to be there, but I had some questions for Yngve. The Foldviks weren't at home, but the front door was open, and I –'

He looks down.

'Did you go inside?'

He looks up again and nods. 'Have you ever visited them?'

Anette takes another sip.

'I had a meeting with Stefan there once – now when was it? Six months ago or something like that. We chatted about his script.'

'Which you were turning into a film?'

'Precisely.'

'And that was the only time?'

She takes another sip and nods.

'We e-mailed and chatted occasionally after that, stuff to do with the film. Which was some way into the future. Everything in the film industry is. To begin with, you meet to agree to have a meeting, and when that meeting comes, you agree to meet another time to have another meeting about meeting up.'

She rolls her eyes. He smiles.

'Why do you ask about that?'

'Oh, I was just curious.'

'Can I ask you a question?'

'Go on.'

'What happened to you?'

She points to his face, to his scars.

'Oh, that.'

He stares down at the table.

'You don't have to tell me,' Anette says, tenderly.

'No, it's just that –'

He twirls his glass again.

'Several people have asked me that recently. I don't really know what to say without –'

He stops and visualises the balcony once more, Jonas's eyes, feels his hands which suddenly aren't there. It's as if he is in a soundproof room with no light. He looks up at her.

'Another time, perhaps.'

Anette holds up her hands.

'Sorry, I didn't mean to –'

'No, no. It's fine.'

Anette looks at him for a long time before she takes another sip of her beer. They drink in silence, watch the diners, watch the door whenever it opens, gaze at the flames.

A question, which has been troubling him, resurfaces.

'Why did you come back?' he says. 'Why did you go to the tent?'

Anette swallows and suppresses a burp.

'Like I said to you: I was curious. You were obviously

up to something. Your face gave it all away. You should have seen yourself. I'm used to thinking in stories and I realised that a very good one was happening right under my nose. It was too tempting not to go back.'

He nods slowly.

'Sorry, I didn't mean to spy on you.'

'How long were you outside before you came in?'

'Not very long. But listen, I've already been through this with that policeman, Brunlanes, or whatever his name is.'

'Brogeland,' Henning corrects her. 'Sorry, I'm just a bit –'

It's his turn to hold up his hands.

'I'm a bit all over the place after a day like today.'

He makes a circular gesture with his finger next to his temple.

'No worries,' she says, mimicking an Australian accent. 'Cheers.'

She raises her glass. They drink.

'What are we drinking to?' he asks.

'That no more lives were lost,' she says and swallows. 'Cheers.'

Chapter 70

They agree to forget about the Foldviks while they eat their Creole-inspired hamburgers with potato boats or potato wedges or whatever they are called. He eats far too much and wolfs his food down. The beer settles like a fermenting layer on the top of his stomach. When they eventually leave, after Henning has paid the bill, he knows he is in troubled waters.

But then again, he likes the sea.

'Thanks for dinner,' Anette says, as they go outside into the June evening. It has started to rain again, tiny, spitting drops.

'My pleasure.'

'Fancy a couple of these?' she says. He lets go of the door, which slams shut behind him. Anette is holding out a bag of Knott sweets.

'These are great after a few beers.'

She pours some of the white, brown and grey pearls into her hand and tips them into her mouth. He smiles and says:

'Yes, please.'

He holds out his hand and gets his own stash. Knott.

Oh, great sweet of my childhood! He has consumed his fair share of them over the years, but he dreads to think how long ago it is since he last tasted the tiny flavour explosions. He takes a brown one, smacks his lips and nods at her with approval.

'You need to eat them all at once. That's what makes them so great.'

He looks at the seven or eight pastilles, if he can call them that, and raises his hand to his mouth. He grins as he does it. One pastille escapes and rolls back into his palm. He looks at the tiny, white, round sweet while he chews and crunches and munches. It looks like a small, white pill.

A small pill, a small, round, white pill.

Small, white –

Oh, hell.

He chews and swallows, never taking his eyes off Anette. She shakes the bag, pours more sweets into her palm and shoves them in her mouth. He looks at the sweets and remembers what Jarle Høgseth always used to say, that the devil is in the detail. It's a huge cliché, but now as he stands there, looking at the white sweet, it's as if the sneaking feeling that has nagged him ever since he stared into Stefan's expressionless eyes, the hook that stirred in his stomach, suddenly takes hold and rips him open.

'What is it?' Anette says. Henning is incapable of

speech. He just stares at her, remembering the white powder under his shoe, the small, round, white pill on the floor in Stefan's bedroom, how the shape and the smell of the pill reminded him of something. He remembers the curtains that were closed, the door which wasn't shut properly.

'Don't you like them?' she asks, still smiling. He is aware that he is nodding. He tries to see if her eyes reveal anything. The mirror of the soul, where the truth can be found. But she merely looks back at him. He looks alternately at the sweets and at her.

'Halloooo?'

Anette waves her hand in front of his face. He holds the sweet between his thumb and index finger and smells it.

'What are you doing?' Anette giggles, munching on.

'No, I –'

His voice is feeble, lacking in air. The number 11 tram pulls into Olaf Ryes Square. Its wheels screech. It sounds like a cross between a pig squealing and a sawmill.

'That's my tram,' Anette says and makes to leave. She scrutinises his face. 'Thanks for dinner. Got to run. See you soon.'

She smiles and she is gone. He stands there looking after her. Her backpack bounces up and down as she jogs. He is still staring at her when she boards the blue-

and-white tram. When the doors close and the tram glides down towards the city centre, she takes a window seat and looks back at him.

Her eyes bore into him like sharp teeth.

It takes him forever to walk home. He can barely lift his legs and has to force them to move. All he can think about is Anette's smile as she left, the backpack which she didn't put on properly, which bounced up and down as she started to run and caused the stickers with the names of exotic, faraway places to perform a peculiar dance before his eyes.

He relives it, over and over, while his shoes make dragging noises against the tarmac, crashing like cymbals. The sound rises, gets wings and mixes with the rain, which has increased in intensity, as he passes the queue outside Villa Paradiso. People inside are eating pizza, drinking, smiling, laughing. He tries to concentrate, he recalls Anette's eyes, the relief in them, the degree of satisfaction, only a few hours after she was knocked out by a stun gun. And he hears Tore Benjaminsen mimicking her voice:

What's the point of being a genius if nobody knows?

Anette, he thinks. You might very well be the smartest woman I've ever met. With the taste of Knott still in his mouth, he turns into Seilduksgate with the feeling that he and everybody else have been conned.

Chapter 71

The pleasant feeling he enjoyed only a few hours ago has been sucked out of him. Back then he was elated, pleased with himself, delighted to have got himself a new source and thrown a bone to Iver Gundersen.

Now his steps are heavy like lead.

He reaches his block and wonders if Anette tricked Stefan into believing that she would also kill herself. Was that was why he lay huddled up against the wall? Because she was lying next to him in the narrow bed?

But why?

Again, he is reminded of Tore Benjaminsen, who thought that Anette was ultimately a lesbian, even though she had had several flings with men. Perhaps it's that simple, Henning speculates. Henriette flirted with Anette, who mistakenly believed that Henriette was genuinely interested in her, only to be rejected. Anette had probably been dumped before, like most people, but not *rejected*. Not by someone she loved. And so she experienced, for the very first time, how much it hurt. The thin, dangerous line between love and hate.

A smart woman, he thinks, as he remembers what

she said in the tent: *her script, too, made it obvious*. This makes him wonder if the script might have been Anette's idea. Perhaps it was *she* who insisted on the Gaarder storyline, so everyone would think that Yngve Foldvik had had an affair with Henriette? Foldvik told Henning that the script was written by Henriette, but that Anette was very likely to have had a say in it.

But when did it start, he wonders? When did her plan take shape?

He remembers what she said about her first meeting with Stefan, after he won the script competition. Perhaps the wheels were set in motion that evening? Perhaps she decided to direct his script to get close to him, so she could manipulate him? She would be the woman who realised his dream. And everything in the film industry takes time. There are meetings about meetings about meetings. It would be relatively easy to pull the wool over Stefan's eyes and, anyway, he would be dead by the time the film was completed.

What had she said to him, what words did she use to trigger his rage? Did she say that women like Henriette turn men into rapists who destroy families? It wouldn't be difficult to inflame Stefan with this kind of logic, given what his mother had been subjected to. The more Henning thinks about it, the more he becomes convinced that Anette guided Stefan the whole way. Like a true director.

He is also convinced that they, or perhaps it was only Anette, tried to implicate Mahmoud Marhoni by texting him from Henriette's mobile, just like in the script. The references to infidelity and the photograph on Henriette's e-mail would be hard to explain away. It would be Marhoni's word against a dead woman's text messages. And no one would have a problem believing that Henriette had two-timed him. After all, she was a great flirt. The one everyone wanted. Including Anette.

He sees Stefan's dead face before him, lying in his bed, pressed up against the wall. Did Anette promise to follow him? Did they make a suicide pact? How did she manage to trick him? Didn't he notice that her pills were different? Why –

Hang on. Henning has an idea. And once the thought is in his head, he unlocks his entrance door fast. He takes no notice of his post, he strides up the stairs, ignoring the pain which screams in his hips and his legs. He opens his front door and sets down his laptop on the kitchen table. He climbs up the stepladder, as quickly as he can, and replaces all the batteries, before he takes off his jacket and opens a drawer in a driftwood cupboard. He sifts through receipts, take-away menus, candles, matchboxes, hellish matchboxes, business cards, but they are not what he is looking for. He comes across a bottle of rum, Bacardi, yuk, more takeaway menus, and there, under an old ice hockey scorecard he has kept for some reason, he finds the business card he knew he hadn't thrown away. He stares at it, sees Dr Helge Bruunsgaard's name printed into the white, textured cardboard.

He takes out his mobile, notices that the battery is low, but thinks it should last for the call he is about to make.

The telephone rings for a long time, before Dr Helge replies. Henning's breathing quickens when the familiar voice exuding enthusiasm and optimism says: 'Is that you, Henning?'

'Hi, Helge,' he says.

'How are you? What's it like to be back at work?'

'Er, good. Listen, I'm not calling this late on a Friday evening to talk about myself. I need your help. Your professional help with a story I'm working on. Can I trouble you for a few minutes? I imagine you're on your way home?'

'Yes, I am, but that's all right, Henning. I'm stuck in heavy traffic, there has been an accident, so tell me, what do you want to know?'

Henning tries to organise his thoughts.

'What I'm about to ask you will sound a bit strange. But I promise you, it's not about me, so don't get worried.'

'What is it, Henning? What is it?'

The sudden concern in Dr Helge's voice is lost on Henning. He takes a deep breath.

And asks his question.

The computer boots up, although somewhat reluctantly, and, as usual, takes a minute or thirty to load. Henning paces up and down while he waits for all the pre-installed programs to get ready, though he won't be using them. The clock in the top right-hand corner of the screen shows 21.01 by the time he sits down and double-clicks on the FireCracker 2.0 icon. Again, it takes ages before the program is up and running. *6tiermes7* is logged on and he double-clicks the name. A window pops up.

MakkaPakka: Hugger?

He waits patiently until the response arrives. Not even *6tiermes7* can be in front of a keyboard all the time.

6tiermes7: Mugger.
Shouldn't you be out celebrating now?

MakkaPakka: Done that. It was no fun.

6tiermes7: You would rather be chatting to me. I completely understand.

460

MakkaPakka: I'm wondering about something.

6tiermes7: You're joking. Now?

MakkaPakka: Now more than ever, possibly.

6tiermes7: That sounds serious. What is it?

MakkaPakka: One of the text messages sent to Henriette
    Hagerup on the day she died came from
    Mozambique. You know from where in Mozambique?

6tiermes7: Hold on a moment, let me check.

His fingers hover over the keyboard, ready to type.
A few minutes pass. Then *6tiermes7* is back.

6tiermes7: A place called Inhambane.

Another large puzzle piece falls into place. It's as if
the gaping hole he has been staring at all day closes and
clangs shut.

MakkaPakka: This case isn't over.

6tiermes7: What?

MakkaPakka: Stefan Foldvik didn't kill himself. Anette
    Skoppum murdered him.

6tiermes7: What makes you think that?

MakkaPakka: Lots of reasons. Too many loose ends. I
need you to do me a few more favours.

6tiermes7: Go on?

MakkaPakka: The samples you took from Stefan's room
– I suppose they're low priority now?

6tiermes7: That's right.

MakkaPakka: That mustn't happen.

6tiermes7: You can't assume I have the power to change
that.

MakkaPakka: No, I know. I'm just telling you what
needs to happen to solve this case.

6tiermes7: If the samples will solve the case in the end,
then surely time isn't of the essence?

MakkaPakka: No, except that Anette could be over the
hills and far away by then. The summer holidays are
about to begin. God knows which far-flung place
she'll visit this time. She has already explored half
the globe. By the time you finish processing the
evidence which could convict her, she could be
anywhere.

6tiermes7: I understand the problem, but I can't do a
whole lot about it. You need to take this up with

Gjerstad or go directly to Nøkleby. Try to convince them. I can always help you afterwards.

MakkaPakka: Okay, I get it. But I've got a couple of other things I know you can help me with.

6tiermes7: What are they?

He takes a deep breath before he starts typing. It does little to calm the galloping beast in his chest.

Chapter 72

The day of Henriette Hagerup's funeral starts off cloudless, clear and beautiful. It is Monday. Henning Juul has dusted down an old suit. He watches himself in the mirror. He adjusts the black tie he hates wearing, and runs his fingers over his scars.

It is a long time since he last looked at them. Really looked at them. But as he does, he thinks they have grown less noticeable. It's like they have sunk into him, somehow.

He takes a deep breath in the bathroom, where the air is still warm and moist after the shower he took half an hour ago. Shaving cream and a razor lie next to the sink which now has a rim of stubble and foam.

Before he leaves, he checks that everything he needs is in place in his pockets. *The most important thing you need to bring is your head,* Jarle Høgseth used to say. That may be true, Henning thinks, but it's not a bad idea to pack some tools as well. He needs to keep his wits about him now, even though he has made good use of them recently. He has reviewed every conversation and every encounter. Dr Helge and *6tiermes7* have both provided invaluable help and pieces for the jigsaw, but he doesn't know if it's enough.

He hopes to know the answer in a couple of hours.

Ris Church was consecrated in 1932. It is a beautiful stone church in Roman style. The church bells, all three of them, are already tolling when Henning arrives by taxi. He gets out and mixes with the mourners.

He enters the church and is given an order of service leaflet with Henriette Hagerup's name and smiling face on the cover. He recognises the photograph. It was displayed on Henriette's shrine outside the college last week. He remembers thinking that she looked intelligent. He takes a seat on a pew right at the back and refrains from staring at the mourners. He doesn't want to look at anyone or talk to anyone. Not yet.

The ceremony is beautiful, dignified, subdued and sad. The vicar's monotonous voice fills the church, accompanied by suppressed sniffling and silent weeping. Henning tries not to think about the last time he was in church, the last time he heard people mourn the loss of a child, but the thoughts are impossible to block out. Even when the vicar is speaking, he can hear the tune of 'Little Friend'.

Fifteen minutes into the ceremony, he gets up and leaves. The atmosphere, the smell, the sounds, the black clothes, the faces, everything takes him two years back in time, to when he sat in another church, at the front, wondering if he could be put back together, if he would ever be human again.

He hasn't moved on, he realises, as he comes out into the porch. He dreads to think about what lies ahead, his future, the unfinished business he has been too traumatised to face. But now that he knows his brain is working again, he can ignore it no longer. I can't let it go, he thinks, I need to do something about the gnawing in my chest, this nagging clockwork which ticks away inside me; it will never release me and let me be swallowed up in the peaceful ground and close my eyes with a feeling of completion.

Because I know I'm right.

He loosens his tie a little as he comes outside and feels the fresh wind on his face. He steps away from the entrance. The vicar's voice carries right through the open doors. A gardener is tidying up a nearby grave and making it look nice. Henning wanders around the graves. The grass is newly mown, its colours lush and green, and all shrubs are trimmed meticulously.

He strolls to the back of the church, where the gravestones are lined up like teeth. He thinks it has been a long time since he last visited Jonas, but pushes the thought aside when he sees her.

Anette is standing in front of the rectangular hole in the ground, where Henriette Hagerup will be laid to rest. Even now, Anette is carrying her backpack. A sudden onset of nerves sweeps through his body as he decides to join her. There is no one around. She is wearing a black skirt and black blazer over her blouse, which is also black.

Anette turns as he approaches from behind.

'So you couldn't stand it inside, either?' she says and flashes him a smile.

'Hi, Anette,' he says, stops next to her and looks down into the hole.

'I hate funerals,' she begins. 'I think it's better to say goodbye like this, out here, before the hysteria begins.'

He nods. Neither of them speaks for a while.

'I hadn't expected to see you here,' she says, finally looking at him. 'Dull day was it?'

'No,' he replies. 'I'm right where I need to be.'

'What do you mean?'

He takes a step closer to the edge of the hole and looks at it again. He is reminded of Kolbein Falkeid's poem, which Vamp set to music:

> When evening falls, I quietly embark
> and my lifeboat is lowered six foot down.

Twenty-three years, he thinks. Henriette Hagerup only lived for twenty-three years. He wonders if she had time to feel that she had had a life.

He sticks his hand into his jacket pocket.

'You thought you had remembered everything,' he says, meeting Anette's eyes. Her cautious smile melts into an uneasy twitch in the corner of her mouth. He can see his words have taken her by surprise. Good, he intended them to. He waits until the dramatic effect is complete.

'What?'

'I couldn't understand why you suddenly became so helpful and obliging. You drove me up to Ekeberg Common, right in the middle of a rainstorm. At that point, Stefan's death wasn't public knowledge. But you knew about it. You knew because you were the last person to see him alive. You knew because you talked him into taking his own life.'

She raises her eyebrows.

'What the hell are you –'

'You suffer from epilepsy, don't you?'

Anette shifts her weight from one leg to the other.

'Can I have a look in your backpack?'

'What – no.'

'Epileptics are often prescribed Orfiril. I bet you have Orfiril in there,' he says, pointing to her backpack. 'Or perhaps you've run out?'

She doesn't reply, but sends him a look that suggests he has wounded her deeply.

'Orfiril tablets look just like this,' he says and pulls

out a bag of Knott from his suit pocket. He takes out a small, white pastille and holds it up.

'Stefan had already let the cat out of the bag to his parents. You were going to prison for a long time, both of you. You saw a chance for Stefan to take all the credit. Or was that your plan all along?'

'What the hell are you talking about?'

'I stepped on one of these, when I found Stefan dead in his bed,' he says, and shows her the sweets. 'Orfiril mixed with alcohol is a lethal cocktail. But the only one who took Orfiril was Stefan. You swallowed a fistful of sweets. Yum. After all, you enjoy eating them all at once. The only problem with Knott is that sometimes they fall out of the bag or you spill some when you're trying to swallow a handful.'

Anette shakes her head and holds up her hands.

'This is beyond me. I'm leaving.'

'I know why you gave me a lift to Ekeberg Common,' he says, following her. She turns and stares at him again. 'You were nervous. You knew that Stefan had blabbed, you were scared he might have told his parents what *really* happened, revealed the name of his partner in crime. You couldn't ask Stefan about it that afternoon – he would have twigged that you were up to something – that the suicide pact wasn't genuine, at least not as far as you were concerned. That's why you offered to drive me: it gave you a reason to be there and find out how much his parents knew. That's why you appeared in the tent.'

Anette puts her hands on her hips. She is about to say something, but she stops.

'And what a performance,' he continues. 'You realised that Ingvild didn't know who you were. You were safe. And you knew that Ingvild had been raped, because Stefan had told you. You also knew that she had taken self-defence classes, that she had a stun gun and that she had been trained to react defensively if someone approached her from behind. Like you did in the tent. Such a compassionate gesture, placing your hand on her back, near her throat, to show kindness, but you did it because you knew what Ingvild would do, she would stun you and surely there can be no better way to remove suspicion from yourself than by becoming the next victim, even if you survive.'

Anette averts her eyes. He can tell from looking at her that it is true, though she hides it well. He is convinced she has been to the Foldviks' flat more than once. That's why she closed the curtains. She knew how it was overlooked from the street, from the flats opposite, and she also knew that the Foldviks had nosy neighbours. Every time a front door was opened, Mrs Steen's curtains would twitch. That was why the front door was almost closed, but not shut. So no one would see or hear her.

Anette scratches her cheek and flicks aside strands of hair that have flopped into her eyes. Henning continues:

'After killing Henriette, you tried to implicate her boyfriend, a man who had won Henriette's heart. You tried to set him up, just like in the script, so you could go free. It didn't *quite* go according to plan, but with Stefan out of the picture, after his confession, all the loose ends were tidied up, as far as you were concerned. You thought you had remembered everything, Anette, but you missed a couple of things,' he says and pauses for dramatic effect again. It appears to be lost on her. She looks at him with expressionless eyes.

'Stefan,' he says and waits a little longer. 'How did Stefan know that Henriette would be in the tent that night?'

He lets the question linger for a long time. Anette doesn't reply.

'No texts were sent from Stefan's mobile to Henriette that day or night. Or from her mobile to his. I know, because I checked.'

She doesn't stir, she simply looks at him. Her face is blank and her breathing indifferent. He straightens up.

'However, a call was made from his telephone to yours on the afternoon he died. It lasted thirty-seven seconds. Was that when he told you he had confessed to his parents? Is that why you drove over? To carry out a little damage limitation?'

Still no reply. He remembers what Anette said to him, outside the college, that Henriette had said she was going to e-mail 'A Sharia Caste' to Foldvik. *6tiermes7*, or someone else from the police, went through Henriette's e-mails and established that she never did. Yngve wasn't lying. Stefan couldn't have found the script at home. There was only one way it could have happened: Anette must have shown, or given, it to him.

Henning watches her. There are no chinks in her armour.

'I'm asking you again: how did Stefan know that Henriette would be in the tent that evening?'

This time, he doesn't wait for a reply.

'Because you told him. Henriette and you had already agreed to meet there. Otherwise, why would she leave her boyfriend's flat? It had to be because of something important, something previously arranged. And you were going to start filming the following day.'

Anette doesn't react.

'What did you say to Stefan that evening?' he continues, unaffected by her stonewalling. 'That you were just going to scare her little? Was that how you made him bring his mother's stun gun?'

Even though Anette doesn't say anything, Henning is convinced that Henriette must have been surprised when Stefan appeared in the tent with Anette. That hadn't been part of her agreement with Anette. But

Stefan still thought that Henriette was the woman his father had had an affair with. Perfect for Anette. And the hole had already been dug, because it was needed for the filming the morning after.

'Did you throw the first stone, or did you provoke him into killing her?'

He looks for sounds of acquiescence or admission, but finds neither. Even so he can't stop now.

'You planned the killing well. And to implicate Marhoni even more deeply, you e-mail Henriette the very day you intend to kill her. You e-mail a photo. Henriette with her arms around an older man. I'm willing to bet that the man in the photo was Yngve.'

'I never sent Henriette a picture of Yngve,' Anette snorts.

'No. You didn't press the *send* button. You got someone else to do that.'

He points to her backpack.

'Inhambane.'

She turns her head, but realises she can't see which sticker Henning is pointing to. It says *Inhambane* in black print against a white background surrounded by a red heart.

'Inhambane is a town in southern Mozambique, on the Inhambane Bay. Great beaches. The day Henriette was killed, she received an e-mail from an Internet café in Inhambane. A text message was also sent to her

473

from a free e-mail account from the same café shortly afterwards, telling her to check her e-mail. This happened while she was with Mahmoud Marhoni.'

'And then?'

'And then? You're telling me it's pure coincidence that you happen to have a Inhambane sticker on your backpack? You've been there, Anette. You've probably got friends there. Inhambane isn't exactly one of Star Tours' top-ten travel destinations.'

Anette doesn't reply.

'The trouble with being partners in crime', he carries on, 'is that you can never be sure that the other one will keep his mouth shut. That's why you were scared, the first time I met you. You were afraid that Stefan would give himself away, give *you* away, that he wouldn't be able to live with what the two of you had done. And you were right. So you tricked him into taking his own life.'

Anette's face dissolves into an enigmatic smile, but she quickly recovers.

'Let me tell you something about Henriette,' she says. 'Henriette wasn't *that* clever. Since her death, everyone has been at pains to say how talented she was, how brilliant.'

Her voice darkens.

'The truth was that she was mediocre. I read the script she sold. It wasn't that good. *Control+Alt+Delete*?

474

– what kind of a title is that? The clever twists in that script were my ideas. But do you think she was going to give me any credit for that?'

She snorts.

'That's why you promised to carry on her work, as you wrote on the card. You felt you had certain rights to the script, to the clever twists. Have you been in contact with Truls Leirvåg yet?'

Anette laughs briefly and then she nods.

'We should make a film together, you and I. You've got a great imagination. But you, too, have forgotten something,' she says. She walks right up to him and whispers:

'The two people who can prove everything you've just described –' she begins and holds a dramatic pause. The coldness in her eyes hits him like an icy slap across his cheeks.

'They're both dead.'

She takes a step back. Then she smiles again. A small, cunning smile.

'So what if they find sweets in Stefan's room?' she continues. 'What does that prove? That he had a visitor who liked sweets? And what if he rang me that afternoon? I was going to direct his film. We were still in contact. None of that proves that I killed Henriette or Stefan. None of it.'

'You're right,' he says. 'The police can only prove

475

that you tried to point the finger at Mahmoud Marhoni, but –'

'What kind of proof do you have?' she interrupts him. 'A sticker on my backpack?'

'It doesn't prove a whole lot, but if you line up enough matches and strike them all, you get a fairly decent flame. When I hand over everything I've discovered to Detective Inspector Brogeland, he and his colleagues will go over everything you have said and done in the last few years. They will turn your life upside down and inside out, every e-mail, text message, receipt and bill will be scrutinised in an effort to link you to a murder and a suspicious death. And when the toxicology report is ready and the police learn that Stefan's body contained Orfiril, the circumstantial evidence will be so overwhelming that it will take a great deal to prevent you from going to prison. One sweet, as you rightly point out, doesn't constitute proof, but remember the Orderud trial. Four people went to prison because of a sock.'

Anette doesn't reply. He looks at her and tries to mirror her frosty smile.

'What's the point of being a genius if nobody knows?' he says, mimicking her voice. She looks up at him. 'Everyone, at some level, wants recognition for what they've done. We want applause. Human beings are like that. That's why you gave me the script. You wanted me to understand. And I do. I understand that you planned it all, and I'm terribly impressed. But you're not going to get a round of applause. Not from me, not from anyone.'

Anette stares at him. He turns around and sees the funeral procession leave the church.

'Like you said, Anette, the hysteria is about to begin.'

She laughs at his remark.

'Wow,' she says, alternately shaking and nodding her head. She comes up to him again. She takes the sweet from his hand and pops it into her mouth.

'Do you know who taught me that they taste best when you eat them all at once?'

She sucks the pastille demonstratively.

'Given how clever you are, I'm sure you can find out,' she says, without waiting for him to reply. She looks at him for a long time. Then she smiles again and walks past him in the direction of the funeral procession. He follows her with his eyes, as she strolls across the grass, past the mourners; she glances at them, nods to some acquaintances, but she doesn't join them. Instead she strolls on, taking her time. As if she doesn't have a care in the world.

And she might well be right, Henning thinks, when Anette disappears from view and the cemetery fills with mourners in black clothes. It may be impossible to prove that she plotted and executed plans that resulted in the deaths of two people. Because she has never admitted to anything, not today or in the tent at Ekeberg Common, and the evidence is, at best, circumstantial.

Jarle Høgseth used to say: *Crimes are rarely delivered giftwrapped to the police.* Sometimes it is straightforward: the evidence speaks an unequivocal language, the perpetrator confesses, either spontaneously or due to evidence presented during interrogations; or in the subsequent trial, the prosecution's version stands in sharp contrast to the explanations given by the defendant. That's the way it is and always will be.

But the truth will never be lost to him. He saw it in Anette's frozen eyes. And plenty can happen during an investigation. New evidence might appear. Witnesses could come forward with testimony that sheds fresh light on Anette's actions. She will have a lot of questions to answer and it is difficult to give consistent replies, time after time after time, to complex questions, no matter how clever you are.

He remains in the churchyard during the interment. He doesn't look up, doesn't listen to what is being said; he only listens when they sing:

> Help me, God, to hum this song
> so my heart will carry on

just one day, one moment at a time
until I reach your good country.

He grits his teeth and swallows the memories and the pain, even though he sees Jonas all the time. He feels that he can finally say goodbye. He hasn't been ready until now. He couldn't manage it back then, because he couldn't, didn't want to accept that Jonas would never again wake him in the morning, at the crack of dawn, would never again snuggle up to him and cuddle, cuddle, cuddle until children's TV began.

It's hard to be grateful for what I had, he thinks, it's hard to remember every day, every moment instead of mourning what will never be. But if I can convince myself that the six years Jonas lived were the finest of my life, then that's a start.

It doesn't feel like much, but it's a start.

He refrains from offering his condolences after Henriette's lifeboat has been lowered six feet into the ground. He knows he won't be able to handle it, won't have the strength to meet her parents and her family without identifying with them. He won't suppress his grief, because he needs to feel it. But not here. Not now.

The time will come.

Just one day, one moment at a time. Until I, Jonas, reach your good country.

Chapter 73

Music is playing from the flat above when he comes home. He stops in front of the entrance door. Arne Halldis is listening to opera. Henning recognises the aria straight away. It is 'Nessun Dorma', from *Turandot*, by Puccini. Henning's favourite aria. Luciano Pavarotti's unmistakable voice fills the stairwell:

> *Ma il mio mistero è chiuso in me*
> *il nome mio nessun saprà!*

Arne Halldis is a multi-faceted man, Henning thinks. Either that or he is a first-class cad who exploits poetry and opera to score with women. He imagines that's why Gunnar Goma is such a big fan of him.

> *No, no! Sulla tua bocca lo dirò*
> *quando la luce splenderà!*

Arne Halldis turns up the volume, as the opera reaches its climax:

All'alba vincerò!
vincerò, vincerò!

The song soars, it travels through walls and concrete, wood and plaster, before hitting Henning right in the middle of his forehead, penetrating his thick skull and rushing through him; his cheeks redden and, before he knows what has happened, the tears are streaming down his face. He can feel them roll down his scars, suddenly he finds himself sobbing.

Only That Which He Doesn't Think About has made him cry since That Which He Doesn't Think About. It feels a little odd, tasting my own salt, he thinks, after so long and knowing that it's Arne Halldis's music that triggered it.

But it doesn't surprise him that music has made him cry again. And he feels the urge to play a chord or two. But he isn't sure if he dares.

He lets himself in as the applause dies down and it grows quiet around him. He replaces the batteries in the smoke alarms, sits down on the sofa and opens up his laptop. It wakes up from its sleep mode. It takes a few seconds, before it finds the wireless signal and he loads FireCracker 2.0. It doesn't take long before *6tiermes7* responds.

6tiermes7: I'm excited. How did it go?

MakkaPakka: As expected. She denied it all.

6tiermes7: Clever girl.

MakkaPakka: The smartest I've ever met.

6tiermes7: You didn't get anything on tape, either?
Nothing we can use?

MakkaPakka: I haven't listened to the recording yet, but
I doubt it.

6tiermes7: Okay. You did the best you could. Now you
need to let us take it from here.

MakkaPakka: I'll try.

6tiermes7: You're not telling me you're planning another
investigation?

Henning ponders this while the cursor blinks in the
chat window. Something has happened to him in the
past week. Though three people have died and families
have been destroyed forever, it has done him good to
work again. Anette hasn't confessed and Hassan's
threats won't be easy to ignore, but Henning has proved
to himself that he still has it. The little grey cells have
woken up again.

He looks at his fingers, before typing the words that
have been smouldering inside him for so long. He

knows that when he writes this, there is no return. He will have fired the starting pistol.

Dr Helge would probably tell me to wait, he thinks, until I'm absolutely certain that I'm ready. But I haven't got time to wait. No one can say if Yasser Shah will be caught, or if Mahmoud Marhoni's evidence will make Hassan and his gang do a Robert De Niro and disappear. No one can tell me when I can walk down the street without looking over my shoulder, or if my nights will be forever filled with sounds that prevent me from sleeping.

That's why he writes:

MakkaPakka: Actually, there was one thing.

He feels cold all over.

6tiermes7: You're joking. What is it?

He takes a deep breath. Almost two years ago I stopped while I was going downhill, he thinks. I pulled the handbrake. He is like Ingvild Foldvik. He has been a zombie since the death of Jonas. But sometimes you need to release the brake, let yourself hurtle towards the abyss, to gain momentum to get back up again. He doesn't know how far down it is, but this time he won't stop until he hits the bottom. No matter how much it hurts.

Henning exhales and starts typing.

MakkaPakka: I need your help.

He looks up at the ceiling. He isn't sure why he does that. Perhaps he is trying to absorb what Pavarotti was singing about. His strength. His will. He looks up a long time; in his head he can hear Luciano's voice again.

> *All'alba vincerò!*
> *vincerò, vincerò!*

At dawn I shall be victorious.
He turns to the screen again. At that moment, he is filled by a resolve, the like of which he has never known. He writes the words with a determination that makes the hairs on his arms stand on end:

MakkaPakka: I need help to find out who torched my flat.

There. The words are out, words only he has been thinking. The police concluded that the fire wasn't suspicious. So Henning buried his words for nearly two years.

Now they are free.

And now that he has written them, now that he has started investigating the toughest story of his life, he might as well say them out loud.

MakkaPakka: Please help me find my son's killer.

Acknowledgements

Burned would never have become a reality without many contributions from friends and family and others who have been willing to read, listen, play ball and share their expertise and experience. Jørn Lier Horst, Erik Werge Bøyesen, Johnny Brenna, Hege Enger, Line Onsrud Buan, Petter Anthon Næss, Torgeir Higraff, Nicolai Ljøgodt, Kristin 'Kikki' Jenssen, Vibeke Ødegård Nohr – a thousand thanks!

An extra special thanks to Benedicte. You are bright. You are great.

Those who know me well also know that the path to my first published book has been long. A final thank you therefore goes to myself. Thank you because you never stopped writing.

Thomas Enger
Oslo, December 2009

ff

Pierced

Book Two in the Henning Juul Series
(Summer 2012)

'[Enger is] one of the most unusual and intense
talents in the field.'
Barry Forshaw, *Independent*

Summer in Oslo. The city is quiet, most people are
away on holiday when an incident occurs that will
dominate the news. Days before his appeal is due to be
heard, Tore Pulli, a notorious double murderer,
collapses and dies during a media interview in one of
Norway's high-security prisons.

The undisputed head of a criminal biker gang, Pulli
had also been something of a media darling, and with
his charm and large amounts of cash had dominated
Oslo's decadent scene before his conviction. But he
always maintained his innocence, claiming that he had
been set up, and that the real killer was still loose.

The police treat his death as suicide, but soon

reporter Henning Juul is digging deeper. He discovers that the murders Pulli was convicted of do not bear his signature, and he is convinced that he would never have taken his own life.

He is deep in the case when he discovers a possible link between Pulli and the fire which killed his six-year-old son, Jonas. With the desperate strength of a grieving father Henning embarks on a dramatic chase where he comes to realise that he himself may be the prey.